Bar Girls

Bar Girls

Jules Kurre

YellowRoseBooks
a Division of
RENAISSANCE ALLIANCE PUBLISHING, INC.
Austin, Texas

ISBN 1-930928-04-1

First Printing 2000

9 8 7 6 5 4 3 2 1

Cover art by Linda A. Callaghan
Cover design by Mary Draganis

Published by:

Renaissance Alliance Publishing, Inc.
PMB 167, 3421 W. William Cannon Dr. # 131
Austin, Texas 78745

Find us on the World Wide Web at
http://www.rapbooks.com

Printed in the United States of America

For Mary

Chapter
1

Keagan looked at her apartment with distaste. The place was a mess and she only had an hour to clean up. If Jill got there and saw the assortment of old newspapers, empty Coke boxes, and random clothing strewn about, Keagan would hear nothing but complaints all evening. "I'll never get this done in time," she said aloud as she rushed about. Dashing into the bathroom she cleaned the shower, toilet, and sink while listening to her CD player which blared Led Zeppelin. As she hurriedly straightened up, Keagan considered why she was going to so much trouble for Jill when she could barely tolerate her presence. They had gone out on two dates, with Jill spending an indecent amount of time criticizing Keagan. Jill was good for one thing: providing material for a story Keagan was writing. The character's main trait was vindictive cattiness, and Jill's personality was a perfect match. Keagan frowned at the thought of another evening with her.

"So what the hell." She turned the music down, picked up the phone, and dialed Jill's number. After three rings, she heard the answering machine: "Hi, this is Jill. My heart goes out to you because your fondest wishes of the moment, being talking to me, are not going to be realized. Leave me a message and maybe I'll fit you into my schedule and return your call. Beep." Keagan's face showed part disgust, part nausea. Hoping to sound ill, she cleared her throat noisily, talking more slowly than usual. "Hi, it's me, Keagan. Um, I'm not going to be—"

Jill picked up the receiver. "Keagan, you sound awful. Are you done cleaning yet?"

"Oh, no. I'm sick and won't be able to go to dinner with you tonight. Sorry." Keagan coughed horrendously for several seconds.

"Hmm. Too bad. Well, feel better and finish up that cleaning, hon! Bye!" Click.

Relief flooded through Keagan as she headed to the back room where her computer was. Calling up the file of her current story, she skim read the first chapter's opening paragraphs. With a frustrated sigh, she took off her reading glasses and rubbed her eyes. Figuring her mental block was due to fatigue, she closed the file.

She went into the bedroom to change into a sleeveless T-shirt and shorts. If she couldn't tackle her writer's block, she could at least do her daily workout. That was something Keagan could immediately accomplish. Returning to the living room, she picked up the 10-lb. dumbbells lying on the floor. She purged her mind of thoughts while lifting, the feeling of muscles stretching and her heightened breathing being more than enough for her to focus on. Her wish to clear her mind was thwarted, however, when her thoughts turned to how important writing had become to her. As a child she had used it as an outlet from reality. But as an adult, it had become her life's ambition. Her one fear was that she would never accomplish anything. As her arms rose and fell in the replaying of this ritual, Keagan felt her thoughts turning negative in spite of the usual comfort and escape lifting weights gave her. Regaining focus, she pushed the possibility of her fears coming true from her mind.

A light sheen of sweat broke out on Keagan's forehead as her workout continued. As she focused on breathing, she considered what her night's objective would be. Keagan always had specific intentions when going to the bar. Although her goal was usually to write about the people there, sometimes it would be to play pool, spend time with friends, or simply get drunk. Getting picked up was never on her agenda. She dated people like Jill because that personality type provided character material for her writing. Whenever a date wanted something more serious, Keagan ended the relationship.

After showering, Keagan dressed in black. She tied the laces to her combat boots, smiling to herself, already knowing what her choice of cologne would be. In the volatile mood she was in, it had to be Polo. There was something about that scent and her being on edge. They went together. Concluding that she needed new ideas for her story and the bar would be a good place to get them, she decided her aim for the evening would be to write.

* * * * * * * * * *

Keagan walked into the Grotto, not spying the usual crowd because it was early. She sat down in her favorite spot without getting a drink, knowing Mabel would be over soon. Looking to the pool table, she happily noted Char's absence. The self-appointed womanizer of the bar frequently hit on her, and Keagan wasn't in the mood to spar.

She glanced up to see Mabel walking toward her table. "Hi, Mabel."

"Hi, hon. What'll ya have?" She smiled at Keagan who grinned back. Mabel was peppy, constantly clearing tables or taking orders, and lending an ear to patrons in the process.

"Just a water." She indicated her notebook.

"Ah, a writing night. And what are you writing about? A woman who's going to walk through that door and change your life perhaps?" She smiled devilishly.

"Oh, I don't think so. But if she arrives, you'll be the first to know."

Mabel chuckled. "Okay, honey." She headed back to the bar to get the water. When she returned, Keagan had a frown on her face and stared at the far wall deep in thought. She set the water in front of her. "That boss of yours giving you a hard time again?"

Keagan looked up with nonchalance. "Nothing I can't handle."

"What happened this time?"

"I got a review full of lies, that's all."

Mabel nodded sympathetically. "How can she get away with that?"

"It's easy enough. She knows I won't complain and that even if I did, nothing would be done. I'm just a little fish in a big pond." Keagan laughed at the bad metaphor.

"But don't they have a higher up manager you can tell?"

Keagan snickered at Mabel's ignorance of retail practices. "It's commonly referred to as inhuman resources. Oh, I mean *human* resources. My complaint would be on the bottom of the list. It's not considered important. They have bigger fish to fry, if you know what I mean."

"But why would your boss do this?"

"Mabel, you will find this very hard to believe, but I'm a big troublemaker."

Mabel looked skeptical, knowing Keagan to be neither a troublemaker, nor someone devoid of a work ethic. "I don't believe it."

"Believe what you want. It's true. You see, I had the gall to complain when she cut my hours and gave them to her cronies she goes out with." Keagan sipped her water.

"How can that happen?"

"Oh, I don't know. Maybe because they've let this evil woman run amok for years. My theory is that she hails from a far off universe, one devoid of all logic, reason, and sensitivity. But her own kind tired of her machinations and banished her to earth as punishment. In response, she's made her life's goal to take revenge on humanity because she can't take revenge on her own kind. Years ago, when I started working at Gigantic, she singled me out, determining to make my life a living hell. Through me, she would achieve the greatest satisfaction she ever knew. This, of course, all culminated by giving me a review that was six points lower than my last. The only question now is what will be her next evil deed?"

Mabel laughed and ruffled Keagan's hair affectionately. "You are something else, you know that?"

Keagan sighed. "So, I've been told. The question is...what?"

"That'll be revealed in time, I'm sure. Now, why don't you try to enjoy yourself and forget about work for awhile?"

"Thanks, Mabel." As the barmaid left, Keagan shook her head wryly, appreciating that she took the time to ask her about work.

The sound of music came from the jukebox since it was the DJ's night off. The bartender controlled the sound level and sometimes it got so loud that Keagan couldn't think, much less write. It was on these occasions that she switched her nightly plan to getting drunk. Tonight wouldn't be such a night because the bartender was Cody, her frequent confidant. If it got too loud, she'd give Cody a look and the music would be turned down. She looked over at the bar and waved to her friend who winked back.

Keagan scanned the bar for potential material when she saw three women come in. Two she recognized as Eileen and Tate, regulars who had been dating for three years and held the "token couple of the bar" title. Keagan didn't know the young woman with them and so began writing about her. She glanced up periodically to take in the developing scene.

Eileen and Tate sat at the bar with their young friend talking quietly. Keagan watched as the young woman smiled or laughed. She couldn't tell her eye color due to the distance between them, but this newcomer was beautiful. Several inches shorter than herself, Keagan pegged her as quite young also; not more than twenty, she guessed. When the young woman caught her eye and smiled, Keagan realized she was staring. She looked away, embarrassed as Char sauntered up to her table. Keagan, so occupied with the young woman, hadn't noticed her nemesis enter the bar.

"Hi, Keag. Notice the new meat at the bar?" Char grinned and directed a purposeful leer toward the young woman.

"Oh, yeah. Now I'm into teenagers." Keagan didn't care for the way Char looked at the young woman. She had a reputation for seducing all the newly out women and then dumping them.

"She's not that young." Char's brow crinkled in worry. "You think?"

"What do you care? You don't look like her type." Char wore a red flannel shirt, old stone washed jeans and cowboy boots. A key ring hung from her belt loop, the keys of which jingled whenever she walked. Keagan often wondered if Char realized that she was providing a built-in alarm for her potential prey. In contrast, the attractive young woman had on khakis and a white, long sleeved blouse. Her shirt buttons were undone, allowing Keagan a view of the tight fitting stretch shirt she had on underneath.

"Opposites attract," said Char.

"Not in your case."

"What is it? You want her for yourself or somethin'?"

"No. Char, can you go away, please? I'm busy tonight." Keagan, surprised at her own bluntness, ignored the fact that it stemmed from her eagerness to continue writing about the beautiful woman at the bar.

"Writing? Why do you do that here, anyway? This is a bar. You're supposed to have fun here."

"This *is* fun to me."

Keagan winced at the odor as Char leaned closer. The smell was a combination of Old Spice aftershave and tobacco. Not at all pleasing to the olfactory nerves. "I could show you a different kind of fun." Her voice held a suggestive lilt that made the writer cringe.

Keagan directed a menacing glare toward Char. "And I could show you many things all of them involving pain."

Char retreated. "Touchy tonight, aren't we?"

"Yeah, you could say that."

"You just need to get laid." Char chuckled as she walked off.

Keagan shook her head in disgust at the insinuation that sex was the answer to her problems. Turning her mind back to the woman, she named her to make things easier on her writing. Since she was a strawberry-blonde, Keagan called her La Roux, a French name meaning red-haired. She watched as La Roux got up and headed toward the jukebox. Keagan's eyes weren't the only ones following her. Char's joined them. When La Roux returned to the bar, k.d. lang could be heard singing, "Big, Big, Love."

Keagan watched Eileen and Tate head for the dance floor. True to character, Char zeroed in for the kill not five seconds after they left. Keagan rolled her eyes and watched the proceedings.

"Hi, I'm Char. You're new here, aren't you?" She held out her hand to La Roux who shook it gingerly.

"Yes."

"What's your name?" Char leaned against the bar and gazed intently at the young woman. Her keys jingled a bit as she shifted.

"I'm Rudy."

"Ah. Short for—?"

"Rudelle."

"That's a very pretty name. Would you like to dance?"

"Um, not really, thanks." Rudy had come to the bar to socialize, not get picked up. And she could tell Char wasn't looking for just a dance.

"Oh, come on, what can one dance hurt?" Char leaned against the bar and put her hand over Rudy's. "C'mon, hon, you've probably never had the opportunity for any real action, have you?"

Rudy's stomach fluttered. She had never encountered a woman that came on this strong. "I don't think—" She noticed a hand placing itself on Char's shoulder. It was the woman who had been looking at her earlier.

"Char, I think Cody wants to buy you a drink...down there...at the other end of the bar."

"Tell her later." Char turned to face Keagan. Her voice tone and facial expression told Keagan that she wouldn't retreat easily.

Keagan put her arm around Char and ushered her away. "C'mon, c'mon, Cody's waiting."

Char glanced longingly back at Rudy. "But, but..."

"Char, she's a young kid, leave her alone for god sakes. Haven't you scarred enough of them for life?"

Char's eyes narrowed and she cocked her head at Keagan. "I'm that much of a heartbreaker, huh?"

"Whatever. Just keep your distance from that one."

She retreated back to her booth in the corner.

Char stewed for awhile but accepted the drink from Cody. She knew it wouldn't be wise to upset Keagan so she scouted around for another target.

A disappointed Rudy watched Keagan retreat to her secluded corner. She wanted to thank her as well as get a better look at those stunning blue eyes. "Cody?"

Cody looked over to the young woman Eileen and Tate introduced to her earlier. They had chatted and Cody found her to be intelligent and witty. She returned to Rudy's end of the bar. "Yes, Rueday?" Cody had begun teasingly drawing out the syllables in Rudy's name during their talk earlier.

"That woman over there, the one in the corner, what's her name?"

"That's Keagan. I'd stay away from her if I were you."

"Why's that?" Rudy asked, intrigued.

"She's pretty introverted, keeps to herself, likes to write. I don't think she's looking for anything."

"Maybe someone needs to introduce her to the concept of serendipity, then." Rudy's eyes twinkled.

"What's that mean?" Cody hated it when people used big words.

"When you find something you're not looking for. What does she like to drink?"

Keagan watched Cody and La Roux talk. After the incident with Char, she lost her concentration and quit writing. La Roux distracted her too much. When Keagan found herself wanting to look into those beautiful green eyes again, she stifled the feeling.

Cody came over with a rum and coke. "This is for you, my dear, compliments of Rudy."

Keagan's eyes widened. "Who?"

"Rudy. The lovely young strawberry-blonde knockout

sitting at the bar. The one you helped earlier?" Cody chuckled. "She asked about you."

Keagan's brow arched in skepticism. "Tell her I said thank you. Wait a minute. She's not old enough to buy alcohol."

"Twenty-one, Keag."

"Hmm. She looks younger."

"Oh, yeah. If I was about fifteen years younger—"

Keagan laughed. "Thank her for me, please, Cody."

"You can thank her yourself, darling. That's how these things usually work."

"Not interested."

"Not interested? She's gorgeous, Keag. Plus, she's really nice. I've been talking to her. She's funny, and she's new, probably doesn't have any baggage. Perfect for you."

"Why are you guys always trying to set me up?"

"Because, deep down, you want to be set up and you know it."

"Oh, sure. Justify your manipulations by saying I want it." Keagan glanced at the bar, her eyes meeting those of the young woman in question. Rudy gave a short wave to Keagan who couldn't help but smile back. She shook her head in disgust at her own weakness. It was time to leave.

"Can you sneak me out the back, Cody?"

"Hell, no! What are you so afraid of? She likes you."

"Damn! I just wanted a nice, sedate, evening."

"A what? You know I hate it when you use words I don't know."

"Why don't you write me a list of all the words you *do* know, and I'll be sure not to use any others around you."

"Snarl, snarl, growl, growl! You just need to get laid, honey." Cody chuckled as she walked back to the bar.

Keagan sighed in frustration. "I really wish people

would quit saying that."

Cody returned to Rudy, enjoying her role of go-between. "Keagan says thanks."

"Hmm." Rudy wondered why Keagan didn't say so herself. She looked over at the solitary woman who scribbled in a notebook. Rudy didn't know that Keagan only pretended to write.

* * * * * * * * * *

Keagan eluded Rudy until the bar got busier. She noticed the strawberry-blonde looking at her, but averted her eyes whenever she did.

By the time her friend Brad Martin arrived, it was approaching midnight and Keagan considered leaving. She had enough material for the night. "So what are you writing about?" Keagan liked Brad for his loyalty. He was a good person to confide in and she couldn't think of one person in her life, including her family members, about whom she could say that.

"I picked out this cute girl at the bar, a new girl, and I've been writing her story all night." Keagan indicated Rudy. Brad turned and looked toward the bar.

"Whoo! Hot stuff. If I was a horny young lesbian, such as yourself, I'd be asking her to tell me her story up close and personal, if you know what I mean." Brad raised his eyebrows suggestively.

"I am not horny. What is it with you people? First Char, then Cody, now you. Maybe you all need to get some. Maybe *you're* the ones with the problem."

"Hmm. You might have a point there."

"So, how's it going with Ted?" Ted was a cute, young man that he met at the bar the previous week. Brad actually went out with him more than once.

"Who?" Brad looked confused.

"Teddy. Cute, little, blonde Teddy? Remember, you were calling him your teddy bear?" Keagan recalled the good-looking young man.

After a few seconds, Brad spoke. "Oh, yeah. Yeah, well, he and I discovered we didn't have one very important thing in common."

"And that was?"

"A belief in monogamy?"

"Are you asking me or telling me?" Keagan laughed at her friend.

"Telling?"

"Someday, you'll date someone more than three times. Then you'll move in together and I'll be coming over for dinner. I can see it."

"I think it would sooner happen for you. Like little hot stuff at the bar up there."

"Nope." Keagan rolled her eyes.

"Why do you come here anyway, if you don't want to meet anyone?"

"You know why."

"To find a story? Nah, I don't believe that."

"Okay. Peace and quiet?"

Brad's eyes lit up. "Ooooh, look, girl, here she comes. She's coming over." Brad jumped up to leave. "Later, girlfriend!"

Keagan grabbed his arm. "No, no, no, wait—" As Brad left, Rudy came over and sat down in his place across from her in the booth. Keagan froze, wondering what La Roux wanted.

"Can I ask you a question?"

"Sure."

"How can you see?"

"Hmm...?"

"To write. Isn't it too dimly lit in here?"

Keagan expected a typical come-on, not a logical

inquiry. "I see all right. I have good eyesight."

Rudy smiled at the straightforward answer. "Good. You wouldn't want to miss anything worth looking at, would you?"

Uneasiness settled in Keagan's stomach, but it was the good type. "No, I wouldn't." The two women continued to stare at each other until Keagan spotted Jill coming into the bar. She didn't like confrontations but knew there would be one when Jill noticed her. She ran her hand through her dark hair and tried to steel her resolve. Her eyes focused on the front of the bar where Jill stood. "Rudy, there's somebody here I need to avoid."

"An old girlfriend, perhaps? I suppose you want me to help you make her jealous?" Rudy was only joking, but the mischievous look in her eyes indicated a willingness to play along.

Keagan allowed a slight grin, not wanting Rudy to know that she found her question amusing. "Yeah, why not." She took her notebook and pen off the table and placed it on the seat beside her.

Rudy turned around, looking toward the front door. "Is that her?" She indicated a drunken, brown-eyed blonde making her way over.

"How ever did you guess?"

Rudy got up and planted herself next to Keagan, sliding close, and putting her arm around her. Keagan inhaled the pleasant smell of her hair and cologne. The scent was subtle, not overbearing. As Rudy put her head on Keagan's shoulder, she found her soft touch welcoming.

Jill stomped over, making a sincere attempt to avoid falling. It was obvious she was drunk. Her entourage stood behind her. Keagan referred to them as the Jill entourage: her group of followers that went wherever she did. "So, Keagan, feeling better?"

"Oh, much better, thanks." Rudy raised her head from

Keagan's shoulder and regarded Jill.

"And what have we here?" Her eyes looked Rudy up and down. "I don't remember seeing you before."

"Hi, I'm Rudy, nice to meet you." She smiled at the woman and offered her hand, which Jill refused. Rudy ignored her lack of manners and continued. "You haven't seen me before because this is my first time here."

"That's obvious. Look, little girl, you're way out of your league here. I wouldn't mess with this one, if I were you."

"Why not? She seems nice to me."

Keagan remained silent, hoping the ordeal would end soon. She admitted to herself that she enjoyed Rudy's attentions, but would not let it go any further.

"Let me give you some advice. She's a liar. She was supposed to go to dinner with me tonight and instead she faked being sick to come here. She can't be trusted!" Jill glared daggers at Keagan, whose eyes focused back at her with calm.

"I can't imagine why she wouldn't want to go out with the likes of you." Rudy tired of being nice to this social pariah.

Jill got up in Rudy's face. "You little slut! I oughta..."

Keagan leaned over and grasped Jill's arm. "Be nice." Hardened, cold blue eyes stared into brown, daring Jill to make one more move.

Jill backed away. Her entourage did the same. "You'll pay for this, Keagan. You could have had the best, and you blew it!"

"Well, I blew you off, that's for sure." Keagan smiled icily at her.

"I'll get you back for this!" She stumbled away. Her entourage followed.

"I'm shivering in my boots." Keagan gave a mock

glare to Jill as she left.

"I was wondering..." Rudy got a contemplative look on her face. "Do you think I have a shot at getting into her group?" She stared guilelessly at Keagan.

Keagan couldn't help it and laughed. "Yeah, but you would need to stay away from me."

Rudy grinned, knowing she wouldn't agree to that stipulation. Thinking it best to change the subject, she scooted away from Keagan, not wanting to invade her space. She continued to sit next to her, though. "That was fun."

"That's your idea of fun?"

Rudy nodded. "Yeah. Sometimes, I don't think I have enough excitement in my life. That really got the old adrenaline going, let me tell you."

"I could suggest something else that might get your adrenaline going, too."

"Oh?" Rudy smiled, and appeared interested.

Keagan thought furiously to come up with a quick answer to cancel out her verbal blunder. "Rock climbing! Yeah, ooh, what a rush."

"You've rock climbed?" Rudy couldn't picture Keagan rock climbing. She could, however, picture her reclining and listening to classical music, something like Bach perhaps.

Keagan gave up. "No. I haven't rock climbed. I have a friend who does it and says it's a real rush. It was nice to meet you but I have to go home. I have to work in the morning at six."

"Oh. Okay." Rudy rose, allowing her to get by. Keagan stood awkwardly for a few seconds, bid Rudy goodbye, and then stopped at the bar to say goodnight to Cody and a few of the others. As she headed out the door, someone touched her arm. It was Rudy.

"You almost forgot your notebook." She grinned and

handed it over to Keagan, who rolled her eyes.

"Thanks."

Rudy smiled and watched her go, thinking she'd be the type to go home and listen to classical music. She was right.

Chapter
2

The cold, late January air made Keagan shiver as she headed to her car the next morning. She grinned, even as her teeth chattered. No snow. It was one of the things she liked about living in Columbus. Usually, there was little of it in that part of Ohio.

She waited for her car to heat up, reflecting on the previous night. Rudy was attractive, charming, and funny. But when she confronted the fact that Rudy might be interested in her, she pushed it to the back of her mind.

When Keagan got home from work that afternoon, she opened her notebook and read over the previous night's notes. Coming to the end, she noticed something scribbled in an unfamiliar hand. The note read, "So, do you think I should go out with Char or not? Rudy." Next to that, she had left her phone number. At first, Keagan feared someone had read her notes, but when she recognized the author as Rudy, she knew the young woman wouldn't have had time to read anything. She was only separated from her notebook briefly.

Rudy's handwriting was neat and orderly for being rushed. Wondering if that revealed anything about the woman herself, she paused in thought. Was everything in Rudy's life as organized as her handwriting? Or did the handwriting indicate a disorder in her life that she tried to compensate for? Keagan chastised herself for her tendency to analyze everything. At the same time, she almost regretted not seeking the answers.

Keagan tore the note out and tacked it onto her corkboard in the kitchen. She didn't know why she did it, except to torment herself. Shaking her head wryly, she glanced a last time at the note, and exited the kitchen, her heart heavy. And then the phone rang.

The answering machine kicked in. Keagan never answered her phone before screening the caller. On those rare occasions when she did answer, it was always someone trying to sell her something or attempting to collect on a late credit card bill. She found these types of people to be annoying more times than not, often finding herself ending such conversations abruptly. The machine was a great way to avoid all this tension. "Hi, Keagan, it's me. I hope you're there. Pick up the phone, it's about mother." Keagan's chest tightened. It was her mom calling to tell her about the latest family catastrophe. This happened at least once a week. She debated on whether or not to answer, before finally picking up the receiver.

"Hellooo." She tried to begin the conversation on an upbeat note.

"Hi, I've got a problem. Your grandmother's out of control and Sean's not answering his phone." Joan Rafferty's tone was frantic. Keagan knew to choose her words carefully or her mother might burst into tears.

"He never answers his phone when there's a problem. What's up?"

"I've had it. I can't live with this anymore. I'm not

going to allow any more alcohol in this house. If she
doesn't like it, she can move."

"What happened now?" Keagan softened her voice in
an attempt to soothe her mother.

"She was supposed to go over to Blanche's house for
that reunion party but when I got home from shopping, she
was sitting there on the couch looking half gone. She
drank the whole bottle. When I told her she was in no condition to go and said I wouldn't take her, she started
screaming at me. We had a fight, I broke a vase of hers,
and then I tried to call your brother, who as usual wasn't
available. Now, she's in her room. I *hate* the sound of that
door slamming!" Keagan could tell that her mother was
close to tears.

Keagan felt trapped with no escape. She couldn't
solve her grandmother's problems any more than she could
make her mother happy. She could only listen and offer
support. But it was never enough. Often, she had a hard
time reconciling her strong feelings of love for her grandmother with the painful reality of her weakness. Her
grandmother should have been one of the best people she
would ever know. Instead, she was often one of the biggest
disappointments in Keagan's life. "You broke a vase?
Which one?"

"You know, the one that's been in the family for over
fifty years. I don't care about it. I just lost control when
she called me a bitch!"

"I'm sorry. Do you want me to come over?"

"No, honey, there's no need for you to do that. I know
how busy you are. I just needed to talk. I'm sorry to
bother you." Joan's voice conveyed genuine remorse. She
regretted venting to Keagan about an impossible situation,
but she didn't have anyone else. A drunken mother was
not considered an appropriate subject for her circle of
friends.

"Please don't apologize. I told you I'm here if you need to talk. I mean that. She'll calm down later."

"Oh, yeah. The 'honeymoon phase.'" Joan laughed to dispel the tension. The honeymoon phase described the aftermath of an argument when the alcoholic offered no apology or acknowledgment of the emotional pain to the family. Things went on normally with false happiness, the wronged family members harboring resentment toward the alcoholic. Of course, another hurtful incident would follow as the pattern continued. "I'll talk to you later."

"Bye." As Keagan hung up the phone, she could feel the tightness in her chest subside. It returned to the back of her heart where it commonly retreated.

She called her brother, Sean. Maybe he would feel like going over to Joan's for awhile. His machine came on. "Sean, it's me. Pick up."

"Yeah, what?" He had just gotten back from a long haul on the road and didn't feel like being bothered with family.

"Did you get a message from Joan?"

"Uh, huh."

"She and Grandma had another fight. It seems to be getting worse, lately. She was pretty upset. Maybe you could go over there and talk to Grandma or something."

"I don't want to get in the middle of this. In fact, there's no way I'm getting in the middle of this. I'm exhausted. I just got back from a three-day trip. The only plans I have are for sleep."

"Well, Sean, I sympathize with you, I really do. I have many things I'd rather be doing, too. Like writing my novel, for one. But—"

"How's *that* going?" Sean had never understood his sister's fondness for that hobby. It seemed like an incredible waste of time to him. She could be out on the road, making $30+ an hour like he did. But instead she chose to pursue a profession that would surely bring her only one thing: nothing.

Keagan considered not answering, but Sean was the only one who ever asked about it. "I've had a bit of a block, lately, but I'll get through it. I'm having a problem establishing the plot, that's all."

He shook his head in response to her nonsense. "Once you figure out what you want to do with your life, it'll all fall into place. What is it you want to do with your life, anyway?"

Keagan resented the question. She had told him repeatedly that she wanted to be a writer. He was in denial. She thought with amusement that wanting to write was very much like being gay. Only tell a select few. "I've told you before that I want to write. How many times do I have to say it?" Keagan knew it was a mistake to show agitation toward her volatile brother, but she didn't care.

"Will you chill? You're too fucking sensitive. I have to get some sleep. Bye!" Click.

Enraged that he would hang up on her, she slammed the phone down. *Why did I even bother?*

She had an overwhelming urge to call Rudy, but stopped herself from doing it. She figured that Rudy might have more interesting things to do than listen to her unsolvable family problems.

****

Later that night, Keagan went to the bar to forget her family problems. Her objective this night would be to get drunk. Not falling down drunk, but pleasantly inebriated. Having the next day off, she was determined to have a good time. No writing, no contemplation, no socialization. The new quarter began in a couple of days and she wouldn't be able to cut loose until it ended, so it was just as well.

She entered the bar with a flourish, determined to be happy, even though her family's problems were not far from her thoughts. Glancing to the bar, she spotted Cody. Avoiding casing the place for familiar faces, she sauntered over to Cody and gave her a smile. "Good evening."

"Hi, Keag. What'll it be?" Cody smiled back, keying in to the false mood her friend portrayed. Knowing it wasn't a good idea to pry into Keagan's problems, she said nothing.

"Rum and coke. More rum than coke." The jukebox played "Big, Big, Love." Recalling that Rudy played that song the night before, Keagan began to turn around.

Before she did, Cody spoke. "Oh, yeah, she's here. Over there, talking to Danielle." The bartender snickered.

Keagan took a big drink of the rum and coke Cody brought her. "Oh?" Her voice drawled out the inquiry. "Who?" She crinkled her eyebrows in confusion, although she knew quite well of whom Cody spoke.

"Very funny. Like you don't know. You better go stake your claim now before somebody snatches her up."

Keagan ignored the comment and went to sit at the end of the bar. From her position, she viewed the booths, tables, and dance floor with ease. Her gaze made its way surreptitiously to where Rudy sat talking to Danielle. Keagan knew of Danielle, but had never dated her. She was okay, Keagan guessed, but never seemed to date anyone for longer than a couple of days or a week at most. It disturbed her to realize that Danielle was a female Brad Martin. Finishing up her drink, she motioned to Cody. "Another, please." She smiled sweetly.

Cody returned in a few seconds with another drink for Keagan. "When she came in, she asked if you were here."

Keagan gave up and grinned. "Who?"

"Don't even—" Cody gave her a knowing look. Sometimes she wished her friend would lay off the sarcasm, but she knew it was a defense and Keagan relied on it. "Then Danielle came swooping over and scooped her up, and they've been talkin' ever since. That was about a half an hour ago."

"You make Dani sound like a vulture." Keagan took a sip of her drink and glanced over at Rudy.

"She is."

"In any case, thanks for the update. The *unsolicited* update."

"Dammit!"

"The update I didn't ask for. Sorry." Keagan looked back over to where Rudy and Danielle sat. They were both laughing. Danielle put her hand on Rudy's arm and squeezed it. She tried to fight down a wave of jealousy that rose in her chest upon seeing this. Without realizing it, she continued to stare at them. As Rudy caught her eye she looked away but didn't miss the smile that came from the young woman. It wasn't difficult for her to smile back and nod out of politeness. Rudy had one of the most endearing smiles she had ever seen. Of course, Cody was observing everything.

"Okay, so now you guys are doing the eye thing. Why don't you just go over and talk to her?"

"First of all, she's talking to someone else, and secondly, I don't see any reason to."

"How about, she's nice, she's sweet, she's attractive, and for completely unknown reasons, she seems to like you." Cody hit Keagan playfully on the side of the head for emphasis.

"I'm not looking for a one night stand."

"I don't think she is, either."

"Or anything more." Keagan reminded herself that there was a reason she didn't have relationships. Breaking her vow to herself would indicate that she couldn't trust her own judgment.

Cody left well enough alone and went to the other end of the bar. As Keagan continued to sit alone, what she feared would happen, did. Rudy left Danielle and within seconds plopped herself down on the barstool next to her. "Hi."

"How's it goin'?"

Rudy smiled, almost as if she knew the affect it would have on Keagan. "Pretty good. Pretty good." She continued to stare at her.

"Oh. By the way, my answer's 'no.'"

This appeared to catch Rudy off guard, as Keagan hoped it would. "Your answer's 'no' to what?" She looked briefly confused before catching on. Keagan referred to the note she left in her notebook. "Why not? Me, Char, we could get a little butch-femme thing going on, don't you think?"

"Nope."

"What? You don't think I'm femme enough?"

"Oh, no, that's definitely not it." Keagan's voice took on an unconscious, sultry edge. "I just don't think she's your type."

"And what's my type?" Rudy found herself responding to Keagan's closeness and shifted a bit. When she did, her knee touched Keagan's. She neglected to move it away not wanting to appear rude. On the other hand, if she left it there, it might send another message. To her surprise, Keagan appeared to ignore the action and continued talking.

"Oh, I don't know," she mused. When Rudy's knee made contact with hers, a pleasurable jolt shot up her leg. She wondered what would happen if Rudy replaced her knee with her hand. Forcing herself to abandon these thoughts, she continued. "You'd probably go for someone more stable, someone like Deb." She pointed out a woman with short, brown, hair sitting in the back by herself next to the dance floor. "Deb met her girlfriend about three years ago, here. That's Kristy." She indicated a tall, demure, blonde sitting at the other end of the bar. "That's Deb's girlfriend."

"But why aren't they sitting together, then?"

"Because they're picking each other up. Watch, you can see them looking at each other. Look." Rudy turned her attention to the two women. Deb caught Kristy's eye and smiled at her. The other woman nodded her head in response. Pretty soon, Deb indicated that Kristy should come over. In a few seconds, both women sat together at Deb's table.

"I don't get it."

"They do it to put excitement into their relationship. Deb explained it to me once. They agree to meet between the hours of eight and ten, but nothing specific. That way, whoever gets there first won't know when the other one will get there. I guess they find it fun. It's one of those relationship things." Keagan shrugged. She had no idea why she disclosed that to Rudy.

"That's kind of sweet."

"If you say so. I think it's kind of sappy, myself. Either you've got it or you don't. No one should have to work that hard at it."

"They seem to be enjoying themselves, though."

"Whatever."

Rudy sensed Keagan retreating. She changed the subject back to their previous verbal play. "Well, you've convinced me. I decided not to go out with Char."

Keagan took a long swig of her drink. "Good. You deserve better than that." It came out of her mouth before she realized it.

"I do?"

Keagan focused on Rudy's green eyes, and sighed. A few years ago, she would have asked her out, but dating no longer interested her except to generate story ideas. She knew Rudy would be someone she wouldn't use like that. "Yes," she replied. Before Rudy could respond, Keagan rose and joined her friends at the pool table.

Rudy watched her retreat with interest. "Hey, Cody! C'mere!" The bartender turned, amused at the lesbian soap opera unfolding by the minute. "Yes, my dear?"

"How do I get a date with Keagan?"

"You don't." At Rudy's sour look, she continued. "But you *can* get her attention."

****

When Keagan spotted Milligan at the pool table, she saw it as a good excuse to relieve herself of Rudy's distracting company and went over to watch her friend play. Milligan was playing against Jackie. Several of the bar patrons nicknamed her "Jackie Daniels," due to her love of whiskey. "Hi, Mill. Jackie Daniels, how's it goin'?"

"Pretty good. I love that name. It's great." Keagan grinned at the shorter woman. She found Jackie's pride in her nickname amusing. Milligan nodded to Keagan, but was concentrating on her shot. It looked like it would be the final one of the game. "Eight ball in the left corner," Milligan called, as she prepared to shoot. The area around the table quieted as Keagan, Jackie, and a few other spectators watched to see if Milligan emerged as the victor. She aimed at the cue ball and brought the cue stick back to strike. Just then, Rudy appeared and stepped up next to Keagan.

"Who's winning?" She looked at the table, wondering if the balls were allowed to hit each other. Rudy didn't know anything about pool, but it seemed to her as if people enjoyed it. She had always wanted to know more about the game and saw this as her opportunity.

Unfortunately, she chose the moment that Milligan was shooting to speak. This break in her concentration caused the cue stick to slip out, barely tapping the cue ball. It didn't go anywhere near the eight ball. "Dammit!" the woman groaned.

"Yes! Yes!" Jackie jumped up and down, knowing she had another chance at winning.

Milligan turned her eyes toward Rudy with an ominous glare. "Who are you?" she drawled. She was the type of pool player who took the game too seriously.

Rudy gulped and her eyes widened, as she realized the woman was quite angry. "I'm really sorry." She glanced at Keagan for support.

Keagan rolled her eyes and tried to keep from grinning. "This is my friend, Rudy. Don't mind her, she can't help being a nuisance."

"Hey. I am not a nuisance!" Rudy's reply was indignant until she realized that Keagan referred to her as a friend. "Friend?"

Keagan said nothing, but stood watching Jackie shoot. The eight ball flew into the left corner pocket, winning the game. Milligan grimaced. She didn't like to lose. "Okay, friend of Keagan, you owe me. You and me, now."

Rudy's face showed confusion, until she realized that Milligan wanted her to play pool. "Um, I, I don't know how to play pool."

"Keagan, you can show her how, I don't mind. I just want to beat her."

Keagan sighed, wondering how she got herself into these situations. *It's because Rudy keeps following me.* She said nothing and went over to the cue sticks aligned on the wall, picking a suitable one for Rudy, who stood looking back at her with disbelief. "Oh, no. I said I don't play pool."

"You only said you didn't know how. Not that you don't play at all." Keagan had a mischievous look in her eye. She handed the cue stick to Rudy, who held it as if it was diseased.

"I can't do this."

"Sure you can. It's easy. I'll show you." Keagan regarded Rudy as if they were conducting a business transaction. What she didn't understand was the way her heart beat faster the moment Rudy stepped up to the table. She ignored it.

"C'mon, I don't have all night. I would like to get in some real action too, not just play and beat some amateur." Milligan racked the balls.

"Oh yeah? What makes you so sure you can beat me?" Rudy took the cue stick in her hands with confidence and strode forward. "C'mon." She indicated Keagan with impatience. "You said you would show me. So, show me."

Keagan raised her eyebrows at Rudy's assertiveness. Milligan stepped back, indicating for Rudy to break. "Okay, La Roux, let's go."

"What did you call me?"

"La Roux. It's my fictional name for you. It's a French name meaning red-haired. I was writing about you last night, and I had to call you something." Keagan deadpanned her whole statement, hoping to make light of the admission as she moved in behind Rudy, and put her arms around her to show her how to shoot. She told herself it wasn't out of line to share this information with Rudy. It didn't mean anything, certainly not that she had any prurient interest in the woman. Not at all.

Rudy's heartbeat sped up with Keagan's closeness and her use of the nickname. If they hadn't been surrounded by a group of women watching their every move, she might have asked if that was akin to a pet name. She might also have asked what Keagan was writing about. Instead, she nodded her head, regarding her companion with a hint of a smile.

"Right now, all you want to do is what's called breaking. You hit the balls with the white ball, the cue. Whoever gets a ball in first, goes first. You can pick stripes or solids, but most people pick the color of the first ball they shoot in. Got it?" As Keagan talked, she positioned Rudy's cue stick to shoot.

Rudy was only aware of Keagan's voice and her hands positioned on top of hers. The pressure Keagan's fingers made on Rudy's hands distracted her. She tried in vain to clear her head and concentrate.

"Got it?" Rudy heard Keagan repeating.

"Oh, yeah, yeah. Gotcha. No problem."

"Okay then, shoot." Keagan moved away from Rudy's body, telling herself she didn't miss the contact.

Rudy hit the cue and saw the four go into the right pocket. She looked to Keagan expectantly. "Now all you have to do is hit the rest of the solids in and hit in the eight ball last and you'll have this loser beat." Keagan directed a challenging look to Milligan, who smirked at her.

"Fat chance of that."

"Um, I'm not sure I have the shooting part down right. Could you show me again, please?" Rudy turned around, smiling sweetly at Keagan. She pretended it was serious business to hide the fact that she wanted Keagan's arms around her again.

Blue eyes met emerald, as Keagan regarded Rudy with suspicion. "Sure." She stepped forward and put her arms around her again. "Now, everyone has their own style, of course, but really what you want to do is position the stick in the way that you have the most control in." As she said this, Keagan glanced downward and noticed that she had a good view of Rudy's bra. Since her top two shirt buttons were undone, Keagan could see that it had lace at the top. She wondered if the rest of the garment was lace. Her eyes traveled of their own volition to Rudy's breasts and she looked back up, hoping no one noticed. Milligan hadn't missed it, though, and directed an amused and knowing smirk to Keagan. She glared at her and continued her instruction. "You can shoot like this." She put the cue stick on top of Rudy's index and middle fingers. "Or like this," she continued, positioning it between her index and thumb. "It all depends on what you feel comfortable with." She stepped back and allowed Rudy to decide which way she wanted to shoot.

"Thanks."

"No problem."

Keagan gave Rudy pointers as she played Milligan. She cut back on their physical interaction, though, because she enjoyed touching her too much.

Rudy, for her part, did well, in spite of her growing attraction to Keagan. She put up a good fight, but every time Keagan spoke it distracted her, making her lose all concentration. She lost the game, but didn't care.

"Good game, kid. I almost forgive you for messing up my other game." Milligan shook Rudy's hand and turned to Jackie. "Doubles next with Sue and Jen," she told her. "We'll play again, sometime, Rudy."

"Okay. Thanks." Rudy turned away from the table and walked to the bar. Keagan stepped in beside her.

"I think you won her over."

"With your help."

"Nah. You have a natural talent for it."

"Really?"

"Yes, really. I thought you were quite good." Keagan spotted an opportunity to leave the situation and took it. "I see my friend, Brad over there. I'm going to go say hello. Later, Rudy."

"See ya." She sat down and Cody brought her a drink. She took a sip. "Thanks, Cody."

"I should keep my big, fat, mouth out of this, but what the hell. She was checking you out, big time, over at the pool table."

Rudy grinned. "She was, huh?"

"Oh, yes. I could see the battle being waged behind those gorgeous baby blues. She likes you."

"I like her, too. But if I tell her, I'm sure she'll bolt like a gazelle or something. She's not exactly approachable."

"Then don't tell her, *show* her."

Rudy smiled and contemplated the bartender's words as she took another sip of her drink. "Hey, do you have any peanuts?"

* * * * * * * * * *

Meanwhile, Keagan bolted like a gazelle over to Brad, who stood near the dance floor. The jukebox was playing, "Enjoy the Silence," by Depeche Mode. As the lyrics ran through her head, she greeted her friend. "Bradley, good evening."

"You're so damn polite, you're going to make a great catch for some lucky, young girl. Wait a minute!" His eyes darted to the bar. "There's a girl right there. How about her?" He indicated Rudy. "She's cute, she's hot, she's happenin'. Ooh, and she's lookin' this way."

"Why don't *you* go out with her, if you like her so much?"

"Because you'd kill me."

"I would not. She can go out with anybody she wants to. I don't care."

"Oh. She doth protesteth too much, methinks."

"Ouch. Did you actually *attend* that Shakespeare

class?"

"Why, certainly. That's where I met that cute guy from the video store, remember?"

"The one who gave you free rentals?"

"Oh, yes. And that's not all he gave to me."

"Didn't he give you about a weekend?"

"Why must you turn every one of my relationships into something sleazy?"

"I'm not the one who makes them sleazy." Keagan laughed at Brad. She enjoyed their light banter, so devoid of tension.

"Ha. Ha." Brad looked to the dance floor. "You want to dance?"

"You know I don't dance."

"I bet you'd dance for little cute stuff at the bar."

"Nope." Keagan leaned against the wall and stared at the dance floor feeling lonely, even though she was in a bar full of people. She didn't think twice about it because it was normal to her.

Closing time came an hour later. Keagan abandoned her earlier plans to get drunk and sat around chatting with Brad. He chose to shift their conversation from Rudy to easier topics, sensing that Keagan's mood was getting worse.

After Brad left, Keagan was the last one in the bar. She got up to leave, and said goodbye to Mabel and Cody. As she stepped outside and zipped up her leather jacket, what she saw both surprised her and made her heartbeat speed up. There was Rudy sitting on the hood of her car, her scarf tied over her lower face, and her gloved hands intertwined. She looked up at Keagan's approach and lowered the scarf from her mouth. "Hey."

"Would you mind telling me what exactly it is that you're doing?"

"I'm praying to Krishna, what does it look like I'm

doing? I locked my keys in my car. Duh." Rudy looked beyond exasperated. She had waited on Keagan for awhile and received plenty of offers for help, but there was only one she wanted to accept.

Keagan snickered. "You need some help?"

"Don't laugh at me. This is not funny. I never do these kinds of things."

"Maybe something distracted you this evening."

"Maybe it did."

Keagan stopped laughing and assessed the situation. It was 2:30 am, on a Sunday morning. Not a great time to call anyone for help. "I take it *all* your keys are in there?"

"Yes, my apartment keys, too."

"You live with anyone?"

"I have a roommate, but—"

"I could take you home, I guess. You could come back in the morning with your extra keys."

"My roommate's gone for the weekend."

Keagan reassessed the situation. Rudy had no keys, her roommate wasn't home, it was the middle of the night, and freezing. She couldn't believe that she was about to ask this woman to spend the night with her. "I guess you could—"

"I could just spend the night at your place." She slid off the hood of the car, her green eyes staring expectantly at Keagan.

"You planned this, La Roux." Keagan walked up close to Rudy, intending to stare her down and make her admit it. She underestimated her opponent.

"Ha! You are full of yourself, aren't you? I did not. And I resent you even suggesting it."

"Yeah, I'll bet you do. How many offers for help did you get before I came out here?"

Rudy remained guileless. "None." She tried to inject sincerity into her voice.

"Oh, right. Here you are, looking so damn beautiful, sitting on the hood of your car and not one single person leaving that bar asked you if you needed help? You think I was born yesterday?"

"You think I'm beautiful?" Rudy's body heated at Keagan's words, in spite of the dropping temperature.

"No! I mean, yes...no." Keagan threw her hands up in irritation. "Let's go." She headed to her car.

Rudy followed Keagan with a hidden smile on her face, and tried not to feel guilty. She didn't have to try very hard.

"My car's a little old." Keagan led Rudy to a 1989 dark burgundy Chevy Cavalier. "The lock on the passenger side is broken, so if you want to get in, you have to ride in the back or climb over the driver's seat to the passenger side. I can't open the door at all because it might not close again." She shrugged, not embarrassed about the car. It got the job done.

Rudy found that endearing. "Oh, I can climb over." Keagan opened the door and Rudy slipped in, climbing over the gearshift to the passenger side.

Keagan got in and put her seatbelt on. She looked expectantly at Rudy. "Well?"

"What?"

"Aren't you going to put your seatbelt on?"

"Nope. I find them limiting in movement." She gazed at Keagan, as if that should have been obvious.

"That's the idea. They're supposed to limit your movement...your movement from the seat onto the pavement with a very brief pit stop through the windshield."

"Are you a pessimist? Or do you just not trust your own driving?" She made no move to buckle her belt, much to Keagan's consternation.

"I trust myself just fine. It's the other drivers I don't trust. Emphatically stated," Keagan drawled out her words, "I'm a very careful driver, I trust my driving. I just think it's wise to exercise a bit of caution—"

"You're an English major, aren't you?"

"Rudy, put the seatbelt on now." Soon it would be three in the morning, and she hadn't even pulled out of the parking lot. And Keagan didn't plan on moving until Rudy put her seatbelt on.

"I knew it. No one uses the word emphatically in common speech." Rudy appeared to totally forget where they were.

"Look, nobody rides with me without putting their seatbelt on. So put it on now."

Rudy frowned. "Okay, okay." She buckled the seatbelt and quieted, looking like a recalcitrant child who had just been admonished.

Keagan pulled out of the parking lot without a word and they drove down High Street. Normally, her mind would be on a thousand different things at once, the stillness of early morning allowing her thoughts free reign. However, with Rudy sitting next to her, she found all her thoughts centered on the silence between them. She fought to say something sensible. "So where are your spare set of keys?" It wasn't poetry, but the question suited Keagan as a way to break the silence.

"I have a set at my mom's. You could take me to get them in the morning. Unless, of course, you find you enjoy my company so much that you want me to hang out with you until my roommate comes home Sunday night." Rudy got a devilish look in her eyes.

"I highly doubt that will happen."

"Stranger things have happened."

Keagan said nothing but Rudy saw a small smirk forming on her lips. Within a couple minutes, they arrived at Keagan's apartment. It was a three-story house that the landlord rented as three apartments. Keagan lived on the second floor, and had to put up with neighborly noises coming from upstairs and downstairs. The rent was reasonable, though, so she didn't complain. The landlord kept the house up and she could have had a garden, but left that to her downstairs neighbor, Rachel, who could frequently be seen outside doing yard work. Keagan considered it a decent place to live for the time being. "You know I expect certain things from the women I bring home with me," she told Rudy, as they walked down the drive to the front door.

"Oh, really?"

"Uh huh."

"And just what is it you expect?" Keagan unlocked the door and they stepped in. She turned on the light and locked the door, putting the deadbolt and chain lock in place.

Keagan yawned as a wave of fatigue swept over her. She knew she must be tired, to be flirting with Rudy. This would definitely not be a good time or place to do that. She glanced idly at the answering machine, but no light flashed. Fleetingly, she thought maybe Sean had called to apologize but thought better of that. That wasn't his style even for something he felt was his fault. And she was certain he would blame her for their previous squabble. Her mind focused back to Rudy's last question.

"I expect them to, um, always wear their seatbelts." She walked to the bedroom down the hall. The second bedroom was used as a study and the only other rooms were a large kitchen, a decent sized bathroom, and the living room.

"Even in the house?" She ignored Keagan's blatant attempts to avoid following through with her flirting and remained in the living room, taking in the place. There was a couch with a furniture throw over it, and one bookcase lined the wall. As Rudy's eyes scanned the contents of the bookcase, a few titles stuck out: Aristotle's *Poetics*, *The Elements of Grammar*, and *The Selected Poetry of Rainer Maria Rilke*. When she glanced into the kitchen, her eyes landed on the corkboard, where Keagan had tacked Rudy's phone number and note. She stored this information away for later. She heard her friend rustling about in the back. "What are you doing?"

"Changing the sheets for you. You can sleep in here."

"I won't kick you out of your bed. I'll be fine on the couch."

Keagan came back into the kitchen. "It's okay, really. You'd be surprised at how many nights I sleep out here. Insomnia."

"I've never had that problem. I have a harder time waking up than going to sleep." She grinned sheepishly at Keagan, who smiled.

"It's settled, then. There are some new toothbrushes in the bathroom drawer, if you want to use one. I also left you a T-shirt and pair of shorts on the bed to wear."

"Thanks." Rudy was impressed at Keagan's attentiveness. "You keep a supply of toothbrushes?"

"Of course. As many women as I bring home, it's a necessity." Keagan winked at her and then went to the living room, plopping on the couch. She covered her head with a pillow and tried to forget Rudy was there.

"Right. Right." Rudy smiled at Keagan's sarcastic comments and went into the bathroom to find a toothbrush. After she brushed her teeth, she changed into the T-shirt and shorts. She laughed at the T-shirt, which said on the front, 2QT2BSTR8. Returning to the living room, she told Keagan, "I *really* like the shirt."

"I thought it would be appropriate." Keagan still had the pillow over her head.

"I noticed you have a Rilke poetry book." When Keagan made no move to take the pillow off her head,

Rudy stepped over and did it for her. She glanced up with surprise. "Yes?"

"I'm talking to you."

"Sorry. When I can't sleep, like right now, I put a pillow on my head."

"What do you mean, sleep? You aren't even undressed yet."

"Oh. Yeah." She gave a half laugh.

"I'm not making you nervous, am I?"

"Oh, no. No. I guess I'll go get undressed now." With that, Keagan got up and headed to the bathroom.

Rudy went over and grabbed the Rilke book. When Keagan came back, dressed in a plain, black, T-shirt and flannel lounging pants, she heard Rudy reading aloud:

> *At first a childhood limitless and free*
> *of any goals. Ah, sweet unconsciousness.*
> *Then sudden terror, schoolrooms, slavery,*
> *the plunge into temptation and deep loss.*

Rudy glanced up and when she saw Keagan standing still and transfixed, her eyes asking for more, she continued with the next stanza.

> *Defiance. The child bent becomes the bender,*
> *inflicts on others what he once went through.*
> *Loved, feared, rescuer, wrestler, victor,*
> *he takes his vengeance, blow by blow.*

"It's one of my favorites."

Keagan smiled faintly, surprised to find Rudy recognizing the book. "There's a bit more." She leaned against the wall and recited with pseudo fervor, almost as if she was making fun of the poetry she enjoyed.

And now in vast, cold, empty space, alone.
Yet hidden deep within the grown-up heart,
a longing for the first world, the ancient one...

"I didn't know you were so poetic."

"I didn't write it."

"But you recite well."

"Thanks. We probably should get to sleep now."

"Hmm." Rudy and Keagan looked at each other for a moment. "Keagan?"

"Yes."

"You wouldn't want to let me read any of your stuff, would you?"

Keagan had wondered when that would come up. "I haven't let anyone read my stuff."

"Why write, then?" Rudy regarded the squirming woman, who sat down to avoid pacing.

"It's not that I wouldn't, I just never have. Except when I was a kid. I'd write these little stories on mini notebooks and let my best friend read them. But that's it."

"You've shared your work in your creative writing classes, though, right?"

Keagan nodded. "It was the most frightening thing I ever did." At Rudy's expectant look, she held up her index finger to indicate for her to wait a moment. She retreated to the back room and came back a few moments later, holding her portfolio in hand. "Here's a couple things I've written for class, if you want to—"

"Thanks." Rudy took them with an enthusiastic smile.

Keagan shrugged. "If you want to waste your time—" She let the phrase ramble off as she once again settled on the couch. "It's my portfolio I used to get into creative writing."

Rudy nodded and got up from the couch, heading for the bedroom. "Thanks. And I don't think it'll be a waste of my time. Good luck with the insomnia."

"Good night, La Roux."

"G'night."   Rudy went into the sparsely decorated room and got in bed, pulling the blankets over herself. A soft light illuminated her surroundings as she looked around trying to get a better sense of the woman she had come home with. The room was immaculate, too much so. Rudy suspected Keagan only spent as much time in it as it took her to sleep. The only things in the room were the bed, a nightstand with a light and alarm clock sitting on it, and a small television. There was nothing on the walls.

She settled in and picked up the portfolio, opening to the first page and seeing a poem. It was called, "thebigjoke." Keagan had intentionally run the words in the title together. The poem rhymed and was vague about its intention. It didn't tell a story, it merely expressed a feeling; one that Rudy thought would be appealing to different types of people for that reason alone.

She read it through three more times, wondering if the poem had a direct inspiration or not. In any case, it revealed another side to Keagan she was grateful to have a glimpse of. In spite of the late hour, she devoured the rest of the portfolio. There were three more poems, two essays, and two short stories. Rudy found each one to have merit. She hoped Keagan would agree to let her read more of her writing.

Chapter
3

An early riser, Keagan was up at 8:00 a.m., heading to the kitchen to make coffee. She showered and changed, not waking Rudy. A little embarrassed at the messy appearance of her apartment, she began to straighten things up when she noticed Rudy's note on the corkboard. "Shit." She tore it down and stuck it in her pocket, hoping Rudy hadn't seen it. In half an hour, the dishes were done, and she had just finished vacuuming when Rudy walked into the living room. One of Bach's *Brandenburg Concertos* was playing.

"I knew it," Rudy said to herself, as she stole a peek at the corkboard. "Good morning." She sat down.

"Morning." Rudy was already dressed. Keagan admitted to enjoying the common interest they shared the night before but was nonetheless relieved that apparently she didn't plan on hanging around long.

"The big joke, huh?" Rudy smiled, as Keagan perked up in recognition of the title.

"Don't hold it against me. It was the only poetry class

I ever took and the assignment was to write a rhyming poem." She poured Rudy a cup of coffee. "Cream and sugar?"

"Yes. Thank you." Keagan handed her a cup. "And rhyme you did. I think it's quite good."

Keagan laughed. "Thanks, but you don't have to say that. I'm not a poet."

"I don't say anything unless I mean it. You may not be a poet, but I enjoyed it." She took a sip of the coffee and averted her eyes from Keagan.

"The only poetry I ever wrote, was because I was forced to," Keagan muttered.

"Then, isn't the world lucky you were forced?" Rudy met Keagan's eyes again, but quickly looked away in respect for her privacy. She knew that showing her writing was a deeply personal thing and that it would be wise not to overdo her praise. "I was wondering," Rudy began, hoping to steer them to a safer subject, "what happened to my note that was on your corkboard last night? Some pesky little varmint didn't sneak in and chew it up, did they?"

Keagan froze in her tracks and returned the vacuum to the closet, happy to have left the poetry subject, but not at all content with the new one. "I don't know what you're talking about."

"You, Keagan—" she began, "by the way, what's your last name?"

"Donovan." Keagan was unaffected by the non sequitur.

"Thank you. When I'm ranting at someone, I prefer to use both their first and last names, for emphasis, you know." Keagan remained silent, thinking she had never seen anyone talk that fast before.

"Now you, Keagan Donovan, are some piece of work. Let me tell you not what I *think* happened, but what I *know* happened. You found my note and not only did you not throw it out, you actually pinned it up, to remind yourself. To remind yourself of me. And right now, I'll bet that note's in your pocket. I'll bet you got up this morning, saw it, panicked, and shoved it into your pocket. Yep, I'll bet that's exactly what happened." Rudy stopped to take a breath.

"Delusions of grandeur."

"What's that supposed to mean?"

"That's what you're having if you think I'm pining away for you or something. You're delusional if you think you saw that note on my corkboard. I threw it out when I found it."

Rudy literally gaped at Keagan's admission. "You are not going to stand there and deny this?"

Keagan shook her head. "Oh, yes, I am."

"Keagan, I know what I saw with my own two eyes."

"You were just tired."

"I was not. Well, I was, but I know I saw that note up there."

"Did not!"

"Did, too!" Rudy was becoming exasperated with this woman. She had never encountered anyone more stubborn. "Okay, then, fine. I'll believe you if you empty your pockets."

"I will not!" Keagan was indignant.

"I'll just have to assume I'm right and you're wrong, then." Rudy smiled impishly, as she rose and headed to the door. "Ready to go?" She was not shy about letting her triumphant smile linger.

"Yeah." A defeated Keagan admitted to herself that Rudy was both beautiful *and* smart. Those qualities made her more attractive all the time.

The phone ringing pulled Keagan out of her contemplation. The machine clicked on and she heard Joan's voice. "Hi, are you there? I'll wait a couple of seconds. I guess you're not. Well, I told your grandmother that I won't allow any more vodka in the house, only beer. She still isn't speaking to me much. I'll talk to you later." The machine clicked off.

"That your mom?"

"Yeah."

"She sounds nice."

"She is nice, sometimes too nice. What she doesn't understand is that the only answer is to allow no alcohol in the house. Beer, vodka, it's all the same." She didn't know why she allowed Rudy that bit of information.

"Your grandma. I take it she's an alcoholic."

"Yep."

Rudy remained silent, knowing that Keagan would offer more information if she wanted to.

"Some people have normal families and some people have what I've got. It took me a few years to realize that."

Rudy sensed that Keagan didn't want to continue discussing her family. As she prepared to change the subject, her stomach growled loudly. The taller woman laughed. Rudy rolled her eyes self-consciously. "I'm *really* hungry. Would you let me buy you breakfast somewhere? It's the least I can do, since you helped me out."

Keagan returned Rudy's intense green-eyed gaze. She couldn't refuse and didn't want to. "All right. Where did you have in mind?"

Rudy's face brightened at the prospect of food. "There's a coffee house on High. They know me there."

* * * * * * * * *

Within minutes, they were seated in the restaurant, sipping cappuccino. On the way over, Rudy explained that The Coffee House was one of her favorite haunts. She often stopped there to have lunch and study. "And every once in awhile, I have breakfast here." Her eyes twinkled as she looked over at Keagan, who was letting her do most of the talking.

"Is this where you take your women after you're done with them?" Keagan grinned sarcastically.

"Oh, yeah. Every last one of them." Rudy played along. "But we don't usually get here this early."

"Oh. Yeah." Nervousness overcame her. Keagan wanted to change the subject but her mind drew a blank.

"So, are you really an English major?" Rudy wanted to break the tension between them.

"Yes."

Rudy realized she was going to have to start asking open-ended questions or all she would get would be mono-syllabic responses. "What a coincidence. So am I. I'm surprised we never ran into each other before. You go to Ohio State?"

"Yep."

"It's a big campus, after all." She laughed under her breath, guessing it came from nervousness because she hadn't found anything particularly funny. "So what classes are you taking this quarter?"

"The one I'm dreading is Traditional Grammar and Usage."

Just as Rudy was congratulating herself on getting more than one word out of Keagan, the waitress brought their orders. Rudy got three large pancakes, four slices of bacon, two eggs, toast, a cream cheese bagel, and a large grapefruit juice. Keagan got an orange juice, a bagel with strawberry jam, and a small side of hash browns. Taking in the slight frame of her companion, Keagan wondered if Rudy could eat all that. She didn't wonder for long. They ate for a few minutes until Rudy broke the silence.

"So, why are you dreading grammar?" She finished up

her pancake, which she had smeared generously with blue-berry syrup.

"Diagramming." Keagan took a bite of bagel. "I just can't do it. It looks like math to me. I'm terrible at math."

"I've made quite a study of English grammar on my own and I've taken Traditional Grammar. I can help you with it, if you want."

"What'd you get?"

"An A."

"Maybe I'll take you up on your offer if I get desperate." Keagan took a last bite of hash brown.

"I'm good with desperate women." Rudy looked down shyly. She reached for her glass of grapefruit juice for something to do, not because she was thirsty.

"You little flirt." Rudy blushed. Keagan thought how adorable it was when she did that.

"I'm not usually a flirt. It must be you."

"Me, bringing out your deviant side, huh?"

"Must be." Rudy and Keagan stared at each other briefly before averting their eyes.

Keagan's gaze fell upon Rudy's lips the next time she looked at her. She wondered what it would be like to kiss them. Pulling herself out of her daze as her eyes met Rudy's again, she suspected Rudy had been watching her every move. She was right.

"You about ready?" Keagan realized that they had been done with their food for a few minutes.

"Yes." Rudy paid the bill, but forgot about the change. Neither she nor Keagan noticed. Later, there was a happy waitress who received a very generous tip.

* * * * * * * * * *

Rudy gave directions to her mom's house as Keagan drove, so there was little opportunity for further talk.

Eventually they arrived and Keagan pulled in the driveway. "Do you need a lift back to your place?" Keagan hoped she did and didn't at the same time.

"Nah. I'll visit with my mom and she can drive me back. I've already put you out enough anyway. Thanks, Keagan. Sorry about all this."

Keagan wasn't sorry but didn't say so. "That's okay."

"Do you want to meet my mom?" It slipped out before Rudy realized the possible implications. "I just thought since you're here—"

Keagan smiled tightly. "I'd like to, but I have some things to do." She paused, and then got out of the car so Rudy could climb over the driver's seat to get out.

Rudy stood awkwardly for a second, and leaned forward to give Keagan a light kiss on the cheek. Rudy could see the shock register on her face as she stepped back from her. "Okay, then. Thanks." She smiled, gave a short wave, and then headed into her mom's house, leaving a flabbergasted Keagan behind.

****

When Keagan got home, she slipped into the den. Calling up her journal folder on her computer, she began to write. It was her usual routine to write in the journal only when she felt like it. Some people allowed themselves to be pressured into keeping one regularly but not Keagan. She wanted the journal to have meaning and so only wrote in it when her inner voice told her to. Now, her voice was screaming for her to write.

Sunday, January 17, 1999, 10:12am

I met this woman at the Grotto. She's attractive and witty. She'll also help me with grammar. Since it makes sense for me to let her help me, I may decide to. As for the attractive and witty parts, they have no bearing on further

*interaction with her. I've already concluded that she
wouldn't be just a "story idea" acquaintance. The only
other alternative is to befriend or date her, both of which
would be bad ideas. She's got a killer smile.*

Keagan saved the file after deleting the last sentence.

She planned on avoiding the bar for a few days, until
her crush on Rudy ended. When that concluded, she'd ask
for her help with grammar. It was a succinct, logical plan.
There was no reason for it not to work. Except that when
Monday night came, she ended up doing the last thing she
intended by going to the Grotto. Her friend Gretchen
called and begged her to come to the bar. She had broken
up with her girlfriend and needed to talk. As Keagan drove
to the bar, she hoped not to run into Rudy.

She arrived around 8:30. As she pulled in, she looked
around the parking lot but didn't see Rudy's car. Figuring
she wasn't there, Keagan walked in with confidence, and
casually gazed over at the pool table. There was Milligan
playing pool with Rudy. Char was standing near, but
looked like she was behaving herself. And Jackie Daniels
was standing nearby drinking a beer. Rudy was concentrating on a shot and didn't notice Keagan, whose heartbeat
sped up the moment she entered her field of vision.
Keagan hated it when that happened. It meant she was losing control of her body and made her edgy. With stealth,
she headed to a booth near the jukebox where Gretchen sat.

"Hi, Keagan." Gretchen was two years older than
Keagan, and was known for her ornery disposition. A
rounded face, and semi long, brown hair framed her gray
eyes. Everyone called her "Big Gretchen" because while
not overweight, she was big boned. She was also an heir-
ess and didn't work, to the envy of many. Keagan recalled
wryly, that Gretchen had once tried to buy her, after she
drank a pitcher of margaritas. Keagan had declined the
offer.

"How are you?"

"Oh, I'm fine, hon." She motioned to Cody at the bar. "My friend needs a drink!" Her voice was loud pitched and obnoxious. As always, Keagan ignored this characteristic of her friend.

"You sounded pretty upset on the phone."

"Keagan, you know I don't like beating around the bush, so I'll be frank. I didn't break up with Kelly."

"Oh. Then why am I here?" Keagan was getting a sick feeling in her stomach. In apparent answer, Cody came over with a rum and coke. She winked at Keagan and returned to the bar.

"You're here because of that cute, adorable woman at the pool table...Rudy. Milligan and the others told me all about it. We're setting you up, since you don't have the sense to do it yourself."

Keagan had a hard time controlling her rising temper. But somehow, she managed to do it. "I can't believe you guys would do this."

"Sure, you can."

"You guys have never gone this far to set me up before. Why now?"

"We're tired of seeing you moping around here scribbling notes in your notebook. We decided you needed companionship." Gretchen grinned with delight and glanced at the pool table. Rudy made no move to come over to see Keagan, much to Gretchen's distress.

Keagan got up. "Guess what? I'm old enough to make my own decisions about what I need, but thanks. Bye." She headed straight for the door, without glancing back or looking anywhere else.

Milligan had watched the proceedings from the pool table. "Keagan?" Reluctant to ignore her friend, in spite of her manipulation, Keagan walked over to the pool table. The game had stopped for the moment. "Can I interest you

in a game of pool?" Milligan tried to look innocent, even
though her plan had been revealed.

Keagan rolled her eyes and took in the scene. "Hi,"
she said to Rudy, who was standing next to Milligan holding a cue stick. "I didn't see your car out back."

"I parked across the street. I have to leave early
tonight and didn't want to get fenced in. I didn't expect to
see you."

"You didn't?"

"You're usually here by now." Rudy paused, sensing
there was more to this. "Why would I expect to see you?"

Keagan was unsure that Rudy was innocent of her
friends' plan. Partially because she suspected that Rudy
intentionally locked her keys up to get her attention. "*You*
tell *me*."

"What do you mean?" Rudy didn't know where
Keagan was heading with this line of conversation.

"As long as you're here, why don't we all play doubles?" Milligan indicated Jackie who was standing nearby.

Keagan, thoroughly disgusted, didn't know whom to
trust. They *all* might have been in on it. "I don't think so.
I was busy until Gretchen called me down here because she
needed to talk. Now that I've discovered she lied and
manipulated me, I don't have any reason to stay."

"What did she lie to you about?"

"Here's the whole story, assuming you didn't already
know. Gretchen told me she broke up with her girlfriend,
Kelly, and needed to talk to someone about it, so I came
down. When I got here, she admitted she was trying to get
me here, while you were here, to set me up with you."

"Oh." It dawned on Rudy that Keagan thought she had
something to do with it. "You certainly don't think I had
anything to do with this?"

"Actually, I do. Aren't you the one who locked your
keys in your car on purpose?"

Milligan sensed that the situation might be getting out
of control soon if she didn't do something. "Who cares
about *why* you're here. You're here. And for the record, it
was us, not Rudy who thought this up. She didn't know
anything about it."

"Of course you're gonna say that," said Keagan.

"Hold on a minute here. Yes, I locked up my keys on
purpose, and for that I'm sorry. I just did it because I was
having a hard time getting your attention."

"You already had my attention."

"I didn't know that."

"I didn't want you to know that. But now, because of
this contrived and manipulated situation, you do. Happy?"

"Not really, no." Rudy felt Keagan's anger, regretting
any part she had in it.

"I've been told that spending an evening with me
makes women very happy, if that's what you're looking
for." Char had been standing nearby, taking in the unfolding confrontation and waiting for an opportunity to step in.
She smiled at Rudy slyly and winked.

"Shut up, Char!" Both Keagan and Rudy said it in unison. At the shocked look on the offending woman's face,
they burst into laughter.

"Okay," began Keagan. "I believe you. I don't know
why, but—"

"I have an honest face?"

"That must be it." Keagan's response held a certain
irony when the only reason she believed Rudy was because
she wanted to.

"Now that we all understand each other, how about
some pool?" said Milligan. For a brief moment, she feared
she made a drastic mistake, by getting Gretchen to call
Keagan. But now it looked like things were shaping up
well.

"Thanks, but I have to go. School tomorrow." Her

gaze lingered on Rudy briefly before she turned and headed for the door.

Rudy stared after her for a few seconds. "You really shouldn't have done that to her. I don't think she's the type that likes to have her decisions made for her like that."

Milligan was racking the balls. "Probably not, but sometimes you just gotta grab people and shake em', ya know? I'm speaking meta—meta—"

"Metaphorically."

"Right. I'm just speaking metaphorically, but I'm sure you get my meaning."

"I'm sure I do. I just don't think Keagan gets it."

"Oh, I think she gets my meaning exactly." Milligan lined her cue stick up to shoot. "That's why she left." She aimed and shot, knocking in a stripe, as the other balls darted around the table.

Rudy looked doubtful. "Maybe she doesn't really like me."

Milligan regarded Rudy, allowing herself a small, knowing, grin. "She likes you. Believe me, I've known her for a long time. She definitely likes you."

Rudy hoped Milligan's words were correct.

****

The next day, Keagan got up earlier than usual for school. Her classes began at a quarter until eight and ran through noon. Being a morning person, this worked out well for her. Grabbing her black leather backpack, she unzipped it and threw a single subject notebook into it. It was her last quarter and she was so thoroughly burned out by school, that she no longer cared about organizing her notes in a multi-subject notebook.

The weather had warmed up over the past few days so

Keagan left her gloves and scarf inside the apartment. As she made her way to the car, the brightly shining sun threatened to improve her mood from lousy to almost enthused. She glanced at her watch and noted that since it was half past seven, she would never make it on time for British Literature. She didn't care since she hated British Literature with a passion.

Arriving at the university, she entered Denney Hall, and hunted down room 115. It wasn't much of a hunt, because she had taken several classes in the same room. Not feeling any guilt at entering late, she stepped in noticing that the class was full. She didn't see any empty seats as her eyes scanned the back of the room. The professor was lecturing about the usual first day things as she did this. Spotting a seat near the back, Keagan trudged toward it. She tuned out everyone in her quest for a place to sit, and was surprised to feel someone touch her arm not a second after she sat down. She almost jumped out of her seat, when she turned to see who it was. Rudy sat directly next to her in the second row. "Hey, Keagan, fancy meeting you here," she whispered. She chuckled as Keagan stared at her in disbelief.

"Are you following me, young lady?"

"More like you would be following me. I was here first."

Keagan grinned. They both turned their attention back to Professor Parnell who was informing them that they would be required to do group presentations later in the semester. Keagan grimaced. She hated working in groups. Parnell said that in a few weeks he would pick each group himself, after he had a chance to review each student's skills. He wanted the groups to be balanced well. Keagan groaned. She didn't like oral presentations.

Parnell dismissed class early and Keagan found herself alone with Rudy as the class filtered out of the room. "You know, this is really kind of funny," said Rudy.

"Oh, yeah. Ha. Ha."

"I mean, imagine the odds, the two of us, having just met at a bar, and with our little ensuing attraction and everything and then...voila, here we are again. Just think of the odds." Rudy was talking fast again. Keagan noted that she tended to do that either when she was nervous or when she felt strongly about something. Or both at once.

Keagan stretched her legs out letting them rest on the seat in front of her. "Ensuing attraction? Nope. Never said I was attracted to you." She enjoyed toying with the beautiful young woman. Keagan knew it was wrong to do, but couldn't help herself.

Rudy inched a bit closer to Keagan, who sat smugly in her seat, her arms folded. The corners of Keagan's mouth came up slightly like she wanted to smile but wouldn't let herself. She smelled Rudy's cologne, the same type she had worn when she had taught her pool. A memory flashed through Keagan's mind of what it had felt like to touch her. "But you said I got your attention."

"Attention. Attraction. Two different words the last time I checked, although similar in many respects. Similar looking, similar sounding—"

"That's it!" Rudy flashed her green eyes at Keagan. "You're impossible! Impossible!" As Keagan inched away in mock fear at her outburst, Rudy rose from her seat and allowed a grin to surface. Keagan was so sexy when she was putting up that sarcastic wall between herself and others. But she was also maddening.

"Nothing's impossible." Keagan's eyes twinkled.

"Good. Bye." Rudy clearly enunciated both words as she started to exit the classroom. "I'll probably be at the bar tonight. Thought I'd be kind to you and let you know, so you could avoid me if you wanted to." She didn't wait for a reply and headed down the hall.

Keagan sat, feeling a twinge of pain at Rudy's biting words. Interpreting this as a sign of her developing feelings for her, she considered how to regain control. She came to no good conclusion. Regardless of whether or not she kept showing up, Rudy was sinking into Keagan's heart.

Later that day, Keagan stopped by her mom's for a visit. Joan wasn't home yet, so Keagan talked to her grandma. She had told her grandma about her sexual orientation five years before when she had broken up with her girlfriend, Terry. Geraldine Rafferty knew something had been bothering Keagan, because her whole personality had changed. Where Keagan used to be lighthearted with a very sarcastic but funny sense of humor, she was now subdued and quiet, the only words coming out of her mouth being ones that were rife with negativity. She almost begged her granddaughter to tell her what the problem was. Keagan was reluctant to tell the truth, that she had a failed relationship with a woman and she was hurting. But Keagan did tell her and never regretted it, because her grandma had been supportive. They had always been close and her grandma had come through for her when she needed it the most. Keagan thought back to that time briefly, as Gerry got her an iced tea.

Keagan never told her grandma how much her support meant. It was one of the main things that helped her get through one of the most painful times of her life. Gerry came back into the living room and handed Keagan the iced tea. She sat down on the couch and her dog, Rosey, jumped up and sat beside her. Rosey put her head on Gerry's leg and looked up with sweet puppy dog eyes. "Yes, sweetheart. You want a treat don't you?" She produced a dog bone from the pocket of her robe and offered it to the dog who took it and munched contentedly.

Keagan sipped her drink and snickered at the dog.

"Unruly beast."

Gerry frowned at Keagan. "She's not a beast, she's my sweetie."

"So are you and Mom speaking yet?"

"Yes, but I can't have any more vodka in the house! I called Sean and he's going to sneak me some." Gerry laughed at this, completely oblivious to the possible consequences of such an action.

"Do you think that's a good idea?"

Gerry put her index finger to her lips, indicating for Keagan to be quiet about it. "Rafferty family secret." She giggled.

"Right." Keagan didn't like keeping things from her mother, but knew the truth would come out soon enough anyway.

"So, how are you?" Gerry took a sip of her beer.

"Fine. I, uh, met this girl at the bar." Keagan didn't know why she brought this up.

"Ah. So, you two are dating now?" Gerry wasn't familiar with gay practices, but she guessed they must be pretty much the same as straight ones.

"Oh, no. No, it's not like that. I guess I don't really know what it's like." Keagan looked down at her feet, feeling silly.

"You like this girl?"

"Yes." Keagan drawled it out slowly, as if she wasn't sure she wanted to reveal this much.

"She pretty?"

"Beautiful." Keagan said this somewhat shyly, not really used to discussing these things with her grandma.

"Nice?"

"Very nice."

"Smart?"

"Yes. She is."

"And she likes you, I take it?"

"I think she does, but—"

"Not buts, Keagan. You must ask her out on a date as soon as you get a chance. What's her name?"

"Rudy." Keagan knew she was about to get encouraged, but wasn't sure she wanted the encouragement.

"Call Rudy and ask her out, Keagan. What have you got to lose?" Gerry was concerned that her granddaughter had been cutting herself off from life. She wanted her to be happy again, and felt this was the way.

"Grandma, we kind of had an argument. I don't think she'd go out with me now if I asked."

"Forget about that. I have a feel for these things. Ask her to go out with you. I guarantee she'll say 'yes.'"

Yeah, right and you're going to win the million dollar lottery, too. "I don't think so." Keagan appreciated her grandma's positive outlook, but didn't share it. It was hopeless. She had no idea how to have a relationship or to treat a woman. That was obvious in the way she had treated Rudy at school.

****

Keagan went to the Grotto that night intent on doing some writing. She took her usual place at the table in the back, hoping to see Rudy and apologize for her actions at school.

Cody came over to see what was going on. She had been involved in the manipulation of the previous evening and felt responsible. "How goes it, Keag?"

"Fine. In spite of you, Gretchen, and Milligan."

"I didn't have anything directly to do with it except, uh, aforeknowledge."

"Malice aforethought." Keagan corrected. "It's okay. I ran into Rudy at school today. We're in the same British Literature class."

Cody respected her friend's feelings enough not to make the sarcastic, teasing comment that was on the top of her tongue. "So, is that good or bad?"

"It's good. And bad. I haven't decided what to do about her yet. I mean, I think I would have a pretty good shot at a date with her—"

Cody laughed outright.

"What?" Keagan looked confused.

She leaned over and touched Keagan's arm, squeezing it in an attempt to make a point. "Rudy took one look at you and fell in love. I know. I was there."

Keagan almost blushed. "Yeah, right."

"My friend, she is *so* into you. It's so obvious." Cody smiled.

Keagan looked over to the door and saw Rudy walk in. She felt a jolt of adrenaline surge through her body. Feeling ridiculous but not knowing what to do about it, she turned back to Cody. "It's not obvious to me."

"That's 'cause you've got this mental block against relationships. Get over it."

"Yeah, yeah."

Keagan watched as Rudy's eyes scanned the bar. The young woman met her eyes and then looked away. Then she watched as Rudy spotted Danielle and started over towards her booth. She decided to sit back and observe for awhile before making her move. Keagan watched as Rudy removed her soft brown, suede jacket revealing underneath a dark blue button-down shirt. Her long blonde hair was tied back in a braid, which accentuated her green eyes. Keagan thought Rudy had never looked more attractive. She watched for a few moments as the young woman chatted with Dani and then felt a strong surge of jealousy when Dani leaned over and kissed her. It wasn't a friendly kiss and Rudy didn't seem to mind too much.

"Ouch," said Cody.

Keagan remained silent, her brain trying to process the feelings she was having without success. She shook her head and tried to clear her thoughts but they were scrambled and filled with dread. "You don't think Rudy likes her, do you?" she asked nonchalantly.

"Do you really care?"

"Just curious."

"I think she likes you, but you won't give her the time of day."

"Yeah, yeah, blah, blah."

"See ya later, kiddo." Cody returned to the bar having made enough attempts to prod Keagan into action. The rest was up to her.

Keagan sat brooding for about an hour, her eyes never far from Rudy. Dani made no further advances, much to Keagan's delight. Eventually, Danielle rose from the booth and left the bar. Rudy's eyes scanned the bar and landed upon Keagan who was pretending to write.

Each table in the bar had a candle on it to make the setting romantic. The cynic in Keagan thought it more likely so that people could see better. She never sought out more light than was provided by the one candle, and so was surprised when a smiling Rudy added two candles to her table. "What's this for?"

"Oh, I just thought I'd bring these over so you could see what you're missing." Rudy slipped into the seat across from Keagan and smiled mischievously.

"Ah." Keagan wondered many things at this point. She wondered why Rudy was there when she tried to avoid her gaze earlier, why she was flirting with her, and why Danielle had gone when it seemed they were getting along so well. But instead of asking the person who knew the answers, she remained silent.

Rudy sensed Keagan's dismay. "Actually, I thought these might help you see better. You know, to write."

Keagan nodded, but her mind wasn't on the candles. "Why did Dani leave?"

"I guess she got tired of me."

"I doubt that."

Rudy wondered if making ambiguous statements was the only way Keagan could express any feeling for her. She hoped not. "She asked me to go out with her and I said I couldn't, so I guess she gave up." She indicated her indifference by shrugging.

"Why aren't you going out with her?"

Rudy stared into the questioning blue eyes and chose to battle Keagan's vulnerability by exposing her own. "I didn't think it would be fair to go out with someone when there's somebody else I'd rather go out with. Do you think that would be fair?"

"No."

"Me neither, so I said 'no.'" This wasn't going the way Rudy envisioned it. Now, Keagan was supposed to ask who it was that she wanted to go out with and Rudy would declare in unequivocal terms that it was Keagan. But she wasn't taking the bait. After a few moments, she realized that Keagan wasn't going to say anything. "You make me so crazy, Keagan, do you have any idea how much?"

Rudy's question, however rhetorical, conveyed to Keagan several things: interest, attraction, and persistence. She also noted that Rudy's voice had dropped to a near whisper that she found appealing. Keagan tried in vain to come up with a snappy comeback, but failed. She was too focused on the nearness of the young woman. She smiled slyly. "How much?" Keagan raised an eyebrow and regarded her challengingly.

Rudy almost gave in to her desire to show Keagan how much by leaning over and kissing her, but couldn't let her have that satisfaction. "Actually, not that much." She averted her gaze, feigning non-interest, and tried with no success to calm her rapidly beating heart.

"Oh?" Keagan enjoyed the game and it was a great way to avoid her feelings.

Rudy had other ideas, though. Forgetting the game, she reached over and placed her hand on Keagan's. Before long their fingers were intertwined. Keagan gazed at her, doing and saying nothing.

"This isn't so bad is it?"

"No." Keagan looked away to get a break from the intensity. As she did, her eyes betrayed her.

Rudy noticed her friend looking toward the door and wondered if she recognized someone. There were three women coming in the door. Noticing Keagan's look of recognition, she asked, "Do you know them?"

Her protective mask settled in and she regarded Rudy coolly again. "Not all of them, just one."

"Oh. Which one?" At her question, Keagan pointed out a tall woman with sandy, blonde hair. She had hazel eyes, a sharp expression, and was turning to look their way. "Her."

Rudy guessed this was someone she had a history with. "How do you know her?"

Keagan pulled her hand away from Rudy's. She snickered. "Her name's Terry. I suppose you could say she's my ex-girlfriend."

Rudy remained turned in the direction of Terry, wanting to get a better look at her. She tried not to make it obvious that she was watching her, but her curiosity about this woman from Keagan's past was getting the best of her and she didn't care. After a few seconds, Terry sat down at the bar. Rudy turned back around to find Keagan regarding her with a puzzled smile on her face.

"So what were you watching her for? You think she's

hot? I could maybe introduce the two of you if you want."

"Ha. Ha. As if."

Keagan remained silent, and remembered where she and Rudy had been before Terry walked in. She missed the feeling of the young woman's hand in hers. Rudy's hands were soft, and the way she rubbed Keagan's fingers gently, comfortingly, was a contact she reveled in. Somewhat hesitantly, she reached across the table toward Rudy who responded by reaching forward and holding Keagan's hand again. Both women appeared to feel comfortable with this mutual action, not speaking about it, but continuing their conversation.

"I was going to tell you before Terry came in that I'm sorry about what happened at school. I was hoping to see you here tonight to tell you that." It was a simple statement, but Keagan delivered it awkwardly.

Rudy was pleasantly surprised at her apology, but tried not to show it. "That's okay. I mean, I know you were just joking around. You do that a lot, you know."

"I know, but sometimes I take it too far."

"That's all right, really."

"No, quit making excuses for me."

Rudy sensed that Keagan was leading to something serious. Her sarcastic demeanor had dropped, revealing a different side to her. She felt that her friend wanted desperately to tell her something, but was having a difficult time doing it. Rudy squeezed her hand. "Okay." She smiled, hoping to put Keagan at ease.

"Despite what I said at school, I—" Keagan stopped, not able to make herself go any further, especially not with Terry sitting at the bar. When her ex-girlfriend walked in, all of Keagan's insecurities returned with her. She tried to push it out of her mind, but it was useless. She stopped and stared blankly at Rudy.

"It's okay. We can talk about it later." Rudy hated to

see Keagan so uncomfortable, and didn't want to be the cause of it. She suspected that Keagan was about to profess some feeling for her, and she didn't think pressuring her about it would be a good idea.

"All right. Later, then." Keagan spotted Terry coming over to their table. She groaned under her breath, but loudly enough for Rudy to hear. A steady pounding began in her head. She put on her indifferent mask and smiled as Terry approached.

"Keagan."

"Hi. Terry isn't it?" Keagan grinned devilishly.

"Nice to see you, too."

Not wanting Keagan to be embarrassed by their intertwined hands, Rudy pulled back. Keagan looked over at her, giving her a mock frown, but accepted the gesture. Remembering her manners, she offered her hand to Terry. "I'm Rudy. Nice to meet you, Terry."

Shaking the young woman's hand, Terry smiled warmly. "Nice to meet you, Rudy."

"I thought you moved down south," said Keagan. Seeing Terry brought back only memories of hurt, not feelings. Keagan wondered if she no longer *could* feel and then glanced at Rudy. She had her answer.

"I'm back visiting my mom. I thought I'd visit Kate while I was here, too."

"Ah." Keagan thought how typical it was of Terry to bring Kate up. Kate was the woman she had left Keagan for. If Terry had an ounce of sensitivity in her, she wouldn't have brought it up. But, sensitivity had never been one of her strong points.

Rudy broke in, sensing the two might want some privacy. "I'm going to go get a water. You want anything?"

"No, thanks. You comin' back?"

"Yeah. I'll be back." Rudy gave her a wink, as she rose and headed off to the bar.

"So," said Terry. "How are you?"

"Fine."

"I see you're just as talkative as ever."

Keagan smiled faintly, feeling both indifference and annoyance. She looked up to the bar, and saw Rudy chatting with Cody. She wished Rudy would come back. "If I remember correctly, the last time we spoke we didn't. Your choice, not mine. So, forgive me if I'm not real talkative or particularly overjoyed to see you."

Terry ran a nervous hand through her light brown tousled hair. "I deserved that."

"Is there some reason you're hanging around?"

"I just thought I'd come over and say hello." Terry's voice took on a defensive tinge.

"Interesting, considering you never had the decency to say goodbye. But don't worry. I got the message."

"Sorry. I didn't mean to hurt you."

"Nobody ever means to hurt anybody, do they? It's no big deal." Once again, Keagan belittled her feelings. It was a pattern she was loath to give up.

Terry was turned off by Keagan's abrasive mood. "I've got to get back to my friends, so I'll see ya around."

"Right," Keagan drawled, watching with relief as she returned to the bar.

Within moments, Rudy reappeared at the table with two glasses of ice water. Keagan had been thirsty but hadn't realized it. She took a big drink. "Thanks."

"Sure."

"So, do you want to hear the story or not?"

"Yes. But this sounds like it might be a long one. Can I go get some popcorn and peanuts, first?" Rudy's green eyes bore into Keagan's inquisitively.

Keagan recalled her voracious appetite. "I'll go get you a snack."

When she returned, she had a bowl of beer nuts, a bag

of popcorn, and two pickled eggs. "Mmm, I love pickled eggs. I didn't know they had them here." Rudy grabbed one and took a bite.

"They don't. I kind of asked Mabel if she had anything in the refrigerator she could spare."

She smiled warmly at Keagan. "Now do I get my story?"

"You get your story."

"I'm sure this will be a good one."

"Why?" Keagan looked confused.

"Because it's about you."

"What makes you think that?"

"I thought you meant you were going to tell me about you and Terry."

"Ah." Keagan leaned back in her chair and contemplated her options. She could bluntly relate the details of her previous relationship or she could make it more interesting. Noting that Rudy had left the other pickled egg on the plate in front of her, she realized it was being saved for her. "Please, have the other one. I'm not hungry."

Rudy snatched it up with a grin. "Thanks." Keagan watched as the young woman devoured the other egg. She found herself happy at her delight.

Keagan smiled. "I'll tell you the story but first you have to tell me something."

"What's that?"

"I don't know your last name." Keagan stared awkwardly at the table for a moment before her eyes met Rudy's again.

"Aw, I didn't know you cared."

Keagan stared back at emerald green eyes that played with her. But instead of her usual denials, she waited patiently.

Rudy laughed. "My last name is Whitman. Rudy Walt."

"Very funny."

"No, really, it *is* Whitman. Just, the middle name's not Walt. It's Lauren."

Keagan chuckled. "That's kind of neat. *I sing the body electric, The armies of those I love engirth me and I engirth them, They will not let me off till I go with them, respond to them, and discorrupt them, and charge them full with the charge of my soul.*"

"*The* soul," corrected Rudy.

"Oh, yeah." Keagan looked sheepish.

"You know, that was pretty impressive. If you were any woman but you, I'd say you were trying to seduce me with poetry."

"Is that what it'll take?" Embarrassed, Keagan tried to cover up her accidental flirtation. "Because there's a place called Xanadu. Maybe you've heard of it?"

Rudy effected a cool façade to hide her shock. The blush on her face and the pleasurable sensation she experienced in her lower body region told her it wasn't working. "You...you mean Charles Foster Kane's home in that movie?" She knew Keagan hadn't meant that.

"No, no. *In Xanadu did Kubla Khan—*"

"If you think reciting 'Kubla Khan' is going to distract me, you're wrong." Rudy folded her arms and took a defensive stance, all the while trying not to smile. It was difficult.

"*A stately pleasure-dome decree,*" continued Keagan.

Rudy was not to be outdone. "*Where Alph, the sacred river ran. Thro—*"

Keagan increased the tempo of her voice in order to get out the whole stanza before Rudy could. "*Through caverns measureless to man d—*"

"*Down to a sunless sea!*" Rudy flashed a triumphant smile, figuring she had won.

Keagan was content to let her think she won, hoping

her mind would focus on that instead of the flirting. "Now, I think I was going to tell a story."

"Fine. Tell your story, but I won't forget what you said."

Keagan frowned, but wished she could grab Rudy and kiss her to shut her up. She took another drink of her ice water, having begun to feel warm.

"Feeling a little hot?"

"No. Why?"

"Oh, I don't know," Rudy began, licking her lips. "You just look a bit flushed. You're not coming down with something are you?" She reached over and pressed the back of her hand to Keagan's forehead.

Keagan gazed back with impassive calm. "So. How do I feel?"

"At last. They're touching." Cody who had sidled up to their table unnoticed pulled both women out of their mutual flirtatious daze. Rudy pulled her hand back as Keagan regarded the bartender with mock annoyance. Cody smiled warmly at both of them, almost regretting her rude interruption. "Can I get you two anything?"

"Yeah. How about taking you and your matchmaking ways outta here."

"Keagan!" Rudy's voice showed her embarrassment.

"It's all right, hon. I'm used to being treated with no respect around here. A person gives up their pickled eggs and not a word of thanks, and then a brush off. I *should* be hurt."

"They were *your* eggs? Gee, thanks." Just then, Keagan spotted the "rose girl," as she was referred to, but Keagan called her Angelique. She was a woman who came in on certain nights and sold single, long stemmed roses. It was considered a nice romantic gesture to buy a rose for the person that one was interested in. The thought entered into Keagan's head, but then disappeared. Rudy would get the wrong idea.

"Oh, you're welcome, dahling."

"Cody, could I have another glass of ice water, please?"

"Sure, Rueday. Looks like you two are gonna need it." Chuckling at her own cleverness, she headed back to the bar, leaving Keagan and Rudy staring at each other in silence.

A few seconds later, Angelique made her way over to their table. "Can I interest one of you in a rose?" She had a perfect selling face. Her eyes danced constantly, complimenting her mirthful demeanor. People felt guilty for turning her down.

Without hesitation, Rudy spoke up. "You got any yellow?"

Angelique produced a crisp full yellow rose and presented it to Rudy, who smiled. "You can give it to my friend." She indicated Keagan. "It's for her." The flower girl handed the rose to a rather startled Keagan who took it graciously. After Rudy paid the woman and she had gone, she watched her friend put the rose to her lips and smell it.

"Nice. Thanks, La Roux."

"It comes with a price, you know."

"What's that?"

"My story?"

Keagan laid the rose on the table, her face turning contemplative. "Ah, yes." She intentionally put on a dramatic air. "The story of a young, naive, nineteen-year-old. Her name was Lola Blankeridge. She was unaware of the evil ways of man and—"

"Lola Blankeridge?"

"Yeah. You know, like that song, "Lola," by the Kinks. '*I'm not dumb but I can't understand why she talks like a woman but walks like a man, oh my Lola. La, la, la, la, Lola...*'"

"Yeah, yeah, I know the song," said Rudy, laughing. "Go ahead."

"So, anyway, this is kind of an ill-fated love story, so beware. Here's my disclaimer: If you don't like sad endings, leave now. This may not be the story for you. Do you want to continue?"

"Yes." Cody came over and deposited two more ice waters onto the table and left, seeing that Keagan and Rudy were involved in a conversation of some substance this time and not wanting to interrupt them.

"Okay, where was I? We have Lola Blankeridge. Most people just call her Lourdes, as a nickname. So—"

"Wait a minute. You mean like Madonna's baby?"

Keagan paused, once again having her train of thought interrupted. "Well, you know." She spoke with haste, anxious to get back to the story. "Kind of. Yeah. Except reversed, all right? May I please continue, now?"

"Yes, please." Rudy gave the lips zipped up sign.

"Lourdes was young, naive, and just coming out as a lesbian. She knew there had been something there ever since she was thirteen and had a hopeless crush on Princess Leia. Luke just didn't do anything for her and neither did Han. Hell, she found Yoda more attractive. But I digress."

Rudy snickered.

"Anyway, one day she was at a lesbian bar with a friend and she met the most amazing woman. Her name was Redd Alert, but people just called her Reddy. Or, Ready, if you know what I mean. Ms. Alert was devious and experienced and she set her sights on the young Lourdes, not realizing or caring how fragile her young heart was. Here's the tragic part: Lourdes's feelings ran deep for this woman who had first shown her what desire could feel like. Who had been the first woman to make her feel attractive? To Reddy, though, Lourdes was little more than a diversion, a distraction, and a reason to end her current relationship. When Lourdes's usefulness ran out, Reddy dropped her like a hot potato, and never looked back. This scarred the young Lourdes who logically maintained that her own rational judgment of people was sorely lacking. She made a vow to herself to have no more relationships, because they weren't compatible with her personality. She roamed the land, a nomad, wandering aimlessly from place to place, remaining a loner. It was a role that fit her well. The End."

"That's a sad story, but I think you could add to it."

"Oh yeah? What would you add?"

"During Lourdes's wanderings, she came across a waif, who latched onto her and followed her. No matter what Lourdes did, the waif, we'll call her, oh, I don't know...how about Gabrielle—"

"Gabrielle? She sounds like a sexpot."

"Get your mind out of the gutter. The sex comes later." Rudy's brow creased, and she looked away, trying to think. Looking directly at Keagan was distracting and not a good idea during the creative process. Keagan, for her part, was drawn in by the addition to her tale. She eagerly anticipated what her friend would come up with next.

"Okay, okay. Lourdes let her hang around, mostly because she was a good cook, but then, it turned into more."

"Don't tell me. They fell deeply in love and rode off into the sunset—"

"Oh, no, no. Keagan, don't you know anything about dramatic tension? I thought you were supposed to be a writer." Rudy gently teased her as Keagan laughed.

"But you're right," Rudy continued. "They did fall in love, but since Lourdes had spent years building up her emotional defenses and Gabrielle didn't have much experience in the fine art of offensive maneuvers, they kind of circled each other for awhile. This dragged on and on, until the smoldering passion between them built up to such a level that even if they had wanted to deny it they couldn't. It had to be satisfied. So, one night, both caught unaware, they made love right there, even though it was a totally inappropriate place." She stopped, looking puzzled.

While Rudy was relating the tale, Keagan had unconsciously placed herself and Rudy in the roles of Lourdes and Gabrielle. "Well...where?"

"I don't know. That's the problem. I can't think of where. It has to be someplace outrageous, you know, to stir things up. The sex, the setting, the eventual release of unfulfilled passion..."

Keagan thought for a moment. "How about an ocean-front beach?"

"Too stereotypical. That's been done a thousand times."

"Okay. How about a car dealership?" She snickered. Why that particular idea had entered into her head, she didn't know. Or care.

"Now that has some real potential."

Surprised at Rudy's comment, Keagan frowned a bit. "It's just something I said off the top of my head."

"I think some of the best ideas come from that kind of thinking, though."

"Whose story is this anyway?" Rudy had taken her sullen tale and turned it into a triumphant love story. Being the cynic she was, she rejected the idea.

"It *was* yours, but I guess it's ours now." Keagan didn't miss double meaning of her words.

"I suppose." She delivered her words cautiously, in spite of her rising excitement. Part of it was sexual attraction but a larger part came from Rudy's willingness to play the game with her. No one had ever dared to meet her in the storytelling arena. Keagan lost count of all the first times with Rudy, but instead of sharing her thoughts with her, she chose to escape from the current setting. "It's getting late. I should go. Work tomorrow."

Rudy nodded her head with no surprise. She had thought Keagan would leave a lot sooner. "Okay. See you at school, then. Or, you could give me a call."

Keagan grinned, knowing that her cover was blown on that subject. "Oh, but I threw your number out, remember?"

"You're sure that's what you did?"

Keagan appeared to contemplate it for a few seconds. "You know what? It might have been salvaged after all." She couldn't help but smile at Rudy, who sat there regarding her with an adorable half-smile. "But, it's probably got a few wrinkles in it."

"I'm sure you'll get them ironed out."

"Yeah. Bye." And then rising, she picked up her rose from the table and sniffed it, her eyes meeting Rudy's once again. Nothing further was said between the two as she turned away, stopping at the bar to say goodnight to a few people. Then, Rudy watched as Keagan scooted out the door, with a little more haste than was necessary.

Chapter
4

As Keagan drove to work the next day, her stray, unorganized thoughts took flight. *My job is meaningless and silly. I work at this place called Gigantic. I put up with rude and obnoxious people, some of whom are my supervisors. Thoughts run rampant through my head all day, and I have no way to satisfy them until I get home. All day I put out junk on a sales floor for people to buy. That's what I get paid for. I put out crap and people pay their presumably hard-earned money to buy it. Money they've earned much in the same way I earn mine. By doing some stupid, meaningless job. I contribute nothing meaningful to society. Except maybe helping Annoying Woman (or AW, as we affectionately refer to her as) understand the difference between the price points of two totally different teapots. Teapots, for godsakes! Who cares about teapots? Why should I? "But why is this one $9.99 and this one's $6.99?" I hold in my temper and smile warmly at her. The woman is a loon, she wears dark sunglasses, a Hawaiian shirt, and a big sun hat all year round. She must think she lives in Maui or something. But I digress. "Well, you see,* *this teapot is larger and it's a different brand. That's why it costs more." She glares daggers at me and raises her voice to a loud, inhuman screech (all right, so it wasn't that loud, and not particularly inhuman, but these are just my random thoughts on the way to work and so I can exaggerate if I want to). "But they're THE SAME TEAPOT! That's FALSE ADVERTISING!!!" Yeah, at this point I wanted to bitch slap her. Not really, of course, because there's not a violent bone in my body, that I know of, but actually I just like the term 'bitch slap' and wanted to use it in my thoughts. Anyway, it's all so insipid and I have to learn the ten sentence patterns for grammar class (abrupt change of subject? Strange). And Rudy said she would help me. Rudy, Rudy, RUDY, RUDY. I have got to stop this interior monologue stuff. Why can't I just focus on driving when I'm driving? And why couldn't Rudy just be the normal type that just hits on me for sex and gets turned down? Why does she have to be so magnetic, intelligent, witty, alluring, sexy, and hot? Oh shit, I'm supposed to be going to work, I have to stop this. Stop thinking about her? Not possible. Not good. Because if it's not possible, it means I've lost all control. And if I've lost all control there's no hope for me and if there's no hope for me...*

A loud horn sounding interrupted Keagan's thoughts. She jumped at the noise, and looked behind her to the driver who was making an obscene gesture and waving his hands in the air. When she turned back around, she noticed the light was green. She had been stopped at a red light and hadn't noticed when it changed. Embarrassed, she started up again. "Okay," she told herself out loud. "Put a lid on it, now." Keagan reached for one of her cassettes, thinking music would turn off her head for awhile. Stepping on the gas with more fervor, she hoped to get to work on time.

****

"I can't believe you kept this from me." Joan refrained from raising her voice, but Keagan knew that her mom was angry. They were sitting in Joan's living room, discussing Gerry, who was passed out on the couch. Keagan took a blanket and covered her grandmother up, placing her hand near Gerry's mouth to make sure she was still breathing. She did this with stealth, so her mother wouldn't see her concern. She knew it was silly to think her grandmother might be dead, but it eased her mind nonetheless.

Joan and Keagan moved into the den. "I try to stay out of your business. She lives here and I don't. It wasn't my place to say anything."

"Is that how you see it? Well, this involves her health, do you realize that? She's drinking herself to death."

"She's been doing that for years. She's not going to stop."

Joan ignored Keagan's comment. "I don't want Sean sneaking her booze. And if you know about it, you have to tell me." Her mom was on the verge of tears. Knowing she wouldn't be able to deal with that, she softened her voice and made sure she told Joan what she wanted to hear.

"The next time I'll tell you, I promise." Keagan gave her mom a hug. "Is there anything you want me to do now?"

"Yes. Tell Sean—"

"Where the hell is my bottle? Joan, you give me that back now or I'll make you pay!" Mother and daughter looked at each other with tense expressions. Gerry had obviously awakened and wasn't too happy that Joan had taken her bottle. They walked back to the living room, but the blanket was crumpled up on the floor, and Gerry was gone.

"Grandma?" Keagan walked around the corner into

the kitchen in an attempt to find Gerry. Joan followed behind with caution. Gerry held a butcher knife, not in a threatening manner, but in a way that told Keagan she might be prepared to use it if she didn't get what she wanted.

"Hi, sweetie."

"Oh my God! She's got a knife!"

"Calm down. She's just holding it. Grandma, will you come sit down so we can talk?" Keagan didn't ask her to put the knife down, wanting to divert attention from it. She hoped that if Gerry agreed to talk, she'd put the knife down on her own.

"The time for talking's long past! This has been building for years! Now I want it back now!" She raised the knife a little.

Keagan knew that she was no longer dealing with her grandma, but with someone else that Gerry became when she drank. Her mind tried to rationalize this, while her heart battled with it. Every time this happened to Gerry, Keagan's heart broke a little bit more.

"I poured it down the drain." Joan's voice was full of contempt and since she tended to react emotionally, she failed to realize the bad choice she had made.

"You bitch! You don't have the right!" Gerry raised the knife in a threatening position and started toward Joan, who was crying and retreating at the same time. Due to the fact that Gerry was quite drunk, however, she tripped, and fell. Keagan dashed over, as the knife fell harmlessly to the floor. She caught her grandma before she hit the floor and was surprised how thin and frail she was.

"C'mon. It's time for bed." Her grandma didn't complain further. Keagan led her stumbling form into Gerry's bedroom and helped her lie down. After covering her up, she noticed that Gerry had fallen asleep. Relieved, she returned to the living room to an extremely upset Joan.

Trying to comfort her mother, Keagan put an arm around Joan who was now seated on the couch. She cried uncontrollably. Although Keagan found such an emotional display distasteful, she reminded herself that Joan was her mother. "I'll go and talk to Sean." Keagan would do anything to make her mom stop crying.

****

After explaining the situation to her brother, Keagan waited for a response. Sean sat quietly, an indifferent look on his face. He was three years older than Keagan, but might as well have been three years younger. Their maturity levels would never come close to meeting.

"I have to be on the road at six tomorrow morning. I don't have time for this. My answer's 'no.' If she wants a drink, I'm going to get it for her. Mom's so damn uptight about it anyway."

"She's just concerned."

"What's the harm if Grandma needs a drink?"

"Apparently she's had a few of those already, thanks to you. And she came at Joan with a butcher knife. So I hope you're happy."

"Fuck you and your self-righteous attitude! You've got some skeletons in your closet just like the rest of us." He glared at her.

"And just what the hell is that supposed to mean?" Keagan wanted him to say it.

"Nothin'." Sean always stopped himself before denouncing her sexual orientation.

"Why don't you just say it for once?"

"Because you're family, even if I don't understand it."

"Bye." She headed out the door, her emotions a jumbled mass of confusion. Getting into her car, she tried to block out everything that happened in the past couple of hours.

Sean watched as she sped away with an annoyed look on his face. He wondered why Keagan went around passing judgment on others when she lived the way she did.

****

When Keagan saw Rudy at school the next day, she put some distance between them. This detached attitude was a shock to Rudy who thought she was making some progress with the beautiful English major. She also had to admit to some disappointment when Keagan didn't call her. Part of her expected it, due to their growing rapport from Tuesday night. Once they were back in class, however, her responses to Rudy's attempts at conversation returned to monosyllabic ones.

Nevertheless, after class, Rudy traipsed along next to Keagan, who didn't acknowledge her presence, but didn't tell her to leave either. The optimist in Rudy took this as a good sign. "What are you doing tonight?"

"Studying for grammar."

"How's it going with that?"

"Since you took it you know that the first thing we do is memorize the ten sentence patterns."

"Are you getting it, then?"

"No. It's going lousy." Keagan stopped walking and went over to a nearby bench. Sitting down, she waited for Rudy to join her. "I'm sorry."

"What for?" She sat next to Keagan.

"For hardly saying two words to you, that's what for."

Rudy smiled. "That's okay. I was kind of used to it anyway."

"It's not you. It's me. It has nothing to do with you."

"It doesn't?"

As Keagan gazed at Rudy, she knew it had a lot to do

with her. What she really wanted to say was that Rudy had done everything right and Keagan didn't know how to react to that. Normalcy was something foreign to her. She had no frame of reference for it.

"Can I ask you a question?"

"You just did."

"I mean a different question." Rudy grinned at her.

"Sure."

"Would you be interested in coming over to my place so I can help you study for grammar?" Rudy knew that Keagan would find this less threatening than if she asked her out on a date.

Keagan exhaled. "Tonight, you mean?"

"Yeah. Why not? You can meet my roommate, Courtney. She's pretty nice, but she doesn't know I'm gay, so, we'll have to keep the gay talk to a minimum."

"Your own roommate doesn't know?"

"No one knows. A few friends, but none of my family. They wouldn't understand. They think I'm the girl-next-door, or something."

"Aren't you? I mean the gay version."

Rudy laughed. "Oh, yeah, the gay version, of course. So, how about it?"

"If I tried, I could probably say no." Keagan grinned.

"Then don't try." Green eyes gazed into blue.

"Okay, I'll come over." Keagan's voice held a mock reluctant tinge to it.

"Don't sound so excited."

"It takes a lot more than that to get me excited."

"Oh, yeah? Like what?"

"Wouldn't you like to know?"

"Still full of ourselves I see, but I could see how someone as attractive as you are would be." Rudy mentally kicked herself for turning their playful flirting serious. Keagan didn't seem to be bothered by it, though.

"I don't know. You don't seem to be too full of yourself."

Rudy shivered. Keagan had lowered her voice, which
made it even sexier than it usually was. Having no
response she blushed, and opened her backpack, getting
out a notebook. After she finished writing down the directions to her apartment, she looked back up to Keagan who
she suspected had been watching her closely the whole
time.

"You live on Forsythe? That's practically right behind
me."

"And down a little ways. I just wanted to make sure
you got there okay."

"I could walk, you're so close."

"Well, then walk. Be there at seven and I might be
nice and feed you."

"I thought this wasn't a date?"

"It's not. It's a study session. Complete with the necessary nourishment: pizza."

"Oh. Okay." Keagan took the piece of paper and put
it in her pocket. They both rose from the bench. "See ya
later," said Keagan.

"Later." Rudy headed off in the direction of the
library as Keagan continued on to her next class.

* * * * * * * * * *

At around 6:45 Keagan still had no idea what to wear.
She kept wondering why it felt like a date when it wasn't.
She scanned the clothes in her closet again, finally decid-
ing on a white tank top and a black banded collar shirt.
Throwing on a pair of button fly jeans, she hastily made
her way back into the living room and put on her boots.
She went back into the bathroom and splashed some
cologne on her neck. Feeling rushed, she grabbed her

backpack and left, not wanting to be late. She tried to calm the excitement she felt, as she made the short trek to Rudy's apartment. She wasn't successful.

In a few short minutes, Keagan reached the address on Forsythe that Rudy had written down for her. Surprised that it was a house, she walked up the front steps of the small porch. She rang the doorbell, and was greeted by a smiling Rudy who opened the door. "Hi. C'mon, in."

Keagan took in the house. "This is nice." Rudy's "apartment" turned out to be a decently furnished two-story house. The furniture wasn't lavish, but it wasn't the most inexpensive type, either. It didn't look to Keagan like the usual college student dwelling.

"I know. You're wondering how I can afford this. Dad pays for it. We have a deal. He pays for everything until I graduate and get a job."

"And that is when?"

"In May. And then there's grad school to look forward to." Rudy caught herself staring at Keagan, who had tied her hair back in a ponytail. That was fine with Rudy, who got a much better look at her face. Admiring the finely chiseled features of her face, she thought that everything on it seemed to be in precisely the correct place. Mentally slapping herself for staring, she averted her eyes, hoping Keagan hadn't noticed.

Keagan had been too busy watching Rudy to notice. She wore an OSU T-shirt with jean cut-offs and looked absolutely adorable. Keagan wondered if coming over to Rudy's house wasn't a mistake.

She sat on the large, overstuffed couch with Rudy next to her. "So, how many patterns do you know?"

Before Keagan could answer, Rudy's roommate, Courtney, sauntered downstairs, clad only in her bra and underwear. Keagan's eyes widened and met Rudy's. "Oh, Courtney, this is my friend, Keagan. She's here to study."

Courtney was blonde, bouncy, and friendly. She came over and shook hands with Keagan, who received a very close up view of the bouncy parts. Averting her eyes, she responded. "Hi, nice to meet you."

"Nice to meet you, too. Well, you two have fun studying. I'm getting ready to go out, so you'll have the place to yourselves soon. Thursday night! It's party night, y'know." She continued on to the kitchen.

"Does she always do that?" Keagan whispered to Rudy.

Rudy snickered under her breath. "We're both girls here, and she doesn't know about me, so what's the problem?"

"Right." Keagan couldn't help but feel a bit jealous that a half-naked, very attractive woman was walking around in front of Rudy daily.

"So how much have you studied?"

"Hardly at all."

"Why don't you study the patterns and while you're doing that, I'll make up some sentences and then you can tell me what pattern they are."

"Sounds like a plan." Keagan opened up her backpack and took out the grammar text, thinking things were going smoothly so far. She actually felt like she could study and not be distracted by Rudy.

Several hours later, they still studied. Rudy allowed a break and they ate pizza, while Keagan complained about the yellow things on top. Rudy had calmly explained that they were banana peppers and that the only way she could eat pizza was if it had banana peppers on it. When Keagan responded by saying that with her appetite she didn't think the lack of banana peppers would stop her, she got a face full of pillow. This escalated into a full-blown pillow fight, which Rudy won. Afterward, Rudy suggested a run through of the ten sentence patterns one more time, and

when Keagan rattled them all off smoothly, she had one
more suggestion.

"I've got a few more sentences for you, and I think
you'll find these fun."

"You sure can tell you want to be a teacher. You've
hardly let me rest all evening." During dinner, Rudy had
disclosed that she wanted to be a literature professor.
Keagan found it an admirable pursuit, if a difficult one.

Rudy grinned, as if she were up to something devious.
"Okay, here's the first one. Now, I'm going to go through
all ten patterns, so don't interrupt me no matter what.
Promise?"

"I promise."

"Number one: *Lourdes is a lesbian.*"

Keagan laughed. "Um, pattern three." She thought it
was cute how Rudy was using the name from her story.

"Sentence number two: *Lourdes yelled at Gabrielle for
putting banana peppers on the pizza.*"

Keagan thought for a moment. "Six?" Sometimes it
took her awhile to see the pattern in her head.

"Right. Very good so far. Number three: *Gabrielle
considers Lourdes cute.*"

Keagan grinned. "That's nine."

Rudy looked down at her notebook and then up at
Keagan whose eyes were riveted on her. She stretched her
legs and moved closer to her friend. Rudy smelled her
cologne and something extra, which must have been
Keagan's unique essence. She liked the feeling it gave her.
"Okay, here's the next one: *Lourdes's muscles are well
defined.*" Rudy told herself she was crazy for doing this
and should stop. In the next minute, she decided to continue.

Keagan felt flushed and her palms were sweating. It
was becoming harder and harder to think with Rudy's
intense gaze, as she rattled off the sentences. "Two."

"Yep." Rudy leaned closer to Keagan, their faces mere inches apart. *"Lourdes looks hot."* They stared deeply into each other's eyes.

Keagan lost all concentration and guessed. "Three."

"No. It's four." Rudy leaned in closer and whispered, "Let me give you one more."

Keagan's heart felt like it was going to beat right out of her chest. "Okay, one more," she breathed.

"Gabrielle gave Lourdes a kiss." Before Keagan could even begin to think of a response, Rudy's lips were covering her own, gently. It wasn't a forceful kiss, but tentative, almost as if Rudy felt Keagan would bolt. She remained in place, however, and found herself responding with an equal passion. When Keagan felt Rudy's tongue slip easily into her mouth, she moaned and returned the gesture, exploring her mouth with fervor. When they parted, Keagan spoke breathlessly. "I thought you said I wasn't supposed to interrupt you no matter what and it turns out you're the one who interrupts."

"That was the plan." Her body was still tingling from Keagan's kiss and she longed for more.

"The plan? You mean—"

"Keagan, will you please shut up and kiss me again?"

Keagan thought it would be unwise to argue and leaned in close for another kiss, but pulled back. "Wait a minute, wait a minute. This is not happening. I just came over to study and, and—"

"And what?" Rudy sighed and leaned back into the overstuffed couch with languor. Her body felt like it was on fire, and her mind was just beginning to refocus on her surroundings. Recalling her kiss with Keagan, she hoped her actions hadn't pushed the reluctant woman too far.

"It's past ten and I should probably leave." She put her grammar text in her backpack and grabbed her jacket. As she stood up, Rudy spoke.

"Okay. Can I ask you a question, though?"

"Sure."

"Did you enjoy it at all? Usually when I kiss someone they don't go running off. They usually stay for a bit." She grinned. "Just my ego, I guess."

Keagan regretted that she might have hurt Rudy's feelings. She glanced toward the table and spotted Rudy's open notebook. Bending down and grabbing a pen, she scribbled something quickly. "This," she began, looking directly into Rudy's eyes, "is my number. I don't give it out to just anybody, because I don't like to be bothered, but for you, I'll make an exception."

"For me, huh?"

"For you." Keagan headed toward the door and Rudy followed behind to see her out. Leaning over she whispered into her ear, "Because you're such a good kisser." Rudy smiled at that, even as her friend's closeness sent shivers down her spine.

"Later." Keagan left and Rudy watched her for awhile as she walked down the street. Then she turned around and headed back for the couch, collapsing onto it, with a silly grin on her face.

Keagan's thoughts didn't stray far from Rudy during the short trek back to her apartment. She accepted her attraction to her, but told herself it was a fluke. One of those things that happened but shouldn't have. As she stepped inside her apartment and flipped on the light, Keagan was hoping to purge her thoughts of Rudy for at least the rest of the evening. Taking off her jacket and throwing it onto a kitchen chair, she glanced at the answering machine, which indicated that there were five messages. There had been none when she left three hours before. Keagan sat down and pushed the message button. "Hi, it's Rudy. Yep, she gave me her *real* number." Click. "You know, your message could use some revamping. Not that it's not good or anything, but there's no subtext in it, you know. You just state everything precisely as it is: *Hi, blah, blah, I'm not available, blah, leave a message.*" Click. "Can you believe your machine cut me off? It's not like I talk that much or anything. Do you think? Oh, well, never mind. Anyway, I was going to say that maybe I can help you come up with a more creative message, if you want." Click. "I got cut off again. You need to get one of those digital answering machines. I bet those don't cut people off. I can't believe you're not there yet. Oh, you left your grammar workbook here. That's why I was calling. Maybe we can—" Click. "Hi, Keagan. I think you need to call me when you get home." Click.

After Keagan stopped laughing, she dug out Rudy's number and dialed it. So much for forgetting about her for the evening. A few seconds later, Rudy answered in a deep voice. "Hello. You've reached the lesbian hotline. This is Mo speaking. How can I help you?"

Keagan played along. "I just came out and I don't know anybody. I'm kind of scared. I'm not sure I know what it is women do with each other."

"What's your name, honey?" Rudy remained in character with the "Mo voice."

"Laura."

"Laura, that's a pretty name. I'd be happy to tell you what women do together. What are you wearing, honey?"

Keagan held back a laugh. She made her voice sound timid and shy. "Okay, Mo, I'll tell you. I'm wearing really short shorts and a skimpy tank top that shows off my bulbous attributes—"

"Bulbous attributes?" Rudy dropped the Mo character. "You just can't help yourself, can you? Bulbous attributes? Do you really think a shy, timid teenager just coming out would say that?"

"Oh, absolutely. *I* would have."

"You're the exception to most rules."

"So what about the way you answered? What if it was your mom?"

"She never calls this late. Besides, caller ID."

"So, you're always going to know it's me calling."

"Does that mean you're going to keep calling?"

"We'll see. So what's up with using up all my tape with your messages?"

"I was just feeling kind of devilish." Rudy laughed. "It must have been your kiss," she added.

"You mean *your* kiss. *You* kissed *me*, remember?"

"I didn't hear you complaining too loudly." When Keagan remained silent, Rudy took a different route. She dropped the competitive banter in her voice. "Look, I like you. Is that so bad?"

Keagan responded to it against her better judgment. "No."

Rudy's mind flashed with a potential book title: *Monosyllabic Women and the Women Who Love Them.* She held back a giggle. "You want to go out with me tomorrow night, then? To dinner?" Rudy crossed her fingers.

"That would be like a date, wouldn't it?"

"I would hope so. C'mon, it won't be so bad. They say I'm a fun date."

"Oh, do they now? Who's they?"

"Oh, you know. All those women I told you about, who end up at The Coffee House with me the next day."

"Ah." Keagan knew she was joking, but wondered why she felt a tinge of jealousy anyway.

"I'll come by your place about seven. Is that okay?"

"Sure." Keagan's response was cool.

"Great. See you tomorrow, Keagan."

"Bye, Rudy."

Keagan hung up the phone slowly and attempted to interpret what happened. She felt both foreboding and excitement. She wanted her and wanted to flee from her. Keagan wished she could settle on *one* feeling.

Chapter
5

The next day, Keagan had a difficult time concentrating at work. Not that her job required much thought, but there were a few simple things that needed attention. Things like putting a new blade into a box cutter without slashing one's fingers, for example.

"Ow! Shit!" Keagan grabbed the index finger of her left hand that was bleeding. "Dammit!" Luckily, she was in the stockroom and there would be no danger of being approached by a customer.

"You incompetent boob!" Her coworker, Nate, who stood near her pricing food, gave a laugh.

"Ha, ha! Thanks for the sympathy." Keagan glared at him and walked over to the utility shelf. Grabbing a few paper towels, she stopped the bleeding and reached into her apron for a Band-Aid. "Cool. One left."

"There'd be more left, if you weren't so incompetent."

"You're on a roll today. I wonder what you'd do if I cut my hand open."

"I'm sure we'll have a chance to find out." His cackle was ornery, the devilment in his eyes affectionate. Nate had been a close friend for years, and their mutual teasing of each other was based on a need to brighten up the atmosphere at work.

"Yeah, yeah. I'm sure." Nate grinned and returned to pricing. Keagan affixed the Band-Aid. "What are you doing tonight?"

"Derek wants to go to the drag queen show at the Garage."

"Sounds like fun." Derek was Nate's boyfriend. Keagan got together with them every once in awhile, but since it often involved some woman they were trying to set her up with, she hadn't seen them recently.

"And you?" He knew Keagan hadn't been very social lately and suspected her answer would be that she was doing nothing.

"I'm meeting a young lady for dinner." Keagan deadpanned the statement, but the corners of her lips upturned ever so slightly.

"A date? A *real* date?" His look was incredulous.

"Yeah, a real date. I can do that too, you know." Keagan's eyes returned to her work, as she sliced open a carton with the box cutter.

"You mean, it's not a story idea date?"

Keagan looked back up with annoyance. "No. A real, bonafide date. Gimme a break."

Nate cackled, seeing this as a prime opportunity to tease his friend. "Where is Keagan and what have you done with her?"

Keagan smirked in response.

"What's her name?"

"Rudy Whitman."

"She related to Walt?"

"No. But she could be. She knows a lot about poetry. She's an English major, too." Keagan stopped, fearing she had started to babble.

"So. You really like her?"

"She's all right." Keagan's look was indifferent.

"Sounds great."

"We'll see."

* * * * * * * * * *

Later, back at her apartment, Keagan lifted weights to alleviate the stress she felt about going out with Rudy. She tried to block out all of her insecure feelings and focus on nothing but exercise. As the phone rang, she listened to her own message with scrutiny. "Hi. I'm not available. Leave a message. Beep." Keagan's brow furrowed as she considered that Rudy might be right. Maybe she did need a more engaging message. "Bonjour, mon amie. C'est Gretchen Fuqua. Keagan pick up."

She wiped the sweat from her brow and picked up the phone. "Hello. I can't talk for long."

"Okay. Neither can I. I was just calling because I'm having a party and I want you to come and I want you to bring, um, Trudy, is that her name?"

"Rudy."

"Oui, oui. Well, it's next Saturday around nine. Can you make it?"

Keagan winced. She *hated* parties. "You know I hate parties."

"But this is my big 80's party. You have to be there." Keagan could almost see her pouting on the other end of the line.

"Maybe if it was 70's—"

"All right. I'll see what I can do about gettin' some 70's in there, okay?"

"Fine, but I'm not staying long."

"Great. And invite Trudy. Bye!"

"Rudy." Keagan hung up the phone, mentally adding

the party to her list of dreaded things to do.

****

Keagan put on some cologne, and glanced at the clock for the last time. She suspected the nervous feeling in the pit of her stomach wasn't going to leave anytime soon. She would go out with Rudy, they would eat dinner, and they would each go home alone. Nothing would come of it. It was just a date.

At around seven o'clock, Keagan heard footsteps. She ran into her bedroom and checked her look once more. Her friends always made fun of her for wearing so much black, but she felt comfortable in the color. She figured it diverted attention from her, especially at the bar. Satisfied that her hair, which she had chosen to wear down, looked okay, she returned to the living room. Not wanting to appear anxious, she waited for Rudy to knock before opening the door. "Hey."

"Hey, yourself." Rudy stepped inside with a smile. "Something smells really good," she said looking directly at Keagan.

"I'm not cooking anything. We're going out to eat, right?"

"I meant you."

"Oh." Keagan looked to the side and grabbed her jacket, which was sitting on a chair.

Rudy smiled, charmed by Keagan's apparent naivete. Taking her arm gently but firmly, she steered her out the door. "C'mon, I want to get you out with me before you change your mind."

Keagan resisted the urge to argue.

****

They bantered briefly over whose car to take. Keagan insisted that since her car must surely be considered an historical vehicle, it would be much more prestigious to take it. Rudy countered by saying that if they took her car, she was going to crawl into the passenger's side *after* Keagan was already seated in the driver's seat. They took Rudy's car.

They went to a gay restaurant Rudy had been to a few times before. She picked it because it had an inviting atmosphere, decent food, and pleasant service. And she wanted Keagan to be comfortable. After they were seated, the waitress came over with menus. "Hi, my name is Brett. I'll be your server this evening. If there's anything you need, just let me know." She addressed them both, but Keagan detected a distinct preference for Rudy in her mannerisms; like the way she winked at her after taking their drink order. As Brett left, she grinned and shook her head.

"What?" Rudy perused the menu. "Ooh. They have escargot."

"She winked at you."

"Jealous?"

"No. And you are not eating snails in front of me."

"She was just being friendly. Why not? What do you have against snails?"

"They belong on the ground. Not in your mouth."

"So you think you know what belongs in my mouth?" Rudy had looked up from her menu to regard Keagan mischievously.

Keagan knew a challenge when she saw one. "No, but if you eat snails, I can tell you what won't be in your mouth."

"Shrimp cocktail, then?"

"Much better."

Brett came back with the bottle of Chardonnay Rudy

ordered. Placing two glasses on the table, she poured a glass for Rudy, smiled at her, and then returned to the back. "Gee, thanks." Keagan frowned.

"She probably thought the wine was just for me."

"Yeah, right. The whole bottle. You wino." Keagan reached for the bottle, but Rudy stopped her.

"Allow me." She courteously poured her a glass.

"Thanks." She took a sip.

"Good?"

Keagan nodded, impressed with Rudy's attentions. "I still say this waitress likes you."

Rudy took a sip of her wine. "Is that so hard to believe?" She gazed guilelessly at Keagan.

"No, but since I'm sitting here it's kind of rude."

Rudy nodded. "Oh, 'cause we're together?"

"Well...yes, since we're sitting here together, eating, presumably, well, we're not eating now but we will be eventually, yes." Keagan wondered where this conversation had sprung from and how she could end it.

"Did anybody ever tell you that you're really cute when you babble?"

"No."

"Hmm. Well, don't you worry about our server. I'll take care of her." Rudy winked at Keagan and spotted Brett coming back to the table.

"Is everything okay?" she asked.

Rudy got a pensive look on her face as she regarded the waitress. "Since you asked, you forgot, earlier, to pour a glass of wine for my lover. She was feeling left out." Rudy smiled sweetly.

Keagan, who had just been attempting to finish her glass of wine, had to swallow quickly and put the glass back down on the table to avoid spilling something. She looked up at Rudy who was looking particularly adorable at that moment and then over at the startled waitress who was regarding her cautiously. "Oh, I'm so sorry. I'll remember next time. Are you ready to order yet?"

"Two shrimp cocktails to start." Brett nodded and went off to get their order. "I told you I was a fun date." She gazed at Keagan, who still had a look of shock on her face.

"I didn't really doubt you would be. I hope she doesn't poison my shrimp cocktail."

"I'll test it for you."

"Make sure she's standing there when you do." Keagan and Rudy realized how silly the whole conversation had become and laughed.

A few minutes after that, Brett returned and took their dinner orders. She had turned extremely solicitous to Keagan. "I guess you handled *her*," said Keagan.

"I know how to handle women." The comment was delivered with false bravado.

"Oh, you do, do you? You're in for a surprise with me, then."

"I don't think I've done too bad with you so far. Let's see, I got you to teach me pool, I've spent the night at your place, I helped you learn the ten sentence patterns, I kissed you, and here's the big one: I got you to go out with me."

"Quite a list of accomplishments. You should be proud." Keagan took a sip of wine and looked up to see Brett bringing the shrimp cocktail. She hoped the conversation would die down for awhile, as Rudy devoured the shrimp.

"Thank you." Rudy picked up a shrimp and dipped it into the cocktail sauce. She licked the sauce clean and gazed up to Keagan, who watched her intently, wondering why she found it so erotic when Rudy ate shrimp. Keagan glanced away.

Rudy popped the shrimp into her mouth. "These are *so* good." Noticing that Keagan had not touched hers yet, she

added, "What do I have to do? Feed them to you?" Before
she could answer, Rudy reached over and plucked one of
Keagan's shrimp from the dish. Smiling with purpose, she
dipped it into the sauce, making sure she got a generous
amount on the piece. Then her eyes returned to Keagan's
who remained sitting quietly, waiting for her next move.
Leaning over, she offered the shrimp to Keagan, whose lips
parted easily. As she drew her hand away, she felt the
slightest sensation of Keagan's tongue against her index
finger. The tingling sensation of pleasure that coursed
through her at this minor action alerted Rudy to the deep-
ening attraction she felt for her. She blushed and returned
to her own shrimp.

Keagan reminded herself that they were in a restaurant
and it wouldn't look nice if she licked the sauce off of
Rudy's fingers. "I must confess, I've never had so much
fun eating shrimp before."

"There's more where that came from." Rudy mentally
kicked herself, wondering why she lost her decorum
around Keagan.

Keagan smiled. Usually someone who flirted the way
Rudy did, had pre-planned sexual intentions, but she didn't
get that feeling from her friend. Instead, a refreshing innocence was conveyed behind her flirtation. Keagan wondered how she did that.

"So, tell me about your family." They had just finished up the shrimp and Rudy wanted to get in some quality conversation before dinner came.

"As you know, my grandma's a drunk and my mom
takes care of her." Keagan laughed to break the tension. It
was her usual way to make light of her family situation.
Rudy wasn't laughing.

"How does that affect *you*?"

"It doesn't."

"Okay. I guess that's fortunate, then, right?" Green

eyes studied blue and they seemed to be offering an invitation.

"Yeah. Look, I'm sure your family's much more interesting than mine. Why don't you tell me about them?"

Rudy accepted that the family was off limits. "You asked. My family's pretty boring, actually. My dad's a lawyer and my mom's in real estate. They divorced when I was eleven. My dad was having an affair with one of his associates. My parents provided the perfect role model for me: what *not* to do in a relationship." Rudy chuckled a bit to break the tension. After all, it was supposed to be a fun, light-hearted date, and not a disclosure of dirty family secrets.

"I never had any kind of role model for a relationship. I just had my mom. I don't know the first thing about it." Keagan stated this matter-of-factly, not in a voice that expected sympathy.

"What happened to your dad?"

"He and my mom got divorced when I was three. He just disappeared from the picture." Keagan took solace in the fact that this no longer hurt her, much like her relationship with Terry. All she had were memories that it had *once* hurt her.

"Do you ever wish you could see him?"

"I used to, but now it would be pretty pointless, don't you think? I'm twenty-four now. He doesn't know me and I don't know him. We'd be strangers. There would never be any way to get those years back that we could have had." Keagan stopped, realizing that she was revealing too much. "And besides, I've come to realize that I never needed a father anyway. Ultimately, you don't really need anybody."

Rudy ignored the wave of sadness that washed through her at Keagan's words. "Maybe not, but it can be a lot more fun *with* somebody."

Keagan reconnected with those beautiful green eyes. "Maybe."

Rudy smiled at her and Keagan had to remind herself to breathe. She took a long breath, feeling relief when she saw Brett coming back with their orders.

The rest of the evening went smoothly. Their conversation, although primarily directed by Rudy, tended to be revealing. They discovered that they both had an affinity for 70's music and classical. They both tended toward outdoor activities, such as hiking, swimming, and white water rafting. And they both *really* liked seafood, but to Keagan's dismay, she discovered that Rudy had never had lobster. She considered whether or not to remedy that.

After they finished desert, the conversation steered back to seafood. "I still can't believe you've never had lobster."

"I guess I just never had the opportunity."

"You'll love it. There's nothing like it. When you dip that succulent piece of lobster meat into the heated butter and place it into your mouth, you'll just be in utter ecstasy." Keagan grinned with mischief, realizing where the tone of the conversation was leading them.

"Really. You'll show me how it's done then?" She gazed intently at Keagan. "I mean, I'm not sure how to get to the meat through the shells. I don't know how people do that."

"Sometimes you can use your hands, that's how I prefer to do it, you can just gently crack open the shell to get what's inside, or you can use a shell cracker, I guess it's called. Looks like a nut cracker to me, though."

"So, your hands play an important part in getting what you want?"

Keagan found herself blushing. "Yes. And it's worth it. Once you taste that sweet meat, you'll never be able to get enough. I guarantee it."

Rudy nodded her head, and barely maintained her decorum. "Hmm, so when are you going to take me out for lobster?"

Keagan's heartbeat sped up. "I haven't had lobster in a long time, so I'm probably a little rusty on the important parts."

"I'm sure we can figure it out together, don't you think?" This time, Rudy made her intentions clear by moving across the table and placing her hand under Keagan's chin.

"Easily done." Rudy kissed her on the lips. Although it wasn't anything passionate due to their public surroundings, it affected her.

"Good." Rudy smiled. "I think it's time to go."

"Right."

* * * * * * * * * *

Since it was still early, they decided to stop by the bar. Neither one of them felt like leaving each other's company just yet. They went over to Keagan's usual table and sat down. Before they knew it, Cody was there, regarding them with a curious smile. "Hi, you two. Did you walk in together?"

"Actually, we planned the whole thing. We saw each other, coincidentally, in the parking lot and said, ooh, let's play a joke on the matchmakers by walking in together. Keep your eyes open. You never know what we might do next just to fool you." Keagan raised an eyebrow and leaned back in her chair, regarding Cody with a cool smile.

"What did you do with this woman?" Cody said to Rudy. "I haven't heard her speak more than two sentences in a row for years."

"My sides are splitting. Have you ever considered stand-up?" Keagan glared at Cody.

Rudy looked innocent. "All I did was take her to dinner."

"Keep up what you're doin' hon."   Cody winked at
Rudy, who smiled in response. "Can I get you something?"

"The usual," said Keagan.

"I'll have what she's having."

"Okay. Any snacks, tonight?"

Rudy put her hands on her stomach. "Oh, no, please.
I'm stuffed after that dinner. I couldn't eat another bite."

"A rare occurrence."

Rudy hit Keagan playfully on the arm. "I heard that
and I'll make you pay for it."

Keagan grinned as Cody chuckled and returned to the
bar. "Thanks for dinner, it was nice."

Rudy wasn't used to straightforward, honest remarks
from Keagan, but instead of teasing her about it, she said,
"You're welcome. Thank *you*. You're a pretty fun date,
yourself."

"You shouldn't come to that conclusion so soon. The
date isn't over yet."

"You mean you have more surprises in store for me?"

As Keagan was about to respond, she heard a loud bellowing coming from near the pool table. "Keagan!" It was
Gretchen Fuqua, waving and making her way over to their
table.

"Oh, joy. She's gonna try and get me to come to her
party next Saturday."

"A party? Sounds like fun."

"Have fun, then. You were invited."

"You won't be there?"

"I *hate* parties."

"Keagan? You're coming to my party, right? Trudy, I
know you'll be there, you're not such a sourpuss like
Keagan here."

"That's a great way to encourage me to come to your

party, by insulting me. And her name is Rudy. Rudy. R-U-D-Y. Okay?"

"Okay." She drawled out her response with mock annoyance. "Forgive me for the faux pas."

"Gretchen, that's okay." Rudy smiled warmly. "I'll come to your party and I'll even convince Keagan to come, too."

"Ha! Good luck with that one. See ya there." She headed for the bar.

"And how do you intend to convince me to go?"

"I have my ways." Rudy got a cryptic look on her face.

"Like what?"

"Being that I'm a young, single, gay girl and I'm going to a presumably gay party, there will probably be other young, single, gay girls there, too. So, I'll probably get picked up if I go alone." Rudy rolled her eyes dramatically.

Keagan laughed. "Yeah, right. You don't look like the type to allow herself to get picked up."

"You never know. A girl gets lonely sometimes." Rudy directed a teasing look to Keagan.

"*Alone, alone, all, all alone, Alone on a wide, wide sea! And never a saint took pity on my soul in agony.*"

Rudy thought hard for a moment. Then, "Coleridge. 'Rime of the Ancient Mariner.' It's going to take a lot more than that to stump me." She regarded Keagan challengingly.

"Okay. *She walks in beauty, like the night. Of cloudless climes and starry skies—*"

Rudy laughed. "Don't insult my intelligence."

"Sorry."

"S'all right."

"*Wild Nights—Wild Nights! Were I with thee Wild Nights should be our luxury!*" Keagan gazed expectantly at Rudy, not quite able to believe they were really doing this.

"Oh, that's a good one. Dickinson, of course. *Futile—the Winds—To a Heart in port—Done with the Compass—Done with the Chart!*"

Keagan lowered her voice. "*Rowing in Eden—Ah, the Sea! Might I but moor—Tonight—In Thee!*"

Rudy's body had a reaction to Keagan reciting poetry and she wished they were in a more private place so she could explore this. Since she couldn't, she said, "I love how she uses metaphors, don't you?"

"Yep." Keagan was trying somewhat unsuccessfully to control her reaction to the poetic rapport she shared with Rudy. She admitted to herself that it was more than just an interest in poetry they shared. The question was whether or not she would allow herself to explore what they could have together.

Cody came back with their drinks, and left quietly. Keagan took a sip of her rum and coke and welcomed the refreshing coolness as it slid down her throat. Gazing back to Rudy, she suspected her friend had come up with a quote of her own, from the look on her face.

"I've got one for you that you're not going to get."

"I highly doubt that." Keagan looked smug.

Rudy took a deep breath. "Here it is. *Tell me, love, how to speed time now, How to slow it then, when I call your name.*"

Keagan felt a shiver go through her as Rudy recited from the love poem. For a brief moment, it seemed as if she was addressing Keagan, herself. And then she racked her brain, trying to come up with poet's name, but couldn't. She didn't know. "You got me."

Rudy smiled. "I don't think they teach that one in any of our English courses. It's Minnie Bruce Pratt. It's a lesbian love poem."

"I figured. I'd like to hear the rest of it."

"I don't know the whole thing by heart. The book's at my house."

"Maybe sometime when I'm over studying for grammar or something."

"Or I could bring it over to your place."

"Sure." The implication being that they'd have more privacy at Keagan's apartment because she didn't have a roommate.

"Tomorrow night?"

"La Roux, whenever you like." Hearing a familiar song, Keagan spoke before thinking. "Dance?" She held out her hand to Rudy, who took it with a smile.

Keagan felt self-conscious as she walked to the dance floor with Rudy. Certainly, her friends would harass her for this. She never danced with her "story idea dates" so everyone would know something was up. She wanted to feel Rudy in her arms, though. If it involved embarrassment, she'd survive it. It was only a dance anyway.

Rudy's arms tightened around Keagan who responded by holding her closer. Focusing on that moment, her thoughts centered on Rudy alone as her eyes closed in contentment. When she opened them again, Rudy gazed up at her. She bent down, their lips meeting slowly at first, with the kiss soon turning passionate. As Rudy's mouth opened beneath hers, thoughts of where they were fled and the only thing that remained were her feelings for Rudy.

Feeling a soft tongue thrusting into her mouth and hands caressing her back caused Keagan to moan. Knowing a further public display could get embarrassing she tore her mouth away from Rudy's reluctantly. Before Keagan gently pulled her back into her arms to finish the dance, she heard a chuckle escape from her dance partner. Keagan flashed her a devilish look as they melded into each other again.

As the song ended, she and Rudy sat back down. "Thanks for the dance," said Keagan.

"Thank *you*."

"Don't tell me I've finally got you speechless."

Rudy gazed into the blue eyes she was coming to adore. "You should know by now there's only one way to get me speechless."

Keagan leaned over and captured her lips swiftly. She couldn't get enough of that sweet mouth. As Rudy pulled her head closer, she felt her tongue seeking entrance again. She wished they were anywhere but the bar. When they parted, Rudy directed a purposeful gaze at her. "Let's go back to my place so I can read that poem to you."

"Right." They made a hasty exit from the bar.

Chapter
6

"So, as a date, what would you rate me on a scale of 1 to 10?" Rudy drove down High Street, heading back to her apartment. Keagan sat silently beside her, lost in her own thoughts.

"So far...I'd give you about a 5." Keagan grinned to herself, knowing she was asking for trouble and loving it.

Rudy flashed Keagan a mock glare and returned her eyes to the road. "Just a 5? That's it?"

"Yep. Until we get back to your place. Then we'll see if you can up your rating." Keagan couldn't help it and snickered.

"And how would I do that?"

"Um..." Keagan found herself unable to come up with a suitable one-liner.

"You...are...bad. But, keep in mind, I don't have sex on the first date. We're going there to read a poem, that's it."

"No sex? You can just take me home, then."

Rudy slapped her on the arm, teasingly, but recognized an opportunity. "Are you saying you want me, then?"

"Oh, yeah, I want you...to take me...to your place and read me that poem." Keagan glanced over at Rudy, who smirked and shook her head.

"You are *such* a tease. What am I going to do with you?"

"Read me a poem."

"I should warn you. This poem's kind of sexy. It might turn you on or something."

Keagan laughed to herself at that comment. She had *already* been turned on during dinner, at the bar, and even right then in the car. "You mean an *intellectual* type of turn-on, right?"

"No, I mean a sexual one. Is that going to be a problem for you?" They were stopped at the light, giving Rudy an opportunity to glance over and look into blue eyes that gazed back with a combination of surprise and excitement.

Keagan feared their playful banter was turning serious but answered honestly. "No."

"I see I've got you back to monosyllabic responses." Rudy grinned.

"You asked a close-ended question. What did you expect?"

"Perhaps I should rephrase the question, then?" Rudy's eyes twinkled as her brain formulated a new question.

"No, no, please don't."

"How would it be a problem for you if I were to read you a sexy poem in my bedroom?"

At the sound of Rudy's voice and the tone her words were conveying, Keagan felt a pleasurable sensation in her lower body. Trying to ignore the distracting feeling, she remembered Rudy was waiting for an answer.

"I guess it would depend where you were in relation to me."

"Hmm?"

"Are you on the bed? Am I in a chair? Or standing? Are we both on the bed? It would also depend if we were touching or not."

"Would it depend on what I was wearing?"

"Definitely."

"How about this? You're lying on my bed, and I'm sitting in front of you, with my back to you, reading, and I'm wearing what I have on now sans the jacket."

Keagan smiled at Rudy's use of the word 'sans.' "We're not facing each other? Do I have my arms around you?" Keagan couldn't think of why Rudy would be reading and not facing her.

"If you want, but you don't have to. That is, if it would be a problem."

Keagan voice lowered. "I could handle that."

"Good."

When they pulled into Rudy's driveway, Keagan heard her date groaning. Apparently, Courtney had decided to have friends over that night.

"I don't care about her having her friends over, most of them are nice, but that looks like Dave's car and he gives me the creeps."

Keagan frowned. "Why's that?" She and Rudy exited the car and strolled slowly toward the front door.

"He likes me, but it's more than that. He asked me out twice now. He just won't take a hint." She shivered. Dave was extremely annoying.

"You want me to tell him you're mine?" Keagan said jokingly.

Rudy felt the sultry reverberations of Keagan's voice seem to trail all the way down her body. She knew Keagan was joking, but secretly wished she wasn't. "How about you just beat him senseless?"

"All right. No problem. Just point him out when we go in and I'll take care of it." Keagan grinned mischievously at Rudy as they reached the front door. Rudy's emerald eyes stared back at her with mirth. She unlocked the door and they stepped inside. Courtney, Dave, and her two other friends, Brenda and Ken were sitting around drinking beer and watching the MTV show, *Loveline.* Keagan glanced with distaste at the television. "Hey," Rudy said to Courtney, and grabbed Keagan's jacket sleeve in an attempt to guide her upstairs.

"Do you two want to watch *Loveline* with us?"

"Thanks, but I consider Dr. Drew to be a pseudo-intellectual shrink who caters to his annoying comic sidekick while they both give out bad advice to a bunch of losers. But, thanks." Keagan grinned to take the edge out of her statement.

Courtney smiled back at Keagan, impressed with her forthrightness. "Actually, I agree with you. *I* just watch it to make fun of it."

"C'mon, let's go to my room." Rudy took off her jacket and threw it over a chair.

"What do you got against Dr. Drew and why are you guys going upstairs for?" Dave, who was seated on the couch, had leaned over to get a look at Rudy's friend. He was shorter than Keagan and fairly stocky with a crew cut and beady, little hazel eyes.

Keagan clenched her jaw and looked dispassionately at Dave. "Answer to the first question: The man is clearly fixated on the family and children and allows this fact to cloud his judgment when giving advice. Answer to the second question: none of your business."

"Rudy, your friend's a real charmer. Where'd you dig her up at? Oh, and what are you doing tomorrow night?"

"Dave, leave her alone," said Courtney. She was tired of Dave asking Rudy out since clearly her roommate wasn't interested.

"This is my friend, Keagan, and we met at...school.

We're in the same BritLit class. And, I have other plans for tomorrow night and *any* night you choose to ask me out. Okay?"

"When are you going to quit playing hard to get?" Dave took a sip of his beer, his sixth of the evening. It was clear he was drunk, a fact that was not lost on Keagan. She held in her ire and responded.

"Playing hard to get carries with it the implication that she really *wants* to go out with you, which she clearly doesn't." Keagan was unable to hide a slight smirk. Picturing Rudy with the likes of Dave was quite funny, actually.

"Who the hell are you anyway?" Dave stood up a bit wobbly.

"Had a little too much to drink, Dave?" Keagan knew she shouldn't taunt him, but he was the kind of person she despised most. Dave was the type that let alcohol lower his inhibitions, which Keagan didn't consider necessarily bad per se. It was the fact that his comments were offensive to others in the process that made her feel contempt for him.

"Sit down and quit bothering my roommate and her friend." Dave looked over at Courtney, frowned, and sat back down.

"Goodnight, you guys," said Rudy nervously as she grabbed Keagan's sleeve and steered them both upstairs.

When they got to Rudy's bedroom, Keagan took off her jacket and draped it over a chair. She had harbored an interest in her friend's room when she had been over to study, but hadn't stayed long enough to get a chance to see it. Being curious about the woman she found so attractive, she took the opportunity to explore it, as Rudy searched for the book. It was a decent sized room, but there seemed to be too much in it for the space allowed. She was only slightly surprised to find that everything in Rudy's room

was far from neatly arranged. She had a lot of books and
only two bookcases. The problem was that she couldn't
defy the laws of physics by fitting all of her books into
such a limited space. Consequently, Keagan noticed more
than a few stacks of books sitting over in the corner by the
window. She smiled to herself. At least Rudy had made an
attempt to keep them pretty much in one place. In the
other corner of the room was a neatly made bed, looking as
if it was being kept separate from the disarray of everything else. Keagan couldn't blame her. If nothing else had
much order, at least a place of rest ought to, right? The
walls were covered in various prints of which her eyes
scanned rapidly. One of them was Monet's waterlillies and
she paused in recognition, gazing at it for a second. Rudy
had some family pictures on top of a bookcase. Keagan
considered asking about them, but didn't want to pry.

Before she knew it, Rudy had turned around with the
book in her hand. "Found it. Sit down, you look like a
deer caught in the headlights. My room's not that scary,
really."

The room *was* scary to Keagan, who continued to fight
her growing attraction to Rudy.

"Take off your shoes and hop on the bed, just like we
talked about. There's really nowhere else to sit anyway."
Rudy grinned shyly at Keagan who looked warily back and
unlaced her boots. As she was doing this, Rudy sat down.
"By the way, thanks for defending me."

"No, problem. That guy's a jerk."

"Why, because he wants to go out with me?"

Keagan looked cautiously at Rudy. "Not just that. It's
because he keeps asking when you've made it clear you're
not interested."

"And he likes *Loveline*."

"Exactly."

"You want to hear the poem now?"

"Sure do."

"Okay." Rudy sat in front of Keagan, who settled back against the pillows. When she turned around to get permission to lean back, the gaze of Keagan's blue eyes distracted her. She almost forgot about the poem to pursue more interesting things, but when Keagan's arms came around her, she leaned back against her friend enjoying the heat from her body. "I need to find the page it's on."

Keagan impatiently waited for Rudy to find the right poem. "Is that the right book?"

"Yes. It's just that, well, this poem isn't like I remembered it. Actually, all I really remembered was the line I quoted you..."

"And the problem is?"

"It's a little more, uh, graphic than I thought."

"Well, you said it could be a turn on."

Rudy turned her head sideways, but didn't look into Keagan's eyes. "I was just teasing, Keagan." She blushed. Fortunately for her, Keagan couldn't see it.

"Should we get into a less intimate position, then?"

Rudy liked the position they were in too much to give it up so quickly. "No. I'll just read it. I promised you, after all."

"That you did, La Roux."

Rudy smiled at Keagan's use of the nickname. "It's called, 'When I Call Your Name.'"

> *July is over, four hot weeks*
> *Of August, two long weeks in September,*
> *And then I'll be in your bedroom, in your bed,*
> *Nibbling your pink earlobe.*

Keagan laughed. Rudy turned around and looked at her directly. "What's so funny?"

"I don't know. 'Nibbling your pink earlobe.' It just

makes me get a vision in my head. I get these visual repre-
sentations in my head from words...not *all* words, just
things that make an impression on me." Keagan shrugged.

"And I would very much like to hear about that, but
can I finish the poem first?"

Keagan gave the zipped lips sign, as Rudy turned back
around, hiding an amused smile.

> *Even in the city, our day will be*
> *Luscious, your hair black and twining*
> *In my hands like the wild muscadine grape.*

"Muscadine grape? Is that really what it says?"

Rudy sighed. "Yes, that's really what it says."

"Oh. Okay. Go on."

"No, no. Comments please? You know you want to."

"Well, there's a comparison between 'black and twining hair' and a 'wild muscadine grape.' Black hair is like
a grape. I just don't get how hair is like a grape, but
maybe I read too much into things..."

"Maybe you need to be educated about muscadine
grapes, then. Don't think of just a single grape, think of a
grape*vine*. Your hair twining in my hands like a grapevine
twines. You see?"

Interesting example, Rudy. Keagan took a moment to
consider this. Maybe she wasn't looking at the big picture.
"Yes, I can see what you mean. I wasn't seeing it that way.
I often have a hard time with poetry."

"Maybe you should try hearing the whole poem, before
you start critiquing it." Rudy's voice carried with it a definite hint of teasing.

"Yes. Please continue."

> *Scuppernong brown, your—*

"What kind of brown?"

"Scuppernong. It's just a variety of muscadine grape. Or the name for the muscadine grapevine." Rudy resolved herself to the fact that Keagan would keep interrupting in spite of herself. It didn't bother her, though. She found her interest in the intricacies of the poem to be alluring.

"Okay. Sorry, I did it again."

"That's okay."

Scuppernong brown, your nipples will be full

Rudy felt Keagan chuckle, but she had no comment for the line in its entirety.

Against my mouth. We will look through
Barred windows at night for the harvest moon.
Equinox soon will diminish the light.

Rudy leaned back further into Keagan's embrace and felt her arms tighten slightly. She sighed with contentment.

Tell me, love, how to speed time now,
How to slow it then, when I call your name.

"I like it," said Keagan. Her mouth was inches away from Rudy's neck, and she convinced herself to ignore this fact.

"Once I explained it to you."

"Thank goodness I have you to tell me these things."

"Without me you wouldn't even have the poem."

"True enough."

Rudy let the book drop to the floor and turned around to face Keagan. Of course, when she did, she was faced with those eyes. They sat facing each other for a few seconds, before Keagan broke the silence. "It's pretty late. I should go."

She started to rise but Rudy's hand stopped her. "You don't have to leave so soon. I could read you another poem." After she said this, she leaned over closer to Keagan, so that their lips were only inches apart.

Keagan stared into suggestive green eyes. She wanted nothing more than to comply with Rudy's suggestion, but she didn't think they would end up just reading another poem and didn't want to rush things. Nevertheless, when she felt her friend's lips meeting hers, she didn't pull back. Rudy gently coaxed Keagan down onto her bed, exploring her body as they kissed. When they parted for air, Keagan panted. "So where's the next poem?"

Rudy gave Keagan a shy look, and tried not to look as mortified as she felt. "Sorry I just attacked you."

"That's all right." They still held each other, Rudy on top looking down at Keagan. She reached forward and brushed a strand of hair out of Keagan's eyes. They both grinned out of recognition that this was what they both wanted. "But, remember," Keagan continued, "you don't have sex on the first date."

"To tell you the truth, I've *never*...had sex."

"You're kidding, right?"

Rudy grinned shyly and buried her head in Keagan's chest. "I kid you not."

Keagan put her arms around Rudy and rubbed her back slowly. "But you're so...so—"

"Flirtatious?"

"I just wouldn't have thought you were."

Rudy laughed. "I just never met anyone I liked that much, to do that with, you know."

"I didn't, either, but that didn't stop me." Keagan rolled her eyes.

"What about Terry?"

"Just a crush. There's a very definite distinction between a crush and love. It wasn't clear to me back then."

"So what's the difference?"

"Crushes go away, love doesn't."

"Oh." Rudy found herself, for once, at a loss for words with Keagan.

"I have to go now." Keagan hoped she had inserted enough clues into her speech to clue Rudy in on what she was trying to say.

"How come? I'd really like to hear about these pictures you get in your head."

"If you'd like to do something tomorrow night, I could tell you."

"Are *you* asking *me* out on a date now?"

"Yep."

"I accept."

"That was quick."

"I don't think much when it comes to you."

Keagan grinned. "You better start, then. How else will you fend off my advances?"

"What if I don't want to?"

Keagan slowed her hand from its position on Rudy's back. Soon, the massage ended entirely. Several things flashed through her mind as potential responses, but she couldn't settle on one. "Sometimes we can't always have what we want," she said. *Like what I want right now.* "I mean, you want to be sure, right?"

"Sure?" If Rudy had been thinking more clearly, she would have known what Keagan was asking, but her closeness was distracting.

"Well, since, you've never..."

Rudy laughed. "Oh, right." She didn't tell Keagan that she had never been more sure about anything.

"I should probably go, then." Keagan sat up. She put

her boots on and stood. Rudy gazed back at her with interest, but remained on the bed.

"I'll drive you back."

"That's all right. I'll walk."

"No you won't." Rudy stood up. "It's too late for you
to walk. Besides, it's raining. Look."

Keagan glanced out the window, and grunted with disgust. "Great. Parties and rain," she muttered.

"Hmm?"

"The two things I hate the most."

Rudy grinned and took her arm. "Next week I'm going
to fix your hatred of parties. Tonight, I get to work on the
rain. C'mon."

Keagan allowed a shy smile to appear as she gazed at
Rudy. She wondered why this younger, less experienced
woman made her feel so nervous.

As Keagan got closer to her apartment, a comfortable
silence settled between her and Rudy. With anyone else, it
would have made her uncomfortable. She watched out the
window as the rain fell a bit harder, not depressing her as
much as it usually did. The side streets were pretty much
abandoned at that time of night, making it peaceful.
Shortly, they pulled into Keagan's driveway and it was
time for words.

"Strange that it's raining in January." Keagan had
enjoyed herself so much that evening that she didn't know
how to say goodbye.

"That doesn't happen very often."

"Yeah." Keagan made an effort to maintain control of
the situation. If she couldn't, it was almost certain that she
would be inviting Rudy inside for the night. And she
wasn't entirely certain that her friend would refuse.
"Thanks for a fun evening." She looked deeply into
Rudy's eyes and smiled. There was a glow from a nearby
streetlight that highlighted her features.

"So, I'm okay as a date?"

The best I've ever had. "Yes."

Rudy grinned and leaned over for a goodnight kiss, but before she reached her destination, she hesitated. "Wait. I think we should do this right."

"And how would that be?"

Rudy opened the door to her car and got out, motioning for Keagan to follow her. Both women could feel the rain, as it pelted them softly. Keagan frowned. Rudy reacted to that by reaching over and pulling Keagan toward her. "I know you hate rain, but I know you like this." She reached up and brought Keagan's head down to meet hers. Their lips met softly and sweetly, but passionately. When they parted, Rudy was surprised to see an almost gaping grin on her friend's face.

"What rain?"

Rudy laughed. "The rain that's getting us both sopping wet. And if I don't leave soon, I'll be too wet and cold to leave."

"And I'll have to provide you with sanctuary for the night." Keagan's arms were around her.

"Yes, which would mean my virtue would be compromised. We couldn't have that." Rudy's arms tightened around Keagan and she hugged her.

"No, we couldn't have that." Keagan hugged her back and placed a chaste kiss on her head. Taking a deep breath, she stepped back. "I'll call you tomorrow."

"Okay." Rudy happily gazed back at Keagan, releasing her with reluctance, and returning to her car.

Keagan stood in the rain, getting increasingly drenched, until Rudy was out of sight. Then, she went inside and wondered how to get over her. Locking the door behind her, she considered why she always felt an odd relief when Rudy was gone. The relief didn't stem from a lack of interest in Rudy. It was the exact opposite. Keagan had a difficult time dealing with feelings she had never had before and didn't know how to voice. She draped her wet jacket over a chair in the kitchen and sighed with confusion. *And I said I'd call her.*

She slept in the next morning. Saturday was one of two days she had an opportunity to do this. She had barely opened her eyes when the phone rang. Snuggling deeper into the covers, she tried to ignore it, but had neglected to turn the sound down on the answering machine. Soon, she was treated to Sean's voice. "Hey, Keagan. Are you there? Are you up? I'll give you some time, if you're not." Groaning, Keagan reached over the edge of the bed and picked up the phone on the floor. "Hello."

"Not up yet?"

"I'm awake. Just not technically up." Keagan yawned and made no attempt to hide the fact.

"Why don't you stop by later? I want to talk to you about Grandma and that whole situation. We'll chat."

Keagan was surprised at his request. "All right. I'll be by around 1:00. How's that?"

"See ya, then. Later."

As Keagan hung up the phone, she couldn't help but wonder what he was up to. Sean almost never initiated the handling of family problems.

When Keagan arrived at Sean's later she wasn't surprised to see that his friend, Greg Spiccoli, was visiting. Sean and Greg had known each other since high school, and although he was a good friend of her brother's, Keagan found him annoying. Greg often used a veil of sarcasm to hide his true dislike of something and in the past his remarks were directed at Keagan.

"Hey." Keagan entered the living room, where Sean and Greg were seated. She took a seat on a chair and noticed that his friend was drinking beer.

"Hey, Keagan, long time, no see. I've missed ya."

Keagan didn't have an opportunity to see Greg much.

"Good to see you." She lied.

Keagan turned to Sean. "How's Grandma?"

"Oh, she's fine. How are things with you?"

"Are you still sneaking her vodka?"

"Where did that come from?" Sean's eyebrows crinkled into a frown.

"Sorry, but it's a logical question don't you think? And you did ask me to come over to discuss the situation, right?"

"Everything's fine with that. Trust me. I just hadn't seen you in awhile and wanted to visit."

"I see." Sean couldn't ask his sister to come over just to chat. He had to make up a family crisis to draw her out. Keagan sighed.

"So, Keagan are you still writing a novel?" Keagan picked up on the condescension in Greg's voice. She smiled to avoid glaring like she would have preferred to do.

"Yep."

"Why so tight-lipped about it?"

Keagan laughed to herself. *Because the few times I have mentioned it, I've gotten a combination of confused stares, inappropriate questions, and just plain ignorance, coupled with a complete disregard for me and the work I do.* "It's not complete."

"What's the plot?" Sean asked.

"I told you before, I was having a bit of trouble with that." Keagan didn't add that her last visit with Sean had hurt her feelings and she had no desire to bring up the subject of writing again. Often, she wasn't sure if her feelings really were hurt, only that they ought to have been.

"Is it about, you know, women, being together?" Greg knew about Keagan's sexual orientation, and seemed tolerant, but never missed an opportunity to sneak the subject into a conversation.

"There are women characters, yes, but if you mean—"

"Any sex in it?"

"There are women characters, and yes, some of them have love relationships with each other." Keagan wondered why she was bothering to explain. She already knew what the response would be.

"Graphic stuff?" Greg laughed. He didn't mean to be lewd, but it came across that way to Keagan. Somehow, she always got the feeling that he saw her as a lesbian and not a person. And it really pissed her off.

"Only as it pertains to the plot." Keagan muttered this last statement under her breath, hoping the subject would be dropped. She felt as if she was in a battlefield and had to come up with a good defensive maneuver.

"Keagan, I don't know why you worry so much about this writing thing. I know you. You'll come up with something. Will you just take your time and quit dwelling on it?"

Keagan smiled tightly, but knew that Sean thought he was being supportive with statements like these. That fact didn't make her any less uncomfortable. "Your friend is the one who asked me about it, and I told you. What do you want me to do? Lie?"

"No, but if you can't do it right now, so what? Forget about it for awhile." Sean smiled over at Greg, who nodded in agreement.

Keagan shook her head. "Look, all I want is for you to tell me that you know I'll get past this, and you know I can do it, that's it." She stood up and headed toward the door to the porch.

"Again my volatile sister. Are you impressed? I used a big word." Sean laughed.

"See ya." Keagan was out the door and heading to her car with a strange sense of deja vu. Hadn't she done the very same thing about a week before? *And I don't have any intention of repeating it anytime soon...if ever.*

When she got back to her apartment, Keagan noticed the answering machine flashing. There were two messages and she didn't feel like hearing either one. Nevertheless, she hit the play button. The first one was from Joan. "Give me a call as soon as you get in. I need your help with Grandma. Bye." Keagan grimaced. With all that had happened at Sean's, she felt her temper flare. "Dammit! Can't I have one peaceful week—" Keagan paused from her tirade as she heard the soft tones of Rudy's voice. She was surprised, because *she* was supposed to call Rudy. "Hi. I know I was supposed to wait for you to call me, but I couldn't. I'm not very good with delayed gratification. <laugh> Give me a call back if you want. It's about 2:00 now. Bye."

Hearing her voice calmed Keagan. But she didn't want to subject Rudy to her bad mood by going out with her that night. It hadn't been that long since she had last seen Rudy and she was convinced she needed more time to get over it. "Might as well get it over with." Picking up the phone, she dialed Rudy's number. After a few rings, she was treated to the sound of Rudy's voice. "Hello. Whitman-Thoreau residence."

"Courtney's last name is Thoreau?" Keagan hadn't even announced herself.

"Hi, Keagan." Rudy smiled. "Nope, I just thought it sounded cool, but probably, only English major types, such as yourself, will get it."

Keagan laughed. "Right." Keagan suddenly felt a pain in her chest at having to stand Rudy up. *I can't. Not tonight.*

"Do you want to do something tonight?"

"Um, I don't think so."

"Oh." Rudy tried not to let the disappointment show

in her voice. "Anything wrong?"

"No, no. Nothing wrong. I just have to study."

"On a Saturday night? Am I being stood up?" Rudy said it lightheartedly, but inside she felt crushed.

"I just can't tonight, Rudy. I'm sorry. Can I call you tomorrow?" Keagan desperately wanted to extricate herself from the conversation, but Rudy made it difficult.

"Sure. See you later, then." Rudy held back a sigh.

"Okay. Bye." Keagan quickly hung up before she changed her mind. She wondered why her heart felt so heavy, but not for long.

Later that night, after a day filled with writing a paper and studying for grammar, Keagan ventured out to the bar. She needed to talk with a friend and hoped Cody would be there. Of course, there was also the chance that she would run into Rudy, but she pushed that possibility from her mind. As she stepped inside, she heaved a relieved sigh. There was Cody at the bar, and no sign of Rudy. Allowing herself a small grin, her heartbeat slowed a bit from its earlier nervousness, and she walked down to the end of the bar and sat down. In a few seconds, Cody was there. "The usual."

Cody came back with a rum and coke and regarded her friend with a mischievous smile. "Well, well, well, trouble in paradise? I'm surprised you're not here with—"

Keagan took a long sip. "Don't."

"You and Rudy seemed to be getting along fine last night."

Keagan finished her drink and motioned for another one. "That's the problem."

Cody came back with a second drink. "Okay, girl, you're going to tell me right now, why that's a problem."

"It's too intense, you know? I need a bit of superficiality."

Cody frowned. "You need what?"

"Let me try to explain. I get really nervous around Rudy. My heart starts beating faster, my palms get sweaty, and I start feeling things I've never felt with anyone before. I just can't deal with this."

"Then you can't deal with the fact that you're falling in love with her."

"No way. I'm not going there."

Cody leaned over and grasped Keagan's chin gently, looking her straight in the eye. "I've got news for you. You're already there. Deal with it."

"I hate when you do that."

"What?" Cody's look was all innocence.

"Get that smug look on your face that says, 'I'm older, I'm wiser, I know all.'"

"I don't know *all*. Just most."

Keagan chuckled. "Then maybe you can advise me. I stood her up tonight. I mean, I canceled our date. I guess that was wrong, huh?" Keagan looked expectantly at Cody, hoping for some guidance.

"Sometimes you are honestly like a babe in the woods, Keag. Yes...that was wrong, but you may get a chance to make it right sooner than you think."

"What? Why?" Keagan looked at the door and spotted Rudy, Eileen, and Tate coming in the door. "Oh, shit! If she sees me, she's going to think...hide me!" Keagan put her head down on the bar as far as it would go, hoping Rudy and her friends would go to the far side of the bar and she could sneak out. Before she knew it, though, a familiar scent made itself known to her senses.

"You obnoxious drunk," the voice said. "And this early in the evening. You should be ashamed. Get your head up off that bar, before you get thrown out." Rudy smiled broadly at Keagan, trying to hold back a laugh.

Keagan slowly brought her head back up and looked at her tormentor. "Hi, La Roux." Keagan raised her eyebrows and tried to put on her best innocent face.

"Don't you 'Hi, La Roux,' me, Keagan Donovan. You stand me up and then come to the bar. Ha!" She focused her green eyes on Keagan with purpose and enjoyed seeing her squirm.

"What's a nice girl like you doing in a place like this, anyway?"

"For starters, I thought maybe I'd try to find a woman who won't cancel on me."

Char, who had been sitting nearby, and listening surreptitiously to the proceedings, recognized her cue. Leaning over toward Rudy, she gazed at her with intent. "I've been told I'm a great date. And I *never* cancel." She wiggled her eyebrows suggestively.

To Keagan's surprise, Rudy turned away from her and regarded Char. "Thanks, Char, but I enjoy a good challenge and I think I've found it." She smiled at Char, who snickered and returned to her drink.

"Is that what I am to you? A challenge?"

Rudy walked right up to Keagan, who was still seated at the bar. She stood between her parted legs. For once, she didn't have to look up at Keagan. Their faces were only inches apart when Rudy finally spoke. "I don't think *you* are in any position to ask questions."

"I guess not." Keagan tried not to be affected by her nearness, but it didn't work. Rudy looked very good. She had on black button-fly jeans and a burgundy sweater that brought out the light red tint to her hair. She wore her hair down and it flowed around her shoulders, where it rested above her breasts. When Keagan realized she had been staring, she looked back into her eyes and shrugged. "I, um—" Not knowing what to say, she gave up and stared at the floor.

"You like what you see?"

Keagan looked back up, mesmerized. "Yes."

"Too bad. You're going to have to work for it this time." Giving Keagan a lingering smile, she turned away and went to join her friends, who were seated at a table.

Keagan watched her walk away, her mouth gaping open. She was used to being the pursued. Now, she had to do the hunting. She wasn't sure she liked that prospect.

"Honey, you better shut your mouth. That's starting to look unbecoming."

Keagan looked up at Cody with shock, and then as things registered again, she closed her mouth and turned around toward the bar. Downing the rest of her drink, she rolled her eyes. "Cody, I believe I've just gotten a taste of my own medicine, as they say. And I don't like it one bit."

"That one's a spitfire, she is."

"And then some."

Keagan stewed for awhile, while Cody waited on some of the other patrons. She noticed Jill and her entourage heading in the door and groaned. Right behind them, came Danielle, who made an immediate beeline for Rudy. Keagan ground her teeth together in irritation.

This is turning out to be a lovely evening. Grimly, she reflected on the fact that all she had to do was keep her date with Rudy and she wouldn't be a part of this turmoil. Presently, Cody came back with a new drink for her friend. "Are you going to sit there and stew all night or are you gonna go get your woman?"

Keagan glared at her. "She's not *my woman.*" She returned her gaze to Dani, who was now seated next to Rudy and her friends.

"Okay, fine. I'm dropping it."

"Cody, do you think I intentionally seek out conflict?"

"Yes. And you're damn good at it, too."

"Gee, thanks."

"You'll get only the truth from me."

"I know." Keagan smirked. "That's why I should quit

talking to you."

"No, that's why you'll *keep* talking to me and you know it." Cody flashed her a smile and went to the other end of the bar to take an order.

Keagan was happy to return to her brooding self, and sighed heavily when she spotted Milligan coming over. "You, too? Can't everyone just leave me alone?"

Milligan brought her hands up and mimicked a cat, complete with claws and beady eyes. "MEOW! What's wrong with you? That chick, Dani, moving in on your territory?"

Keagan put her head down on the bar with a sigh. When would the torture end?

"I got just the way to get revenge. Pool. You and me against, uh, blondie, what's her name—"

"RUDY."

"Yeah, Rudy. Against Rudy and Dani. We could beat the pants off of 'em. How about it?" Keagan didn't see it, but Milligan motioned to Jackie Daniels, with a nod of her head. Jackie made her way over to Rudy's table.

"Yeah, we'll make that little tramp pay for stealin' your woman."

"She is *not* my woman." Keagan groaned in misery. When would be a good time to escape unnoticed?

"Not anymore. We've been watching...everything. We know exactly what's going on, me and the girls." As Keagan lifted her head, she looked over to the women seated next to the pool table. There sat Sue, Jen, Gretchen, and Jackie who had just rejoined them. When they saw Keagan glancing over, they all gave her sympathetic looks.

"This is like some kind of grotesque nightmare. I *knew* there was another reason for me not wanting a girlfriend, besides my brooding disposition and loner tendencies."

"And what's that?"

"The fact that all of you seem to be along for the ride, too."

Milligan appeared to consider this. "Yeah. How can we resist? It's the classic 'opposites attract' thing, you know? The sweet, young, inexperienced, thing, finds herself strangely drawn to the tall, dark, brooding, older woman hardened by time and too many failed relationships."

"I haven't had that many relationships. And I'm only three years older than she is. Sheesh!" Keagan raised her head up wondering if she ought to be offended.

Milligan smiled and took her arm. "C'mon, let's play pool." For some reason, Keagan allowed Milligan to drag her over to the table where Jackie Daniels was standing next to Dani and Rudy. She told herself it wasn't because she had a desire to be near Rudy.

"All right, let's get this over with." Keagan couldn't help but deliver a glare in the direction of Dani. Rudy observed this with interest.

"Keagan, you don't sound very enthusiastic," said Dani.

"I just agreed to play to help out my friend."

"You're not here because of the scenery?" Dani smiled at Keagan, in an attempt to convey that she knew exactly why she was there.

"Sorry. You're not my type." Keagan grinned tightly.

"Oh, I know what your 'type' is." Dani threw a glance in Rudy's direction. Rudy remained silent, watching the proceedings. She didn't think it would be a good idea to interrupt the two.

"Probably 'cause it's the same as yours."

"Maybe, but I follow through with my dates. Can you say the same for yourself?"

Keagan flashed a questioning look at Rudy. Surely she hadn't told Dani about the date cancellation. She wasn't the type to succumb to bar gossip, was she? She had been wrong before about other people. What made Rudy any different? Rudy shook her head slowly to tell Keagan that she hadn't said anything. Against her better judgment, Keagan believed her, but there was still a nagging doubt in her mind.

"Why don't you sheath those claws before you scratch somebody?" Keagan said to Dani. At that, Rudy laughed out loud, which caused Keagan to laugh, too. Dani was not amused.

"Why don't we settle this with a game?"

"I don't think so." Keagan changed her mind, quickly, upon realizing that Dani wanted to "fight" her for Rudy. She wasn't into that kind of thing. In fact, she despised that kind of thinking and everything it stood for. If Dani wasn't careful, Keagan was prepared to tell her exactly why.

"How about, the winner gets Rudy?"

"Excuse me?" Rudy recognized her cue to enter the conversation. *This is starting to get way out of control.*

Keagan walked over to where Dani was standing, so that their faces were mere inches apart. She tried with great effort to control the ire she was feeling. "Don't ever suggest anything like that, even jokingly, ever again. Got it?"

Dani would not be defeated so easily. "Don't play the intimidation card with me, Keagan. I know a lot about you. Remember, Terry? I went out with her last week and got an earful about you. You're all talk and no action, right?"

"Feel like testing me?"

"I don't think you're worth it." With that, she stepped back, and snickering, went over to join Jill and the entourage.

Keagan exhaled strongly and glanced over at Rudy,

who was speechless. Milligan, who decided she didn't want to face her friend's wrath, had made a hasty retreat a few seconds before.

"Keagan, Jackie told me it was you and me against Milligan and Dani. It wasn't?"

Keagan laughed, partly to relieve the tension she felt and partly because it was funny. "No, it wasn't."

"So, Milligan and Jackie set this whole thing up as some kind of competition?"

"Looks like it."

"I suppose they thought they were helping you?"

"Yes. They don't seem to think I can handle you." Blue eyes gazed cautiously into twinkling green ones.

"I've been trying to get you to handle me since we met." Rudy laughed, almost shyly. She couldn't help it that she had always been an obnoxious flirt.

"So I still have a *chance* at handling you?"

"Not if you keep running away from me." Rudy reached over and took Keagan's sleeve, maneuvering her into a nearby booth. When they were seated, she waited for Keagan to speak. After about ten seconds, she realized that she was going to have to reinitiate talk, because Keagan wasn't going to. Although she often found it frustrating dealing with her, there was simply no place else she'd rather be or anyone she'd rather be with. Somewhere along the line, the deep attraction that she felt for Keagan from the moment she laid eyes on her, had turned into something more profound. Rudy realized that she was falling in love with her, and probably already had. And although now probably wouldn't be the best time to discuss that, it *would* be a good time to clear the air about Danielle. If she knew Keagan, she was probably still wondering and stewing about it. "You know I didn't say anything about you canceling our date, right?"

"Then why did she imply it so strongly?"

Rudy shook her head a little in exasperation. "I'm supposed to be the inexperienced one, here, but it doesn't take a rocket scientist or even someone with as little experience as me to pick up on the grapevine at this bar. A lot of these women are gossips, and I know this is going to surprise you, they actually *like* it when someone's having a hard time with a date. Then they can chatter about it all night and it diverts attention from themselves. You know, Char may come on pretty strong sometimes, but I don't fear that she's talking about me behind my back." Rudy directed a warm smile toward Keagan, who listened intently.

"How can you be so sure?"

"I can read people. I suspect, actually, that Char is just a softy inside and just needs someone to come along and respond to that."

Keagan allowed a small grin to surface. "Someone like you."

"I've already got it kind of bad for this other chick. She's dark, she's brooding, she's infuriating, but I like her."

"Sounds like a real loser to me. Not worth your time." In spite of Keagan's sarcastic delivery, she almost seemed to mean the words.

"Oh, she's definitely worth my time. She's a very talented writer, she's into poetry, she's a good dancer, not to mention a fantastic kisser."

"So what are you sittin' here with me for?" Keagan's quip broke the tension and they both laughed.

"I can't believe this." Rudy glared at Keagan.

"What?" Keagan's look was all innocence.

"I said you would have to work for it this time, and here I am giving you the out again. Not fair." Rudy folded her arms and feigned indignation.

For Keagan it was a sheepish look. Then she recalled

just whom it was she was dealing with and turned her look to a smug one. "That's just how irresistible I am. All the women are the same, you know. They can't help themselves."

"Oh, yeah, they're all lined up at the door trying to get to you. It's gonna get ugly before it gets better." Rudy smiled with relief. She had finally brought the real Keagan out again. The problem was making sure she stayed there.

"You might have to hide me."

"You could hide in my bedroom." If the lighting in the bar had been better, Rudy might have seen the blush that colored Keagan's face.

"And why would I want to do that?"

"Fringe benefits."

"Such as?"

"Well, first of all, you get to sleep with me. And, I did say *sleep*, so don't get any ideas. You know I'm not that kind of girl."

"I know, I know. I wonder why I stick around."

Rudy lowered her voice a bit. "Because all this teasing and taunting will make it that much better when I finally give in."

Once again, Keagan was amazed at Rudy's ability to affect her with mere words. Not being able to resist any longer, Keagan leaned over the table, until their lips met gently. It wasn't a kiss filled with passion, but was meant to reassure. As Rudy brought her hands up to Keagan's face, to prolong the kiss a bit, the two of them heard cheering and clapping. Where it was coming from they weren't really sure, being more occupied with each other at that moment. When they parted, Rudy chuckled softly. Keagan gave one last look to Rudy and then her head was down on the table again...for the second...or was it the third time that evening? She had lost count. Milligan, Gretchen, and the rest of the gang were cheering elatedly. Keagan covered up her head with her arms and whined. "Why me? Why me?"

Rudy continued to laugh. "You realize that at some point you're going to have to raise your head up again, right?" she asked. The gang seemed content to leave them alone for the time being, their goal accomplished. Keagan, however, remained hiding, arms crossed and lying on the table, her head buried in them.

Keagan's head rose slowly as she sensed the worst was over. She was met with a pleasant sight as she looked at Rudy. Her friend grinned at her. "You're enjoying this too much," said Keagan.

"And if I am, remember this was all your fault anyway."

Keagan raised her eyebrows in surprise. "And just exactly why is it my fault that the gang was sitting over there, and probably still is, gawking at my personal business?" She glanced at the pool table and surrounding area quickly enough to see Milligan, Jackie, and the others look away as if not wanting to get caught spying.

"All you had to do was keep your date with me and none of this would have happened."

"It all gets back to that, doesn't it?"

"Oh, absolutely, and I'm not letting you forget it anytime soon. Don't think one little kiss is going to smooth things over just like that."

"Why not? I thought the sensitive types like you always fell for that kind of stuff." Keagan found her comment to be amusing. The problem was that her companion didn't.

"Oh, really, is that what you thought now? You're in for a rude awakening."

"That was a joke."

"I know. That's the problem." Rudy looked away. She could ignore Keagan's avoidance issues and have a pleasant evening with her. Or she could make things more interesting. "Look, I came with Eileen and Tate and I haven't seen them in awhile so I'm going to go back and join them. When you're ready to confront why it is that you're making jokes about hurting my feelings, then give me a call." Rudy waited in vain for Keagan to stop her.

"Bye, then." Keagan glanced down at the table as Rudy went back to her friends.

Shortly after that, Cody came over and sat down. "Things were looking good. What happened?"

"I happened. I open my mouth and before I know it, I've screwed things up. There's a reason we silent types are silent, you know."

"Yeah, I know. Fear. You just need more practice expressing your feelings, that's all."

"But every time I have a feeling, I push it to the back of my mind, and a sarcastic comment comes out. I think I hurt her feelings."

"Apologize, then."

"I wouldn't know what to say."

"How about, 'I'm sorry, Rudy, for hurting your feelings.'"

Keagan shook her head and stood up. "Thanks for the advice, but I think I've done enough damage for one evening. See ya later."

"Bye, kiddo." Cody watched Keagan leave, and sympathized with the pain her friend felt. Then she rose and returned to the bar.

* * * * * * * * *

The rest of the weekend was a blur to Keagan. She thought about calling Rudy several times but didn't. When she considered the possible things she could say and how they might come out wrong, she always changed her mind.

When Tuesday came, her stomach was on edge. She skipped breakfast, too nervous to eat. Hoping to regain control soon, she headed out, confronted with weather that was anything but inspiring. Keagan hated snow almost as much as rain, and there was plenty of it that morning. In spite of this, she got to school early and decided to catch up on the novel she had to read for American Literature.

Rudy went to school early, hoping to get a chance to talk to Keagan before class. Although it didn't surprise her, she was disappointed that her friend hadn't called over the weekend. Sometimes she wished she could get inside the frustrating woman's mind for just five minutes. Rudy longed to understand Keagan, but it became increasingly difficult to chase someone who found it easier to run and it became downright depressing when she considered that most people did what was easier.

Rudy peeked into the classroom. Although she was pleased to see Keagan sitting in the back reading, she was nervous at the prospect of talking to her. The side of Keagan's body faced the door and her feet were propped up in an empty seat, so she didn't sense Rudy's approach. She was focused intently on what she was reading, and Rudy stopped to watch her. She felt the familiar pounding of her heart upon gazing at Keagan, but was reluctant to break away too soon from watching her unobserved. It was a pleasure she didn't get much of a chance to indulge in, and Keagan looked cute with her brow furrowed and her eyes rooted in one direction. "Are you going to just stand there, or come on in and join the fun?"

Rudy jumped upon hearing the familiar voice. Keagan had sensed her the entire time. Pushing aside her embarrassment, she grinned and entered the room, sitting down next to her friend. "Hi. Whatcha reading?"

"She's still talking to me. That's a good sign."

"That's one of the longest titles I've heard in a long

time. Is it a classic or mainstream, current, balderdash that
I'll find on the New York Times bestseller list?"

Keagan gazed up at Rudy with a shyness that made
Rudy's heart flutter. "It's a classic. In fact, it's Melville's
timeless classic, *Moby Dick*. And hi, yourself. Why are
you here so early?"

"I could ask the same of you."

"You could ask..." Keagan flashed her a devilish grin.
"Let me read this to you. I want to know what you think.
Have you read *Moby Dick*?"

Rudy groaned. "Unfortunately, yes."

"Okay. '*Man and wife, they say, there open the very
bottom of their souls to each other; and some old couples
often lie and chat over old times till nearly morning. Thus,
then, in our hearts' honeymoon, lay I and Queequeg—a
cosy, loving pair.*'"

"How sweet, and they're both men." Rudy winked at
her.

"Exactly. I find it interesting that in class we don't
discuss it in regards to the potential homoerotic subtext."

Rudy laughed. "You can't be serious."

Keagan got a sly look on her face that barely managed
to veil her sarcasm. "Well, when you think about it, the
friendship between Ishmael and Queequeg happens very
quickly. They just meet and are suddenly best friends.
Sounds a lot like love at first sight to me."

"And do you believe in love at first sight?"

"You're digressing."

"So."

Keagan put up her hand. "I'll answer that...later."

"Yeah, sure you will." Rudy gazed guilelessly at
Keagan.

"No, I will, but what I wanted to say was look at the
words that are used. Words like 'married,' when Queequeg
says that's what he considers he and Ishmael to be."

"Yes, but 'married' has a different meaning in his culture and he says so."

"I know, but I'm talking about just the wording, in and of itself, taken out of context—"

"If you take it out of context, it can mean anything you want." Rudy laughed.

"Right, but look at the other words that are used. 'Hearts honeymoon' and he compares them to old couples." Keagan looked smug. "I think there could be something there. I mean, subtext is about what's below the surface, waiting to burst forth. I'm suggesting a reading of *Moby Dick* whereby Ishmael and Queequeg are lovers and we're given these obvious hints in order to throw us off, to makes us think it's too obvious, you know? All these blatant marriage metaphors. Ha! I see right through it."

"Why don't you write a paper on it, then?" Rudy knew Keagan was joking, but had no doubt she could actually write a convincing and properly academic paper on the subject.

"Because as it is, I'll never even get the book read. I haven't read much of it and there's..." She flipped to the end. "478 pages."

"You have the whole quarter, right?"

"True, but my attention span wanders after about an hour of reading this. You know if you've read it."

"I've heard that it takes about twenty-four hours to read, which is about twenty pages per hour." Rudy paused as she did the calculation in her head. "So really all you have to do is read three hours a week for eight weeks and you'll be done in time for the exam. Does that make it sound easier?"

"Yes, it does. Thanks." Rudy's calculations, if followed carefully, would make it possible for her to finish the book on time. "Even though I don't deserve your help." Keagan thought of her actions a few days before.

"Look, I'm not—"

"Wait. I just need to say one thing. I'm really sorry for what I said. And that it hurt your feelings. I never want to do that. Sometimes, things come out the wrong way with me. I don't know what else to say."

"You don't have to say anything else. Thank you." Rudy was touched by Keagan's words and wished they had time to discuss it further. Since they didn't, she figured it best to change the subject. "By the way, you never answered my question about love at first sight."

"I know." Keagan drawled it out teasingly.

Rudy settled back into her seat and prepared to pursue the subject later.

In a few minutes, the class had settled down and the instructor came in. It was her grammar teacher, Dr. V.M. Addison. What was she doing here? And where was Parnell?

Dr. Addison had dark, shoulder-length hair and looked to be in her late forties. Today, she was wearing one of her signature outfits that always looked to Keagan like a riding outfit. Dark black boots came up to her knees, where tan trousers met them. A white, banded collar shirt and a short, black blazer complemented this. "Why is Dr. Addison here?" she whispered to Rudy, who shrugged having no idea. Keagan considered Dr. Addison a menace in grammar. The woman was always calling on her when she wasn't prepared and Keagan had no desire to have her for any other classes. "Looks like she just came from the racetrack." Rudy couldn't help but laugh, because she did look like a jockey.

"Good morning, everyone. I'm taking over this class for Dr. Parnell, who had to go and do some, oh, research, or some such nonsense. I'm Dr. V.M. Addison for those of you who don't know me. For those of you who do...well, I'll be calling on you first so be ready." Dr. Addison laughed, but to Keagan it was an evil cackle. She slipped down into her seat, trying to hide behind the student in front of her. Rudy looked over at her in amusement, and then glanced up front again. Dr. Addison had a grammar book, not the British Literature text. Seeing the professor catch her eye, she smiled. Rudy had taken grammar with her. "Rudy? Didn't you already take grammar?" The woman looked genuinely confused.

"Dr. Addison. Yes, I did. But this is British Literature."

"British *what*? You're kidding." The professor scowled.

"We were reading 'The Passionate Shepherd.'"

"You're sure this isn't grammar?"

"I'm sure."

"It appears I've been duped again. They told me it was grammar. What do I know about British Literature? Would anyone like to read Homer's *Iliad* in Greek? I can do that." The class laughed and Keagan smiled to herself. A teacher who doesn't know squat about the subject. She could deal with that. She got out her notebook and began to write. This class would be a breeze.

"Thanks, Rudy. And the poem was...?"

"'The Passionate Shepherd to His Love,' by Christopher Marlowe. It's on page 767."

Keagan cringed. She absolutely despised that poem.

"Thank you. Well, class, since I am less than prepared today, I don't have a text. So, would someone like to read the poem for us?" Dr. Addison scanned the room and spotted none other than her reluctant grammar student, Keagan. "Keagan, would you read it for us, please?"

Keagan's jaw clenched. "I'm just observing today." She faced Dr. Addison, smiling brightly, hoping that her charming wit would spare her the agony of reading the poem aloud.

"How about observing *the poem* and sharing it aloud with the class?"

By this time, Rudy's attempts to hold in her amusement failed. She laughed, but quickly clamped her mouth shut, and put her hand over her mouth in an attempt to keep it that way.

"Something funny, Ms. Whitman?"

"No, nothing."

"Well, then, Keagan the class is waiting."

Keagan glared at no one in particular. "*Come live with me and be my love, and we will all the pleasures prove...*"

After class, Keagan was still grumbling. She didn't care to read aloud and certainly not cheesy, love poems. Love poems were okay, but cheesy ones were off-limits. "Oh, it wasn't that bad was it?" Rudy asked her as they strolled along the sidewalk outside Denney. It was snowy and cold, but sunny and an altogether pleasant day. The state of the weather was causing Rudy's mischievous side to surface. Keagan frowned in response.

"You read that beautifully."

"Gee, thanks."

"No, *really,* Keagan," she continued in a dramatic voice. "When you said, 'Come live with me and be my love,' I was ready to drop everything right there and follow you." Rudy laughed.

"So that's all I have to do to get you, is just recite a cheesy, love poem?"

"And quit canceling our dates."

"Touché."

"Would you do it?" Rudy got a contemplative look on her face as another idea came to mind. "In fact, I think you owe me. I think you should read me this poem to make it up to me for breaking our date."

Keagan considered it for a moment. "Yes, I'll do it. And then we're even. Deal?"

A huge smile came to Rudy's face. "Deal."

"Why don't you come over tonight? If you're not doing anything. We can study grammar. Or rather, *you* can help me study. The first exam's next week."

Rudy nodded. "Okay. I'll bring dinner. What do you like?"

"Chinese. I like—"

"No, no, don't tell me. I plan on surprising you." She grinned with purpose.

"Why does that scare me?"

Silently appreciating the guarded look on Keagan's face, Rudy steered things back to the other subject. "So, do you believe in love at first sight?"

"Huh?"

"My question from earlier that you promised you'd answer."

"Oh. Um..." Keagan was coming to learn that Rudy didn't forget anything.

"Rudy. Hi." Keagan was saved from answering when a friendly looking woman with blue eyes and light brown hair approached them. They stopped walking to talk to her.

"Hi, Jodi. How are you?" Rudy had dated Jodi briefly a few months before. She liked her well enough, but there was no chemistry between them. Jodi's overly aggressive advances had turned her off. They hadn't remained friends, but not for lack of Jodi's trying.

"Just fine. I called you last week. Didn't you get my message?"

I got all five. The woman couldn't take a hint. "My roommate sometimes forgets to give them to me." Rudy wondered where this conversation was going. And hoping that it went there soon. "This is my friend, Keagan. We've got to get going. Nice to see you." Rudy gave her a friendly smile, hoping she'd leave.

Jodi was busy taking in Keagan. Keagan didn't notice,

however, because she was staring at the ground, not having anything to add to the conversation. "Nice to see you, too. I'll give you a call."

"I've been busy lately with school and I probably won't have time to do anything."

Jodi smiled, almost condescendingly. "We're just talking about a phone call, Rudy. I didn't propose marriage or anything."

Rudy didn't know how to respond to that. Her experience didn't often involve coming up with clever one-liners to deal with rude people.

That got Keagan's attention. She casually draped her arm around Rudy. "No, but if you did, I might have a problem with it." She put on her best glare. Rudy tried not to laugh.

"Ah. I see what you mean when you say you've been busy. And I can't say that I really blame you." Jodi looked Keagan up and down once more, smiled leeringly, and left.

Keagan and Rudy both laughed. "She's not bad looking, actually," Keagan said. "It's just...when she speaks."

"Yes. She was checking you out big time, you know."

"Really? You think I'd have a shot with her?" Keagan grinned as they strolled to Rudy's car. A light snow was falling.

"I think I still want my chance first. If that's okay."

They reached the car and Rudy leaned against it waiting for Keagan's answer. "Still?"

"Still."

"Yeah, that's okay." Keagan felt warm inside, in spite of the cold. "So, see you tonight?"

Rudy smiled and licked her lips with pleasure. "Oh, yeah. Can't wait for that Chinese."

"Always thinking of food."

"That's not all I think about."

"And what else do you think about?"

"You and me in a clinch."

Keagan felt a jolt of pleasure go through her and felt heated in spite of the weather. And in spite of their public surroundings, she reached forward and put her arms around Rudy, not too tightly, but securely. "Like this?"

Rudy's arms tightened around Keagan and she nestled her head under the taller woman's neck. "Yeah, just like this."

Keagan laughed and settled her head upon Rudy's before having an unnerving thought. *What am I turning into?* Giving her a last squeeze, she pulled away with an unsure look on her face, but hid it before Rudy could notice by grinning. "Later, Rudy." Keagan gave a short wave and walked in the other direction. It left Rudy wondering if what they had planned was a date or a study session. There was always something to ponder when it came to Keagan but that was how she liked it.

****

"Hi, Grandma." Keagan sat comfortably at home, after having skipped grammar class. One day of Dr. V.M. Addison was quite enough for her. She called to see how Gerry was doing. In the past few days, they hadn't talked much and Keagan knew her grandma got lonely sometimes, being alone all day. Rosey was there, but sometimes a human voice was nice, too.

"Hi, sweetie," said the familiar friendly voice.

"How are things with you and Mom?" Keagan neglected to add that she hadn't returned Joan's latest message. Since Joan hadn't called back, it couldn't have been an emergency and she didn't feel any guilt over it.

"Oh, about the same, but she doesn't know Sean's been sneaking me vodka again...as if he should have to. I'm a grown woman and I'm not hurting anyone. If I want to have a drink, what's wrong with that?"

"Nothing." It was a lie, but she couldn't tell Gerry how she really felt about it. If she told her the truth, Gerry would become angry and refuse to speak to her.

When Keagan was young, Gerry took her to school because Joan worked third shift. The twelve-year-old didn't think it at all odd when Gerry stopped at a bar at eight in the morning to have a couple of drinks; even though she was heading to work after dropping Keagan off at school. She didn't even think it was odd that every morning they would stop and get two donuts for Keagan. Gerry had told her that it wouldn't be a good idea to tell Joan about the morning bar stop. Years later, a more older and cynical Keagan felt that the donuts were a bribe. It took time and maturity for her to understand that it wasn't normal for people to drink before work and it wasn't normal for a grandmother to ask her granddaughter not to tell her mother something. Keagan's adulthood had brought on many revelations.

"Oh, well, enough about that. How are things with you? Do you need any money?"

Keagan smiled. Even though all Gerry received for income was a meager social security check, she always helped out Keagan when she needed it. "No, I'm doing okay, but thanks."

"And what about your little girlfriend, Rudy? How's she?"

"Oh, fine." Keagan didn't want to talk about Rudy. "But she's not really my girlfriend. We just went out once."

"I want to meet her."

"You do?"

"Yes, and then I can judge for myself about you two. Since you won't tell me." She knew Keagan well, and that meant understanding how introverted she was. "Just bring her by. You don't have to stay all evening. I just want to meet her. Promise you'll do it soon."

"Sure, Grandma."

"Good. Take care, Keagan. I love you."

"Me too. Goodbye."

****

Later that evening since it was just a "study session," Keagan put on a Nine Inch Nails T-shirt and faded jeans, which sported a gaping hole in the left knee. Since she owned a pair of slippers but always seemed to lose them, she wore socks. She was listening to a new radio station. It was an oldies station, but it wasn't *old* oldies, it played music from very late sixties, all the way through the seventies, with a bit of early eighties thrown in. Just what Keagan liked. The only drawback was that since it was a new station, it didn't have the funding to play a wide range of music. Consequently, Keagan had listened to the theme to *Fame* at least twenty-five times in the last three weeks. Chuckling to herself, she sang, *"Fame!!! I'm gonna live forever...I'm gonna learn how to fly....HIGH! I feel it coming together...people will see me and..."* Her singing was interrupted by a knock at the door. Keagan opened the door to a smiling Rudy, her hands full of Chinese takeout. "Were you singing?"

"Nope." Keagan took one of the bags from her and placed it on the kitchen table. "So, what did you get? Shrimp eggrolls, I hope?" Keagan looked to Rudy like a little kid let loose in a candy shop.

"Hi, Rudy. It's so nice you came over to help me study and you know what? It's nice to see you." Keagan looked up from the food to take in Rudy thoroughly for the first time since she came in. Rudy grinned and took off her jacket.

"You look great," Keagan told her. Rudy was only wearing a dark blue sweater and jeans, but to Keagan, she was beautiful no matter what she wore. Appreciatively glancing at Rudy's body, she continued to stare for a moment, falling speechless.

"Something wrong?"

"No."

"Did you want to do something?"

"Yes, this." And then she reached forward to pull Rudy into her arms, but before their lips could meet, Rudy put a hesitant finger up to Keagan's lips. "I was wondering. Is this a date or a study session?"

"That depends on what it is you'd like to study. It could be both, you know." Keagan grinned mischievously. She continued to hold Rudy in her arms.

"What if I'd like to study every inch of your body?"

"Well, then—"

Rudy kicked herself for her flirtatious nature that popped out at the most inopportune of times. "What I really was trying to tell you was that I have a rule for this evening."

"A rule?"

"Yes. No kissing until you read me that poem. Then I'll know you're serious about our deal and about *me*."

Keagan was familiar with vulnerability enough to recognize it when she saw it. "Fair enough. I think we should eat now." She relinquished her hold on Rudy, albeit reluctantly.

"You do, do you? Don't worry, I have no plans to capitalize on the obvious double entendre just sitting there waiting to be used. And I did bring shrimp eggrolls." Rudy grinned.

Keagan smiled. "And that really good sweet orange sauce, too?"

"Of course."

"And the hot mustard?"

"The hottest."

"You really know what I like."

"Yeah, I do. And I'm going to give you exactly what you want eventually." Rudy looked down into one of the bags trying to hide a smile.

Keagan rolled her eyes. "Right, but not until I read the poem." Rudy didn't reply. Instead, she took a shrimp eggroll out of the bag, doused it with hot mustard, and placed it against Keagan's lips. She opened her mouth and took a bite. "Oh. That's hot." There was something so ambiguous about Chinese hot mustard. It gave both pleasure and discomfort at the same time. Keagan had never been able to rationalize it and didn't even try. She chewed gratefully.

"So are you." Rudy's voice was sultry, but then she laughed. "I'm just teasing you."

Keagan finished eating her eggroll, and then focused back on Rudy. "Don't be a tease."

Rudy laughed, finding it amusing that Keagan was calling *her* the tease.

Keagan got a cautious look on her face. "Thanks for bringing dinner. Let's eat and then I can read you the poem."

"Let's eat fast. I really want to hear you read that poem."

Keagan sighed, imagining herself reading the dreaded poem aloud to Rudy. "Why did I agree to this?"

"Because you like me?"

"Of course. You're the gay girl-next-door, after all."

"Right." Rudy reached forward and took the soup out of the bag. She took the lid off and Keagan smelled the aroma.

"Wow," Keagan said in response to seeing the hot and

sour soup. "Thanks. I love soup and I especially love hot soup, as in spicy hot."

"Good." Rudy smiled. "I got us Kung Bao chicken. Do you like it?"

"Never had it."

"Then I can introduce you to something new."

"Like what?" Keagan raised her eyebrows suggestively.

"And rule number two," Rudy began, backing away from Keagan. "No flirting until after the poem. Flirting would only lead to kissing, you know."

Keagan laughed. "All right. Whatever you say." These "rules" that Rudy came up with revealed a new side to her friend that Keagan found extremely attractive.

They ate in the kitchen. Keagan's kitchen was actually quite large for the small apartment that she lived in. There were three windows that let in a great deal of light and it was a pleasant room. The kitchen table was inherited from Gerry, who no longer needed it, living with Joan. Consequently, it was shaky because of its age. A couple of legs had been replaced, but the shakiness was still there.

Keagan left the stereo on in the living room and the sounds of the oldies station drifted into the kitchen as the two ate their dinner. Rudy held two cookies, wrapped in plastic, in her hands. "Our fortunes for after dinner." She grinned mischievously.

"Great."

"I brought some white zinfandel, too. You interested?"

Keagan nodded and produced two wineglasses from the cupboard. She got a couple of napkins and sat down as Rudy poured the wine and handed a glass to her. Keagan looked down at the table shyly.

Rudy smiled. Keagan began eating the chicken and looked back at her, shaking her head to indicate that she liked it. The two ate for a few minutes in companionable silence until Keagan got a simultaneous look of fright and surprise on her face. "Ah!" Hardly able to move, she motioned for Rudy to hand her the wine. The younger woman complied immediately and watched as her friend downed the glass and motioned for more. As Rudy was refilling her glass, she realized what had happened. Keagan had never had Kung Boa and didn't know about the non-edible hot peppers that were included in the dish. Drinking down a second glass of wine, Keagan felt better and the hotness of the peppers was almost gone. "I can't believe how hot those peppers were," she eventually said.

Rudy got a sympathetic look on her face. "I'm really sorry. I should have told you about that. I didn't think about it. You're not supposed to eat the peppers."

"Maybe not, but now that I have, I feel great." Keagan smiled.

Rudy laughed. "That's only because you downed two glasses of wine to counteract the effects of the pepper."

"Or maybe because I'm with you." Keagan grinned shyly at the admission. "Well, now I can finish dinner safely? Or is there anything else you should warn me against."

Rudy was still feeling her heart's reaction to Keagan's admission. "I could warn you against me."

"Really? And why should I be warned against you?"

"Because when I see something I want, I don't give up until I get it."

"Watch it. You said no flirting." Keagan grinned.

"That's not flirting. That's just me telling you something about myself. If we're going to get through this dinner until the poem, you're going to have to distinguish between mere admissions and me just being an obnoxious flirt...not that I'm going to give you an opportunity to point out any flirtations again." Rudy took a sip of her wine and gazed back at Keagan, noticing that she wasn't speaking, just thinking. *What's going on in that head of hers?*

Keagan considered what Rudy had said. She had never had a woman pursue her quite like Rudy did and certainly not one who was a virgin. Not that her lack of sexual credentials necessarily guaranteed timidity, but Rudy's method of pursuit almost always indicated experience. At least in the women Keagan was used to dealing with. Of course, it was possible that she had experience, but had just never made love. Keagan felt confused by the scenarios going through her head, especially in light of having met Jodi earlier that day. "Rudy, can I ask you something?"

Rudy looked momentarily surprised by Keagan's question. "Sure."

"How many girlfriends have you had?"

Rudy thought for a moment. "What's your definition of girlfriend?"

"I don't know." Keagan thought hard for a moment. "Maybe...someone you're in love with?"

"I've had girlfriends, but I've never really been in love."

"Oh."

"Just crushes, you know."

"Right. I know. So, what would she be like?"

Rudy looked momentarily perplexed. "What would who be like?"

"Never mind. Let's just finish eating."

"Keagan." Rudy knew she was asking a substantial question and then downplaying it. "Are you asking what the woman I fall in love with will be like?"

Keagan turned away. "Yes."

Rudy looked pensive. "Okay. Let me think about this." She paused then, almost too long for Keagan's comfort. "She would have to be smart, considerate, and caring, have a really good sense of humor, and preferably be a creative type. That would be nice. And if she was beautiful, that wouldn't hurt, either."

"So, you've never met anyone like that yet?"

Rudy recognized it as the loaded question it was. "Up until a couple of weeks ago...no." She would have to teach Keagan that if she were going to ask, then Rudy would answer honestly.

Briefly, the insecure part of Keagan wondered who it was. Kicking herself for drinking the wine instead of grabbing a glass of water, she knew she should change the subject fast. *Alcohol makes me more open.* Keagan merely gave Rudy an enigmatic look and began eating again.

Rudy respected her reluctance to continue and said nothing further. The conversation through the remainder of the dinner was fairly ordinary, not getting personal again. Rudy knew that Keagan felt more secure discussing things that were already known and decided. Realizing this, she didn't invade her space, although she knew that eventually she would have to break through the barriers to Keagan's isolation.

Later on, they retired to the living room to begin studying. Keagan was still distant and Rudy still animated in spite of it. When they sat down on the couch, Keagan grabbed for the grammar book and opened it. Rudy held the fortune cookies in her hand, holding them up in front of her face with a grin. "Aren't you forgetting something?"

Keagan groaned. "Oh, great. Now my whole future and ultimate destiny will be revealed, right? Inside of a mere cookie."

"No, but you might have some...fun...reading it. I know you have a big problem with fun, but I think you can handle it." She tossed her one of the cookies.

Keagan caught the cookie and unwrapped it. "I don't

even like fortune cookies. They have no flavor."

"That doesn't matter. What matters is what's inside."

"I feel a metaphorical statement coming on..."

Rudy laughed. "Nope. Just a reminder. To make it more fun, you need to add "in bed" after whatever your fortune is. Okay?"

Keagan looked incredulous. "What? Why?"

"Don't tell me you've never done that."

"Nooo, I've never done that."

"There's a first time for everything." She laughed with pleasure at Keagan's discomfort. Not that she enjoyed seeing her uncomfortable, but in a way it was cute. "I'll go first." Rudy unwrapped her cookie. Reading it quickly, she grinned and looked back to Keagan. "Accept the next proposition you hear...in bed!" She started laughing as Keagan shook her head slowly and smiled.

"That's worded strangely, don't you think?" Keagan's sense and awareness of the way words went together caused her to automatically replay the phrase in her mind several times and it didn't make complete sense.

"How so?"

"It says, 'accept the next proposition you hear,' not 'receive' or even 'get.' The implication being that you should accept any proposition you hear, even if it's not directed at you. If you were to do that, I would think the person who was actually offered the proposition might get a little bit peeved, don't you?" Keagan stated this matter-of-factly. Rudy noted that she wasn't at all being facetious. She had to admit that Keagan was absolutely right.

"You're right." She thought for a moment and came up with an idea. "That's why, especially in this case, it's fun to add 'in bed.' Because, if you do, you can assume that there are only two people in bed together and if one hears a proposition, then it must have come from the other person, being directed toward the first."

Keagan grinned mischievously. "Is this your way of telling me you're not into threesomes?"

"Disappointed?"

"I have a difficult time dealing with just one person."

"Knowing you, I could imagine." Rudy's teasing was affectionate.

Keagan rolled her eyes, held up her cookie, and shook it. "I'll open mine now." She read it and scrunched up the paper. She put it quickly in her pocket, looked back at Rudy and shrugged.

"Oh, no you don't." Rudy leaned over closer. "What does it say?"

"Oh, nothing."

"If you don't let me see it right now I'll tickle you until you give it up. And I'm not kidding." She moved her hands threateningly toward Keagan.

"You want me to 'give it up'? Why didn't you just say so? You know I'm always ready, willing, and able." Keagan grinned evilly and backed up farther against the couch as Rudy moved over closer. They weren't touching yet.

"The flirting rule! Now *you* broke it! Just let me see it...please?"

Keagan looked into Rudy's eyes with purpose and resolve. "No... way." She stated it firmly. And before she knew it, Rudy had pounced on top of her and tickled her. Keagan tried to hold in her laughter and even tried to fight back, but all her efforts were futile. Rudy ended up on top straddling Keagan and pinning her arms over her head playfully. "Okay, okay! I surrender! Please stop!" She descended into helpless laughter and Rudy joined her. When they stopped tussling, both were breathing heavily. Rudy's position on Keagan's stomach caused her to feel very pleasant sensations in the lower part of her body. Keagan felt something similar, especially when Rudy moved her legs slightly to allow her to move closer. They gazed deeply into each other's eyes, as Rudy felt her breasts brush against Keagan's. She leaned forward to kiss Keagan and then her stubbornness made her remember the rule. Releasing Keagan's arms, she sat up and moved away with a heavy sigh, holding out her hand. "You're not going to make me break my resolve. Hand it over." A flushed and heavily breathing Keagan dug the fortune out of her pocket and gave it to her. It said, "The love of your life will appear in front of you unexpectedly...in bed." Rudy giggled.

Keagan sat quietly, still debating after their close encounter, whether or not to try breaking Rudy's resolve, but decided against it. "You know, the word 'appear' is rather deceiving in that one."

"Are you gonna critique every Chinese fortune we read?" Rudy had never gone out with anyone who paid such close attention to words as Keagan did.

Keagan shook her head. "Well, how many are we going to read tonight? By my calculations, we only have two fortune cookies, thus two fortunes, thus I'll only be critiquing two. Right?"

"You are so arrogant." Rudy enjoyed Keagan's arrogance and found it attractive, but she wasn't going to let her know that.

"I just state things as they are."

"Right." Rudy smirked.

"You don't think so?"

"I didn't say that."

"Okay. Here's a good example. This party of Gretchen's. I'm not going and do you know why?"

Rudy sank back on the couch. She laughed at the song playing on the radio, "Fire," by the Pointer Sisters. "I'm sorry, this song is so hilarious!"

Keagan grinned in recognition. *"I'm ridin' in your*

car..." she sang in a lampooning way. "*You turn on the radio...you're pullin' me close...I just say no...I say I don't like it, but you know I'm a liar....*"

"*'Cause when we kiss...oooh...FIRE!!!*" Both Keagan and Rudy sang this part together. And then both dissolved into a fit of laughter.

Since Keagan could never resist the urge to make fun of silly lyrics, she continued to sing and Rudy continued to laugh. "*Late at night...you're takin' me home...you say you wanna stay...I say I want to be alone...I say I don't love you...*" Keagan gave a fleeting glance at Rudy whose eyes were focused on her, in spite of her laughter. "*But you know I'm a liar...*"

"*Cause when we kiss...oooh...FIRE!!!*" Both women collapsed into a fit of laughter as the song continued. Keagan held her stomach, as she laughed so hard, she could hardly speak.

Rudy stopped laughing before Keagan did. "You know, it might not be that funny. I've had kisses that were like fire."

"Oh, really? Who is it? I'll kill 'em!" Making fun of the song had propelled Keagan into a goofy mood that she didn't often find herself in. Rudy found it refreshing.

"Are you going to commit suicide, then?"

Keagan did a huge double take and settled her eyes upon Rudy. "No, but I really don't think we should go there, right now, with the kissing rule and all."

"I know." Rudy got a guileless look on her face. "You wouldn't be able to control yourself."

"No, it's you who would have the problem. You almost kissed me after you tickled me. Admit it."

"And you almost kissed me back."

"Why does that not make any sense, when we're talking about something that never happened?"

Rudy grinned, hoping to steer the conversation back to

the party and away from kissing before what was left of her resolve was gone. "My point exactly. So why aren't you going to the party?"

"Because, honestly, I don't see any reason for parties. All I see at parties is a bunch of people getting drunk, looking for someone to take home, or promoting their status as part of an entity." Keagan gave Rudy a look of utter disgust and settled back onto the couch.

"An 'entity'?"

"You know, those inseparable couples like Eileen and Tate sort of. No offense meant, I know they're your friends."

"None taken. I just don't know what you mean."

"There are some couples, actually like my friend from work, Nate and his boyfriend, Derek. They can't do anything apart. They're always together, no matter what friends they see. It would be unheard of for Nate to go out with me without Derek. I just think it's dysfunctional to be that dependent on one person."

"It could be. I see what you mean." Rudy was getting a better understanding of Keagan's insecurities by her admission.

"What it amounts to is what if that person dies or leaves. They're not around anymore and then what happens to the person left?" Keagan shrugged. She hadn't meant to reveal that much but felt comfortable with Rudy.

"That's the risk we take when we give our heart to someone. If we don't risk it, we never experience the joy of loving someone."

"I suppose, but I'm still not going. I have no intention of sitting there all night listening to that drivel. Oh, and I forgot to tell you another thing I despise...the gossip."

Rudy grinned and had no intention of trying to persuade Keagan to go. "Okay. I'll try to have a good time without you."

"I'm sure you'll manage."

"I'm quite capable of managing without you. It's just that I'd rather not."

Keagan picked up a nearby pillow and pelted Rudy with it. A startled Rudy retaliated by picking up the pillow near her and bopping Keagan over the head with it. A fierce pillow fight ensued, with Rudy emerging as the victor. "I see you've found a new way to avoid things."

"I'm not avoiding anything. Just havin' some fun!" Keagan grinned evilly. She held Rudy at arm's length and decided to get daring. "My grandma wants to meet you."

Rudy looked shocked. "She does?"

"Yeah, so think about it, okay?" Keagan looked away, indicating that she didn't want to continue the subject further.

"Okay."

"Good, let me know."

"No. I mean, okay, I'll meet her."

"Oh. Cool. She's a really neat lady." Keagan looked away, slightly surprised that Rudy agreed so quickly.

"I have no doubt." Rudy smiled.

****

Rudy helped Keagan with her grammar for a couple of hours. They reviewed the ten sentence patterns again, and Keagan got them all correct. Rudy tried in vain to eliminate the flirtatious tactics she used the last time they studied. Her friend pointed out to her several times that she was breaking the flirting rule, but she just smiled and said it didn't apply to sample sentences used for studying purposes. Keagan said that she couldn't make "addendums" to the rules, but Rudy insisted she could, because they were *her* rules. Near the end of their study session, one of the sample sentences practically screamed at Keagan to break the kissing rule. "Some teacher you are. Trying to get your student to kiss you all the time."

"Excuse me? I don't have to *try* to get you to kiss me. It's what you want and you know it."

"You don't know what I want."

Rudy leaned closer to Keagan so that their shoulders were touching. "Oh yes, I do." Her voice lowered.

"And what's that?"

"You want to keep your part of our deal."

"Huh?"

"Hello? Paybacks for standing me up. You recite the infamous poem, 'The Passionate Shepherd to His Love.' Remember?"

Keagan paused to try and clear her head. "I was hoping you'd forget."

"But if I forgot, we'd never be able to break the two rules I made. And besides, I never forget—"

"Anything. Yeah, I know."

Rudy smiled, pleased with herself, as Keagan reached for the British literature anthology. She opened the book to where Rudy had strategically placed the bookmark: right to "The Passionate Shepherd."

"Wait. One condition," Rudy said.

"What's that?" Keagan glared suspiciously at Rudy.

"You can't lampoon it, you can't parody it, you can't make fun of it. You have to read it seriously."

"Oh, joy. I should have known you'd say that."

"Yes, you should have." Rudy grinned.

"But, how can I? You know what the poem is. It's completely cheesy—"

"For our time and place, yes, but it has its place in the realm of pastoral poetry. In any case, a good orator will make it good, right?"

"I don't know where you got that idea, but I'll try." Keagan picked up the book and read it the way she felt

Rudy wanted her to.

> *Come live with me and be my love,*
> *And we will all the pleasures prove*
> *That valleys, groves, hills, and fields,*
> *Woods, or steepy mountain yields.*
>
> *And we will sit upon the rocks,*
> *Seeing the shepherds feed their flocks,*
> *By shallow rivers to whose falls*
> *Melodious birds sing madrigals.*

Keagan laughed. Rudy gave her a stern look. "I'm sorry, but I'm doing okay so far, right?"

"No, you're not, because you stopped and laughed. The deal was for you to read it through to the end...seriously." Rudy raised her eyebrows and tried to avoid smiling. The truth was that she was just curious as to how far Keagan would go to please her.

"Okay." She continued with the poem.

> *And I will make thee beds of roses*
> *And a thousand fragrant posies,*
> *A cap of flowers, and a kirtle*
> *Embroidered all with leaves of myrtle;*
>
> *A belt of straw and ivy buds,*
> *With coral clasps and amber studs*
> *And if these pleasures may thee move,*
> *Come live with me, and be my love.*

Rudy sighed audibly. "That was beautiful. You did a wonderful job. And now I have a reply for you."

> *If all the world and love were young,*

And truth in every shepherd's tongue,
These pretty pleasures might me move
To live with thee and be thy love.

"Oh, no you don't." Rudy had just gotten Keagan to recite to her an extremely passionate pastoral poem and now she was offering the reply from the nymph, the object of the shepherd's affection. "You know damn well the nymph's reply comes over as cynical." Rudy grinned with pleasure and continued reciting.

Thy gowns, thy shoes, thy beds of roses,
Thy cap, thy kirtle, and thy posies
Soon break, soon wither, soon forgotten—
In folly ripe, in reason rotten.

Keagan realized Rudy was joking around, but she had a serious thought when considering the shepherd and the nymph. "So, what does this mean? You're the nymph and I'm the shepherd?"

"More like *you're* the nymph."

"Well, maybe I can become more like the shepherd."

"Nah. The shepherd likes the nymph just the way she is." Rudy smiled.

Keagan didn't reply, just gazed back at Rudy. "It's pretty late." Keagan glanced at the clock. It was one in the morning.

"I'm sorry. You have to work tomorrow don't you?"

"Don't remind me." Keagan grimaced at the mere thought.

"Where do you work, anyway? You never told me."

Keagan hated it when people asked where she worked. Gigantic was not exactly the most glamorous of retail establishments and the service left something to be desired. "It's a store called Gigantic. We sell cheap junk.

My job is to put it out."

Rudy's face brightened in recognition. "Hey, I shop there. They have a lot of good deals, but there's this one woman up front who's really mean. I tried to return something once, but I lost my receipt. She was pretty scary."

"Don't tell me. Bleached blonde, beady eyes, too much makeup, string for hair..."

"Yeah, that's her."

"That's my boss. She's completely incompetent."

"Yes. So, I take it you don't like working there?"

"That's an understatement. The job is boring, the management doesn't communicate, and they constantly expect us to work these obscure shifts. The only reason I've stayed is that the company pays for part of my tuition and I couldn't stay in school without it." Keagan didn't feel like discussing work anymore. It was depressing.

Rudy thought for a second and then grinned at Keagan, who was frowning. "I could call up and ask for the manager and tell them I had some great customer service from someone named Keagan. I could make up a whole story about how you helped me."

"I'm sure you could, but it wouldn't matter. They don't like employees who threaten them in any way. And me doing anything well is a threat to their authority, even though they're all twenty years older than me." She shrugged. "But thanks for the thought." She smiled at Rudy.

"Okay, then...okay. How about this? I call up and complain about this boss of yours. I'll tell them she treated me abominably and I'm never shopping there again." Rudy's eyes lit up at the prospect and she got an adorable, devilish look on her face.

Keagan laughed. "Two problems with that; first, they wouldn't know what abominable meant and second, it's normal for her to treat people like crap. They wouldn't think twice about it."

"I tried."

"Thanks." Keagan usually didn't tell anyone about work, but was glad she told Rudy, who was inexplicably able to make her laugh about it.

"So, you kickin' me out now?"

"No. You can stay here if you want, but I expect certain things from my overnight female guests." She snickered.

"So you've said. What do you expect?"

"No snoring and no blanket hogging."

"Well, I don't know if I snore or not, but...wait a minute. You're not suggesting we sleep *together*, are you?" Rudy smiled and looked suspiciously at Keagan.

"I have a big enough bed, there's no reason why we can't sleep together." Keagan's response was delivered in her usual rational tone, but inside she felt nervous at the prospect. "And anyway, I kept my part of our deal and read the poem. So, anything's allowed to happen now. Flirting, kissing, whatever."

"Oh, I see what you're getting at. You just want a kiss." Rudy leaned closer.

"That's not what I said."

"I've come to realize you don't always say what you mean."

"You have?"

"Yes. And sometimes what you say is in fact the opposite of what you really feel." Rudy was so close that Keagan could feel her breath on her face. She took a moment to study Rudy's verdant eyes, and thought how pretty they were. She had never seen quite that color of green before. Shaking her head to clear it, she felt her body responding to the close proximity of the woman. She felt her rational side take over, telling her to back off. Her mind flashed into the near future and the scenario that arose in her head made her feel uneasy about sleeping with Rudy. "You take the bed, *again,* and I'll take the couch. I already changed the sheets." She smirked.

"Scared of me, huh?" Rudy wondered why Keagan had changed the sheets on a Tuesday.

"Yes. Maybe just a little." Normally, she wouldn't have admitted that much, but since knowing Rudy, some of her actions had been anything but normal ones. "There's something for you to wear on the bed. Goodnight."

Rudy chose not to explore Keagan's admission, but to file it away for later. "Now wait a minute. You changed the sheets and you already have something for me to wear. Did you plan this?"

"No, *I'm* not the one who *plans* things," she began, raising her eyebrows to indicate she hadn't forgotten Rudy's previous scheme to spend the night with her. "I just like to be prepared. And when I knew you were coming over to study, I realized you might stay late and might even stay all night. That's all."

Rudy was surprised at Keagan's actions, but impressed as well. "Okay, but you're the one who has to work, so you take the bed." When Keagan tried to protest, Rudy held up her hand. "I'm not taking no for an answer." She agreed then, but with reluctance. Rudy fleetingly wondered when the last time was that someone had taken care of her. Keagan fell into the role of caretaker easily, but didn't seem to be as eager to be taken care of herself.

Rudy leaned over and gave Keagan a goodnight kiss. It was short and friendly almost, but contained a hint of passion in it. Although Keagan might have prolonged it, she realized it wouldn't be a good time for that kind of exploration. "Didn't want you to have to go to sleep without that kiss you've been waiting for." Rudy grinned mischievously.

It was on the tip of her tongue to tell Rudy that

although it was a nice kiss, she was hoping for something more passionate, but she remained silent. Best not to go there now. She grinned at Rudy and rose, going to her bedroom. Returning in a few seconds, she threw a pair of shorts and a T-shirt at her, which Rudy gratefully caught. "Thanks." Looking at the T-shirt, she laughed. It was the 2QT2BSTR8 shirt.

Keagan shrugged and feigned indifference. "It's just you, I guess." She allowed a small grin to surface. "Goodnight."

"G'night." As Rudy watched Keagan return to her bedroom, she entertained a thought of following her, but that's all she did. She hoped that sometime soon she would be able to act on her frequently entertained thoughts involving the dark-haired, enigmatic, English major.

Chapter 7

Keagan drowsily awakened upon hearing the alarm. She glanced at the clock, which said 4:00 am, and closed her eyes again, looking forward to thirty more minutes of sleep until she really had to get up. Thinking of Rudy who spent the night on her uncomfortable, lumpy couch, an idea occurred to her and she forced herself to rise. She used the restroom and then went to the kitchen to make coffee. Glancing into the living room, she could tell that Rudy was far from comfortable. She was lying on her stomach, her left arm draped over the edge of the couch. Her right arm was lopped over the top of the couch unnaturally, she was squirming, and the blanket was lying on the floor. Keagan wasn't sure if she was asleep or still trying to get there. She regretted not letting Rudy sleep in her bed. Why should she be uncomfortable all night just because Keagan was wildly attracted to her and afraid of things becoming too physical? She went over to the couch and knelt down, gently touching her friend's shoulder. Rudy's eyes opened and she gave a half grin. "Hi."

"Hi." Rudy's hair was tousled and her T-shirt was

pushed up her stomach several inches. Keagan thought how cute she looked in the morning. "I've got to get ready for work. If you want, you can sleep in my bed."

Rudy yawned. "It's about time you asked me into your bed."

"But we've only known each other for two weeks. That would be scandalous."

Although still exhausted from tossing and turning on the couch all night, Rudy came up with a suitable reply. "Somehow, I think I'd get over that aspect of it pretty quick." She gave Keagan a lazy grin and yawned.

Keagan's only response was a short grin. "C'mon." Before Rudy knew it, she had been guided into the bedroom and tucked in. "You can hang out as long as you want, doesn't matter to me." She turned to leave but felt a hand on her arm.

"I need to ask you something."

"Sure. What?"

"I had this dream last night about your story. You know, the one that you write at the bar, and well...I was wondering. What's it about? The one you were writing the night we met."

Keagan sat down on the bed. "I don't have a lot of time."

"In a nutshell, then."

Keagan turned away. It wasn't yet dawn and the dark shades in her room added to the feeling of concealment. She was grateful for the low lighting and that Rudy couldn't see the slight blush that colored her cheeks. "Actually, you'll laugh. It's about two English majors who fall in love." She laughed uneasily.

"It is, really?"

"Yeah, it is really."

"That's not what I expected."

Rudy could see Keagan's smile, even in the darkness.

"Right. I have to get ready for work. I can tell you more about it later, if you'd like." She stood up and headed for the door.

"I'd like." Rudy settled back comfortably into the bed, letting her thoughts wander briefly before falling into a deep relaxing sleep.

* * * * * * * * * *

The day passed quickly for Keagan. She divided her mental musings between thinking about her story and devising conversation starters at parties. She still didn't intend to go to Gretchen's party, but felt it was a useful mental exercise nonetheless. So far she had come up with several things to chat about that avoided the label she hated the most...small talk. *Why do people slow down for cops? A cop can be coming in the other direction and everybody slows down. Do people really think that cop's going to do a U-turn and stop them for speeding? More likely she's heading for the donut shop. Or he. And what is it with the cereal aisle in grocery stores anyway? All those cheesy toys they have displayed at every four-foot section that cost three times as much as any toy in the regular toy aisle. Do retailers really think parents are going to shell out their hard-earned money for that crap? And what is with these bowls that come with built-in straws? How lazy has society become anyway? Now we're too lazy to pick up the bowl and drink the milk left over from our cereal? And this new yogurt that comes complete with a collapsible, easily assembled spoon. What the hell is that? We can't bring our own spoon along with our lunch?*

Keagan was making a bale of used cardboard as she had these thoughts. As the stockers emptied their cartons, they placed them into a machine called a baler and when it filled up, the cardboard was extracted from the machine and sold to a company that recycled it. All the job really involved was opening up the machine, threading some wires through the bottom to the back and up through the top again. Then the wires were tied around the bale to keep the cardboard in place and the whole thing was removed from the machine onto a pallet so it could be moved. Keagan didn't mind volunteering for this because she could hang out in the stockroom for fifteen minutes and avoid customers. There was also something that appealed to her sense of creativity about making a bale. Every bale was unique. She could always devise new ways to twist the wires together; she could even crisscross them. Although the one time she had done that her boss, Slone, wasn't very pleased. Keagan hadn't done it again.

After she threaded the wires to the back, she stood and moved to the rear of the machine. Her thoughts wandered again as she pushed the wires back through to the front. *And what is with those coffee filter extractors, or whatever they're called?* Keagan had been surprised when she had picked up a package of coffee filters only to find a free filter extractor inside. It was a small piece of blue plastic that resembled a mini set of tongs except it had little white rubber pieces on the end, presumably to allow the device to adhere to the filter. It was about three inches in length. *When I tried to use one, it didn't work. The filters were stuck together so tightly I had to use my hand to get one anyway. The whole process took much longer trying to use the device than simply not using it. Where's the sense in that?* Keagan didn't have much patience for useless things. Working in retail, she was exposed everyday to ridiculous items that people didn't need. People were constantly spending their money on useless junk. *Why? Why? Stop the insanity!* She came back to the front of the machine and twisted the wires together. *What kind of tie today?* She decided on the neat, small twist that took longer but made the bale more secure. *And I like how it looks.*

With great effort, she let her mind go blank for a few minutes as she tied the wires. She would have to go wash her hands when done, because they were oily and turned her hands black. When she was on the fourth wire, her thoughts went to Rudy. *I told her what the story was about. Mistake. What's she going to think now?* The truth be told, when Keagan saw Rudy that first night at the Grotto, she began writing a story about a young vivacious woman who has an encounter in a bar. There wasn't really any point to it. To Keagan it was just a writing exercise with a live subject. Only later, when she discovered that Rudy was an English major did the idea occur to make the protagonists English majors. And then, the more she got into the story, she realized that her characters really liked each other a lot. *I got this grand idea to write a love story. Where did I get that idea? I don't really mind well written love stories, but didn't ever think about writing one...until I met Rudy. Strange.* As she finished tying the wires, she stood and turned toward the controls on the machine. It was at that moment that her boss, Madeline Slone, approached.

"Um, Keagan, what are you doing?"

Keagan turned around. *What does it look like I'm doing?* "I'm making a bale." Keagan stated it matter-of-factly with little intonation in her voice, not wanting to show her irritation.

"It's too small and you tied the wires wrong again." Slone's beady, little eyes bored into Keagan's.

"So what did you want me to do? I can either complete the bale or I can untie all the wires and see if I can force the door shut again, which is unlikely. Or if your problem with it is more that the wires are tied wrong I can just untie them and retie them the way you would like them

to be tied. On the other hand, if it's more important that
the bale be bigger, I should probably stick to my second
option, which probably won't work as I've said." Keagan
stated all of this in a dispassionate voice, but she could see
Slone's face turning red as she spoke. She didn't intentionally set out to piss off her boss. It just happened.

"Oh, just finish it!" Slone stomped off in the other
direction. Keagan couldn't help but smile.

****

Rudy ended up sleeping in at Keagan's for three more
hours. She didn't have anything planned that day, except
studying, so when she got up and saw that Keagan's
kitchen was messy, she decided to clean it. One thing led
to another, and eventually she had cleaned the bathroom,
mopped the kitchen floor, and vacuumed and dusted the
living room. She finished around one o'clock and left
Keagan a note:

> *Hi. Now don't get mad. I just wanted to do*
> *something nice for you, since you gave up*
> *your bed for me and all. (Although you*
> *might have decided to do that last night...ha,*
> *ha) I'll see you tomorrow at school or you*
> *can always give me a call.*
> *Love,*
> *La Roux*

Rudy smiled to herself when she got a mental picture
of Keagan coming home, seeing what she had done, and
reading the note. *She'll get that dumbfounded look on her*
face that says, "what the hell happened?" Then she'll go
into a mock glare, but eventually allow a small grin. Too
bad I can't be here to see it. Rudy considered hanging
around until Keagan returned, but didn't want to invade

her space.

She returned home to the sight of Courtney on the living room floor scrubbing. She had a scowl on her face and looked agitated. Rudy approached her. "Spill something?"

Courtney sighed disgustedly. "You're lucky you weren't here last night. Where were you, anyway?"

"At Keagan's." Rudy sat on the couch.

"Oh. Jake decided to have a last-minute party. *Here*! He brought about ten people over here, who I didn't even know."

Rudy laughed. "Have you ever heard of the word, 'no'?"

"Yes, I just have a hard time using it. Anyway, they spilled beer and I'm trying to get the smell out of the carpet. It's awful!" Courtney leaned down and sniffed the rug. With a scowl, she resumed scrubbing.

"I think we should make a rule. No more beer in the house."

"Ha, ha! And I'd have no more friends."

"Sure you would. They'd just be quiet, reserved types who like to stay in the background and not get boisterous."

Courtney laughed. "That sounds like *your* friend."

"Keagan?"

"Yeah, her. I've only met her a couple of times but that's how she comes off." As she continued scrubbing, Courtney periodically sniffed the rug to test her progress.

"She is a little shy, but she's different when you know her."

"Bring her over again. I'd like to get to know her better. You two *are* dating, right?" The whole time Courtney talked she was still scrubbing the floor and so Rudy couldn't see her eyes.

Rudy was shocked at her roommate's question because they had never discussed her sexual orientation. It just never came up. True, Rudy's best friends were Eileen and

Tate, an openly lesbian couple that had been over to the house a few times and Rudy never showed an interest in the opposite sex, but how had Courtney figured it out?

"You could say we are. How did you know?"

Courtney stopped scrubbing and sat on the couch next to Rudy, appearing to contemplate the question. "The main thing was that you turned down the irresistible Dave. I mean what more could you want in a man than that? And he's very talented. He can drink anyone under the table and he can crush a beer can with one hand."

Rudy was relieved to know that her roommate wasn't going to have a problem with it.

"Seriously, I suspected it for awhile, but then the night I met Keagan I knew."

"How?"

"You and she have chemistry, you know? It's very obvious." Courtney shrugged, not being able to explain further. "So, now that I know, we can do girl talk, right?"

"Sure." Rudy felt like Keagan for a second, with her monosyllabic responses.

"Rudy. How serious is it?"

Rudy thought about her question for a second. "We've only known each other for a couple of weeks. I—I don't know. I do think about her all the time." Rudy's voice quieted as she made the last admission.

"Okay. I have an idea. You bring her over for dinner. I'll invite Jake and we can double date. Then I'll get the lowdown on you two."

"I don't know if I could get her to do that. She's not much into social stuff."

"Oh, I think you'll find some way to convince her."

Rudy grinned mischievously, contemplating the possibilities.

****

Gerry called Keagan at work that day and asked if she could stop by and take her to the store. So, after work, she and her grandma got lottery tickets, cigarettes, and vodka. Keagan tried to talk her out of getting it and suggested beer instead, but Gerry insisted on it. Joan would be furious when she found out. She was not looking forward to the impending confrontation with her. She was continually torn between them and the only way to eliminate that feeling would be to distance herself from both of them which she was unwilling to do. Keagan reminisced about spending the weekends with her grandma when she was a child. They would go to the store and Gerry would buy her a toy. Of course, then she had to endure sitting in a bar for hours. Gerry's kindness to her granddaughter usually always outweighed her weaknesses...usually.

****

When she finally returned home, it was to a sparklingly clean apartment. Shaking her head with amusement, she thought about how Rudy never failed to surprise her. Reading her note, she smiled and said aloud, "Now, La Roux, why would I be mad? I hate housework."

She dialed Rudy's number. After a couple of rings she heard a voice say, "Shakespeare's den of iniquity. Dark lady speaking. Can I help you?"

Keagan held in a laugh. *Does she come up with these spontaneously or plan them?* "This is the rival poet. Is Bill in?"

"Wouldn't you rather speak with me?" Rudy lowered her voice into a seductive tone.

"That depends on what you're offering."

"How about a fun filled evening of frivolity? Petrarch is having a party. If you came, you, he, and Bill could discuss sonnet styles."

"English, Italian, they're all the same to me. And anyway, I'm not much for parties, unless they're private. I might be interested if it was our own little party...just you and me."

"Oh, really? What would we talk about? I'm just the dark lady, not a poet."

"And that is a problem...why?"

Rudy hesitated momentarily. Was Keagan turning into a flirt? Could it be possible? Tempted to remain in character and continue their banter, she nevertheless reverted back to her real persona. "It's not a problem at all, but you surprise me."

"And why's that?" Keagan was grinning broadly in spite of herself.

"So flirtatious. And more bold about it."

"We're on the phone. It's easier."

"Ah."

"Rudy, thank you for what you did."

"No problem. I like doing things for you."

"Oh." Keagan didn't know how to respond to that. No woman had ever said that she liked doing things for her with no ulterior motive. And she knew Rudy had none.

Sensing that Keagan was uncomfortable, Rudy changed the subject. "Courtney knows I'm gay."

"She does? Did you tell her or—"

"She guessed."

"It must be because you're so butch."

Rudy laughed. "Actually, it was because of you."

"Because *I'm* so butch?"

"Nooo...it's probably going to embarrass you, but I'll tell you anyway. The couple of times she's met you, she's sensed a chemistry between you and me. That's what she said."

"Hmm..."

"She, uh, was really cool with it. She even suggested

you and I having dinner with her and her boyfriend, Jake, but I said—"

"Sure."

"Sure...what?"

"I'll do that."

"You will?" Rudy's voice was filled with incredulity.

"Why not? It won't kill me, right?" Keagan couldn't believe what she heard herself saying. She only knew that pleasing Rudy had become important to her.

Rudy laughed. "No, it won't kill you. I promise. And it's only for a few hours..."

"You don't have to convince me. I already said yes."

Rudy decided to change the subject before Keagan changed her mind. "So what about the party?"

"Still not goin'."

"Aw." Rudy tried to communicate a pout over the phone but failed miserably. "And I thought you would decide to go."

"You're such a nag."

"I'm pouting."

"I don't care. That won't work."

"What will?"

"Nothing, nada, zip."

"How about bribery. Seafood?"

"Nope."

"Chinese?"

"Forget it!"

"Sex?"

"Hmm, now that depends. Who with?" Keagan snickered.

"What do you mean, 'who with'? You're impossible! I hope you have a nice, sedate, lonely Saturday evening...alone. I hope you enjoy yourself."

"Oh, I intend to." Keagan sounded smug, although a part of her wished she could go to the party with Rudy.

Parties just weren't her thing, though. The phone conversation with Rudy ended, and she found herself feeling uncharacteristically lonely.

****

Keagan saw Rudy Thursday at school, but she didn't bring up the party again. She found this odd because usually, women she dated tended to be needy and nagged her until she gave in. *Sounds like some of my family members.* Keagan didn't want to admit it, but Rudy's decision not to pursue the matter made her want to go to the party. Her seeming indifference had a reversed psychological effect.

Keagan spent the day Saturday catching up on schoolwork and writing her story. There was one particular part that was giving her problems, so she left the computer and headed into the living room to think about it. She glanced out the window and noted that it was sunny, but probably freezing cold. *It looks lovely outside, but if I go out I'll freeze.* She didn't know why but that made her think of Rudy. She rubbed her eyes with irritation and sank onto the couch. *Why do I always think in metaphors?* She was almost glad when the phone rang.

As usual, the answering machine clicked on. "It's your mother, Keagan. Pick up the phone." Joan didn't sound happy. "I found your grandmother with a bottle of vodka again. Sean must be buying it for her. You're going to need to talk to him again for me. I can't believe he would do this. Bye."

Keagan sighed. "The continuing turmoil of my loving family." Keagan didn't think about how angry Joan would be if she discovered that it was she who let Gerry buy alcohol. Pushing it to the back of her mind, she returned to the computer room.

****

"Cody, I'm surprised you got the night off." Gretchen Fuqua, social animal that she was, enjoyed being in her element. Spotting the bartender in a far corner of the spacious living room, she approached her.

"Even career bartenders like myself get nights off." Cody smiled and scanned the room. The CD player was squawking out an early 80's Boy George song. Most of the people there were from the bar, but there were several she didn't recognize. It was around nine-thirty and there were already about forty people there. The house was immense and Gretchen had it suitably decorated with 80's paraphernalia. Pictures of rock stars adorned the walls and there were streamers and balloons everywhere. On the coffee table, Cody spotted an unsolved Rubik's cube.

"Mabel took pity on you, huh?" Gretchen took a sip of her punch. "Don't forget to try the punch. It's an old family recipe and it's just to die for."

"Okay, but what's in it?"

"Secret." Gretchen grinned devilishly.

"So, whose house is this again?" Cody walked over to the snack table. Among the treats were shrimp, crab cakes, eggrolls, and spinach dip with an assortment of vegetables and crackers. That could wait until later. She was interested in the punch.

"It's my stepdad's. He's out of town this weekend and gave me the keys." The house was impressive. It was a four bedroom three story dwelling with a two-car garage, swimming pool, and hot tub. The floors were all natural wood and obviously shined and well maintained and the place was lavishly decorated. Expensive hand-blown glass pieces were scattered about and several rare art prints decorated the walls. Gretchen left everything as it was for the party. If something happened, she'd deal with it. That was just life.

"And naturally he gave permission for you to have a wild party." Cody poured herself a cupful of the green substance. "Green," she commented, sniffing it gingerly.

"That's the lime sherbet." Watching as Cody took a sip, Gretchen's eyes widened with anticipation. "Well?"

Cody swished the cool fluid around her mouth before swallowing. Definitely vodka, but well hidden. "It's good. My compliments to the bartender."

"Thanks, hon!"

Cody's brow creased and she regarded the substance cautiously. "I'd be careful with that stuff, though. It tastes great and goes down too easily." She chuckled under her breath.

"That's the whole point!"

****

Rudy rode with Eileen and Tate to the party. When they arrived, Gretchen swooped over and led Rudy to the infamous Murphy's punch. "I hope it's not anything like 'Murphy's Law'," said Rudy, sniffing the green beverage. Tate and Eileen went off in search of Milligan and the pool table.

"It's divine, I promise, hon." Gretchen watched as she took a rather large sip. Rudy's eyes widened a bit and she shook her head slowly up and down with approval. "Ooh, you were right, this *is* good."

"I told you. And now for the real question. Where's your datemate? Miss-I-am-a-reclusive-dark-brooding-English-major, hmm?"

"Home I suppose." Rudy poured herself another cup of Murphy's punch.

"And you didn't convince her to come? I thought you were going to."

"I guess my powers of persuasion aren't as good as I thought."

Gretchen rolled her eyes and shook her head. "Let me give you some advice with that one, dear. She needs to be forced into almost everything. Keagan never learned how to have fun. You have to make her have fun. It's the only way with her."

"I'm not at all comfortable with the word 'force'."

"How about persuade, entice, suggest, then?"

Rudy smiled at Gretchen. She had actually become quite fond of her, even if her methods seemed rambunctious. "I see your point but in the end, Keagan will do what she wants to do."

"You don't get it do you? She has to be *shown* what she wants. Oh, she knows, deep down somewhere but she needs an instigator, a catalyst, you know?"

Rudy imagined herself as that instigator or catalyst.

"Here, have some more punch, hon. The night is young!"

Not knowing that she had a natural non-tolerance for alcohol, Rudy agreed because the punch tasted so good. It tasted like Kool-Aid. "Oh...sure, why not."

****

Nate and Derek arrived fashionably late at around ten-thirty. Not expecting to see Keagan they scanned the room, looking for a familiar face. They saw Brad lurking in the back by himself, drinking a Miller Genuine Draft, and looking forlorn. "C'mon, let's see what's up with Brad," said Nate.

"You're looking rather contemplative this evening, Bradley." Nate smiled at the moody young man.

"Oh, hi. I was just thinking that maybe Keagan's got the right idea."

"About?"

"Keagan's at home right now all by herself and I'm here at this party all by myself. What's the difference?"

"You're not by yourself. We're here." Derek rolled his eyes at Nate's attempt to make him feel better and scanned the room. Soon, he spotted Char and an unfamiliar woman sitting in the back of the room singing to each other. "What's Char doing?"

Brad looked disinterestedly at the two women. "Oh, that's the flower lady from the bar. Angelique, I think is her name. Apparently, she hit it off with Char. They're singing..." He paused for a second to determine the song. "Oh, yes. Now it's Chaka Khan's 'I feel for you.'" He shrugged. Derek and Nate chuckled. "Hell, you should have been here when they were singing Mister Mister's 'Broken Wings.' That was a real hoot."

"You're a veritable fountain of 80's music trivia," Nate commented.

"I did a little research to impress partygoers. By the way, stay away from that punch. That stuff's potent."

"What punch?"

"The great Gretchen Fuqua hasn't introduced you to her family's secret recipe of Murphy's punch?"

"Nah, we haven't seen her yet."

"Judging from what it's done to sweet, innocent Rudy, I'd steer clear of it."

"Rudy Whitman? The girl Keagan went out with?"

"Yeah. Her. Oh, no, now they're singing 'Head over Heels' by the GoGo's." Brad cringed.

"Which one is she?"

Brad pointed out Rudy, who could be seen sitting in a circle surrounded by several women and at least two drag queens. "Oh, she's the one reciting all the poetry." He snickered.

Nate laughed. "You really only came here just to

watch people, didn't you? You're more like Keagan than
you realize."

Brad only looked at the floor and grinned.

****

Rudy attracted quite an audience. It started out inno-
cently enough. She had been chatting with Jen about
school and they discovered a mutual affinity for poetry. It
wasn't like the affinity she and Keagan shared. This
mutual interest involved Rudy reciting and Jen listening.
Rudy enjoyed it, though, and it took her mind off of
Keagan, which she had been trying to do unsuccessfully all
night. When Danielle came over and sat next to her, she
didn't protest, not wanting to make a scene.

Rudy recited several classic poems and as she was trying to think of another one, Jackie Daniels spoke up. "Do
you know any lesbian ones?"

"Several." Rudy continued to drink the punch, but
was starting to feel a bit different. *Hmm, I hope I'm not
getting drunk.*

Dani put her arm around Rudy. "Why don't you recite
one of those for us?"

Rudy felt pressured and her head felt fuzzy. Consequently, the only one she could think of was the poem she
read to Keagan after their date. She had memorized it the
day after, because they both had liked it so much. *So much
for the poetry distracting me.* Eventually, she got to the
final lines, "*Tell me love, how to speed time now, how to
slow it then, when I call your name.*"

The group applauded and Rudy decided she was finished reciting poetry for the night. As she turned around
and stood up, she noticed a tall, dark figure standing near
the corner, leaning against the wall. Her arms were folded
and she stood looking at Rudy curiously.

Rudy felt a range of emotions that spanned the gamut from surprise to happiness to irritation and back again. How long had Keagan been standing there?

When Dani noticed that Keagan wasn't making any move to approach Rudy she touched her arm. "Can I get you some more punch?"

"I don't think so. I've had enough." Her eyes never left Keagan's who continued to stare. "Will you excuse me, please?"

As the rest of the group broke up, Rudy approached Keagan gingerly and watched as a small grin surfaced on her face. "Hi."

"Hi, yourself. How did you sneak in here without me seeing you?" Rudy stepped forward and almost stumbled into Keagan, who caught her effortlessly. She put her arm around Rudy and laughed.

"You haven't been into Gretchen's punch, have you?"

"Oh, no. Just drunk on life." She giggled.

Sensing that Rudy needed help to keep standing straight, Keagan put her arms around her, holding her from behind. She whispered into Rudy's ear. "I thought that was our special poem. And you shared it with all of them."

Rudy leaned back into Keagan and felt like she was floating. "You smell so good."

"Let's sit down." She took Rudy's hand and guided her over to the couch.

Rudy put her head on Keagan's chest as a strong arm encircled her, pulling her close. "It was the only poem I could think of. They wanted a lesbian one."

"Yeah, I know, I was there the whole time, remember?"

"Why didn't you say anything?"

"I enjoyed watching you. And didn't want to interrupt."

Rudy considered that for a moment. "So why did you

come? I thought you hated parties."

"I do hate parties, but when I considered my options for what to do this evening, rationality won out."

Rudy lifted her head up and gazed into Keagan's eyes. "And what were your options?"

Keagan looked over to the table and spotted the Rubik's cube. Removing her arm from around Rudy, she picked it up and played with it. "I could sit at home and brood, the idea of which I actually found quite appealing, try to write my story which I have a mental block about, or go to the party which could be a chance to get some great material. It just seemed to make the most sense to come to the party, considering the options."

Rudy nodded her head and hid her disappointment that she didn't figure into the options. "I still want to know more about this story." Her stomach grumbled loudly and she looked away in embarrassment.

"Hungry? Stay here and I'll bring you something. I saw a few delectable treats over there. This isn't a Chex Mix party, apparently." She set the puzzle down on the couch and took off.

****

As Keagan put crab cakes and shrimp on a plate, she heard a bellowing noise. "Keagannnnn!!!" It was Gretchen and she was heading over to the table.

"Hi, Gretchen. Great party."

"'Hi, Gretchen. Great party.' Don't sound so enthusiastic."

"Believe me, I'm trying not to." She glanced over to the couch to see Dani approaching Rudy and sitting down beside her. Couldn't that woman take a hint?

"You can't leave little miss cutie pie alone for a minute can you? You better claim her soon, hon, before somebody scoops her up."

"You make Rudy sound like a piece of land."

"Excuses, excuses!   Now go on back over there and mark your territory."   She gave Keagan an affectionate shove.

When Keagan returned, Dani was chatting and Rudy was looking uncomfortable. She realized that her younger friend was too polite to tell her to leave. "Danielle." Keagan handed the plate to Rudy whose eyes widened with pleasure upon seeing the shrimp and crab cakes.

"Keagan."

"You mind if I ask you a question?"

Dani looked suspicious. "No, I suppose not."

"I was just wondering why you had the gall to think Rudy would want to talk to you when you tried to win her in a pool game. That's all."

"What?!"

"You know, you tried to win her like she was a prize. That's really low. And what's really sad is that she's too polite to tell you that. But you know what? I'm not." Keagan kept her voice low and unwavering with her eyes boring straight into Dani's. And then she motioned with her hand for Dani to leave.

Dani stood up, glaring at Keagan. "You'll pay for this, Keagan!" She stomped off, hoping to find Jill and the entourage.

Keagan plopped down next to Rudy who was chewing contentedly on her shrimp. She picked up the Rubik's cube and played with it again. "Why do all the women say that to me? 'You'll pay for this!' I did nothing but bring the truth to light."

"People don't like dealing with the truth. *You can't deal with the truth!*" Keagan cringed at Rudy's lame attempt at a Jack Nicholson imitation and they both laughed. Rudy dipped a piece of shrimp into the cocktail sauce and offered it to Keagan who took it between her lips and chewed.

"Great shrimp," she murmured.

"That's your reward for standing up for me."

Keagan swallowed the shrimp. "Is that all I get?"

"Is that all you want?"

"No, but you're drunk."

"I know. Isn't it great? I don't think I've ever been drunk before. All my feelings feel exposed and on display."

Keagan laughed but felt the irony of her words. She knew first-hand what the abuse of alcohol did to people and here was Rudy, saying it was great. "So you've never made love before, you've never been drunk before. What else haven't you done?"

"Lots of things and I want to do them all with you." Rudy leaned over and put her hand on Keagan's face, caressing the soft skin she found there. Barry White could be heard crooning in the background. "Oh! I just love Barry White!"

"You're crazy. Barry White. Hey, that's 70's. I guess Gretchen kept her promise to me, but I didn't think it would be Barry White." She chuckled lightly, but kept staring into Rudy's eyes. Rudy leaned closer for a kiss, but Keagan could see Brad approaching out of the corner of her eye. "Rudy, this is my friend, Brad." Rudy, who had been focused on Keagan shook her head and turned to greet him.

Brad held out his hand. "I know *of* you, but I don't think we've actually met." He smiled warmly and shook Rudy's hand.

"Nice to finally meet you, Brad."

"You have impeccable timing," said Keagan.

"Sorry. I was just about to head out but couldn't resist the urge to meet this very special, lovely woman who has attracted my friend's attention. And now that I have, I shall be off. Rudy, I would very much like it if you and the big, brooding one—"

"Why does everyone always call me that?" Keagan frowned.

Brad cleared his throat noisily. "Would have dinner with Michael and myself sometime soon."

"Michael?"

Brad shrugged. "My latest."

"Oh. Cute?"

"Not bad. And he works at The Garage. Free beers and no cover." He smiled gleefully.

"Must your 'companions' always provide you with some free service?"

Brad grinned evilly. "Nope, but it doesn't hurt, right? Goodnight, ladies. Enjoy your evening." And he was off.

"He certainly is charming."

"He's a good friend. A bit complicated, but we all are to a certain extent."

"And you'd know complicated when you saw it, huh? Now where were we?" Rudy leaned over but before she could capture Keagan's lips, two more visitors interrupted them. "Nate, Derek, this is Rudy." Keagan completely took her hands off of Rudy and gave up.

"Hi. We are really so happy for you two." They almost said it in unison.

"Happy? Why?" Keagan was confused.

Rudy ignored Keagan. "Nice to meet you both."

"What do you mean, 'happy, why'? You can be so dense sometimes, you incompetent boob." As Nate said this, Derek just rolled his eyes and prepared for Nate to be his typical, nosy self. Nate extended his hand to Rudy who shook it. "I work with Keagan."

"Oh. I hear it's an interesting place to work."

"That's an understatement or too big of a compliment

for the place, I don't know which. We have fun, though, don't we?" He glanced at Keagan and their eyes locked.

"Stop the odiousity!" They both said it in unison and then laughed. Derek shrugged his shoulders, sighed and gazed at Rudy sympathetically. Obviously, they were witnessing an in-joke between co-workers.

"You had to be there, I guess," said Keagan meekly.

Rudy grinned. "Probably, but I'd like to hear the story behind that one."

"I'm sure you'll get it out of me eventually."

"Well," Nate said, "I think Keagan has finally found someone to keep her in line. Goodnight to you both. We've got to leave."

"Bye." Keagan watched her friends go. "This is so cool. I've managed to avoid the small talk." Keagan smiled with delight.

"And what's wrong with small talk? It can be very revealing, you know."

"I can think of a lot more revealing things than small talk."

"Oh, really? Like what?" She leaned over and kissed Keagan's neck and felt her breathing catch. She didn't stop until she reached her lips and then her tongue entered Keagan's mouth and she felt her moan. They parted and Rudy placed her hand at the top of Keagan's chest to feel her heartbeat. "Your heart's beating fast."

"It's your fault."

"And why exactly is that?"

"Um..."

"Keagan, Rudy?"

The women both looked up to see none other than the infamous Dr. V.M. Addison standing before them. To Keagan, it was some sort of warped, reversed, poetic justice, vindicated upon her for not being the best grammar student she could be. And for not being into British Literature. Of all the people to interrupt a private moment. Rudy, however, even in her inebriated and embarrassed state, managed to be pleasant and friendly. She smiled brightly at the professor and casually removed her hand from Keagan's chest.

"Dr. Addison, how nice to see you. I wasn't aware that you knew Gretchen."

"Oh, I'm an old friend of her stepdad. And when he let me know she was having a party, I couldn't resist stopping by to see what damage would be done." She chuckled lightly, giving no indication that the situation she had intruded upon had at all affected her. "So, what are you two up to?"

Rudy chimed in promptly. "We were just discussing Freneau. Right?"

Keagan, still in a state of confusion, embarrassment, and mortification, nodded silently. She reached for another piece of shrimp and chewed on it to have something to do other than to come up with something to say.

"Certainly you could come up with a more stimulating topic than that. I know. How about another recitation of 'The Passionate Shepherd'?" Dr. Addison laughed.

"We're not in school now." Keagan regarded Dr. Addison for the first time.

"Sentence pattern?" Dr. Addison meant for Keagan to name the sentence pattern of her statement.

Keagan put her hands on her head and buried it in the pillow on the couch.

"I think it might be pattern one," she heard Rudy whisper.

"See you girls in class!" And with that, Dr. Addison was off to mingle with the other partygoers.

After Dr. Addison was well out of earshot, Keagan and Rudy looked at each other and exploded into hysterics. "So, what do you think the V stands for?"

Keagan appeared to consider the question carefully. "I think Vicky. Definitely Vicky. Like, Dr. Vicky Marie Addison."

"Not Veronica? Or Violet...or Vivian?"

"What do you think of Vega, Vanessa, Venus, Verbenia, Viola, Virginia, or Volupia...that one means sensual pleasure. Yep, I'll bet that could be it, too. She's a woman of mystery anyway. And then she shows up at a gay party. Hmm."

Rudy was too busy laughing at Keagan's long list of V names to comment. "How did you know all those?"

Keagan shrugged. "I'm a writer. It's my business to know a lot of different names. I have this great little book with over 20,000 names in it. That's where I get them."

"Ah." Rudy smiled and glanced down at Keagan's hands, which had been working the puzzle almost non-stop since she had picked it up again.

With no bravado, she set down the solved Rubik's cube. "You want to get out of here?" Keagan didn't want to know what would happen next if she hung around at the party and she didn't think she could handle much more stress in one night...or much more embarrassment.

"I came with Eileen and Tate. You could drive me home if you want."

"All right. Let's get out of here."

After Rudy let her friends know that Keagan was driving her home, they headed for the door. "Leaving so soon?"

Keagan turned and was startled to see Jill and Terry standing together, blocking her way. "A match made in heaven," she remarked.

"I never thought you were one to resort to cliches," said Terry.

"If the shoe fits..." Keagan couldn't help but smile upon hearing Rudy's laughter at her remark.

"Thought I'd give you some advice about your new girlfriend, Rudely." Terry had obviously had both too much punch and too much of Jill's influence.

Rudy actually laughed at the mispronunciation of her name, but Keagan didn't. "Her name is Rudy."

Jill chimed in. "Rudely Witless, right?"

Rudy glared at Jill, not seeing the humor in that one.

Looking at the two women she had once dated, Keagan had only one comment. "Remind me never to date again."

Rudy took hold of Keagan's arm. "You could just date me, if you want. Then you wouldn't have to worry about dating anyone else."

Keagan glanced down at her, but said nothing.

"Have fun with your little girl-toy, Keagan. Eventually she'll see what you're really like."

"I'm surprised at you, Terry. Still carrying a torch after all these years?" Keagan tried to make her voice sound light. If she didn't, her anger would show and she didn't want to give Terry the satisfaction. She had a lot of nerve making such comments after she had dumped Keagan and left town.

"Nah. I never was in the first place. I just like to watch out for sweet, young things like her."

"Interesting. You never watched out for me when I was a sweet young thing." As both Jill and Terry glared back at them, Keagan said, "Now do you see why I hate parties?"

"I actually do now. And remind me to have a talk with you about your taste in women." Rudy grinned at her companion.

"It's improving. Don't you think?"

"Oh, definitely. Let's go."

As Rudy and Keagan exited the house, she could feel Keagan's arm around her shoulders. Her consumption of the shrimp and crab cakes had improved her ability to focus on her surroundings, even if it didn't improve her ability to maneuver. In any case, she felt herself sobering up, but decided she liked the attention being drunk got her and didn't want to give it up yet. "You souse!" Keagan snickered, unable to stop herself from teasing Rudy.

Rudy slapped Keagan in the stomach playfully. "Hey, that's not fair! I didn't know how potent that punch was." They continued down the steps to the front porch, with Keagan guiding her.

"I know." When they reached the car, Keagan realized that Rudy would either have to ride in the backseat or climb over the driver's seat. Deciding to give her a choice, she looked to Rudy questioningly.

"What?" Keagan simply raised her eyebrows and gazed at Rudy guilelessly. The streetlight illuminated Keagan's blue eyes in just the right way for them to have an effect on her, causing her to almost forget about the broken lock on the vehicle's passenger side door. "Oh." She laughed. "I almost forgot. I can climb over, no problem." Rudy plopped into the driver's seat and Keagan gazed at her with amusement as she tried to get the upper part of her body into the passenger seat first, which left her sprawled over the gearshift with her legs trapped beneath the steering wheel.

"It usually works better if you put your feet and legs over first."

From her uncomfortable position, she managed to twist her head around to face her friend. "Are you going to just stand there gawking or are you going to give me a hand?"

Keagan grinned evilly and clapped, howled, and whistled. "Sure. You deserve a hand after contorting your body like that!"

"I think you're enjoying this." Rudy grunted. Her right foot was cramping.

"Why would I enjoy seeing a young woman with brains, talent, and beauty get sloshed and then get herself stuck in a vehicle because she tried to climb over in a completely illogical way?"

Rudy didn't know if she should be flattered or insulted. She decided on flattered, but directed a glare in Keagan's direction anyway.

"Okay, okay." She moved forward, intending to help but stopped. "I think if you just start over you could get over easier. Just come out—"

"I can't!"

"All right, all right." Keagan leaned down into the driver's seat, thinking how funny the two of them must look to anyone watching. "This isn't going to be easy. I'm going to try and pick you up a bit, and when I do *you* are going to have to move your legs up and over to your seat. Okay?"

Rudy laughed. "That sounds like fun."

Keagan moved the driver's seat back as far as it would go to give them more room. "Just think of the fun we'll have trying to get you back out."

"Oh, I know, umph—" Before Rudy was prepared, Keagan embraced her from behind around her stomach and pulled up. It was an intimate position due to the lack of space. For a brief moment, their bodies pressed tightly together. Rudy was barely able to concentrate enough to pull her legs up and over the gearshift onto the floor. Before their maneuver was completed, however, Keagan's hands accidentally slipped down to caress Rudy's hips.

"Sorry." Keagan gazed over sheepishly.

Once Rudy was settled into her seat, she gazed over at her companion with mirth, and ignored her apology. "So, was it good for you?"

Keagan realized that she could play openly with Rudy because, simply put, she was still drunk and absolutely nothing was going to happen between them. "Oh, baby, I've had it better."

"Give me another chance, then. I'm new at this."

She pointed at the seatbelt and Rudy had the sense to reach for it and buckle up. When she had difficulty doing it, Keagan did it for her. Then she directed a sultry smile toward her and started the car. "So, what do you want? Lessons?"

"You mean love lessons? Sure if you're offering."

"Oh, honey, I think it's you who will be doing the offering." As she pulled into the street, Keagan reconsidered this kind of conversation while driving.

"Oh, really? And just what do you think I'll be offering you?"

"Your body, your heart, your soul." Keagan grinned a little and refused to look in Rudy's direction.

"You must be really good."

"I haven't had any complaints."

"None?"

Keagan appeared to think for a second. "There was this one woman who didn't share my *appetites* if you know what I mean."

Rudy played innocent. "Um, no, what do you mean?"

Keagan glanced over and met the mischievous green eyes of her companion. She knew that Rudy wasn't that naive. And that it would be a perfect time to end the conversation. "Okay, that's enough of that. I think we're almost at your place anyway."

Rudy remained silent and considered why her attraction to this woman seemed to grow every time Keagan clammed up. The more reclusive her friend became, the more Rudy wanted to break through that isolation. *I must be one of those women who like the hard to get types. If she threw herself at me, I'd probably take three steps back and bolt. On second thought, at this point, I probably wouldn't.* Gazing over at Keagan and taking in her delicate features and strong hands on the steering wheel she felt her heart begin to pound. *Nope. Definitely not.*

****

Rudy came home to an empty house as Courtney was out for the evening. This pleased her because she wanted to be alone with Keagan. Although Rudy's coordination was improving rapidly, she didn't say anything, enjoying the touch of her friend too much.

After Keagan helped Rudy off with her coat, she insisted on helping her to the bedroom and Rudy didn't argue. As they got in the door, Rudy plopped onto the bed with a sigh. Keagan stood in the doorway. "I guess I'll leave now if you're okay."

"Could you help me undress please?" Rudy gazed at her with such a sincere look that Keagan almost didn't suspect any underlying motives in the question.

"Uh, what do you need? Your shirt unbuttoned or—"

Rudy laughed. "If it makes you too nervous I can try and do it myself."

"I'm not nervous." Keagan walked over to the chair sitting in front of Rudy's desk and picked up a nightshirt draped over the back. "You want this?"

Rudy nodded. This was starting to get interesting. Keagan came over to the bed, nightshirt in hand, and laid it down. With a guarded look on her face she reached forward but then stopped. "Can you sit up?"

"I don't think so." Rudy's eyes looked back at Keagan challengingly.

Keagan almost grinned, but held back. She knew Rudy was playing with her. *Two can play that game.* Swiftly she reached over and unbuttoned Rudy's blouse, never breaking eye contact. "How hot do you keep it in here anyway?"

After four buttons, she leaned back and took off her leather jacket, letting it lie on the floor. Returning her attention to Rudy, she finished unbuttoning the shirt, but did it agonizingly slowly. Too slowly for Rudy whose eyes remained riveted on Keagan, who was turning a simple undressing into a seduction. "You'll have to lean up a little so I can take it off. Can you do that?" Keagan's face was inches away from Rudy's and she never let her darkened blue eyes leave Rudy's green ones.

Rudy nodded as her breathing increased. She leaned up a bit and Keagan helped her the rest of the way, slipping the blouse from her shoulders easily. Maintaining her eye contact with the now aroused young woman, she allowed Rudy to lean against her while she reached for the nightshirt. Not wanting to embarrass Rudy, whose upper body was now clothed in just a bra, she tried to speed the process along a bit. "Keep leaning against me and I'll put it on for you." Every time Keagan spoke, her voice was a whisper, a sultry mixture of low, seductive intonations. Having avoided looking directly at a topless Rudy initially, her eyes eventually betrayed her and she glanced briefly down, just as she brought the nightshirt around her and Rudy slipped her arms into it. *Total lace. I had wondered.* "Have I got you speechless again?" Keagan was buttoning up the flannel nightshirt.

Rudy was breathing hard. "I think so. And you didn't even kiss me this time."

Keagan just smiled. *Play with me, will you? I'm the master at this game.* Without warning, she reached her arms around Rudy to unhook her bra, but found no clasp. She leaned back only to see a smiling look of triumph.

"The clasp's in the front."

Keagan realized that if she put her hands anywhere near Rudy's breasts, it would be extremely difficult to remove them again. However, she wouldn't, *couldn't* let her win the game. "Oh," she said with nonchalance. Her hands moved under the nightshirt and very deftly undid the clasp, barely touching her friend's overheated skin. Within a couple of seconds, Rudy slipped her bra off with a still attentive Keagan helping her.

Rudy knew exactly what Keagan was doing and that she was losing. She had never been so turned on by anyone and now wished that Keagan had left. Or at least that she hadn't asked her friend to undress her.

"I'll get your pants now." Keagan didn't wait for a signal from Rudy, she just leaned over and reached for the top button to her jeans. When she did, Rudy felt a sensation of heat centered somewhere between her legs. She exhaled a little too loudly.

"No, no. That's okay. You've done enough, really. Thanks. I think I can get that." She tried not to pant, tried to control her erratic breathing.

Keagan smiled with mock seductive intent. "Oh, no. I always finish what I start. And I did agree to *undress* you. Didn't I?"

"I'm sure you always finish what you've started, but undressing me isn't all you've started." Rudy mentally kicked herself for admitting it. *Face it, she beat you at your own game.*

Keagan almost sat back, but decided to remain leaning close to Rudy. The verbal banter was too much fun for her to give up easily. "Oh, really? And just what else have I started?"

"You made me want to feel you close to me, you made me want—"

"I'm sorry." Keagan interrupted because things were going beyond flirtation and getting serious. She didn't do serious.

"Sorry for what?" Rudy felt a dull ache deep within her upon hearing Keagan's words.

Keagan grabbed her jacket and headed for the door. "I'm just sorry but I can't deal with this right now." She turned and left the room.

Rudy felt her heart breaking and knew she had to make a decision and quickly. Should she follow Keagan and stop her, thereby admitting that she wasn't really that drunk anymore or let her go and risk not seeing her for days? Jumping out of bed, she headed for the door and ran down the steps. "Keagan, wait."

Keagan turned around to see Rudy at the bottom of the steps; the same woman who couldn't even undress herself ten minutes earlier. "Feeling better?" The sarcasm dripped from her voice.

"I think my little buzz wore off."

"Right. It stayed just long enough to manipulate me into undressing you." Keagan remained standing at the door.

"Did you really hate it so much?" When Keagan didn't respond, but just locked her gaze with Rudy's, she continued. "Why don't you sit down so we can talk."

"About what? About how you faked being drunk to toy with me?"

"What?" Rudy's green eyes widened. "That's not what I did. And even if I did, it wasn't as bad as what *you* did."

"I only did what you asked."

"That's not all you did. You made sure I got excited in the process."

"What's the matter? You can't handle what you've been asking for all along?"

"It's not me that can't handle it."

"I can handle anything, even a little flirtatious tart like you."

"That's what you'd like me to be, isn't it? You wouldn't find that so threatening."

"I don't find you threatening. I don't know what you're talking about." Keagan turned around and reached for the door, but as she did Rudy went over and stood in front of it blocking her exit. "Get out of my way. We're having a fight and I'm leaving!"

"We're having a fight because *you* say so? I say we're having a discussion and I'm not finished yet!"

"Fight!"

"Discussion!"

"*Major* argument!"

"Disagreement!"

"You're impossible!" Keagan's eyes blazed with anger.

"Not half as impossible as you!"

Realizing that Rudy wouldn't move, Keagan leaned forward and brushed her lips against Rudy's. Her intent was to get Rudy to move away from the door by distracting her, but it was she who became distracted by the feeling of arms reaching around her. The kiss deepened and Keagan pushed her up against the front door. When Keagan pulled back, it was only briefly and then her lips found Rudy's neck and she planted long, lingering kisses up and down it. Rudy struggled a bit, because it was expected, but her moans of pleasure that she couldn't help suppressing let Keagan know her original plan was failing miserably. She'd have to stop soon, but at that moment everything felt too good.

She finally pulled back with Rudy still firmly ensconced in front of the door. They were both breathing heavily, having enjoyed the kiss, but neither one was through being angry. "Your meager attempt to get me away from the door failed miserably. Care to try plan B?"

"I don't know. Plan B might be a little too much for you."

"For me or for you?"

Keagan paused, her mind reeling. She had never encountered anyone that challenged her the way Rudy did. What they had been doing together was pleasant and although she had never been much for physical expressions of affection she enjoyed it. It was more than that, though. It was so totally irrational that it left Keagan feeling unstable, unsure, and always on the edge. And she desperately wanted to be safely secured far away from that edge. She wasn't even able to avoid the party. Oh, she rationalized her reasoning for going, but the only reason she went was to see Rudy. Rudy knew it and so did everyone else. "I have a confession to make."

Green eyes looked at her calmly. "Yes?"

"I knew you had sobered up."

"You did?"

"I have an alcoholic family member. I can tell if someone's really drunk or not."

Rudy blushed. *Of course she'd be able to.*

"I just want to know one thing. Why did you do it?"

"I have a confession, too. I wanted to see if you'd really help me undress or if you'd be too shy. I got my answer, didn't I?" Rudy kept to herself the fact that she had very much enjoyed Keagan taking her clothes off her, even if it left her frustrated.

"You didn't think I would?"

"Honestly, no. I thought you'd just bolt, but you saved that for later." She smiled at Keagan for the first time in minutes.

"I missed that."

"What?"

"Your smile. You do it often enough, that when you don't I miss it."

"Hmm. C'mere, sit down with me. Let's chat." Rudy held her hand out to Keagan who took it gingerly, but allowed her friend to lead them to the couch. Once seated, they unlinked their hands.

"Now let's get a few things straight, Keagan Donovan."

Rudy's habit of using her first and last names when annoyed got a chuckle out of Keagan.

"I like you. I think you like me, too or I wouldn't even make the effort to discuss this. We've been playing games with each other that are a lot of fun, but the games have been turning real and that's where you seem to have a problem. I don't. So, you have to decide if you want to continue to play games with me only or if you want something more. I think we shouldn't see each other until you decide." Rudy exhaled, relieved to have finally said it.

"Where did you get all that wisdom at such a young age?"

"It must be a gift."

"I didn't mean to hurt your feelings."

"I know, but you do and you have. Keagan, I'm very interested in you. Do you understand what I'm saying?"

"Yes, yes." Keagan sighed. "I'm not that emotionally crippled."

"I don't think you are but I can't read your mind and when you don't say anything I don't know what to think."

"I've heard everything you've said, believe me, and I understand. Don't know how I'm going to get through that grammar exam without you, but I'll manage." She gave a short laugh, trying to expel the pain she felt.

"I'll still help you with—"

"C'mon, Rudy. That's not going to work and you know it."

"I know." Rudy's voice was quiet.

"I suppose we shouldn't sit together in class, then."

"Probably not." The idealistic part of Rudy hoped Keagan would say that she didn't need any time.

Keagan got up, wanting to get it over with. "I'll see

you, then." She headed for the door and didn't look back at Rudy as she exited the house. After she got outside, the fierce cold bit into her face like a portent, telling her she had made an unwise decision. Keagan tried to convince herself that her decision was the correct one on the short drive home.

* * * * * * * * * *

The next day, Keagan awoke with a headache but that wasn't all. Her entire body joined in as well. She was congested and her throat was sore. Joan called around one o'clock and the childlike part of Keagan answered hoping to get some motherly sympathy.

"No, Mom, I'm fine, really." Keagan paused to cough. "I don't need anything, really."

"You don't sound good."

"It's probably my own fault anyway."

"What do you mean?"

"Oh, nothing." Keagan didn't elaborate on her belief that personal stress affected health. After her encounter with Rudy the night before she was convinced that was the cause.

"Do you feel well enough to talk to Sean on the phone, sweetie?"

Keagan turned away from the phone and blew her nose. "About what?"

"About him buying vodka for your grandmother, remember?"

Keagan considered asking her mother why she couldn't do it herself. "I don't want to get involved in that."

"This has to stop! And I don't know any other way." Joan burst into tears.

Keagan rubbed her head and reached for an aspirin.

"Okay. I'll call him. Just don't cry please."

"Thank you. I hope you feel better."

"Yeah, me too." When Keagan hung up the phone she felt like the dog of the family. What was the harm in telling Joan that she'd talk to Sean even though she had no intention of doing so? It didn't matter who allowed Gerry to get vodka. She'd get it one way or another.

****

"So, *what?*" Brad Martin stopped by Keagan's with some Chinese hot and sour soup when he learned she was sick. He brought three pints, convinced that the spicy soup would burn through her illness. As she sipped at it, the conversation steered to her relationship with Rudy.

"We're not seeing each other. She wants me to decide to stop playing games or something. I don't know."

"I like her, Keagan. And I haven't liked *any* of the women you've dated."

"None of them? Why didn't you tell me?"

"You don't tell your friend that you don't like their date, it's uncouth. You wait until the friend figures it out for themselves and then you give support."

"Oh. Yeah, right."

"I can tell she's the one for you. You shouldn't let her go."

"How do *you* know? You've only met her once."

"I felt the chemistry, the connection, the rapport between you, the—"

"Okay, I get the point." Keagan felt cranky from being sick. The last thing she wanted to do was discuss her love life.

"I have to go meet my date, girlfriend. Enjoy your soup." He headed for the door.

"Thanks, Brad."

****

Monday was a cold, snowy day, the first of February. Rudy pulled her scarf around her face and enjoyed the feeling of a light snow falling. *I must be crazy to take a walk in this kind of weather, but right now I'm simply too restless to stay in and too distracted to study.* She ended up on Neil Avenue, the street where Keagan lived. Knowing it wouldn't be a good idea to stroll past her house, she turned around when she knew she was too close. As she was strolling back, a car pulled up along the street and stopped. A door opened and a long arm thrust something into the snow. Rudy couldn't see what it was, but when the car took off speeding down the road, she approached it.

"Mew! Mew!" An orange tabby was walking in two inches of snow and failing miserably. Rudy immediately ran over to the small, abandoned animal when she saw it was a cat. She picked it up and cradled it to her. "Aw, it's okay, kitty." She saw that the animal was wet from the snow and felt a flash of anger at the people who had thrown it out of the car. How could people be so cruel? "Mew, mew!" Rudy petted the small head and felt the creature purr. "It's okay, sweetie, I'll find a place for you to stay." She didn't think the kitten could be more than eight weeks old at the most. "But you can't stay with me. I wish you could but my roommate's allergic." Rudy smiled as an idea occurred to her. She turned and walked in the direction she had just come from.

****

Keagan sat on the couch drinking from a bottle of Nyquil. She thought it was a waste of time to measure out the substance in the plastic cup when she'd probably take the whole bottle anyway. She hated being sick and sleep-

ing was preferable to being awake and miserable. Nyquil
always did the trick.

   She picked up the remote and channel surfed, finally
landing on the *Jerry Springer* show. Jerry was introducing
his guests. *Why not? This show is like a really bad auto-
mobile accident. You can't help but look at it.* A woman
came onto the stage and professed to be a lesbian. She had
silky, long hair, lanky legs, and wore enough makeup to
supply a bordello for a year. She was wearing a short, sil-
ver mini-skirt and pumps. "No way." Keagan took another
sip of the Nyquil, feeling the thick liquid coat her throat.
*Hopefully, I'll be asleep soon and will no longer be sub-
jected to this tripe. 'Keagan, just turn the channel,' her
inner voice told her. I don't feel like it. Besides, there's
nothing on at four in the afternoon except sitcom repeats.*
Keagan hated sitcoms because although some were funny
almost all of them followed a pattern and a formula that
she found limiting.

   "So, Trudy, what secret did you want to reveal today?"
Springer asked. Keagan chuckled. Trudy was the name
Gretchen kept calling Rudy by mistake. Trying not to
think of Rudy, she focused back on the show. "Well,"
began Trudy, with fake tears in her eyes. It was easy to tell
when television tears were fake, Keagan thought. The
tears always streamed from the middle of the eye. Anybody who has ever cried knows that tears almost always
fall from the sides of the eye. "I cheated on my boyfriend.
I slept with—" she paused for dramatic effect, "my boyfriend's cousin's mother's brother's ex-lesbian friend."
She began crying and Keagan laughed. "*Ex*-lesbian?
Why's she sleeping with a woman, then?" She shook her
head and questioned her mental state. Why was she trying
to make sense of the show?

   "And let's bring her out, now!" said Springer. He
motioned to the side of the stage. "Everyone, please meet

Mo!" Keagan groaned at yet another reminder of Rudy. She recalled the evening they role-played over the phone, with Rudy taking on the role of a character named Mo. Out walked a woman with short hair and bulging muscles, wearing a flannel shirt with the sleeves cut off. She had a scowl on her face. Complementing her outfit were black leather pants and combat boots. "Char?" Keagan laughed. "Nah, no keys." At least the show was amusing her.

It was at that point that she heard a knock on the door. With a groan she got up, wondering who could be dropping by. Most of her friends knew she didn't like unexpected visitors. She looked through the peephole, and saw Rudy standing there. *I could just pretend I'm not here. Maybe she'd go away. But my car's out there. That probably wouldn't work.* Slowly she opened the door to reveal a snow covered Rudy standing there with a slight smile on her face holding a cat. "Hi."

"Hi." They stood regarding each other for several seconds. "Can I come in please?"

"Sure." Keagan stepped aside as Rudy walked in, taking in her appearance. She had sweat pants on and a T-shirt. Her hair was a bit disheveled and she looked pale. On the coffee table sat the Nyquil, a bottle of aspirin and a glass of grapefruit juice. Keagan sat back down on the couch as if it had taken all her energy to answer the door.

"Are you sick?" As she asked this, the kitten mewed.

"Just a little under the weather, nothing incapacitating. What's that and why are you here?" Keagan didn't try to hide the irritation in her voice. The only thing she hated more than being sick was being visited when she was. Brad was just lucky he brought the soup when he came over. In any case, she didn't want to see Rudy due to their current situation. At least not until she had figured out how to handle it and she definitely hadn't figured it out yet.

"Aren't we in a great mood." Rudy walked over to Keagan and put the kitten in her lap.

"Hey!" She protested the intrusion, but soon found herself petting the small creature. Soon, the kitten had fallen asleep on Keagan's lap.

"I think she likes you. It's a mystery to me *why*, but—" Keagan frowned and looked at Rudy for an explanation. "Look, I'm sorry to just drop by like this, especially since we're not supposed to see each other but I was taking a walk and found her. She's just a baby, look at her, and I can't take her with me because Courtney's allergic and I thought maybe she could stay with you until I find some-one who'll take her? Please?"

"Sure." Keagan was too exhausted and weak to refuse.

"Thank you. Thank you so much. And now for the other matter. You look terrible."

"You really know how to flatter a girl." Keagan coughed. She felt drowsy as the medication took effect.

"Who's taking care of you?"

"Do you see anyone besides me around? I don't need anyone to take care of me."

"Sure you do. Everyone does. I'm going to go to the store and get some cat food and a litter box for our little bundle of joy. Is there anything I can get you?"

"I don't need anything." Keagan grumbled out her words. The little kitten stretched and yawned contentedly. Keagan rolled her eyes. The cat was kind of cute.

Rudy grinned. Keagan was sort of cute sick, in a help-less, pathetic kind of way. She glanced at the television. "What is this tripe you're watching?"

"I'll have you know that Springer is high quality tripe."

"Ah." Rudy watched a few seconds. "Oh, I see they've got lesbians on today."

"Please. They have lesbians on *every* day." Keagan's

eyes remained glued to the television.

"But everyone knows they're not real ones." Keagan nodded in amused agreement, and Rudy added, "I thought you didn't like TV."

"I only watch it when I'm sick."

"Which explains why you know that Springer has lesbians on everyday."

The blue eyes turned back to Rudy, whose own were twinkling mischievously. "You said you walked here?"

"Yeah." Rudy headed for the door, hiding a smile. She could take a hint.

"Take my car if you want. It's cold and there's no reason you should walk back to your place for yours. The keys are hanging on that hook by the door."

"Okay. Thanks. I'll be back." Rudy grabbed the keys and headed out the door.

****

When Rudy returned, she was treated to the sight of Keagan sleeping on the couch and the kitten perched on her stomach. It was so cute she wished she could take a picture of it. Smiling, she went into the kitchen and put the groceries away. A short time later, she had prepared the litter box and stowed it away in Keagan's closet. The kitten was waking up. "Perfect timing." Walking over to the couch she picked her up, being careful not to disturb Keagan. "Okay, little cutie, let me show you how this works." She set the cat into the box and the creature stood there for awhile, before scratching the litter. "I'll get you some food while you're becoming acquainted with that." When Rudy had finished filling two bowls with food and water, she heard the familiar mewing sound, as the kitten walked out of the closet. Soon, she was munching contentedly. "Now that you're settled, I can go check on your friend on the couch."

Sitting on the edge of the couch, Rudy put her cheek against Keagan's forehead. Noticing that she had a fever, Rudy wondered if she should stay for awhile. When the blue eyes suddenly opened, she leaned back with surprise and slight embarrassment.

"Trying to take advantage of me in my feeble condition?" Keagan smiled weakly. She was a light sleeper. It didn't take much to wake her although she was surprised that Rudy's touch was able to break through the effects of the Nyquil.

"You should be so lucky." Keagan laughed lightly at Rudy's words. "You have a fever, I think."

"Oh."

"I think I should stay here and make sure you're okay. I can—"

"No, that's all right. Can you just get the grammar homework for me from Dr. Vicky Marie Addison?" Rudy rolled her eyes. Keagan loved referring to their teacher using the fictional name she gave her. "I don't think I'll make it to school tomorrow." Rudy put her hand back on Keagan's forehead and looked into her eyes, realizing that when Keagan felt badly, she did, too. She had an overwhelming desire to stay there and take care of her, but she knew she had to respect her friend's wishes.

"Of course I can. I—"

"Thanks, Nurse Rudy."

"I would be if you let me."

"Really, I'll be okay. Besides, you said we shouldn't see each other until I figure out my feelings and this definitely qualifies as seeing each other."

"But we're not *seeing* each other. I'd just make you some soup, feed it to you if you want, give you medicine, change your sheets, bring you lots of beverages—"

Keagan couldn't help but laugh. "Wow. I should get

sick more often with that kind of an offer."

"No, you shouldn't. I don't like this one bit."

Keagan couldn't help but be touched by Rudy's concern, which she felt undeserving of. She looked back at
her but didn't speak further.

With reluctance, Rudy headed for the door. "If you
need anything just call me. And if you get hungry anytime
soon, I brought you two pints of hot and sour soup.
They're on the kitchen table. It should stay hot for a little
while yet."

Keagan was amused, wondering if it was possible to
eat five pints of soup in one day.

"Oh and your new little friend's litter box is in the
closet. She's got plenty of food and water, so she's all set.
You might try to think of a name, so we don't have to keep
calling her cat or kitty." Rudy grinned.

"Or beast. Although I like that name." Hearing a
mewing noise, Keagan looked toward the kitchen to see the
small animal wobbling out and into the living room. Rudy
bent down and picked her up, heading toward Keagan. She
deposited the kitten on Keagan's lap and the animal purred.

"Now, kitty, your job is to take care of Keagan. She's
a very good friend of mine and I don't want to have to
worry about her. Okay?" In seeming response, the animal
mewed. Rudy laughed. "Kitten's meows are so much cuter
than grown cats, aren't they?"

"Yeah."

"I'll see you later. Take care of yourself."

"Bye, Rudy." Keagan watched her leave. It would
have been nice to have Rudy stay but she wasn't ready to
face what the implications of that would be. Wondering if
she ever would be, she stared at the little kitten that had
fallen asleep again and joined her in slumber.

****

The next day, although she had to miss school, Keagan was feeling better by late afternoon. She finished her third pint of hot and sour soup and took the cold medicine Rudy brought. She was also surprised to see that her refrigerator was restocked with food. She made a mental note to repay Rudy.

The kitten was still nameless. Keagan thought how silly that was when she was a writer who had a book with 20,000 names in it. Finally, since she was tired of calling her "cat" or "kitty", she began calling her Rudy. Keagan told herself it was just temporary, until she thought of another name, but the more she thought about it, the more appropriate the name seemed. Picking up the kitten, she stared into her eyes and when the sunlight streaming in from the window reflected off of them, they almost looked green. The orange of the cat's coat wasn't quite the same tone as Rudy's reddish-blonde hair, but it was close enough. The cat liked to talk a lot. In cat language, of course. The most notable similarity to Rudy was the cat's voracious appetite. This cat liked to eat and Keagan had to remind herself to ask Rudy how many times a day a cat should be fed. Was five too much? The cat was small like Rudy, too, and she liked to torment Keagan. She smiled deviously, looking forward to Rudy's reaction when she found out.

At around four o'clock, there was a knock at the door. She got up and answered it, surprise lighting her features when she saw Rudy standing there holding her backpack and smiling. "Hey. I've got a grammar practice test for you. Thought you'd want it." Noticing that Keagan looked much better and less pale, she felt relieved. Thinking of her being alone and sick bothered Rudy.

"C'mon, in." As Rudy walked in, Rudy walked

out...or rather ran. "Rudy, come back here!"

Rudy got an immediate look of confusion on her face. "Hmm?"

"Rudy, Rudy, here kitty, kitty!" The kitten hadn't gone far and upon hearing Keagan's voice walked slowly back into the apartment. Rudy shut the door.

"Please don't tell me you named this cat Rudy."

"Why not? It seemed appropriate." Keagan snickered.

"Why you—" Rudy slapped her on the arm. "And just *why* is it appropriate?"

"Well, she just kind of showed up out of nowhere, and she seemed to take a liking to me instantly, and she won't leave. And she likes to sleep in my bed." Keagan grinned.

"Anything else?"

"She likes Chinese food and she's, um...soft and cuddly."

"Oh, really? I think I'm getting jealous." The kitten rubbed Keagan's leg and mewed.

Keagan smiled and her features softened a bit. She wondered where this conversation was headed.

"Does she like lobster?"

"I don't think she's ever had any."

"There's a first time for everything. Maybe you should get her some."

"She might not like it. The real thing often pales in comparison to the anticipation."

"Or vice versa. How will you know if you don't try?"

"I won't know." Sometimes the only way to answer a question was in a forthright way.

"That's right. You won't know." Unzipping her backpack, she took out the practice test and handed it to Keagan. "Here you go. See you later. I'm glad you're feeling better."

"Um, did you want to stay for a few minutes, or—"

"I can't. I've got a study group at four thirty." Rudy

leaned up and kissed her on the cheek, whispering in her ear, "Besides, you've got Rudy to keep you company." Grinning at the unreadable look on Keagan's face, she turned around and left.

"See you later." Keagan looked at the practice test and went to get her grammar book, but knew her concentration level would be very low.

****

Keagan returned to work on Wednesday, feeling quite back to normal. When she got home, there was a whining furball waiting for her. She fed the kitten and watched her eat, enjoying the feeling of caring for something. Walking into the kitchen, she glanced at the answering machine, which indicated she had three messages. Hitting the play button and retrieving a 7-up from the refrigerator, she sat down to listen. "Hello girlfriend. Brad here. I hope you're feeling more spiffy than when I last saw you. And I hope you made up with the little, red-haired, spitfire. <laughter> Call me if you need anything more. Ciao, babe." Click. "Keagan, it's me. Call me when you get in. I know all about you buying booze for your grandmother. We need to talk." Click. "Hi, this is Rudy #1, the one that isn't a cat. <laugh> Just calling to see how you're doing, for purely caretaking reasons, of course. You know where to reach me if you need anything. Bye."

Keagan thought it was funny that her friends inquired about her health, but her mother didn't. In any case, Joan sounded much too calm and that could only mean trouble. Sighing, she picked up the phone, dialing slowly, wanting to delay the inevitable as long as possible. "Hi, Mom."

"Hello. When I found out you hadn't talked to Sean I got suspicious. Then I had a fight with your grandmother while she was drunk on the vodka you bought for her and she admitted it was you! How could you?"

"I'm feeling a lot better, Mom. Thanks. And I didn't buy anything for her, she bought it herself!" Keagan felt the usual tension building in her chest.

"You know that's not what I'm talking about. You took her to the liquor store. You *allowed* her to do it! I can't even trust my own daughter anymore."

"She's a grown woman who has a lot of years over me. Who am I to tell her what to do? To set limits on her activities? She asked me to take her to the store. I—I did try to persuade her to just buy beer—"

"That's noble. Why don't I just send her over there to live with you? That would be really good for your little lifestyle, wouldn't it?"

Joan never made comments about her daughter's sexual orientation. Keagan reasoned that she was angry and wanted to get back at her and this was the tool she was using. Her mother didn't mean it. "I won't discuss that."

"Why not? I think you need to take a good look at your own life, before you start passing judgment on me and my decisions!"

"I'm not—" Keagan began to formulate a rational response in her head as she always did, but stopped half-way through. "Have to go. Bye." She set the receiver down. There was no need to be rude to her mother by hanging up on her. But there was also no need for her to bother coming up with a suitable response, when her mother treated her with such disrespect.

****

On Thursday, in spite of their earlier interaction, Keagan and Rudy kept to their resolution and didn't sit together in class. In spite of this, each ended up sitting in positions that gave them almost perfect views of each other. The first couple of times their eyes met they looked down embarrassedly, each thinking the other had seen her staring, neither one understanding that they were both guilty of staring at each other. Eventually, both women realized what was going on. When class ended, Rudy, who had been sitting closer to the door, quickly exited the room. Keagan considered going after her but didn't.

Friday night found Keagan sitting at home with Rudy the cat. She sat in front of the computer, knowing what she wanted to write, but not knowing how to write it. Shaking her head ruefully, she picked up the phone, dialing the number of the bar. Cody answered. "Hi, Cody, it's Keagan. Got a question for ya."

"Yep, honey, what is it?"

"I just need you to look around the bar and see if Rudy is there, that's all."

There was a pause for a few seconds and then Keagan heard Cody's voice again. "No, I don't see her. You two have a fight?"

"No, just an agreement that we've resolved to stand by. I'll see you in a few." Keagan hung up the phone, not privy to the confused look on the bartender's face.

****

Twenty minutes later, notebook in hand, Keagan was sitting at the end of the bar, chatting with Cody. "So, let me get this straight. You aren't seeing each other because she says although the games are fun, she's tired of just that and wants more?"

"Yeah." Keagan scratched her head. "I haven't an inkling of what she really means, though, but I need to figure it out soon."

Cody shook her head in exasperation. "What exactly did she say?"

"I don't know. Something like, 'I'm very interested in you. Do you know what that means?' or something..."

"Do *you*?"

"Huh?"

Cody reached over and knocked her fist gently on Keagan's head. "Do you know what it means when a woman says she's interested in you? A woman you've dated and presumably kissed?"

Keagan averted her eyes. "I guess so."

"You *guess* so?"

"I think maybe she's become attached to me because we have the English major thing in common." Keagan took a drink of her rum and coke and glanced back to Cody, who was shaking her head. "What?"

"What, what, what? I will spell it out for you. In fact, why don't I write it out for you. Give me that." Cody grabbed Keagan's notebook and pen. She wrote something down and in a couple of minutes gave the notebook back to Keagan. "Now you've got it in writing, my friend." Grinning, Cody went to the other end of the bar to help a patron.

Keagan read what Cody wrote and sighed, labeling her as another meddling matchmaker. She sought out Milligan and played a few games of pool with her, but remained distracted and irritated. Milligan tried to lighten Keagan's mood with small talk but that only made her more annoyed. Eventually, she returned to the bar and the sanctuary of Cody. Sighing heavily, she asked for another drink and contemplated her plans for the remainder of the evening. She opened the notebook and read Cody's words again. "What are you looking at?" asked the bartender as she sidled up to her, placing a drink on the bar.

"A great work of fiction."

"I don't think so." Cody glanced at the door. "Oops! Speak of the devil. I think it's your La Roux."

Keagan's head shot around to see Rudy walking in and heading for the other end of the bar. She stared at her, hoping to make eye contact. Rudy ignored her. "Cody, Cody, c'mere." The bartender shuffled over. "I want to buy Rudy a drink." Shaking her head knowingly, Cody sauntered down to Rudy.

"Hi, Rueday. That very attractive, raven-haired knockout would like to buy you a drink. What would you like?"

Rudy smiled. "Tell her thanks, but that's not what I want from her."

Grinning, Cody returned to Keagan's end. "She said to tell you thanks, but a drink isn't what she wants from you."

"Ask her what she wants then."

"Why don't *you*?"

"Cody, please. It's a game we play. Please?"

"Okay, okay." Cody returned to Rudy's end. "She wants to know what you want."

Rudy smiled slyly and gazed down at Keagan. "Tell her if she wants to know that, she has to come down here."

Cody dutifully returned to Keagan. "She says you have to talk to her if you want to know."

"I think she's trying to reel me in."

The bartender chuckled. "I think so, too. The question is, will you let her?"

Ignoring Cody's question, Keagan walked to the end of the bar and sat next to Rudy. "You know, you're not a very easy woman to pick up."

"And you're not very easy to forget, you heart-breaker."

"I thought you didn't want to play games anymore."

"I'm not." Keagan detected a tinge of vulnerability in Rudy's voice.

"What about our arrangement? We probably shouldn't

be speaking at all."

"I think it's okay. We can pretend we just met and that I was asking you a stereotypical question."

Ignoring the obvious fact that it would be playing another game, Keagan asked, "Okay, then. What question?"

"Do you believe in love at first sight?"

Keagan smiled. Indeed, she had never gotten around to explaining as she had promised. "I don't even know if I believe in love."

"Why not?"

"Lots of reasons, but where love fails in the real world, it never has to fail in mine." Staying within the role, Rudy gave a look of mock confusion. "I'm a writer, you see. I can create any world I want to and manipulate anything. I can always have a happy ending."

"And what are you writing about now?" Keagan leaned on the bar and stared at Rudy as the smell of her cologne and the fresh scent of shampoo in her hair assaulted her senses. She had to remind herself to answer the question.

"It's a story about two people, two women who are quite different, but discover they have a lot in common and—"

"Oh, don't tell me. A love story." Rudy features softened.

"Yes, but it's not that bad really. I'm just having a problem with them getting together. I don't know how to write it." Keagan sighed.

"You don't know how to write a love scene?"

Keagan nodded, embarrassed. "Everything I write comes out overly melodramatic."

"Maybe I could help you."

"And how could you help me?"

"You could just make love to me and then write about

what we did." Green eyes met blue as the recognition of what was really going on registered with them both, but neither said a word nor stepped out of character.

"That's an amazing offer but what if it isn't any good?"

Rudy leaned a bit closer and then whispered, "It will be."

Keagan felt a heat burn inside her. "It happens in an unconventional place."

"Where at?" Rudy's breathing picked up.

"I can't give away all my secrets." Keagan smiled mischievously and turned away. Things were getting out of hand.

Rudy on the other hand, felt her desire quickly changing to anger. How many times would Keagan do this push and pull act? And how many times would she fall for it? "What the hell do you mean you can't give away all of your secrets? As if you've even given away any! You know what? I'm through with you. Yeah, I actually am." She paused for a second as if needing to convince herself. "I'm tired of being manipulated like one of your characters. Either you want me or you don't want me and the signals you're sending me are telling me you don't."

"Are we still in character?" Keagan had never seen Rudy that angry.

"That was *not* the right thing to say right now!" On the verge of tears and yet seething, Rudy got up and headed for the restroom, leaving a totally baffled Keagan behind. Some of the bar patrons watched the scene and then went back about their business. Keagan was glad it was still early in the evening and most of the regular gossips weren't there yet. Rising, she followed Rudy, while trying not to make it apparent that she was following her.

"Rudy?" Keagan walked into the empty restroom. There were four stalls but she didn't know which one her friend was in.

"I came in here to get my composure back and you being here isn't going to help."

Keagan made her way down to the end. Rudy was in the fourth stall near the wall. The door was locked. "If you open the door, we can talk."

"I'm not opening the door. And since when have you ever wanted to talk?"

"Open the door."

"I'm through!"

"I'm not."

"What? Now that I'm no longer interested, you're going to chase me? That's really shallow."

"I don't think that's the case."

"That you're shallow?"

"No. That you're no longer interested."

"Still full of ourselves, I see!"

"No, just stating things as I see them. I've been known to do that."

"Right. When you actually *allow* yourself to see them!"

"Are you going to come out of there or do I have to come in?"

Rudy wondered if this was another game that Keagan was intent on winning. If it was, she intended to win. "I'd like to see you try!"

Glancing down at the floor, Keagan decided in a split second that she could fit through the opening in the bottom. It would take a little maneuvering, but it was possible. Moving her body gracefully to the floor, she let her legs slip through first and then crawled the rest of the way under. In a second, she was standing before Rudy in the confined space. Looking at her friend's astonished eyes, she took another step forward until their bodies were touching.

"Can't give up the chance to win the game, can you?" Rudy asked.

"Does *this* feel like a game to you?"   With that, Keagan leaned down, capturing Rudy's lips with her own. Her arms enfolded Rudy who struggled a bit and then relaxed, but Keagan had other ideas. Her tongue entered a willing mouth, as she turned Rudy around and pinned her against the door. They parted after a few long minutes of heated exploration, both panting heavily, and forgetting where they were momentarily.

"No more games?"   Rudy reached up and touched Keagan's face, caressing it, thinking of how beautiful she was and of how she was so totally unaware of her allure.

Keagan slowly came back to her senses and they told her that she was in a bathroom stall in a bar, and that she was considering doing things that probably shouldn't be done there. "I'm sorry, Rudy. I—"

Rudy pressed her body against Keagan's, putting her arms around her waist possessively. Laying her head on the taller woman's chest and inhaling her sweet scent, she placed a kiss on Keagan's collarbone. "I don't want to hear that again." Her voice was a low whisper and it did very interesting things to Keagan's mind, body, and emotions.

"We should get out of here."

"Why? We have so much to catch up on and it's much more private in here than out there, don't you think?"

Rudy drew the dark head toward her, capturing Keagan's lips.   She pushed her tongue roughly into Keagan's mouth and felt her moan. When they parted, she kissed her neck while exploring her body. Moving her hands to the top of her shirt, she undid the buttons, never breaking eye contact with Keagan. "You never told me how you did on the grammar exam."

"No, I didn't." Keagan's voice was strained, her rising

desire for Rudy taking control of her body. She reached out and ran her fingers through Rudy's reddish-blonde locks, her hand stopping to caress her left cheek.

Rudy moved her hands underneath Keagan's opened shirt, feeling the soft, flushed skin there. "So how did you do?" She kissed down her neck and planted kisses along her collarbone. Keagan gasped.

"Did you like that? That's good, because you know I'm kind of new at this." Rudy maneuvered them around so that now Keagan was against the door. As she did this, her hands never ended their exploration of her stomach and they moved upward to caress a breast. "Oh," was the only sound heard out of Keagan before Rudy kissed her again, this time tantalizingly slow, with long thorough strokes of her tongue lingering deep inside Keagan's mouth. The taller woman matched her stroke for stroke, as Rudy continued to caress her breasts in spite of the barriers of her bra. The entire time, Keagan's hands had moved to Rudy's hips, softly kneading them.

"So, how did the exam go?"

It took Keagan a moment to register that Rudy was asking an intelligible question. Panting, she tried to speak as the sensual assault on her body continued. "I think I did all right," she managed to breathe out with effort.

"Just all right?"

"I would have done a lot better if I had you to help me." Rudy's hands reached around Keagan's back and unhooked her bra. Pushing it up and over her breasts she wasted no time in teasing a nipple with her tongue. "Ahh."

"I know you would've but that's okay because you have me now." Rudy was now down on her knees with Keagan slumped against the door straddling her. Leaning forward she took her left breast in her mouth never breaking eye contact with Keagan and began a slow, steady, sucking. Keagan didn't think she had ever felt such pleasure. Breaking away from her with effort, she tried to speak coherently. "We can't do this here. It's not—"

Rudy's hands moved over to Keagan's jeans and unzipped them slowly. Leaning over so that her lips were right against Keagan's, she stared into her eyes with unmistakable desire and love. "Will you stop fighting me? When will you stop fighting me?" And then her lips were crushing against Keagan's who opened her mouth fully to take in all Rudy had to give. Somewhere in between her passion and her body's betrayal of it, Keagan could hear Rudy reciting something. Although her hands were busily stroking Keagan's firm stomach, she kept speaking. "*And yet I dream of dreams fulfilled and rest somewhere before this restless heart is stilled and all its fancies blown to air.*"

As her lips found Keagan's neck again, she heard Keagan breathing heavily but speaking in between pants. "Bliss Carman, 'The Vagabonds', ah. I can't believe you did that *now.*"

"And you've just proven how good you are." She nipped at Keagan's ear.

"I haven't proven anything yet. You're the one who's good." Her hands massaged Rudy's thighs as they stared at each other.

Rudy's breathing increased and she felt the familiar pleasurable sensation building between her legs. "C'mon, Keagan, give me one, please."

"As if I could think." She leaned forward and kissed Rudy having been denied the pleasure of her lips for too long. It turned into another long exploration as she slowly moved her tongue inside Rudy's mouth in desperation. Rudy intentionally avoided letting her tongue connect with Keagan's because she hadn't yet granted her request. They broke apart roughly. "You're such a tease."

"Just give me what I want and I won't be." Rudy's

lips met Keagan's neck and planted small kisses beginning from slightly under her ear down to her collarbone.

"I think you've developed a fondness for my neck. Not that I mind. "

"Among other things. Please? Just one."

Keagan wondered how Rudy expected her to come up with a poetry quote when the young woman's lips were affixed to her neck sucking soundly and her hands were busy exploring her lower body. In spite of her passion, though, she thought of one, hoping to impress Rudy who she figured didn't really expect her to think of one anyway. "*Divine am I inside and out, and I make holy whatever I touch or am touched from,* oh...oh, Rudy."

"Go on...ah...please."

"*The scent of these arm-pits aroma finer than prayer, this head more than churches, bibles, and all the creeds.*"

Rudy backed away from Keagan's neck to gaze into azure eyes now blazing with need. "Oh, you bad girl, how sacrilegious. It's Whitman, of course, 'Song of Myself.' Such an easy one."

"Thought I'd pick one from your namesake. Didn't mean for it to be that easy."

Rudy smiled, leaning over to whisper into Keagan's ear. "Sometimes easy isn't all that bad." Seeing Keagan's look of amusement at the double meaning, she laughed a little under her breath. "Honey, stand up a second." Keagan scooted up a bit, trying to focus on anything but the heated sensations moving straight to her center. Rudy pulled her jeans down a bit and placed her hand right above Keagan's underwear. She moved her hand in slow circles all around the area. "I like your underwear. I should've known you'd wear black." Her lips moved back to Keagan's neck and sucked hard.

"Sometimes I wear red...oh...or blue or green, I like colors." Keagan thought it odd that Rudy continued to talk. No one she had been with had talked much before. It was like nothing she had felt before and it was at the hands of this young, inexperienced woman. "Oh, you must be a natural, La Roux," she breathed.

"I think it's just you." Rudy slipped her hand inside Keagan's underwear and made no move to take them off, but massaged the area underneath. Keagan closed her eyes, the pleasure almost too great for her to accept. *Is this really happening? And is it happening in a place like this? And do I want it to stop? No.* Rudy reached up and caressed the side of her face. "Open your eyes." She did as Rudy asked. "I want to hear you say it. Say it, please, Keagan."

Looking into Rudy's verdant eyes and taking in all that was happening, Keagan could barely speak much less know what Rudy meant. Closing her eyes again, she moaned as the caresses continued. Rudy leaned in close and she felt a warm tongue enter her ear softly. "Oh, that's good," Keagan moaned. Rudy swirled her tongue around Keagan's ear all the while continuing to stroke her firmly below. Keagan's hands were around her the whole time, but she was far too distracted to do much. "I want to feel more of you, Rudy."

"I know. Tell me." Her voice was a sultry whisper in Keagan's ear.

"I want you...so much." With those words, Rudy leaned back and kissed Keagan on the mouth, more of a reassuring kiss than one designed to spark further passion. And then Rudy slipped a finger inside her moving slowly in and out as Keagan cried out softly. Rudy was both sur- prised and turned on at the wetness she felt. "I think you won this time, ah—"

"I think we both won this time." Rudy pulled down on the underwear to get better access. Keagan was very help- ful, pulling them down the rest of the way. "So eager," said Rudy. "I like that in my women."

Keagan laughed in spite of herself and her situation. "What women?"

"I'll tell you all about it sometime when I'm not so busy." Rudy looked into Keagan's eyes and placed another finger on her. Unsure, she asked, "Do you want—?"

"Uh, huh." Taking in the light sheen of sweat on Keagan's body and her flushed appearance, Rudy decided she was doing something right and that it was time to finish it. Keagan was still leaning against the door with Rudy stroking her firmly, gently. Rudy loved the way she felt and the pleasurable sounds she was making. Deciding to get bold, she inserted a third finger and felt her lover tensing around her fingers. Moving slowly in and out, Rudy watched Keagan's face contort in pleasure and ecstasy as she reached the edge and went over it. Rudy stayed inside wanting to feel what Keagan did, until the waves had subsided and then bringing her hand up to her face, she erotically licked the digits, her eyes never leaving Keagan's, who was still breathing heavily with a smile forming on her face. The sight of Rudy doing this excited Keagan all over again. Remembering they were still in a public place, Rudy quickly reached down and pulled up Keagan's underwear and jeans. Keagan was very little help at all but did manage to zip her jeans. She laid her head on Rudy's chest and the younger woman wrapped her arms around her tightly and kissed her head. "I think I've just been made love to by a virgin." Rudy stroked Keagan's hair and started to chuckle.

"And it was really good," Keagan added. Then she reached up and kissed Rudy, this time their tongues meeting and connecting passionately.

"What did you expect? That I wouldn't do any research before undertaking such an arduous task?"

"Research? What research? And it wasn't that arduous, was it?"

Rudy put Keagan's bra back in place and then buttoned her shirt up. "I would really love to discuss this in more depth, but I'd rather do it in a more private surrounding...you see," she leaned over and kissed Keagan's neck sending instant shudders down her spine, "there are a lot of other things I'd like to do to you and I can't do them all here."

Keagan pulled Rudy to her and kissed her. "Not half as many things as I want to do to you, La Roux."

"Let's go back to your place." Rudy had unabashed lust in her eyes.

Keagan looked amused. "I wonder what they're going to say about us out in the bar. I'm pretty sure I heard at least two people come in."

"They're probably cheering you on for deflowering me." She laughed. "Little do they really know." As they stood up, Keagan put her arm around Rudy.

"Uh, huh. That *you're* the beast, not me."

"That remains to be seen."

Keagan flashed Rudy a mysterious smile. "Let's go." Suddenly, facing the reality of exiting the stall and indeed the restroom itself, she developed a sense of propriety. "We can't just both walk out at the same time, what if someone walks in? They'll think—"

Unlocking the door, Rudy stepped through it without further discussion. "Honey, I think everybody's figured it out by now and if they didn't they can always look at your neck." Rudy began laughing.

"My neck? Oh, shit!" Keagan went over to the mirror. Sure enough, there was a hickey on the side of her neck. A big one. "I feel so cheap!"

Rudy leered at Keagan appreciatively. She was quite sexy all disheveled. "I know. So do I. Isn't it great?"

Keagan looked at Rudy finding that she had only one

conscious, lingering thought at that moment. She hoped to indulge that thought very soon. "Oh, yeah."

Rudy and Keagan looked at each other and collapsed into hysterics. They had just succumbed to the ultimate stereotype: the bathroom tryst.

Rudy walked out of the restroom first and Keagan followed behind, remembering that she had left her jacket and notebook at the end of the bar and would have to get them before they could leave. "I have to get my jacket," she whispered into Rudy's ear.

"Okay. I'll meet you outside." Rudy winked at Keagan and walked to the end of the bar she'd been sitting at, grabbed her own jacket and left.

Several people sitting at a table nearby started laughing. Scowling, Keagan made her way back to Cody and her jacket. As she grabbed the notebook, she put on her jacket and made a beeline for the door. "Um, honey?" Cody asked.

Keagan turned back around with a heavy sigh. "Yes?"

Cody flashed her a lascivious smile. "I take it you two made up?"

"You could say that." With a slight grin, she began to head for the door but turned back. "Thanks, Cody."

"Anytime, hon." Cody watched as Keagan headed out the door.

****

Keagan walked out of the bar and looked for Rudy, but before long she was embraced from behind. Small hands moved their way up her stomach under her jacket and moved to caress her breasts. "What took you so long?"

"I was just looking for my date. I don't think you should do that. She might not like it."

Rudy explored Keagan's upper chest area, enjoying the

effect it was having. "I don't care if *she* likes it or not. Do you like it?"

"It might be more fun if you took my shirt off."

"That can be arranged."

Keagan turned around and kissed Rudy, pressing her up against the brick of the building. "How about at my place this time?" she breathed when they parted.

"Okay, but you might have to talk me into it."

"Believe me, I was counting on it."

"A verbal seduction. I like that idea."

Keagan glanced around to make sure no one was around. "Or," she leaned up close to Rudy, cradling her head, "I could just give you what you gave me right here, right now." She kissed Rudy again, not stopping until their tongues had enjoyed a thorough exploration.

"Too commonplace," breathed Rudy as they parted. "You'll think of something more creative than imitating what I did." Her hands caressed Keagan's body as she spoke.

"I know. I can't let you win." Keagan smiled evilly.

Growing tired of this extended foreplay, Rudy leaned in close and peered up into the blue eyes sparkling in the moonlight. She whispered. "I want to feel your body against mine, and I don't want any barriers. I want it soon. I want to feel your bare skin against mine and I want to writhe in passion at your hands. Let's go *now*."

"You know, you kind of sound like one of those cheesy romantic novels." She snickered.

Rudy hit her playfully. "Oh, yeah? Like the one *you're* writing?"

"Oh, no mine won't be cheesy, it'll be *realistic*."

"Hopefully, not *too* realistic."

Keagan leaned down and nuzzled Rudy's neck. "I don't know. I like the realism I've experienced lately." She leaned back up and gazed into Rudy's eyes.

Rudy couldn't help but be touched by the sentiment. "You do?"

Keagan simply nodded. "Let's go."

****

It was still fairly early when they got back to the apartment. Keagan opened the door cautiously, not wanting the kitten to fly out the door as she often did. Sure enough, the kitten was right there, but they managed to get in and shut the door before she escaped. "She always tries to escape."

"Just like her owner."

Rudy the cat mewed and looked up at the humans for attention, but at that moment their attention was riveted on each other. "Good one. And I am not her owner. This is only temporary." Little Rudy purred and rubbed up against Keagan's leg. She sighed heavily and gazed down into Rudy's beautiful, green eyes. "So, what do you want to do? It's still early—" Keagan felt it would be rude to grab Rudy, take her into the bedroom, and slowly remove all of her clothes, although it was exactly what she felt like doing. Feeling her heart rate increase with her uncertainty, she took the opportunity to take off her jacket, which she flung onto a chair.

"We could watch TV." Rudy's eyes twinkled with mischief.

"Yeah."

"Or we could read poetry." Rudy took off her jacket and stepped closer. Reaching out, she took Keagan's right hand and brought it to her mouth. Taking an index finger into it, she slowly explored the finger with her tongue. "Or you could just kiss me."

Keagan wasted no time bringing her lips down to meet Rudy's in a passionate kiss. It continued for a few seconds until they parted for air. "Now are you going to tell me about this 'research' you did?"

"I'd rather show you. C'mon." Rudy took Keagan's hand and led her into the bedroom. Shoving her playfully onto the bed she looked down into blue eyes that stared back with uncertainty. She wasted no time climbing on top of Keagan, whose arms came around her gently. "You know, La Roux, if you don't watch it, people are going to start calling you the butch in this relationship. I mean, first you seduce me in the bathroom stall, and now you've cleverly maneuvered me into the bedroom and pounced on me."

Rudy chuckled and kissed Keagan on the neck. "I guess you're going to have to start taking over then, hmm? Wouldn't want to ruin my reputation as the inexperienced, virginal, compliant femme now would I?" Before Keagan could respond Rudy kissed her, this time longer and harder. Their tongues met as the two women explored each other's bodies in earnest. Soon, Rudy undid the buttons to Keagan's shirt. "Déjà vu," she murmured, as she listened to her lover moan.

Getting a brief flash of Dionne Warwick on *The Psychic Friends Network*, Keagan laughed. Rudy had her shirt undone and was planting a kiss above her breasts. The blonde glanced up with a confused look on her face. "What's so funny?"

"When you said that, it reminded me of Dionne Warwick, that's all." She continued to laugh.

"There's just no shutting down that mind of yours, is there?" Rudy reached behind Keagan to undo her bra.

"I guess not."

"Don't worry. I plan on seeing what I can do about that." As Rudy pulled off Keagan's shirt and bra with more enthusiasm than was necessary, Keagan was treated to the sensation of a hot tongue teasing her breast. "Oh,

that feels really good but my mind's still turned on full
throttle." Rudy moved her hands to Keagan's jeans,
unzipped them quickly and began pulling them down.

"You know what I think your problem is?"

"What?" Keagan felt a tongue dart in her ear.

"You need to get with me." Rudy kissed her with passion and allowed her tongue to dart in forcefully to express
her point.

"It's a problem that I need to get with you?" Keagan
asked after they parted. Her face showed a devilish smile.

"No, that you haven't gotten with me *yet*!" To make
her point, Rudy tickled Keagan's now bare stomach and
watched with pleasure as she giggled uncontrollably.

"I *have* gotten with you. Right?"

"Nope so far we just had an unplanned liaison in a
public bathroom. That does not a relationship make." She
smiled mischievously and Keagan didn't miss her meaning.

"Are you sure that's what you want?"

Rudy paused and appeared to seriously contemplate
the question. "Not really. I thought I'd wait until after the
sex and make up my mind. You know. See how it is first.
But I'm getting kind of impatient now, so could you please
get on with it?"

They both laughed at Rudy's quip. "Get on with it?
Oh, by all means, I intend to get on with it." Keagan
grabbed her playfully and threw her on the bed so that she
was now on top, her legs straddling Rudy's waist. Leaning
down, she whispered in her ear, "I'm tired of you having
all the fun." Before Rudy's shock had totally registered
and her laughter completely subsided, Keagan's lips had
found her neck and she sucked, slowly and steadily, all the
while enjoying the soft moans coming from her lover. Her
hands moved to Rudy's blouse and she slowly unbuttoned
it. Feeling her own body responding to what she was doing
to Rudy, she stopped momentarily, leaning back and look-

ing into the green eyes now rife with passion. "Rudy?"

"Hmm...?" Rudy was speechless, her body tingling all over from Keagan's attentions.

"I didn't think you were going to turn me on this much."

Rudy laughed. Sometimes, she didn't know whether to take Keagan's admissions as compliments or not. "You didn't think I'd turn you on?"

Keagan kissed her. "Oh, no, that's not it. I just didn't think anyone could ever make me feel this good." Rudy leaned up and pulled her shirt the rest of the way off. Their eyes met and Keagan reached forward and almost gingerly undid the front clasp to Rudy's bra. "Memories..." Keagan's laugh ended when Rudy swatted her playfully. She leaned over and gently massaged Rudy's right breast while her tongue found the other one. Listening with pleasure to the soft moans coming from Rudy, she remained staring deeply into her green eyes the entire time. Leaning back, she exhaled loudly, her eyes riveted on Rudy who panted softly. "I think I've built up this moment in my mind so much that I can't believe I'm touching you."

"You've touched me before."

"But I've never touched your breasts." She smiled almost shyly, but kept her hands firmly on Rudy.

"So," Rudy felt her heart pounding, "what do you think of them?"

"I'm finding it hard to think at all."

"Then why bother trying?" Rudy placed her hand gently on Keagan's cheek and drew her back down. Another heated kiss ended. "So is this lesson one?" she asked.

"Lesson one?" Keagan reached down to unbutton Rudy's jeans and began pulling them off. Rudy squirmed, attempting to help. When they were completely off, Keagan placed kisses on her stomach.

"Of the love lessons you promised. Remember?"

Rudy stroked through strands of silky, dark hair. Keagan sighed in pleasure and made no attempt to move beyond her current actions.

"I didn't promise you love lessons. You just asked for them." She stroked Rudy's legs marveling at how toned they were.

In spite of her rising excitement, Rudy managed a small laugh. "Okay, fair enough, but just, ah, theoretically, if you were giving them, what would the first one be?"

Weren't they supposed to be making love? Why all the talk? In spite of these questions that went through her mind, Keagan admitted to enjoying it. The chatter added a dimension that was missing from her other relationships. She found the mental stimulation appealing. Moving up, she took each of Rudy's hands in her own, guided her arms over her head, and pinned her down. "Lesson number one would be, how to get your lover prone." She moved her hands back to Rudy's breasts and kissed her collarbone in earnest.

In spite of her body's response to Keagan's skillful attentions, Rudy couldn't let go of their dialogue. It was too much fun. "And just how would you...ah...do that?"

Keagan looked back up. "Apparently very easily." She laughed.

"You calling me easy?" Mock indignation laced her words.

"What if I am?" Keagan had been denied the pleasure of Rudy's lips for too long. How long had it been? Two minutes? Three? As she kissed Rudy, her tongue slipped out, attempting to gain entrance, but Rudy kept her mouth shut tightly after Keagan's last remark. Briefly frustrated, but formulating a plan, she turned away and planted long, sensuous, affecting kisses on her neck. This continued for a few moments until Rudy's breathing heightened considerably and her cries of pleasure increased. At that point,

Keagan moved back to her mouth now completely open
from the panting. Dipping down quickly, her tongue
entered Rudy's mouth and they shared a long kiss, their
tongues moving together, and their craving for each other
escalating. They parted at last, after what seemed like
minutes but was only a few seconds. Both breathing
heavily, they stared at each other, Rudy recognizing the
usual triumphant smile forming on Keagan's face.

"Okay, okay. So I *am* easy. So what?" At this, they
both collapsed into laughter.

"Nothing wrong with easy. Nothing at all." Keagan
remained leaning over Rudy, her eyes turning serious.

"I suppose that's how you like your women, right?"

"What women? There are no other women. Just you."

"There aren't?"

"No. You're the only one."

"I am?"

Keagan rolled off of Rudy and pulled down her jeans.
Repositioning herself near her, the only barrier remaining
was their respective underwear. Making no further
attempts at seduction, Keagan leaned over and kissed Rudy
almost tentatively, waiting for her next comment. None
was forthcoming. They shared a mutual grin, as their eyes
both traveled southward. "The underwear." They said it in
unison. Both tried to stifle another laugh, because this was
making love, right? It was supposed to be dramatic and
passionate, not funny. Rudy and Keagan were both coming
to realize that sex *was* funny. A very funny thing to do.

Finally, as they both reached for their own underwear,
Keagan stopped. "Lesson two would be how to undress
your lover. Shall I?"

"Yes...please."

Keagan leaned over and placed an almost chaste kiss
on Rudy's cheek. She slowly reached forward and began
pulling Rudy's underwear off. Apparently, she did it too

slowly for Rudy who reached down herself and pulled it
off the rest of the way. As Rudy threw the underwear
against one of the bedroom walls, she pulled Keagan's
head back down and kissed her. They came up for breath
presently. "Too slow, huh?" Keagan asked.

Rudy nodded. "And don't worry about me being a virgin." At Keagan's surprised look, she continued, "I know
you are, but don't be." She tenderly caressed Keagan's
face and kissed her softly. "I'm right where I want to be
with the person I want to be with. I just...I love you."

Keagan's eyes widened, her heart picking up in speed.
"Hey, La Roux..."

Rudy's fingers were instantly at her lips. "Don't say
anything." They stared at each other for what seemed like
a short eternity. Rudy's next words were whispered
against Keagan's lips. "I don't want anything to ruin this
moment."

"Nothing could ruin this moment because you're a part
of it." She remained still until Rudy took her hand and
kissed it. She noticed Keagan shaking.

"Why are you shaking? I'm supposed to be the virgin
here."

"I've never felt like this before."

"Then we have our own special feeling together
because I've never felt this way, either." Words failing
her, Keagan leaned forward and kissed Rudy again, feeling
her mouth opening. For the first time she allowed herself
to revel in how good it felt to feel her body against Rudy's.
The sensation of flesh on flesh was something she had felt
before, but not in this way. This time it was different. She
felt a sense of belonging and rightness she had never
known before. It both scared and excited her. She let herself succumb to the feeling of Rudy's tongue in her mouth.
It was so soft, so sweet, and so inviting. And she tasted so
wonderful. She had to have more. They parted breath-

lessly, and Keagan spoke with a slight smile on her face. "I think something's—"

Rudy nodded her head vigorously. "Off, now." Not waiting for Keagan to take off her underwear, she reached forward and pulled them down. Before Keagan knew it, Rudy had maneuvered herself on top again and was kissing her passionately. "You feel so good," Rudy panted in between kisses. "Please don't tell me this is a dream..."

"Sorry, but it *is* a dream. It's *my* dream come true."

"A dream come true is a dream no more."

"That sounds like one of those famous quotations." Keagan moaned as she felt Rudy's lips on her neck and hands on her breasts.

"Not yet, but maybe someday." They both laughed at this.

"I can see it now. 'This quote was inspired by Rudy Whitman's first foray into sensual pleasure.' And—"

"And that foray was long delayed because Rudy's talkative lover couldn't shut up long enough to—"

"Me? Talkative? Come now." The double entendre inherent in her own words was not lost on Keagan. She flipped Rudy over regaining the top position, and allowed her hands to explore lower on Rudy's body.

"Ah." Rudy smiled and closed her eyes. "I've been waiting for you to say that."

"I wonder if you'll stop flirting at the ultimate moment of passion," Keagan whispered, as she allowed her hand to slowly massage Rudy. Dipping her finger in briefly, she felt the wetness of her arousal.

"Why don't we see? Ah, that feels so good." She felt Keagan's finger slip in again and stroke her slowly. "So," she began in between pants, "how many women have you done this to?"

"What?" Keagan sat back in exasperation. She wasn't the only one who had trouble shutting down her mind during sex.

Regretting that her inquiry had caused Keagan to stop, Rudy looked guilty. "I was just wondering—"

"La Roux, can we make a pact?" Keagan leaned down and gently kissed the tender skin between Rudy's breasts, reveling in the heartbeat she felt speed up.

"Yes." Her reply was breathless.

"No more talking."

"Awww—"

"I mean it. You promise?"

"So if I don't promise you'll quit what you were doing?"

"Yep."

"Does this mean you aren't going to answer my question?" Although Rudy gazed at Keagan guilelessly, her eyes still held a mischievous glint.

"Yes. That's what it means." Keagan tried to look stern but realized she was failing miserably. "From right now at this moment. No more words, Rudy, I mean it."

"Ooh, I like it when you take charge." She laughed.

Keagan put her hand over Rudy's mouth. "Now what did I say?" She could feel Rudy about to speak and continued quickly. "Don't answer that!" In spite of the mock glare she received, Keagan knew she could have some fun with this. "Now," she began, as her hands moved over Rudy's hips, massaging them thoroughly, "You can moan, you can cry out, you can even scream if you want. Just no talking." She leaned down and planted kisses along the bottom of Rudy's stomach. Working her way up, her lips eventually found a breast. Flicking her tongue out, she teased the nipple for a few seconds before placing her mouth firmly around the breast and sucking with ardor. "It'll be worth it, I promise," she whispered. A short moan was the only response, as green eyes locked with blue. Keagan knew she would pay for this later and she wholeheartedly looked forward to it. She treated Rudy to an in-depth exploration of her body, her mouth and hands seeking out places she had always wanted to go. Her fear seemingly fled, and in its place was a burning desire to please this woman who offered her love freely, for reasons Keagan was still trying to understand.

Keeping her eyes riveted on Rudy's, her hand once again found the source of her desire as she continued stroking. "You feel wonderful," she couldn't help telling her.

"Wow, that's so different." Rudy averted her eyes, knowing she'd be in trouble for breaking the pact.

"What's different?" Keagan didn't tease her about breaking the pact. She had missed the sound of Rudy's voice and welcomed it.

As Keagan continued her slow stroking, Rudy found it hard to focus on coherent thoughts. "Oh...oh, ah...from when I've touched myself." Rudy couldn't hold back and laughed.

Keagan was amazed at this woman's ability to be forthright, even while making love. "That's good, isn't it?" She could feel Rudy getting closer and increased her thrusts a little. "Just tell me if there's anything you want me to—"

"You're doing just fine and yes, that is good." Rudy's breathing became labored at that point and although her intellectual thoughts were fleeing with the pleasure she was feeling, one request came to mind. "There is something I want."

"Anything." Keagan continued to touch her, enjoying the feeling of warmth and wetness exuding from Rudy, who was so open, needing, and giving.

"Kiss me."

Now panting herself, Keagan leaned up until their lips connected gently. She deepened it, enjoying the feeling of Rudy's soft cries entering into her mouth as their tongues met. This continued until Keagan felt Rudy's release around her fingers. She had never felt anything so sweet. Staying with her until the contractions subsided, she kissed her forehead and then her mouth gently. Rudy's eyes were closed and she was smiling broadly. "Can I talk now?"

"You talked before." Keagan stroked her hair, and chuckled lightly.

"I know, but—" She flung herself into Keagan's arms and they held each other tightly. Rudy wanted to profess her love again, but didn't. She had done it once and that was enough for now. "That was so good." She leaned back and kissed her lover passionately. "When can we do it again?"

Keagan felt her body reacting to Rudy. "No time like the present, right?"

* * * * * * * * *

"So, that's all there is to it? That's what the big hoopla was about?" Sometime later, after Keagan and Rudy had enjoyed a thorough exploration of each other's bodies, they lay together quite sated. Keagan had her head on Rudy's stomach and her arm wrapped around her. With a chuckle, she sighed contentedly feeling fingers in her hair stroking gently.

"Yep. That's all there is to it."

"Too bad. I was hoping you'd give me more lessons."

"What do I look like? A love instructor?"

"You could pass for one in a pinch."

"You think so, huh?" Keagan turned over and met green eyes. She continued to rest her head on Rudy's stomach. Gazing up at her lover, the only thought she had at that moment was that Rudy looked like an angel that had come to rescue her.

"Yep." In spite of her apparent nonchalance, her fin-

gers stroked Keagan's face. Keeping her eyes focused on
blue the entire time, she touched every facet of her face,
ending with her lips. She felt Keagan's breathing increase
as her finger found its way into her mouth. Keagan gave
equal attention to Rudy's other fingers, sucking each one
sensuously. "Oh, yeah, definitely in a pinch," Rudy said
with a sigh.

"You have beautiful hands." She placed a gentle kiss
on Rudy's palm.

"C'mere." Rudy took hold of Keagan's face, and felt
her lover crawl up her body, positioning her arms on either
side of her. Almost not knowing how to react to such a
sweet sentiment coming from Keagan, she kissed her.
Soon the kiss deepened, and soon after that they were both
breathless.

"And beautiful lips." Keagan traced them with her
finger. "And beautiful eyes." She looked deeply into
them. "In fact, there isn't an inch of you that isn't beautiful."

Rudy buried her face in Keagan's chest. "You better
watch it. You're going to ruin your reputation as the taci-
turn loner."

Keagan wrapped her arms around her. "Oh, damn.
What a loss." They both laughed. A few seconds after
that, a noise could be heard coming from the hall.

"Mew!" Rudy the cat hobbled into the bedroom. She
stared at the bed and tried to jump up, but failed miserably.
Keagan laughed. "You wimpy, little beast! You're too
small to jump up."

Rudy hit her on the arm playfully. "You're so mean.
Making fun of a sweet, little kitten. Put her up here."

"Nah, I enjoy watching her pitiful attempts." Keagan
snickered with glee.

"If you're not nicer to Rudy the cat, then Rudy the
woman might not be so nice to you if you know what I

mean." She had an evil grin on her face.

Keagan scowled. "Mew! Mew!" She looked to the cat and then to Rudy. Soon, she scooped up the little kitten and placed her on the bed. The small animal looked around cautiously, taking in the new surroundings. Then she curled into a ball and fell asleep. "I'm *so* sure. Withholding sexual favors for a beast." She sighed with mock disgust.

Rudy leaned over and climbed back on top of Keagan with a mischievous glint in her eye. "You're more of a beast than she is, you know." Before she could respond, Rudy kissed her, her tongue darting in and out of Keagan's mouth passionately. "Again? You're insatiable."

Rudy took her hand off of a breast she was beginning to massage. "Well, if you'd rather not—"

Keagan put her hand back in place on her breast. "No, no. I didn't say that."

Rudy sobered. "It *is* getting kind of late."

"Stay."

"All night?"

"It's not like you haven't before."

"Yeah. Well, right, but before we weren't—"

"Giving in to the undeniable cravings of the flesh?" Keagan flashed Rudy a saucy grin.

Rudy smiled at the clever choice of words. "Right, but—"

"I want you to."

"Are you sure?"

"Of course, I'm sure. What do you think I am? Some heartless seductress who preys on young, innocent women and then throws them out of her bedroom when she's done with them?" Keagan put on a mock look of indignation.

"No. I don't think you'd throw me out. You like me too much."

"I don't think I could ever throw you out."

Rudy leaned over for another kiss. Soon, they were engaging in another dialogue that led to another heated session of their new favorite activity.

****

"*You raise your face from mine, parting my breath like water, hair falling away in its own wind, and your eyes— green in the light like honey—surfacing on my body, awed with desire, speechless, this common dream...*" Keagan whispered the phrase from a favorite poem into Rudy's ear and watched as she awakened, her eyes blinking slowly. Rudy smiled.

"What a nice way to wake up."

"I always aim to please."

They were facing each other, not touching. "You pleased." Rudy leaned over and touched the side of Keagan's face running her hand down her cheek.

Keagan closed her eyes at Rudy's caress and considered how to proceed. Declarations of love were not her style, but she knew that Rudy deserved that if that's where they were headed. *Is that where we're headed? I have no idea. She told me she loved me, but it could have meant anything and she could have said it for any number of reasons. I could just ask her. Nah, no way.*

"Can I ask you a question?"

It took a few moments for it to register with Keagan that Rudy had spoken. She was lost in thought. "Sure."

"Does this mean I'm your girlfriend, now?" Rudy didn't want to make any presumptions.

Blue eyes gazed back at her pensively. "Do you want to be?"

Rudy smiled and shook her head slightly. "I think yes, after what we just shared, I would like to be very much." *Actually, way before we shared that.*

"Is this the part you were talking about where you make up your mind after the sex?" Keagan grinned.

"Exactly. And I've had all night to think about it, and my answer is yes."

"As I recall, we didn't do much thinking." Keagan smiled that sexy grin Rudy adored.

"Oh, I don't know. I thought quite a bit." She leaned over and kissed Keagan's neck and whispered into her ear. "I thought about what I wanted to do to you next, what I wanted you to do to me—" Rudy stopped to give more complete attention to the smooth, tempting neck she was sucking on.

"Umm, so is this exclusive?" Keagan found it both challenging and exciting to carry on a lucid conversation while being aroused.

Rudy tore herself away from Keagan's neck to look deeply into her eyes. "As in we only sleep with each other? Yes, I want that, too."

Keagan held open her arms. Rudy snuggled into them, placing her head under Keagan's chin and smiling into her chest. "You sure have a lot of demands."

"I'm a very demanding woman."

"Oh, I know. Believe me, I know."

Rudy grinned. "Can we eat breakfast now?" Her stomach had been growling for the last half-hour.

"And yet another demand." Keagan got up, grabbing a T-shirt and shorts from her dresser. She put them on quickly and headed for the kitchen. Coffee sounded really good.

****

"You look so different with clothes on." Rudy, now clad in Keagan's dark green terrycloth robe, chuckled as she made her way into the kitchen. She was holding Rudy and petting her. "I kind of got used to seeing you without them."

Keagan stood at the stove preparing eggs and bacon. She allowed a small smile to surface, which Rudy couldn't see. "We could always set aside some time for them to be removed again." She started laughing and turned around to see green eyes gazing at her with amusement. Spotting the robe, she noted that it was way too big on Rudy, but it made her look very cute.

"But we have an exam to study for, remember?"

"Can't we study in bed?"

"Oh, right, and just how much studying do you think we'd get done?"

Keagan grinned. "A great deal, I'm sure." She turned back to the stove and flipped the bacon, while continuing to keep an eye on the scrambled eggs. "We'd be in a much closer space. We'd be able to focus more. You know, when going over the quotes."

"And you wouldn't get distracted?"

Keagan grinned evilly. "Oh, certainly not."

"What if I was naked, would you get distracted, then?"

Keagan appeared to think about that. "Only if you were trying to seduce me."

"Oh, I wouldn't do that. Not while you were studying anyway. I'm supposed to be an aspiring teacher, remember?"

"Yes and surprisingly you've taught me more than I thought you'd be able to." Keagan raised her eyebrows.

"My research, you know—"

"You haven't told me about that yet."

"A girl has to have some secrets." Rudy poured two cups of coffee.

"If I recall correctly, you seemed to have a major problem with me and my secrets."

Rudy rolled her eyes and shook her head with disgust. "That's because you were being pigheaded. I'm just being alluringly coy." With a mischievous smile, she deposited Rudy on the floor and went to the refrigerator for the orange juice. The little kitten mewed and went over to her bowl to eat.

"Oh, is that what it's called?" Finishing up her cooking, Keagan prepared their plates, setting them on the table. Rudy got the bagels as they popped out of the toaster. As they sat down, Keagan spoke again. "Why is it that when I have secrets, I'm being pigheaded and when you have them, you're being alluringly coy?" Rudy poured two glasses of orange juice, not immediately answering. She glanced down at her eggs, smiling slightly. As she salted them, she looked back up to meet challenging blue eyes staring back waiting for an answer. "Because extroverts are allowed more cryptic moments than introverts."

"Oh, is that so?" Keagan grabbed the grape jelly and put some on her bagel.

"Yep." Rudy smiled with satisfaction and began eating her eggs.

"And who made up these rules?"

Rudy snorted. "Me, of course. It only makes sense. We extroverts constantly wear our hearts on our sleeves. Sometimes, it can get a bit overwhelming, even for us. It's then that we need a secret or two to keep us balanced. See?"

Keagan felt a warmth that couldn't be explained by the hot coffee trailing down her throat. She didn't think it was possible for her to become more attracted to Rudy, but it happened whenever she turned an ordinary conversation into something thought provoking. "And about the pigheaded introverts?" As she bit into her bagel, her eyes never left Rudy's.

"You see, introverts are pigheaded because they never give an inch. Everything stays inside until it feels like they'll burst. That's why just as it's healthy for you to divulge some of your secrets, it's healthy for me to keep some of mine."

"I see." Keagan got up and came to Rudy's side of the table, kneeling down and leaning very close to her face, their eyes meeting. "And there's nothing I could do to persuade you to...divulge...your secret?" Tangling her hands in Rudy's long, blonde hair she bent her head back gently and kissed her neck softly.

Rudy's breathing increased. "Well, um, there could be something...maybe."

Keagan kissed the other side of her neck, this time lingering longer. "Do you like grape jelly?" She whispered it into Rudy's ear, hearing her sigh. Keagan enjoyed the effect she had on her. Reaching over to the jelly, her hand scooped out a generous amount of the tasty substance, which she smeared onto Rudy's neck. As she licked and bit at it tantalizingly, she recognized the familiar soft moans coming from her lover. The taste combined with Rudy was heavenly.

"Ah, that's going to be so...messy," said Rudy as she eagerly surrendered to Keagan's lips and tongue which were making it very hard for her to think coherently.

"But so delicious." She kissed Rudy thoroughly on the lips, then, enjoying the sensation of her tongue combined with the grape jelly.

They parted both panting. "You're crazy," said Rudy.

"You made me that way." Keagan's mouth found Rudy's neck again and lapped up the rest of the jelly. Soon, her hands wandered underneath the green robe, exploring as her lips found Rudy's again.

When they parted, Keagan breathed heavily and her body tingled. She definitely wanted to take their conversation where it was apparently heading. "We haven't even finished eating yet."

Rudy got up from her chair in a rush, and pushed

Keagan to the kitchen floor with no objections from her
lover. "I don't care. I know what I want and at the
moment it's not eggs and bacon."

Keagan almost laughed but before she could, Rudy's
lips found hers again, as they surrendered to yet another
passionate embrace. Keagan reached up and undid the belt
to the robe. Surprisingly, she didn't notice any discomfort
at being prone on the hard surface.

Chapter
8

Rudy sat on the couch trying unsuccessfully to study for the British literature exam. She and Keagan decided it wouldn't be the best idea for them to study together. It would be entirely too distracting. They had already skipped breakfast due to their newly awakened passion. Trying to study would be futile.

Reading over a poem by Sir Thomas Wyatt the Elder, she sighed with disinterest. She liked to read the stanzas out loud, being able to internalize more that way. On the exam, she'd be required to identify a quote by listing the title and the author as well as telling what the significance of the quote was. *"My Lute, Awake! Perform the last Labour that—"* Groaning, she gave up trying to read the poem. Nothing was making an impression anyway. Rudy flipped through the pages, but it seemed like every poem she came to was suggestive and reminded her of Keagan. "The Ecstasy," by John Donne. "That's it! I've had it! I can't study anymore." She slammed the book closed.

Just then, there was a knock at the door. Courtney, ever the social animal, came barreling down the steps to answer it. Still clad in her robe, her hair was a bit disheveled and she quickly tried to fix it. Noticing Rudy sitting on the couch, a brief flicker of surprise crossed her face. "When did you get in?"

"A few hours ago." It was almost two o'clock and Rudy grinned at her roommate's state of dress that late into the day. *Must have been a long night,* she thought wryly.

Figuring it was one of Courtney's friends, Rudy opened the book again and decided to give it another shot. Trying to block out the voices at the door, she nonetheless looked up when a few seconds later Courtney closed the door and was holding a long box in her hands. It was obviously a delivery of flowers. Her roommate stared at her expectantly, heading over with the package. "I see someone got flowers. How sweet. Aren't you going to open them?"

Courtney plopped down next to Rudy and grinned with delight. "Why would I open up *your* flowers?"

Rudy's eyes widened. "Mine? No way! Give it here quick!" Opening the box, her eyes were treated to a dozen yellow roses with one sweetheart red rose in the middle of the bunch. "I can't believe she did this."

Courtney was getting impatient. "Open the card. See what it says."

Rudy looked at Courtney amusedly. "You're almost more excited than I am." She opened the card and read, "*Thanks for a fun evening. L., K.*" Smiling a bit, she put the card back into the envelope.

"That is so romantic."

"Hmm..."

"What do you mean, 'hmm'?"

"I wish I knew what she was trying to say." As an afterthought, she added, "we slept together last night."

Courtney laughed. "I already figured that out. You don't come home last night and when you do, you have this big thing on your neck."

Rudy almost blushed. "It's called a hickey. And quit trying to change the subject."

"So what's bothering you about this, then?"

"Keagan and I had a very exciting, passionate very sexual night and morning together and all she says is, 'thanks for a fun evening.' And she can't even write 'love.' Why do people always do that? Write L. when they mean 'love.' It's not like love's that big of a word that it needs an abbreviation. I never got that."

"So you don't know how she feels?"

"No, I don't and it really bugs me, you know? I know I shouldn't worry about it and I told myself it wasn't going to be a problem but I told her I loved her, and she didn't tell me. So, what are these flowers supposed to mean? All I am is a good time?"

Courtney put her hand on Rudy's shoulder and squeezed it. "I'm sure that's not it. Why don't you call her?"

"What if this is her way of saying, 'I really like you, but—'?"

"Somehow, I don't think so. Let me put these in water for you and you give her a call, okay? And if things don't go your way we'll get a gallon of mint chocolate chip and talk."

"Thanks." Rudy watched her roommate go into the kitchen. Picking up the phone she dialed Keagan's number and got the answering machine. After leaving a message, she tried to concentrate on studying again.

****

"Flowers. I sent her yellow roses." Keagan gave up the idea of studying. Instead, she went over to Brad's. He was getting ready for "Drag Queen Night" at the bar and was trying on outfits as they talked. He sported a long, golden wig and wore a short, strapless, black dress. Keagan tried not to laugh as Brad placed two balloons into his dress to serve as breasts.

"Oh, that's good girl. You gotta keep 'em happy. You know, the only time, and I mean the only time I ever sent anyone flowers I was really in love. Are you—?"

Keagan threw her hands up in the air. "Of course! Yes, yes, yes, okay? I've thought about this and the only conclusion I can come to is that yes, I am."

"Ah. Young love. It's so sweet."

Keagan groaned.

"What do you think of my boobs?" Brad thrust his chest into Keagan's face. The balloon size he used made his false appendages look like a size D.

"I must say, you are really stacked, sweet thing." Getting a mock lecherous look on her face, she reached over and with both hands "fondled" his balloons. "But a little too pliant, methinks."

"Hey, stop that! I'm not that kind of girl." He backed up in mock horror. "And besides, what if little Rudy found out? It'd break her heart."

"Yes, I'm sure it would break her heart if she found out I was fooling around with a drag queen." They both laughed at the utter absurdity of her statement. "What is 'Drag Queen Night,' anyway?"

"Oh, it's simply divine! Everyone who's ever wanted to be a drag queen but didn't have the guts—"

"Sounds like a book title. '*Everyone Who Ever Wanted to Be a*'—"

Brad frowned and glared at his friend. "Do you want to know or not?"

Obediently keeping her mouth shut, Keagan gestured for Brad to continue. "Like I was saying, anyone who never had the guts to go out and strut her stuff can do so this one night, and do it in relative anonymity, since everyone there will be dressed up."

"You mean, you can't get in unless you're in drag?"

"Of course not. That would ruin the whole idea."

"Aren't the real drag queens going to get offended?"

"Oh, certainly not! It's the highest form of flattery."

Keagan looked skeptical. "Just like being spoofed on *Saturday Night Live*? Is that kind of what it's like?"

Brad clapped his hands and pointed his index finger at Keagan. "Exactly, my friend."

"Hmm."

"So, do tell. What did you put in the note? Something like, 'My darling, Rudy. Last night was so perfect and you were so divine that I can do nothing but pledge my eternal love and devotion to you forever. With every bit of love I have in my heart, Keagan.'" As he said this, his eyes turned intense and he swayed his arms dramatically through the air.

Keagan rolled her eyes and sighed in mock disgust. "Nope, I just told her thanks for a fun evening." She shrugged.

"You told her what? That's it? Haven't I taught you anything? Now we're going to have to do damage control, girlfriend."

"I was just being honest. It *was* a fun evening." *And morning.*

"You were just being honest, you were just being *honest*?" His voice rose considerably in pitch and tone. "Love isn't about HONESTY! Don't you know anything?" Shaking his head in disgust, he began formulating a plan to help Keagan.

Keagan laughed. She almost thought that Brad believed what he was saying and that was the scary part. "I felt other things, too, besides it being a fun evening, I just didn't say."

"You didn't say, you didn't say! You *never* say.

You're going to have to say soon, girl, or you'll lose that
one. I had her pegged right when I met her. She's the type
that needs commitment, I can tell." He took off the wig
and looked for another one. *I just don't make a good
blonde.*

"Of course, you would know. Being that you have
such a vast experience with relationships and all. When
was your last one?"

Brad thought for a moment. That moment stretched
into several. "Um, 198—just kidding. It was 1993. So
there."

"Oooh, six years ago. I apologize for doubting you."

"That six years is by choice, I might add."

"Of course." Keagan smiled knowingly.

"We're getting off the subject here. What are you
going to do to make this up to her?"

"Make what up? I sent her flowers, for godsakes. She
should be *thanking* me."

Brad shook his head, now sporting a bright reddish-
blonde wig, and patted his friend on the back sympathetically. "You don't get it do you? What you wrote on the
card is incongruous with sending the flowers. Do you realize that people send flowers for all kinds of things? Not
just because they're in love. People send them to congrat-
ulate, for holidays, for weddings and for funerals and I'm
sure there's other reasons, too. Now, unless you make it
clear in the card what your intentions are, the person
receiving the flowers is liable to be confused."

Keagan thought for a second. It almost made sense in
a twisted sort of way. "Do you think Rudy might be confused?"

"If the sender is confused, the recipient will be, too,
most likely. Correct?"

"Maybe. Let me ask you something. A theoretical situation. You've dated someone for three weeks, and then

you have sex in a bathroom stall in a bar—"

"That *was* you?"

"What? How did you know? I didn't tell you."

"Jackie Daniels came to The Garage last night and was telling some story she heard from someone about an encounter going on in the bathroom at the Grotto. She said the rumor was that it was you, but I defended you saying you were too rational and in control to ever do something like that."

"Oh, terrific." Keagan put her head in her hands. "The infamous grapevine is in full force, I see. I'll never be able to go back to the bar again."

"Are you kidding? They were lovin' it! Everybody was applauding you for finally getting la—"

"Stop. Please." An even worse thought occurred to Keagan, one that outweighed her own embarrassment. "Did anybody mention Rudy's name?"

"No."

"Good. I wouldn't want her to be embarrassed. Or unwittingly develop some kind of reputation."

"Sounds like you care." He smiled warmly and reached for a pair of high-heeled shoes. As he put them on, Brad winced at the tightness. "Ah! These are way too tight."

"If it sounds like a queen and acts like a queen—" She grinned evilly.

"Ha, ha. Now tell me the theoretical situation." He pulled the tight shoes off.

"Okay. You dated the person for three weeks, you have an unplanned sexual liaison, you go home together and make love for most of the night and part of the morning, then you decide neither one of you will get any studying done if you stay together that day so she goes home, you send her flowers and you write what I put in the card. If you're Rudy, what do you think?"

"I think, 'Oops. She's backing off and trying to be nice with the flower gesture, but she doesn't really want to start anything.'"

"But I had them put the red sweetheart rose in. Doesn't that count for anything?"

"Yeah, it makes it look like you sent a dozen yellow roses, that symbolize friendship, by the way, and then made a nice gesture with the smaller red rose. It looks like you're saying, 'we should just be friends.'"

Keagan sighed in frustration. She now wished she had never sent the damn flowers. *I should have known better than to make a stereotypical, romantic gesture. I should have known it would backfire.* "All right. What should I do?"

Brad pressed the speaker button on his phone so Keagan could make a call and they could both hear it. "She's probably called you by now. Call and hear her message. That way, I can tell for sure how much work we need to do."

Frowning at her friend, Keagan did as she was told. There was a message from Joan apologizing for their last conversation, a message from work telling her that her shift had been changed to 4:00 am for the week, and at last a message from Rudy: "Hi, Keagan. These roses are beautiful. Thank you. Uh, I needed to talk with you. Well, we'll just talk later. <deep sigh> Bye, bye."

"Uh, oh. Big trouble, girlfriend, big trouble."

"What? She thanked me, she said she wanted to talk to me which is obvious because she called and she said we would talk later which we will. And she said 'bye.' I don't see the problem."

Brad rolled his eyes dramatically. "Don't you know how to read between the lines? This girl is hurting. Didn't you hear the *sigh*?"

"Sigh, sigh? What sigh? What are you talking

about?" Keagan was a patient person, but Brad thoroughly tested her ability to maintain her temper. *What the hell is he talking about?*

"Do I have to play it again? Right before she said 'bye' she sighed, indicating a struggle over what kind of closing to use. Do I say, 'I love you, I miss you, I hope to talk to you soon, do I call her honey, sweetie,love kitten-'"

"Love kitten?" Keagan looked aghast.

"Okay, drop the 'love kitten.' I'm trying to make a point here, girlfriend."

"All right, so since I've screwed everything up so badly, what should I say to her?"

"Say nothing. Yet. I know exactly what you need to do." Brad grinned and raised his eyebrows. Keagan knew that he was up to no good, but that she'd probably go along with it anyway.

****

Later that evening, after Rudy and Courtney had eaten ice cream, made a crockpot of chili for dinner and talked about relationships, Rudy found herself answering yet another knock at the door. Looking through the peephole, she saw a young man standing there with a box of flowers. Shaking her head in disbelief, she opened the door.

"Delivery for Ms. Rudy Whitman." He handed her a clipboard and she smiled at him and signed it.

"You're a very popular woman today. Is it your birthday?" He smiled pleasantly at her.

She couldn't help but laugh. "It's not my birthday. I think I must have an admirer."

"He's very persistent." He took the clipboard back from her.

"Thank you." Choosing not to tell the deliveryman that he had the wrong gender, she took the box inside, but before opening it, looked at the card first. It said, "*Last night was special. So are you. Love, Keagan.*" Smiling broadly this time, she opened the box to see a dozen red roses. "Courtney! Get down here!"

After a few moments, her roommate came barreling down the steps. "What? What happened?"

"She sent me red roses this time."

"*This* time? Geez," Courtney sighed. "Why can't I find a man like Keagan?"

Giggling, Rudy handed the box to Courtney. "Would you mind please? I have a phone call to make."

* * * * * * * * * *

"*Oh, cruel time! Which takes in trust our youth, our joys, and all we have, and pays us but with age and dust; who in the dark and silent grave when we have wandered all our ways shuts up the story of our days.*" Keagan recited the stanza from Sir Walter Raleigh's poem, with no enthusiasm. "How depressing," she said aloud. "Why did I become an English major?"

Hearing the phone ring, Keagan perked up. She walked over to her answering machine as it clicked on. "Good evening. You have reached Keagan's Den of Lesbian Desire. If you are anyone but Rudy, please leave me a message and I'll get back to you. If you are Rudy, don't leave a message. Just hang up and come over immediately. The Den requires your presence. Ciao." Beep. Click. Hangup. "Hope that was her."

In less than ten minutes, there was a knock on her door. She looked through the peephole to see Rudy standing there. "Who is it?"

"Is this Keagan's Den of Lesbian Desire? I don't have the wrong place do I?"

"Yes it is and no you don't."

"Can I come in?"

"Is your name Rudy?"

"Yes, and I think I have something you want."

Keagan opened the door. "Like—?"

"Like this." Rudy stepped inside, and was instantly enveloped into Keagan's arms. Their lips met forcefully as she felt her lover's tongue inside her mouth while she straddled Keagan's thigh. Strong arms picked her up and lips found her neck. "Why don't you...come...inside?" she heard Keagan say. As Rudy was drawn in, she sensed her lover shutting the door with her leg.

"If you insist." They collapsed onto the couch.

"I want to show you something." Their bodies writhed together, the heat between them increasing.

Green eyes stared into blue. Rudy's frustration showed in her actions. She held onto Keagan, breathing heavily, both wanting what was being done to her and knowing that they should be talking, not ravishing each other. "What?"

"This." Keagan maneuvered herself underneath Rudy and gazed into her eyes. She kissed her and Rudy responded ardently, wondering if she wouldn't come from that alone. Keagan's hands found her breasts through her shirt and fondled them. Her lips found Rudy's neck and she heard a welcoming sigh as they feasted on a familiar place.

"Wait a minute, wait." Rudy tore her neck from Keagan's lips with reluctance.

Keagan tried to get her breathing under control. "What's wrong?"

"We are not doing this. I came over here to talk, not just jump into bed."

"We're not in bed." She kissed Rudy on the neck.

Rudy glared at Keagan, not at all impressed with her tendency to be literal. She climbed off her lover and sat at the other end of the couch. "Because I don't want to feel like our relationship is just about sex."

"It's not." Keagan sat up on the couch and looked over at Rudy, hoping they weren't about to have a revealing conversation, but fearing they were about to. "I'm sorry. You're just so attractive to me. I can't keep from touching you. Please don't think it's just about sex."

"Is that all I am? Just attractive to you?" The tone of her voice was not accusatory, but honestly questioning.

"Oh, no. You're much more than that. You're my grammar tutor." Knowing that it wasn't the right response, Keagan averted her eyes. When Rudy didn't respond but sat watching her, with a hint of a smile on her face, Keagan took that as a sign that she wasn't angry. "Did you like the roses?"

That got the smile to grow broader. "The first or second bunch?"

"Second."

"I liked the first."

"Better than the second? Why?"

"The first bunch was more you. The second bunch was like somebody stepped in and said, 'this is how to be romantic, Keagan. Now do it right this time.'"

Keagan looked at the floor. "Brad said the flowers and the card were ambiguous." He didn't know that the yellow roses were supposed to tie in with a theme she had in mind. They were the same color as the rose Rudy gave to Keagan at the bar.

"Yes, but that's you, right?"

"Ambiguous?"

"Not exactly, you just don't wear your heart on your sleeve, but I know you care."

Keagan smiled. "Shall we try to get some studying done, now?"

"Let's."

* * * * * * * * * *

Keagan laid on her back, a floor pillow supporting her head, with her eyes closed, trying to concentrate. Rudy sat on her lover's stomach, her legs straddling Keagan's torso. This studying arrangement worked well. It suited their desire for physical contact, while precluding anything physical happening due to Rudy's rules. They were clear on this subject. The only touching allowed was the touching made necessary by Rudy's position. And they had to study for at least three hours, not including breaks. Rudy even went so far as to deduct the time used for bathroom and snack breaks. Keagan avoided eye contact as much as she could. That always got her into trouble.

Flipping through her notes, Rudy located another quote. " *'But, ah,' Desire still cries, 'give me some food.'* " Keagan looked up into her companion's green eyes and grinned. "That's from 'Astrophil and Stella,' but it's not on our study list."

"So what?" Rudy put her notebook on the floor. She leaned down closely to Keagan, face to face, so their lips were almost touching. Keagan put her arms around her and moved their bodies together, rubbing against her playfully. She could feel Rudy's pelvic area grinding against her own, causing familiar sensations to course through her body.

"Oops," Keagan chastised, as Rudy's hands moved to her hips. "I think you're breaking the touching rule."

"It's been three hours. Time's up." Rudy's lips captured Keagan's in a passionate kiss. Soon, her hands moved to Keagan's shirt to pull it out of her jeans, but a hand stopped her.

"Just leave our clothes on." Keagan whispered the request into Rudy's ear.

"But I want—"

"Trust me. You'll like this." Keagan brought her hands around to touch Rudy's breasts through her shirt. The sensation of what lay beneath her shirt and bra was arousing to Keagan as she melded her body into Rudy's and kissed her neck.

After a brief look of confusion, Rudy gave into the sensations their fully clothed activity created. She stared into Keagan's eyes, as their bodies moved together. She felt hands move to grasp the backs of her legs tightly, as they both felt their arousal heighten. Keagan's lips moved back to meet hers once again and their tongues met hotly. Only a few moments later they were both on the edge and almost came together, Rudy beating out Keagan by a few seconds. Panting and still aroused they collapsed together on the floor. Keagan spoke first.

"You're amazing." She held Rudy close, enjoying the feeling of their entwined bodies.

Still gasping, Rudy spoke with effort. "That was incredible. We didn't even strip. I never knew it could be done that way."

"There are lots of ways to do it." Keagan grinned.

Rudy turned her head up to gaze into azure eyes. "Feel like showing me?"

"Yes." Remembering that they had more studying to do, Keagan began to feel guilty, but that didn't stop her lips from seeking Rudy's again. As the kiss deepened and their mutual arousal returned, Keagan reached behind her lover and grabbed her butt playfully. The grab soon turned into a tickle. Rudy laughed. "Ticklish? There?"

Rudy laughed again. "It's even worse when my jeans are off."

"Naturally. I guess we'll have to take them off then."

After another heated kiss, they parted, Rudy trying in vain to retain her self-control. "We should study some more, you know."

Keagan kissed Rudy's neck, slowly, torturously. "Study your body? I'm for that." She moved her hands around to the button-fly of Rudy's jeans, giving a mock growl. "These take forever to unbutton."

"It's better that way." Rudy panted. "It heightens the anticipation."

Keagan undid one button. She ran her hands across Rudy's back and kissed her again.

"Ah, oh, that was good, but we should finish studying first or we might not get to it."

"You don't think?" Keagan nuzzled Rudy's neck and breathed in her scent with pleasure. Her hair smelled fresh. "What shampoo do you use?"

Rudy was slowly grinding herself into Keagan. "What?" She couldn't focus on thinking.

Keagan undid two more buttons. "Is it Pert? It kind of smells like that, but it's different." She slipped her hand inside Rudy's jeans and massaged the area above her underwear, enjoying the sound of her moans.

"Uh, huh. Yeah." Rudy's only thought centered on her desire for Keagan to rip her clothes off.

"It smells great." Keagan kissed Rudy on the cheek before moving her kisses lower and fulfilling Rudy's unvoiced desire.

****

Some time later, Keagan was awakened by the sound of a telephone. She opened her eyes with annoyance and noticed that it was dark outside. Rudy rested half on top of her and Rudy was lying at the foot of the bed purring softly. The phone rang twice, and the message clicked on. Not taking notice of it, she preferred to stare at her beautiful, slumbering lover. "Good Evening. You have reached Keagan's Den of Lesbian—"

"Oh, shit!" She was up like a shot, trying to gently but quickly ease Rudy off of her and onto the bed, while barreling into the kitchen. Not bothering to grab her robe, she ducked down as she approached the machine, the blinds from her window being open. "Desire. If you are anyone but Rudy—"

The whole commotion woke Rudy up. "What? What is it?"

"The message!" Keagan bellowed from the kitchen. "I forgot to change it back!" Reaching the machine in good time, she pressed the on/off button. The message continued to play anyway. "Please leave a message and I'll get back to you. If you are Rudy, don't leave a message. Just hang up—" Desperately, she pressed the on/off button a second time. It continued to play. "And come over immediately. The den requires your presence. Ciao." Finally remembering that she was supposed to press the stop, not the on/off button, she glared with irritation at the machine and listened as it beeped. She sighed with relief upon hearing Brad's voice. "Hi, girlfriend. I'm at the bar. Just thought I'd check on your progress. Nice message. <snicker> Not really my style at all, but I'm sure your babe will appreciate it. Gotta go. And please remember to change that. I could have been your mother, Keagan!" After an overly dramatic sigh, he hung up. She could hear laughing coming from her bedroom.

"No laughing! It's not funny!" She pressed the record key. "Call back later. I'm busy. Thanks. Bye." Feeling a chill coming on, she bolted back into the bedroom and under the covers.

Rudy was still laughing. "It's very funny. That's what you get for being so clever."

Keagan looked over at her quite naked companion and graced her with a mischievous smile. "And this is what you get for laughing." With no further warning, Keagan pounced on Rudy and tickled her without mercy. As Rudy's laughter subsided, her tickling turned to slow caresses. Rudy ran her fingers through Keagan's long, dark hair and pulled her head down to lay on her chest. They stayed like that for a few seconds until Keagan's arms tightened around Rudy for a small hug. "Did I tell you I have to work at four in the morning?"

"That's inhuman. You would have to get up at—"

"Three in the morning." Keagan laughed.

"Why so early?"

"Our freight processing...isn't."

"Do you enjoy it at all?"

Keagan moved out of her arms and leaned up against the pillow. It was past ten o'clock, and if she had any intention of being awake the next day, she should have been in bed at seven sleeping. Normally, she wouldn't consider not going in. The first time she called off in a couple of years had been the Monday before. However, the place she was in at the moment was so comfortable that she began to consider it. Rudy made her feel safe and she wasn't ready to leave that safety yet. "I used to convince myself that merchandising was somehow artistic. I used to enjoy it a lot, but after awhile, I realized that everything I created was soon torn apart. There's no immortality in the retail world." She chuckled lightly.

"Is that what you want? Immortality?"

"No. I just want somehow to know that everything inside of me isn't worthless." Keagan shrugged and wondered what had caused her to voice such thoughts.

"Look at me." She turned her gaze back to Rudy. "I'm sure someday everyone will know that, but until then, would you settle for me?"

"That wouldn't be settling." Rudy smiled gently. She marveled at how time and again, Keagan revealed so much through saying so little. She fell back into Keagan's arms, then, but instead of sleeping they talked.

* * * * * * * * *

Keagan forced herself to get up and go to work. She and Rudy had talked for almost an hour the night before and they didn't get to sleep until half past eleven. She was exhausted in the morning, but didn't regret her evening with Rudy, who was fulfilling many roles for Keagan, the least of which was lover. Although the lover part was incredible, the role of friend was equally important. Being lovers would have been devoid of substance without their growing friendship. Rudy also, through her actions, functioned as a teacher. She taught Keagan that expressing emotions didn't always have to hurt. It was an unconscious revelation to Keagan who slowly internalized the idea.

At around noon that day, Keagan was called to the manager's office. Wondering what they wanted, she made her way back to find both Madeline Slone and the store manager, Nelson Johnson in attendance. *Nelson Johnson. What kind of parents would name their kid that? It's almost as bad as naming your kid William Williams or Jacqueline Jackson or David Davidson or...*

"Um, Keagan, what were you doing?" That annoying buzzing sound dragged Keagan right out of her thoughts. Shaking her head, she realized it only *resembled* a buzzing sound. It was just Slone. "Packing the defects on a skid." *Like you told me to do an hour ago. What did you think I was doing?*

"I need you to record about 10 adcasters by the time you leave. Here's a list of the items and the sales." Nelson handed over the list to Keagan as he spoke. Adcasters were short, brief advertisements that played on the store's PA system. When Nelson said "record" what he really meant was that she needed to write and record ten of them. This would take time and she hadn't finished skidding the defects yet. Staying over was out of the question because she had some last minute studying to do for British literature, and a nap to squeeze in as well. She had been doing the adcasters for years, and it was always the same. Thirty minutes left of her shift and they'd ask her to do them.

"I'll need more than a half an hour to do these."

"You can stay over. We need these done," said Slone. Her beady eyes bore into Keagan's, who never could figure out the color of them. It almost seemed to Keagan that each eye was a different color. A scary thought and one that she quickly abandoned.

Keagan grinned. Obviously, being an English major meant that she was the only possible candidate to do the adcasters. Probably the only literate one. The only one who could write, the only one who could speak. *Should have told them I was an engineering major. Nah. They'd just ask me to fix the baler when it breaks!*

"I can't. I have an ex—"

"I'll let you out early on Friday. Or you can come in later. Becker's on my case because we don't have any ads playing." Becker, the district manager, was an anal retentive, pain in the ass. Keagan sighed. Becker couldn't help it. Every district manager she had ever worked with had no common sense and lived to make everyone's job more difficult. Taking pity on her boss, she finally replied, "Sure. The defects—"

"Um—" When Slone said "um" it carried with it a connotation of annoyance, superiority and tyrannical intentions. She was annoyed at life to begin with, wanted to flaunt her self-created superiority, and enjoyed acting the tyrant. So, her "um" wasn't stumbled over in the normal way. It wasn't used to mask her inability to form thoughts into words (although she did have this problem as well).

She actually made it into a word. A word that meant, *You are lowly hourly employee scum and I will see you one day scrubbing the stockroom floor with a toothbrush!* "Um," she repeated for emphasis, "you can finish those Friday."

"Okey-dokey." Upon saying that, Keagan had a fleeting thought of how irrational her behavior often was at work. When she heard herself saying things like, "okey-dokey" it only reminded her.

As Nelson and Slone left the office, Keagan sat down at the desk and perused the list of items. A 12-pack of toilet paper, grape jelly *(Now what does that remind me of?)*, personal massagers *(Just a cover for vibrators)*, foam cups *(How unenvironmentally conscious!)*, boy/girl diapers *(Does that mean they're for hermaphroditic children? Hmm, I may have to inquire about that one.)* Non-wet roll-on deodorant *(I can't believe it actually says 'non-wet'!')*, condoms *(In the adcaster? They asked for it!)*, douches *(This is like a dream come true!)*, ladies bras *(Ooh, baby! I'll have fun with this one!)*, and men's bikini briefs. Keagan smiled with glee. The list was a veritable fountain of lewd material just waiting to be exploited. She picked up her pen. *I know. I can tie them all into a common theme.* Smiling again, her eyes took on an evil glint, as she wrote.

Keagan decided that if she was going to tie all the ads into a theme, she could do it by using a common character. One the shoppers would identify with. Being that the Gigantic "mascot" was a hare *(It looks like a hare to me and it's pictured next to the official store logo)*, she called the character, O'Hare. Now, the customers could join O'Hare as O'Hare (she let the character remain genderless, to add more mystique*)* shopped the store.

An hour and a half later, having completed writing and recording the adcasters, Keagan found herself back in the manager's office after the first ad played. She had almost made it out the door when she heard the page. Returning to the office, she saw Nelson looking perplexed, and Slone seething with rage (kind of like she usually looked but with a red face). "Who is this...*O'Hare*?" Slone asked, suspicion lacing her voice.

Keagan took one breath and began slowly. "O'Hare is a character I created for fun to tell the shoppers about the items. I felt that if I introduced myself by a name, the shoppers would be more likely to listen, first of all, and, secondly, if they liked me, maybe they would take my advice about buying the items. See?"

Nelson squinted his eyes. "So...*you* are O'Hare?" He couldn't hide the confusion on his face. Not that he was even trying. Slone continued to stare at Keagan with contempt.

"No. I'm not O'Hare. O'Hare is a character I created." *So far so good, Keagan.*

"But in the ad, you say, 'Take it from me, O'Hare.'"

Keagan tried to hide her sigh of frustration. "Right. I just portray O'Hare, so I would say that. Does that make sense?"

"Nobody's going to know who he is anyway!" Slone interjected with ire in her voice.

At least she understands the character part. "Um, no. O'Hare isn't gender specific. O'Hare is simply...O'Hare."

"What does that mean? Do you know that people are coming up to me and asking who he is? I'm sick of their prying questions." If it were possible, Slone's face would have turned redder.

"After only one announcement?"

"Yes!"

"That's great! See, that's my whole point. People were listening. They were listening enough to ask you."

"Keagan, I understand that part." Nelson, if not the brightest man, could usually be reasoned with. If things were explained to him at least twice he almost always understood. "It's this drag queen announcement." He indicated Keagan's adcaster notebook that she left lying on the desk, in her haste to leave. "We read your announcements and some of them I'm not sure about." As if on cue, that very announcement began to play: *"Hi, shoppers, it's just me, O'Hare again, with more great deals! Check out our ladies department this week where we've got a special on bras. That's right! This week only you can get an UltraFlex sportsbra with extra lace for only $1.99! So pick a few up today for the man, woman, or drag queen in your life while they last! As always, thanks for shopping Gigantic and remember you'll only get the truth from me...O'Hare!"*

"Um, that is barbaric!" *Barbaric?* "Men don't wear bras! It's, it's...OH!"

"Were I not to include men and drag queens, it would be excluding a portion of our customer base."

"I think you should turn that one off, though." Nelson tried to look apologetic.

"Sure."

"I thought drag queens were men," said Nelson.

"They are, but they also have egos. I wanted to cater to that by naming them."

Filled with rage, not unlike her usual state, Slone confronted Keagan. "You have an answer for everything, don't you?"

Keagan projected her best smug look. "Just about everything, yes." *Would you rather have an imbecile for an employee,* she added silently.

"Um, um...Keagan I want you to turn off the massager one, too."

"Aww, that was my favorite." Keagan allowed herself to grin then. As if on cue, the announcement began to play: *"O'Hare, here. Ohhh, I just hate the feeling of sore muscles at the end of the day. And all that built up tension that simply can't be eliminated in the workplace. That probing, deep-seated feeling that no amount of willpower can defeat. That all encompassing need for utter physical bliss that the demands of a post-college, entry level accounting job tend to create...* <sigh> *So you know what I did? I went to Gigantic and purchased a personal massager! Today for only $3.99 you can get the travel size and for only $7.99 the mega size! Get 'em while we got 'em and feel your tension drift away! Take it from me...O'Hare!"*

Nelson snickered. Slone slapped him on the arm. "Stop that! That announcement is obscene."

"Only from a certain point of view," said Keagan. "I realize that the target audience may be a bit narrow, but—"

"That's very creative, but I'm afraid you'll have to take that one off, too." Nelson shook his head trying to convey sympathy. He was the type that hated to disappoint anyone.

"Sure." Keagan stood patiently, waiting for them to continue. How much more of her work would they tear apart? "But I must state in my defense, such as it is, that my announcements promote the item, and also get people's attention. You can't deny that."

"No, it's just the way you do it—"

"They're awful! Especially the one about the condoms." Slone looked aghast.

Funny, I thought she'd relate to that one. As if on cue, the announcement began. Keagan began to worry about the perfect timing. It was eerie. Almost unreal. *"Hi, it's me O'Hare again. Picture this: You're out on a date and things turn interesting. It begins to rain, but you don't have any protection. A little wetness won't bother you, but you don't want to get drenched, right? Of course not. Make sure you're always covered by shopping Gigantic.*

This week only we have a special on condoms! Only $2.99 a pack! And remember, it's not cool to get caught in the rain! Take it from me...O'Hare! As always, thanks for shopping Gigantic!"

"I know," Keagan began. "A little heavy on the metaphor. I could kill the metaphor if you like." She spoke matter-of-factly as if they were in a negotiation.

"Kill them all!" Madeline Slone's screech could be heard as far as the breakroom, which was located a considerable distance from the manager's office. Keagan had to fight to keep from shivering at her brutal tone. It was all quite scary. Time to go home for the day.

* * * * * * * * * *

After she got home, Keagan took a nap and by the time she awoke there was a message on her machine. It was Rudy asking if she was in the mood for Chinese. A starving Keagan had agreed enthusiastically. They had eaten their dinner, chatted about the day, and then retired to the living room as Keagan related each and every one of her announcements to Rudy except one.

After Keagan had stretched one too many times trying to ease her sore muscles, Rudy took over. "Turn around."

"Why?"

Rudy grinned at her clueless lover. "Better yet, take your sweater off and turn around. I'm going to give you a shoulder massage." Keagan admitted to herself that it would feel great and did what Rudy asked. Feeling the small but adept fingers probing into her aching flesh was like heaven. She moaned with pleasure.

"That feels great. Thank you."

"I live to bring you pleasure." Rudy laughed. "What about the jelly one? You didn't tell me that one."

Keagan had a difficult time thinking due to the pleasure she was feeling. "I'll try. Let's see." She thought a moment and then switched into O'Hare mode. "Hi there, shoppers. It's me, O'Hare again and have I got a deal for you! Do you feel like enhancing your sexual pleasure? Want to hear your lover moan while reaching unknown heights of ecstasy? We've got just the thing here at Gigantic! This week only, pick up a jar of Gigantic brand grape jelly! It's not only great with peanut butter! Take it from me...O'Hare!"

Rudy laughed and swatted Keagan playfully. "You did not say that! You're awful."

"I most certainly did." Keagan feigned indifference. "That's the one that almost got me fired."

"As if. Not even *you* would allow an announcement like that to play."

"That's what you think."

Rudy stopped her massage as Keagan turned around to face her. "Admit it now, oh great guru of advertisements. You're in a real vulnerable place here, you know." It was true. She was topless and could very easily be tickled senselessly.

"Nope. Never." Keagan smiled evilly as Rudy tickled her stomach and pushed her back. Then she jumped on top of Keagan and straddled her stomach while continuing the torture.

"I think you're really enjoying this. You aren't even fighting this time."

"Why wouldn't I enjoy your sweet hands all over my naked torso?" The low tone of Keagan's words caused Rudy to shiver involuntarily. Their eyes met and locked as Rudy moved her hands to the sides of Keagan's face.

"All you had to do was ask." Their lips met softly as Rudy settled her body on top of Keagan's. She felt strong arms settle around her as their tongues moved together slowly, passionately.

The sound of the phone ringing was the only thing that brought them out of their exploration. They parted and Keagan listened as the answering machine clicked on. "Call back later. I'm busy. Thanks. Bye."

"I see you also forgot to change your flippant message." Rudy laid her head on Keagan's chest and chuckled.

"It's still appropriate. Seems I'm always busy when you're here lately." She tightened her arms around Rudy and sighed as the machine finally beeped. It was Gerry. "Okay, you old grump. Sorry you're busy. <laughter> If you and your little girlfriend want to come by tomorrow, please do. I really want to meet her. Hope to see you tomorrow, sweetie. Bye."

Keagan averted her eyes, embarrassed. "So, are we going, sweetie?" Rudy's eyes gleamed with mischief.

"Oh, no. Not two of you." Keagan groaned.

"Well, you get to call me La Roux."

"That's a nickname!"

"Pet name!"

"Is not!"

"Is too!"

"Okay," said Keagan. "I give up." She kissed Rudy.

"Good." Rudy smiled. "Are we going?"

"If you want to."

"I told you I would like to meet your grandma."

Keagan nuzzled her neck. "My mom might be there, too."

Rudy moved her neck to give Keagan better access. "Uh, oh. Is this where you take me home to meet your family?" Keagan planted kisses up and down her neck.

"Sure."

Rudy sighed with pleasure as Keagan added to her actions by pulling her closer and massaging her back. "Your grandma seems like such a nice lady."

"She is." As Keagan kissed Rudy again she thought

fleetingly of the fact that Gerry was a nice woman, but only when she was sober. *Let's hope she's that way tomorrow.*

As the kiss ended, Rudy ran her fingers through Keagan's hair and got a devious look on her face. "So, Keagan, why did your grandma call me your girlfriend, hmm?"

"Rudy?"

"Hmm?"

Keagan's answer was to kiss her again quite thoroughly, but Rudy broke away with effort.

"Won't work." Rudy laughed. "But that's okay. I'll let you off the hook like I always do."

"You make me sound like a fish."

"Nope. A fish would be easier to reel in."

"Ooh! Touché! You are too clever for me, darling." *God, did I just say that? How did that slip out? I sound like a drag queen!*

"What did you just call me?" Rudy moved her hands to Keagan's hips.

"Um...darling? But it was my drag queen impression."

Rudy playfully punched her arm. "You are *so* unromantic."

"Then why are you with me?"

Because I'm so in love with you I can hardly breathe when you're near me. "I like unromantic women. I like the challenge."

"Hmm." Keagan sensed that wasn't necessarily Rudy's first choice for an answer. As she felt warm hands begin to wander her body she wondered if she could ever give Rudy what she needed. Her responding heartfelt kiss to Rudy attempted to convey everything her words couldn't.

Chapter
9

Keagan opened her eyes drowsily; her attempt to stretch instantly thwarted by Rudy's very solid, warm, and welcoming presence lying almost on top of her. Instead of stretching, she tightened her arms around the still slumbering woman, breathing in the scent of her.

As her mind gradually came into focus, she could hear something in her head. Not that it was any surprise to her. She always heard so many things in her mind at so many different times and in so many different ways, that as a child she had suspected schizophrenia as the cause. Some minor research had led her to the conclusion that she was simply weird, not schizophrenic. Adulthood had labeled her mental musings as imagination but this time it was the jitters she got before an exam and it was manifesting itself by running the opening lines to "Goblin Market" over and over again in her head. Hoping to shut off the poem brandishing mechanism in her head, she recited aloud: "*Morning and evening, maids heard the goblins cry: Come buy our orchard fruits, come buy, come buy: apples and quinces, lemons and oranges, plump unpecked cherries,*

melons and raspberries, bloom-down-cheeked peaches."
She paused. "Bloom-down-cheeked. I love that." Glancing over at the clock, she frowned briefly and continued her recitation. *"Swart-headed mulberries, wild free-born cranberries, crab-apples, dewberries, pine-apples, blackberries—"*

"Is it time for breakfast?" a very sleepy voice asked. All that was registering at that moment was the sound of various fruits being recited. It made her hungry.

Keagan glanced over at the green eyes, now fully open. She leaned over, her lips finding a neck. "Uh huh. This is breakfast." She explored the soft area underneath Rudy's chin with small but lingering kisses, ending her journey by licking at the pulse point at the bottom of her neck.

"Uh. That's *your* breakfast. Where's mine?" Rudy felt her body's response to Keagan and shivered. It was a very pleasant way to wake up.

"Right here." Keagan cupped Rudy's face in her hands and kissed her thoroughly. When they parted, Rudy moved over to completely lie on top of Keagan. They stared at each other with knowing smiles on their faces. Rudy got a very thoughtful look on her face, as if she was seriously considering something. "You know, I must say that was the best sex I ever had last night."

Keagan snorted. "It's the *only* sex you ever had."

"Not with *you*." Rudy moved her hands down to Keagan's stomach as if threatening to tickle her.

Keagan quickly grabbed both of her hands and held them, a devilish grin on her face. "So what are you doing? *Rating* it each time? Sheesh!"

"No, but it's definitely improving." She deadpanned the remark.

"Improving?" Keagan released Rudy's hands and tickled her. Soon, Rudy was on her back and pleading for mercy. As spasms of laughter overtook her lover, Keagan whispered into her ear. "Like it was *so* bad at first. I feel so sorry for you."

"You should." Rudy knew that remark was inviting even more trouble than she had already started, but didn't care.

"I would really love to continue this conversation but I think we're gonna have to get going. Seeing as that it's already a quarter after seven." Keagan knew that if she didn't stop tickling Rudy, they would be even later than they were already going to be.

"7:15?" Rudy instantly jumped out of bed and glanced at the clock in horror. "That's means we only have thirty minutes to get to the exam." She grabbed her clothes and rushed into the bathroom.

Keagan remained characteristically calm. Being late for an exam wasn't the worst thing in the world, right? Shrugging, she rose and stretched languorously. "I suppose this means we'll have to skip the shower?" she called after Rudy, not really expecting her lover to hear or respond. "I *hate* skipping showers."

* * * * * * * * *

"I thought you set the alarm for six." Keagan's car sped toward the university. She was, trying to purge her mind of poetry by listening to the Rolling Stones. She hated walking into an exam with poetry running through her mind haphazardly and that's what often happened. So she began a ritual that involved singing songs in the car on the way to class. That way her stress level subsided and her brain felt clearer. "*Is there nothing I can say, nothing I can do to change your mind, I'm so in love with you—*"

"Keagan?" Rudy moved her hand in front of her lover's face with annoyance.

"Hmm?"

"Didn't you set the alarm?"

"*I'll be your savior, steadfast and true, I'll come to your emotional rescue, I'll come to your emotional rescue—*"

"Will you quit singing that song and answer me?"

Keagan sobered and turned down the volume. "Yes. I set the alarm for six. There are a few possibilities as to what happened, but we'll only be ten minutes late, fifteen at the most anyway."

Keagan's lack of concern over their impending tardiness calmed Rudy considerably. "I want to know what the possibilities are." She requested it more because she liked to hear Keagan talk and reason out things than because she really cared.

"You would." Keagan allowed herself a brief glance at Rudy's now twinkling green eyes. "Anything for you. Here we go. Possibility one: the alarm went off, but we were really tired and turned it off quickly and fell back into a deep, winter slumber. Possibility two: the alarm clock is crap and malfunctioned. Possibility three: you and I were in the throes of such a deeply passionate embrace that we neither heard nor cared about the alarm, the exam, or getting out of bed at all."

Rudy laughed and joined in. "Possibility number four: I was too busy giving you that big love bite on your neck to notice and you were too busy enjoying it to hear."

Keagan pulled into the parking lot. "Oh, no. Did you get a chance to—?"

Rudy flashed her lover a cocky smile and displayed the left side of her neck, which was no longer blemished by the hickey that Keagan knew was there. "Liquid makeup. And of course I got a chance to put it on. You think I want to go around looking like a cheap hussy?"

In spite of the embarrassment Keagan knew she would

soon be subjected to, she couldn't help but laugh. "Oh. You mean looking like *I* look, right?"

"You really need to tell that girlfriend, uh, that woman of yours to control herself better."

"I would, but she has no control. She's so into me she can't help herself. I can hardly blame the poor wench. I am pretty irresistible." Snickering, Keagan pulled into a parking spot and turned the car off.

"Poor wench? I'll show you who's a poor wench," said Rudy, placing her hand possessively on the side of Keagan's neck and smoothly guiding her lover's lips to her own. Her kiss was teasing, but long and deep letting Keagan know that she wasn't the only one that was irresistible.

Keagan took several deep breaths, trying to regain the composure that Rudy's kiss had stolen. "First you're complaining about being late, now you're making us even later." Keagan's tone was chastising, but her sexy grin told Rudy she was joking.

"Don't press your luck, you veritable fountain of sarcasm, you." Rudy's eyes took on a dangerous glint as she grabbed her backpack.

"Yes, but that sarcasm's good for something." Keagan got out of the car and watched with amusement as Rudy scrambled quickly over the driver's seat. She locked the door and they walked together fast.

"Oh and what's that?" Rudy sprinted ahead.

"It got me one hell of a kiss," came the whispered reply from Keagan, who had easily caught up with Rudy. She smirked in response and Keagan winked at her as they took off running toward Denney hall, ignoring the stares they were getting.

****

"I hate being late," Rudy grumbled as they finally

entered the building. The halls were cleared of students, which confirmed their tardiness. Keagan, walking along calmly, had to jog to catch up with Rudy who was sprinting down the hall.

"It's not like the classroom's going anywhere."

Ignoring Keagan's lackadaisical attitude, Rudy nonetheless did not spare her lover a scathing glare as they finally reached the room. As they entered the quieted classroom, Keagan mockingly shook as if out of fear and saw this as a prime opportunity to tease Rudy. "*I loafe and invite my soul,*" she whispered. "*I lean and loaf at my ease observing a spear of summer grass.*"

"Shhh."

"Apparently, Ms. Donovan, you've been loafing *too* much." Keagan's devious smile ended upon being faced with her nemesis, Dr. V.M. Addison. Dr. Addison picked up two exams, handing one to Rudy and then to Keagan. Keagan smiled at the professor, trying in futility to charm her into lenience. "Good morning, Dr. Addison." With an even brighter smile this time, she took the offered exam.

Dr. Addison smirked slightly and Keagan winced as the professor's eyes obviously spotted something. Something large and purplish-blue on Keagan's neck. "Have too much fun last night, Ms. Donovan?" To the professor's credit, she whispered her teasing comment low enough so that no one else heard. This fact, however, didn't stop the blush that immediately appeared on Rudy's face. The professor had seen them at the party after all.

"Oh, that." Keagan rolled her eyes with nonchalance. "Cat bit me."

Dr. Addison leaned closer to the two women, her eyes sparkling impishly. "Funny how a mere cat bite makes your friend blush so."

As a thoroughly embarrassed Rudy took off in pursuit of a seat, Keagan tried hard to contain the laughter welling up inside of her. Smiling to herself, she sat down deciding that appearing to be a cheap hussy was fun after all.

* * * * * * * * * *

Later that afternoon, Keagan, in spite of her great anxiety, took Rudy to meet her family. She wisely chose to stop at home and dig out the one turtleneck sweater she owned. She hated turtlenecks but sometimes they came in handy. It just wouldn't do to be sporting a hickey in front of one's relatives.

As they pulled in the driveway, Keagan found herself shaking. She had taken a couple of aspirin for the nausea but it wasn't having any affect. Overall, she felt quite ill.

As they headed to the front door Rudy spoke. "I'm actually kind of nervous."

"Why?"

"What if they don't like me?"

"I guess I'll have to dump you and date somebody new, then." Keagan glanced at Rudy challengingly.

Rudy punched her on the arm. "Good luck finding somebody to put up with you."

"I would definitely need it." Before Rudy had a chance to react to Keagan's sober response, her lover had stepped forward and opened the door, which was unlocked. *The faster we get this over with, the better.* Peeking her head in, Keagan was greeted by an enthusiastic Rosey, who jumped off the couch where she was sitting next to Gerry and bolted over. "Hi, Grandma."

"Hi, sweetie."

Keagan decided to do the introductions first, before assessing the situation. "This is Rudy." As Rudy began to step forward to shake Gerry's hand, Rosey positioned herself right in front of her and jumped up in a friendly, playful way. Rudy laughed and petted the animal's soft head.

The dog soon settled down having gotten some attention.

"Meet Rosey, my other sweetie. Rosey, get down now! You're not making a good first impression."

Rudy smiled at Gerry and politely reached forward after placating the dog. She shook Gerry's hand. "It's very nice to meet you, Mrs. Rafferty."

Keagan's eyes darted to the coffee table in front of Gerry. Sure enough, a glass of liquor was sitting on the table and this time it wasn't vodka, it was whiskey. "Please, please call me Gerry. Mrs. Rafferty was my mother-in-law and God knows I don't need any reminders of that witch!"

Rudy chuckled. "Okay."

To further test the situation, Keagan approached her grandmother and gave her a kiss on the cheek. "Nice to see you, Grandma." Her breath reeked of whiskey. This hadn't been her first drink. *You can't even stay sober to meet my girlfriend.* "We can't stay very long," she announced as she and Rudy took a seat on the loveseat across from Gerry. At Rudy's look of confusion, she added, "We've got an exam to study for."

Rudy wondered why Keagan lied, but felt it best not to ask. There was a palpable tension in the air and although she didn't know what had started it, she had no desire to add to it.

"You? Study? I didn't think you did. Isn't that why you've been in school so long?" Gerry chuckled as if it was a joke, but Keagan clearly didn't take it as one.

"Ha. Ha." Inside, Keagan was seething. She was used to attacks that were masked as jokes and tired of them as well.

Rudy, for her part, felt her protective instincts kicking in. She saw through the veneer of humor and then spotted the whiskey. "Keagan's actually a more diligent student than I am. I tend to want to goof off a lot." She smiled at the elderly woman, in an attempt to make the conversation lighter and shift the focus from Keagan.

"You must be a lousy student then, if she beats out you!" Gerry exploded into hysterics and Keagan laughed lightly. Rudy wondered why she accepted this kind of abuse.

"I've been helping Keagan study grammar. She's picked it up very quickly. She's doing a great job." Rudy looked at Keagan as she said this and thought she saw appreciation in her blue eyes.

"Grammar? What's there to study with that? Grammar's easy!"

Oh, no. Now she's done it. Keagan knew instantly that her lover was going to come up with one hell of an answer to that one.

Rudy took a deep breath and began. "Well, first a mastering of the ten sentence patterns is necessary, followed by an understanding of modal auxiliaries which are extremely important to understand in order to grasp the verb-expansion rule. After that, it's necessary to completely master expanded determiners, expletives, nonrestrictive modifiers, relative clauses and pronouns, and *do* transformations. And none of that even begins to take into account phonology, which in my opinion should be a required study along with grammar. Studying things like alveolar stops, labio-dental fricatives and affricates. Yes, Keagan's doing quite well with it all." Rudy smiled sweetly and secretly enjoyed the look of utter confusion on Gerry's face. Keagan remained silent, but Rudy thought she heard a small groan coming from her.

"My, my, it appears you've picked a brain Keagan. Congratulations. Maybe she can support you when you insist on sitting at home and writing." Gerry laughed and Keagan followed suit.

"I'm not a brain, Mrs. Rafferty. I'm just someone who

really enjoys the study of English grammar. And as for supporting Keagan, I would be happy to do it if it were financially possible. I want her to do what she loves to do." Keagan cast a startled glance at Rudy and met the sincere green eyes looking back.

"I said you could call me Gerry, dear."

"Yes, I know." Rudy knew her mouth was probably getting her into big trouble, but the alternative was to sit passively and allow the woman she loved to be attacked by her own family member.

As if on cue to break the uncomfortable silence, Joan came in the back door. Keagan tensed involuntarily, knowing what was coming next and dreading the fact that Rudy had to be there to see it. In a few seconds Joan entered the living room holding a bottle of Seagram's in her hand.

"Hi, Mom. I'd like you to meet...my friend, Rudy." Ignoring the introduction and Rudy altogether, Joan focused on Keagan alone. It was obvious what she was thinking.

Her mother had such a dour look, that Keagan felt an instinctual need to lighten things up. "Mom? You haven't started drinking have you?" Keagan's brow furrowed to simulate mock suspicion. Gerry and Keagan both laughed. Rudy remained silent, wanting to stay out of the impending family argument.

"Shut up, Keagan. You're not cute anymore. I can't believe you would bring this poison into my house."

Keagan instantly sobered. "Then don't believe it."

"What am I supposed to think? You're sitting here, she's drinking that, and there's a bottle in my kitchen. I know how to put two and two together."

"Apparently you do. Let's go, Rudy." Standing up, she headed for the door, expecting Rudy to follow, but she remained standing in front of the couch. *Here's the part where I break my resolution to stay out of things.*

"Not going to defend yourself, huh?"

"No. Let's go."

In the meantime, Gerry and Joan had begun a heated argument about the whiskey. As usual, Gerry was defending her right to drink however much she wanted and Joan was telling her to stop or get out. They both completely ignored the presence of Keagan and Rudy.

"Rudy, let's go." Keagan knew the only way to stop the pain in her stomach was to leave. What was Rudy waiting for?

"Um, excuse me!" Rudy pitched her voice a bit higher than usual to get Joan's and Gerry's attention. They went silent for a second and looked at her, Gerry angry with her for interrupting and Joan wondering who she was.

"Just to set the record straight, Keagan didn't bring the whiskey. I think it's really unfair of you to treat her this way. Nice meeting you both." Then she turned to join Keagan who was waiting impatiently at the door, but not before one final bellow from Joan.

"Don't tell me about my daughter. I think I know her a little bit better than you do. Who are you anyway? Her latest fling or another one-night-stand that she uses to come up with plot ideas for her writing? Hmm?"

"With all due respect, ma'am, if you had allowed yourself to be introduced to me, you would have seen that I'm someone who cares about your daughter very much. And you wouldn't have had to ask that question." Another glare was all she got from Joan who turned from her and began arguing with Gerry again.

****

When they returned to the car, Keagan was the first to speak. "So what did you think? They're warm, friendly, and outgoing. Just like me, huh?" Keagan started the engine and they began the short trek back from German Village.

"I don't think they're anything like you."

Keagan forced herself to laugh through her hurt. "I'm really sorry they treated you so rudely. It was a bad idea to take you over there."

Rudy put a reassuring hand on Keagan's thigh. The blue eyes met hers. "Well, since taking me over there didn't work, how about taking me somewhere else? Like my bedroom."

Keagan laughed. "You endless flirt."

"No. I'm not flirting. I'm serious. I want to hold you right now."

"I want that, too." Keagan was touched by the concern showing in Rudy's eyes. It almost made her forget about the latest family incident as the tension in her stomach dissipated. Taking Rudy's hand, she brought it to her lips, placing a kiss upon it.

****

When they got back to Rudy's house, Courtney was cooking for her boyfriend, Jake. She invited them to dinner and to Rudy's surprise, her lover agreed. They retreated to Rudy's bedroom when Courtney said dinner wouldn't be ready for another half-hour.

"You must really be hungry," Rudy teased. She was lying with her back against the headboard of her bed, reclining into the pillows. Keagan's head lay against her chest, Rudy's arms protectively around her. She moved her hand to Keagan's dark hair and gently stroked it, loving the touch and feel of the soft, beautiful strands.

Keagan's breathing was even and relaxed, at last returned to normal from the earlier altercation. She listened contentedly to Rudy's steady heartbeat. "Why?"

"Because you agreed to dinner with Courtney who you don't know that well and Jake, who you don't know at all."

"Well," Keagan placed her hand on Rudy's thigh and stroked it gently, "the way I see it, I know you and you know them, so I think I'll make it through."

"I think you will, too." Rudy smiled and gave Keagan a small, reassuring hug. Her feelings felt raw and exposed holding her lover like this. She longed to tell her how she felt but didn't think it would be a good time. Keagan was too vulnerable at the moment and telling her how much she loved her would only make her more so.

"You know what will happen now?" Keagan considered raising her head to look into the green eyes, but decided it would be easier to discuss these things in her current position.

"What?"

"Probably tomorrow I'll get a message on my machine from Grandma saying she's sorry Joan ruined our visit, and would we please come back and to give her a call. And then I'll get a message from Joan saying she's sorry Gerry ruined our visit and for the things she said to you about me, that she really does want to meet you and she really doesn't have a problem with me being gay and to please give her a call. It's always the same thing. They think an apology will heal it every time they hurt me." Keagan's breathing began to catch and she tried to keep from crying.

Rudy tightened her arms around Keagan, feeling contempt for a family that would so heartlessly dole out such emotional abuse. Her feelings of ire lessened when she considered the seriousness of the illness that wasn't being dealt with in Keagan's family. She felt compassion for them, even while they hurt Keagan. "Honey, if you want to cry, go ahead. You might feel better."

"It makes me feel ashamed to cry." There was no way she could look at Rudy now.

"You've never cried with *me* around." She lovingly stroked Keagan's hair and moved her hand down to her cheek where she felt a single tear fall.

Keagan felt her composure leaving her. "I can't risk my big, butch image by crying in front of you." She attempted to laugh, hoping to stifle down the impending tears that she felt coming.

Rudy's voice was soft and quiet. "Sure you can. You're not that butch anyway, so you won't be ruining any image. Right?"

Keagan was touched at Rudy's attempt to spare her embarrassment, even as wracking sobs overtook her. The last time she had cried it had been with her grandmother. Now she was crying *because* of her grandmother. She held tighter to Rudy as the tears fell down her face. She heard words of comfort as gentle fingers brushed away her teardrops. She clung to Rudy for several minutes until finally the tears stopped and her composure returned. Feeling Rudy's hands still in her hair, she wondered how she had lived without this woman's touch. She lifted up her head and gazed into green eyes full of compassion. "Funny," she began with a small smile, "I wasn't ashamed this time."

Moved by Keagan's display of vulnerability and her willingness to share it with her, Rudy brought her lips to Keagan's for a kiss. And then she pulled Keagan back into her arms where she held her in silence until it was time for dinner.

* * * * * * * * * *

Dinner was pleasant and Courtney turned out to be a nice host. After about twenty minutes of friendly conversation with both Rudy's roommate and Jake, Keagan felt more comfortable around them. When discovering that

Keagan wanted to be a writer, they responded positively and demanded an autographed copy of her first book. That got a genuine smile out of Keagan who immediately promised them both.

Eventually, the conversation turned to the subject of Valentine's Day, which was in five days. Keagan *hated* Valentine's Day. She found all the hoopla over love to be quite nauseating and hypocritical. People rushing to the greeting card shops at the last minute to purchase cards. And what for? If showing love meant buying a piece of thin cardboard folded in half with a cheesy verse written inside, then what was the point of love at all? She didn't understand it.

"So, what are you two doing for Valentine's Day?" Courtney had a romantic streak in her and she very much enjoyed the holiday and the gift giving it inspired. She also hoped that by asking, it would stir Jake's memory. Hearing the question, Jake groaned. Keagan followed suit.

"I suspect we have a couple of kindred spirits, here." Rudy flashed a small smile to Keagan who sat across from her at the table.

"I just don't see any point to Valentine's Day," said Keagan dispassionately.

"Hear, hear!" Jake liked Keagan more and more.

"And why not?"

"Are you sure you want to ask her that, Courtney? I'll just bet she'll come up with some long diatribe about how Valentine's Day is just a commercial holiday invented so greeting card shops can make tons of money off the hopeless romantic saps that feed into the disgustingly sweet drivel about finding your one, true love." Rudy gazed back to Keagan who was regarding her with amusement.

"Thanks, La Roux. I couldn't have said it better myself." With a pensive look on her face, she continued. "Well, of *course* I could have, but you did okay."

"Are you a Leo? That's some ego on display there."
Everybody laughed at Courtney's teasing banter. Keagan
didn't mind it. It made her feel more at ease.

"If you've got it, flaunt it I always say."

"Libra," said Rudy. Rudy recalled discussing their
birthdays the other day, which naturally lead to mentioning
their astrological signs. Neither Keagan nor Rudy knew
much beyond what sign they were, however. This wasn't
the case with Courtney.

"Libra. Uh, huh. I can see it."

"Oh, no. Here she goes," said Jake. He grinned good-
naturedly at his girlfriend and sat back preparing for
Courtney's in-depth analysis of all that was Keagan.

"Do tell more." Rudy grinned evilly at her lover, as
Keagan cringed. She hated parties, British Literature, Valentine's Day, and *Astrology*.

"Libras hate displays of intense emotionality and prefer detached, intellectual discussions of life."

"That's me." Keagan nodded her head smugly.

"And...Libras tend to use passive aggression instead
of confronting things openly. Like provoking others to act,
rather than acting themselves."

"Moi?"

"Yeah, *you*." Rudy directed an intense but teasing
gaze toward Keagan.

"Example?"

Courtney and Jake observed the banter between the
couple with amusement. They seemed very comfortable
with each other.

"Like last Saturday," Rudy began, immediately noticing the flustered look that appeared on Keagan's face. "We
ran into each other at the bar. We ended up actually having
this discussion in the bathroom..."

"Right. Good example. All my fault. I'm just pas-
sive-aggressive. I'll try to work on that." Keagan deliv-

ered her words quickly, hoping Rudy would abandon that train of thought. She wasn't going to mention them being in the stall together was she?

"The bathroom? How did you end up in there?" asked Jake.

"Oh, well, you see—" Rudy paused as she noted the look of unease on Keagan's face. Grinning broadly, she started to continue.

"Why does *anyone* go to a bathroom?" Keagan laughed uneasily.

Courtney and Jake looked confused.

"Actually, when you're in a bar, the bathroom is a great place to talk if you need quiet...and privacy." Rudy looked over at the now squirming Keagan and winked.

"Oh, I agree," piped in a totally oblivious Courtney. "Sometimes when I go out with my friends we escape to the bathroom to talk about guys and stuff. I know *just* what you mean."

"What guys?" asked Jake.

Courtney laughed. "The guys my friends are dating." She rolled her eyes.

Directing a dangerous glare toward Rudy, Keagan decided to change the subject. "So, what are Sagittarians like?"

"They're nearly perfect. There's hardly anything they can do wrong. They devote their lives to pleasing others, expecting nothing in return. They'd give the shirt off their back to—"

Courtney and Rudy laughed, while a confused Jake got a puzzled look on his face. "Oh, I get it. Rudy's a Sagittarian." That only made them laugh harder.

"I think I'm being ganged up on by two roommates." Keagan allowed a small grin to surface upon seeing both Rudy and Courtney get innocent looks on their faces, complete with fluttering eyelashes. She shook her head, accepting the teasing good-naturedly.

****

When they finally found themselves alone together in Rudy's room, Keagan wasted no time getting revenge. She picked Rudy up, threw her on the bed, and tickled her without mercy. "Stop! Oh, please. Please, please." Although Rudy laughed uncontrollably, she enjoyed the feeling of Keagan's hands on her body. Trying to tickle her lover back, she discovered, was futile. Keagan was simply too fast and Rudy had already lost her composure after being unceremoniously dumped on the bed and pounced upon.

"This is apparently the only way I can teach you to behave." Keagan whispered her words into Rudy's ear and felt her tremble. She stopped tickling her after a few seconds and relaxed into the pillows, laughing as she did so. Rudy tried to catch her breathing, and slumped down feigning exhaustion. Believing Rudy to be worn out, Keagan was caught unaware when she felt swift hands on her stomach that tickled her ruthlessly. With a yelp, she soon found herself being straddled by a triumphant Rudy who held down her arms. The look of utter astoundment on Keagan's face caused Rudy to laugh. "You're not going anywhere unless I let you." She raised her eyebrows, her grin wily.

"Oh, really? I'm bigger than you are. I could get you off of me easily if I wanted to." Keagan made no move to do so.

"Do you want to?" Rudy leaned closer so that their lips were almost touching.

"Not really." They enjoyed a long, thorough kiss during which Keagan took advantage of Rudy's distraction to flip her over on her back and pin her arms over her head. "Now you're *my* prisoner." Keagan chuckled and kissed

Rudy's neck in earnest.

"And what do you do to your prisoners?" Keagan moved her body against Rudy's, her hands exploring.

Rudy felt a hot tongue enter her mouth. "I discipline them." Keagan's hands came up to the top of Rudy's sweater and unbuttoned it.

"What kind of discipline?" Rudy moaned as Keagan's lips traveled down the front of her neck.

Not wanting to interrupt what she started, Keagan nonetheless allowed herself a glance at the clock. She scowled. "I have to go soon. I'm still on that early shift." Groaning with frustration, she pulled away from Rudy.

Rudy was breathing heavily, the fire begun by Keagan not anywhere near being put out. "You can *not* leave me like this."

Keagan's eyes raked up and down the now aroused body of the woman she couldn't get enough of. "Oh, I don't intend to, but I do need to go home since I have to work so early. You up for continuing this at my place?"

"I'm up!" And she was, heading out the bedroom door to run downstairs and grab her jacket, not even remembering to bring a night bag. Keagan ran after her.

****

A couple of hours later, a very contented Rudy was reading what Cody wrote in Keagan's notebook the previous Saturday. Keagan was lying across from her, waiting for her reaction. She figured that Rudy's response would give her some insight into how she really felt.

Young Rudy (two Rudys were too confusing) was trying to knock a ball of yarn off the bed with limited success.

"Cody's very insightful." Rudy wanted to wait for Keagan's input before she commented further.

"Yes. She's a neat lady."

"I like her a lot."

Keagan picked up Young Rudy with one hand and hoisted her above her head. The little kitten squirmed and then mewed. She brought the small animal back down and set her upon her chest. After a few moments, the kitten was clawing it. "Oww." Keagan groaned but didn't remove her.

"Sweetie, don't do that." Rudy leaned over and pulled the kitten's clawed feet free of her lover's chest. "You can just move her, you know. You shouldn't have to experience pain just because she's a cat."

"It's her nature. I don't mind."

"I *do* mind." Rudy looked into Keagan's eyes. "I don't want anything to hurt you."

Keagan averted her eyes from Rudy's. "You can't protect me from everything."

"No, but I'll protect you from what I can."

Keagan smiled as the little kitten settled herself onto her chest and slept no longer clawing. She gazed into Rudy's green eyes. "Thank you."

"Anytime."

Keagan felt the kitten purring and sighed. She was cute. *Maybe I'll keep her.* "So, um, what do you think?"

Rudy put the notebook on the floor and stared back at Keagan with guileless eyes. "About what?"

"About what? About what you just read."

"I don't know. You tell me." Rudy's eyes twinkled at Keagan.

"No. You tell me."

"All right, I'll tell you." Rudy took a deep breath and tried to fight down the very uneasy feeling she was now getting in her stomach. *Here goes nothing.* "I think Cody is right-on, at least the part involving me."

"You *think*?" Keagan reminded herself that she had asked for this. It was *her* curiosity that brought them to this point. Picking up the sleeping Young Rudy, she placed the animal at the foot of the bed where she yawned and fell back into slumber.

"I *know*."

"Hmm."

"What do you mean, 'hmm'?'" Rudy threw an exasperated look to Keagan who covered her face with a pillow. "Oh, no, you don't." Rudy reached over and grabbed the pillow off of Keagan's head and then bopped her with it. Keagan's eyes remained closed, but a huge smile was forming on her face. "Let me tell you something. Something I don't think you're aware of." She straddled the prone form of her lover and then leaned down close, their faces almost touching. Keagan kept her eyes closed. "I would have slept with you the first night I met you."

"Damn!" Keagan opened her eyes. "I *knew* I should have tried something."

"You are so awful!" Reaching over, Rudy grabbed the pillow and hit her again, but Keagan didn't fight back, she just laughed.

Keagan sobered. "But you didn't even know me."

"You're wrong. I knew you the first time I saw you."

Keagan reached up and touched Rudy's lips and then drew their bodies closer together. She could feel the familiar surge of adrenaline that intimate contact with Rudy always caused. She knew it was something she wanted to feel for a long time, but her cynicism wouldn't let it be. "Let's see. They saw each other...across a crowded room—"

Rudy groaned. "*Please* don't go there."

Seeing that Rudy was serious, she fell silent. Keagan had learned from past mistakes that sometimes her mouth got her into trouble and this might turn out to be one of those times.

Rudy laid her head down on Keagan's chest to rest it

snugly in the crook of her neck and felt strong hands stroking her hair. Her voice became quiet. "I meant what I said
when I told you I loved you, you know."

"Hmm." Several people had told Keagan that and
most of them probably didn't mean it. The word was frequently bandied about.

Ignoring Keagan's noncommittal response, Rudy continued anyway. *No sense in doing things half-assed, right?*
"I'm so in love with you, I can't think." She chuckled
softly. "I know I probably flunked that BritLit exam.
Lucky that's not my concentration."

"But we studied for it all night." It was true. In spite
of the two English majors' mutual desire to pursue more
stimulating activities, they had studied quite thoroughly.

Rudy gazed into darkened blue eyes that were watching her closely. "True enough, but all I could think about
the whole time was getting your hands on me. That tended
to cancel out just about everything that went into my
brain." Embarrassed a little, she put her head down again.

Keagan considered this. "Hmm." She suddenly felt a
need for distance from Rudy, but didn't know why. Anyone else's heart would be soaring with happiness over such
an admission. Keagan could only feel suffocation, fear,
and love. The question remained as to which would domi-
nate. "Thank you."

"For what?" Rudy felt strong arms tightening around
her for a hug.

"For feeling that way about me."

When the embrace ended, Rudy drew back and looked
into Keagan's eyes. They seemed to be trying to say something without words. "You don't need to thank me for loving you. It's not something I chose. It's just what I feel. I
don't have any control over it."

"Yeah, I know." *Neither do I.* That was the one thing
that frightened Keagan more than anything.

****

Rudy and Keagan were pleasantly surprised to discover on Thursday that they both had passed the exam, just barely. Luckily, there would be the rest of the quarter to bring their grades up. Rudy was thrilled that she scored a point higher than Keagan and didn't let one opportunity to mention it slip by. Keagan defended herself and her great mental reserve of poetry quotes by telling Rudy that she must have been thinking about her way too much during the exam. Although they hadn't spoken about their feelings for each other since Tuesday night, and Keagan hadn't made any declarations, Rudy noticed that she had been more open in expressing affection for her. The comment about the exam was just one example.

As for Valentine's Day, Keagan refused to attend the party thrown at the bar. Rudy tried to use her powers of persuasion to convince her to go, but it was just like Gretchen's party. The answer was always no.

As expected, Keagan received the obligatory calls of apology from her family. She accepted with grace, but decided to distance herself from them for awhile. Being hurt was something she no longer had to endure because she had a choice. Her resolution was to set permanent limits with them.

Sunday evening saw the Grotto bristling with action and decorations. Rudy sat at the end of the bar, sipping a Coke and chatting with Cody. She took in the unfolding scene. Large three-dimensional red hearts hung from the ceiling. Red, white, and pink helium-filled balloons floated throughout the bar. Most of the people in attendance were wearing red or pink. Rudy had on white jeans and a soft, red cassimere sweater, accented with red hoop earrings. Less noticeable were the heart-spotted white socks she had on underneath her shoes. She chuckled to herself at the razzing she would get when Keagan saw them. Taking another sip of her Coke, she glanced up to see Cody coming her way. The bartender was dressed as Cupid; complete with arrows stored on her back.

"Cody? You didn't by any chance shoot Char and Angelique did you?" She indicated the former predator Char who was sitting at a table near the dance floor with the flower girl, Angelique. Char was feeding her chocolates and their gazes never left each other.

"No, I didn't have to." Directing a wry grin in their direction, the bartender scooped up two empty beer bottles and disposed of them. "You know what Keagan would say about this, don't you?"

Rudy held up her hand. "Wait. Let me take a shot." She crinkled her brow as if in deep thought and then her features took on the best imitation of a dispassionate Keagan. "'I really don't see the need for such a sugary sweet display of affection in public. When people don't do those kinds of things in private, it makes me think they have an agenda. That agenda being to force their relationship down my throat. I *hate* entities!'"

Cody burst into laughter and Rudy followed. "Honey, you are good. Where is the elusive Ms. Keagan anyway? I know she hates Valentine's Day, but now she has you."

Rudy smiled. "I think she still hates it, but I'm hoping she'll show up since we didn't make plans."

"She'll show up. She *always* shows up. This is my theory. I think Keagan likes the attention she gets for showing up late. She doesn't know she likes it, but deep down I think she does."

"You may be right." Rudy glanced around the bar and spotted several people she knew. Milligan and Jackie Daniels were playing pool, Jill and Dani were in the midst of their latest scheme, Gretchen was attempting to stir up new controversy, and Brad was near the back just lurking around brooding. She spotted him and waved. In a few moments, he joined her at the bar. "How's it going, Brad?"

He sighed. "Same old, same old. None of my boyfriends want anything more than sex."

"Maybe someday you'll find someone who does." Rudy smiled encouragingly.

"What makes you think I want someone who does, girlfriend? I was just saying that all my boyfriends just want sex. I didn't say I had a problem with it." He grinned leeringly.

Rudy laughed. "Ah. Okay. Sorry I misunderstood you."

"S'all right. I'll forgive you just this once. You waiting for tall, dark, and brooding?"

"You know, I could use the same terms to describe *you*."

"You might." He paused and ordered a drink. "Keagan and I *are* a bit alike. Except she wants more than sex in a relationship."

"You think so?"

"I *know* so." Cody brought over a whiskey sour for Brad. "Thank you my darling!" He took a sip as the bartender sauntered off. "She told me."

"She did?" Rudy didn't want to pry information out of Keagan's best friend, but she was understandably curious about things her lover had not yet revealed.

"Sure." He said it nonchalantly and reached for some popcorn. It was tinted pink. Rolling his eyes and grimacing, he popped some into his mouth. *They really go over- board for some of the V-Day hoopla.* "Not in so many words, but she told me she loves you."

"She what? What did she say exactly?" Rudy wasn't proud of encouraging Brad to betray his friend's confidence, but she had to know.

Brad was almost touched by Rudy's curiosity. Ordinarily, he would never give away any of Keagan's secrets, but this wasn't just anyone. Rudy was the woman his best friend was in love with and aside from that, Brad liked her. With Keagan finally having a likeable girlfriend, Brad's life would be easier as well. "Okay, let me think a minute here. What did she say, what did she say." He remembered exactly what Keagan said, but the sadistic part of him enjoyed Rudy's trepidation. *Okay, Brad, stop it and put her out of her misery.* "Ah, yes. I told her the only time I ever sent flowers to someone was when I was in love. And then I asked her if she was. She said something along the lines of 'Yes, yes, yes, of course I am. I've thought about this and it's the only conclusion I can come to.'"

"That sounds like Keagan all right."

"She's nuts about you, okay? Don't worry about it." He grinned at her and then his ever-travelling eyes spotted someone he knew on the other side of the dance floor. "Gotta go, girlfriend. I'll catch ya later."

As Rudy watched him go, she considered her relationship with her lover. Would Keagan ever be able to express her feelings for her verbally? And did it really matter that much? She realized there were no easy answers to these questions. Her eyes scanned the bar again. She noticed that Deb and Kristy were sitting on other sides of the bar. Kristy had just kissed another woman and it was clearly a romantic kiss. She remembered the night that Keagan had told her about their "pickup" ritual to keep their relationship stimulating.

Noticing where Rudy was looking, Cody spoke in a low voice. "They broke up."

"Hmm." Keagan told her they were the token couple of the bar. They weren't supposed to break up. "I think I'd avoid Valentine's Day at the bar if I were them, but to each her own."

"That's what I say, Rueday. It's sad, though. They

were together three years."

Rudy nodded but didn't say anything.

****

Rudy visited with several other people before Keagan finally made an appearance. She stifled down a laugh as she saw her lover enter the bar clad in a red blazer, pink shirt and black jeans. *I suppose she had to sneak black in there somehow.* Rudy was genuinely surprised that Keagan indulged the inclination to wear red on Valentine's Day. It seemed like she was carrying something, too, but Rudy couldn't make out what.

Keagan's eyes didn't meet hers. Instead, she went straight for the bar and got a drink. Then she went over to the other side of the bar and sat down at a table by herself. Rudy's eyes remained riveted on her.

Keagan made sure to find a table with an excellent view of Rudy so she could easily get her attention. She glanced up at Rudy to see her smiling with interest. Keagan merely grinned in response and remained seated.

Rudy watched as Cody went over to Keagan's table. She could see her lover handing a couple of things to Cody, but couldn't make out what they were. She did detect a smirk on Cody's face as the bartender sauntered back to the bar. In seconds, Cody had placed a glass of red wine in front of her, along with a large red rose and a note folded in half. "Compliments of the rival poet from Shakespeare's den of iniquity." Cody shook her head and walked off. She had no idea what she had just said to Rudy, but those had been Keagan's instructions. She figured it was an English major thing.

Rudy glanced to Keagan whose eyes had never left her. Casting her lover a suspicious look, she opened the note and read: "I was just sitting here minding my own business when my eyes set upon the loveliest vision they ever had the fortune to gaze upon. Would you like to bring your beauty and splendor a bit closer and relieve the waves of loneliness that wash over and through me every time your eyes leave mine?" It was signed, The Rival Poet. Rudy laughed and looked over to Keagan who was smiling at her and getting that adorable expression on her face that seemed to say, "Who? Me?"

Rudy sniffed the rose, enjoying the fragrance. Picking up her glass of wine, she started over to Keagan's table, wondering what she had planned. "Are you the rival poet who requested my presence?"

"Oh, yes." Keagan flashed her a saucy grin.

"From the den of iniquity?" Rudy remained standing.

"Uh, huh. Please, have a seat."

"I don't know if a woman of my virtue can allow herself to associate with a complete stranger who claims to be from a den of iniquity. No offense meant."

"No disrespect is meant, La Roux, but then why did you come over at all?"

Rudy arched an eyebrow at Keagan, but chose to ignore her use of the nickname. She sat down and took a sip of the wine. "Yum. This is good." *If she can slip out of character, so can I.* Meeting Keagan's eyes, she reverted to her role. "You remind me of someone."

"Oh, and who would that be? An old lover perhaps?"

"No, my current lover." Rudy sniffed the rose again and smiled almost shyly.

"What's she like?"

Rudy thought briefly and then brought the rose to her lips for a second. "Absolutely impossible." She smiled devilishly.

"Good one."

"Thanks. I thought so." Leaning over, she kissed Keagan on the lips. "You look very nice this evening."

"What? You're not going to make fun of me?"

Rudy snorted. "Are you kidding? My girlfriend who says she hates Valentine's Day, shows up at the bar I'm at, picks me up in a very sexy way, gives me a rose, and a romantic note. And to top it all off, she's dressed in red and pink and looking so good that I can't take my eyes off of her. Why would I make fun of that?"

Keagan gazed down embarrassed. "I see your point." When she looked back up, her gaze was devious. "I'm pretty good at picking up chicks. Glad you like my technique."

Rudy laughed and hit her on the arm. "Sometimes I think you'd fit in better at a sports bar. You could just sit there with all the jocks and talk about picking up chicks."

"Nah. That'd be boring. No women." Keagan winked at her. "I noticed you called me your girlfriend. I think I like that idea." Keagan looked her squarely in the eyes.

"Oh you do?"

"Uh huh. There are just too many logical reasons *for* you to be and no compelling enough ones for you *not* to be."

"And what would these reasons be?"

"Number one: you're really hot." Keagan snickered. Being bad was so much fun.

Rudy rolled her eyes. "Gee, thanks. Anything else?"

"You like poetry and literature and stuff. And you're a grammar guru. That could help me with my writing career, you know." Keagan paused as if she had to think really hard to come up with something else.

"And—?"

I know I am going to get slapped for this one, but I don't care! "You're pretty good in bed." Keagan smiled broadly and raised her eyebrows lecherously.

"*Pretty* good?"

"Well, sweetie, you're still new to this stuff. I don't

blame you." Keagan tried to duck as Rudy leaned over and slapped her across the head teasingly.

"She finally calls me 'sweetie' and she's being a lech! I think I *will* ship you to a sports bar."

"Okay, you're *great* in bed." Keagan reached over and squeezed her hand to reassure her that she was just being facetious.

"That's better." When Keagan didn't add anything, Rudy inquired further. "Is that it?"

"No, there's more." Keagan took a deep breath. *No use in doing things half-assed.* "I think we fit together well."

"Yeah, we do, don't we?"

"I mean, you...fit inside my heart. Somehow you know me. And you make me happy."

"You make me happy, too."

Keagan felt a fullness in her heart that was unknown before Rudy. "So, ya want to be my Valentine, then?" She grinned crookedly and tried without success to avoid feeling silly.

"I thought you felt that Valentine's Day was a cheesy, commercial holiday with no redeeming value."

Keagan nodded in the affirmative and grinned. "I still think that, but I want you to be my Valentine anyway."

"Okay, then, it's settled. One Valentine coming up. Just let me know when you want me."

"Oh, I will. Count on it." Keagan leaned over and kissed Rudy. When they parted, Keagan's gaze fell upon Char and Angelique who were still feeding each other candy but were now licking chocolate off of each other's fingers. She sighed in disgust.

Cody came over with new glasses of wine for them both and chuckled upon seeing what Keagan was watching. "What do you think of them, Keag?"

Keagan frowned. "I don't see the need for such a disgustingly sweet display of affection in public. When people don't do those kinds of things in private, it makes me think they have an agenda to try and force their relationship down my throat. I *hate* entities!"

Cody looked at Rudy and winked. They both laughed. "You were close, Rueday. Very close. Almost word for word. Not bad, honey." She headed back to the bar.

"What was *she* talking about?"

"Never mind. I'll tell you later. Do you mind if we go? I want to be alone with you right now."

Keagan leaned over and whispered into Rudy's ear. "If you want to be alone, the bathroom's only about ten feet away. What da ya say?" Their eyes locked.

Rudy wondered if she was serious. Keagan motioned with her head toward the bathroom, to indicate she was. "I'll consider it, but only if you use the door this time."

"Deal." Keagan felt relief that she wouldn't have to defy physics to crawl under the door again. Her back was thankful.

Coming next from
Yellow Rose Books

Tumbleweed Fever
By LJ Maas

In the Oklahoma Territory of the old west Devlin Brown is trying to redeem herself for her past as an outlaw, and is now working as a rider on a cattle ranch. Sarah Tolliver is a widow with two children and a successful ranch, but no way to protect it from the ruthless men who would rather see her fail. When the two come together sparks fly, as a former outlaw loses her heart to a beautiful yet headstrong young woman.

Available November 2000.

Available soon from
Yellow Rose Books

Seasons: Book Two
By Anne Azel

Book Two, containing the stories Spring Rains and Summer Heat, continues the saga of Robbie and Janet Williams. Robbie has a career in the film industry while Janet is an educator. Seasons examines the crises that can come into the average woman's life, and focuses on the courage it takes to be female and/or gay in today's society.

Lost Paradise
By Francine Quesnel

Kristina Von Deering is a young, wealthy Austrian stuntwoman working on an Austrian/Canadian film project in Montreal. On location, she meets and eventually falls in love with a young gopher and aspiring camerawoman named Nicole McGrail. Their friendship and love is threatened by Nicole's father who sees their relationship as deviant and unnatural. He does everything in his power to put an end to it.

None So Blind
By LJ Maas

It's been almost 15 years since Chicago writer, Torrey Gray has set eyes on the woman she fell in love with so long ago. Taylor Kent has become one of the most celebrated artists in the country, and has spent the last 15 years trying to, unsuccessfully, forget the young woman that walked out of her life, stealing Taylor's heart in the process. Best friends forever, neither woman has ever been able to find the courage to speak about the growing passion they felt for one another. Now an unusual, but desperate request will throw the old friends together again, but this time, will either of them be able to voice their unspoken desires, or has time become their enemy?

Encounters
By Anne Azel

Encounters is a series of five stories: Amazon Encounter, Turkish Encounter, P.N.G. Encounter, Egyptian Encounter, and Peruvian Encounter. The stories are interrelated by the characters who all share a common ancestor. A loop in the space/time continium allows the couples of today to help their ancestors find their own troubled path to happiness.

Other titles to look for in the
coming months from
Yellow Rose Books

Safe Harbor By Radclyffe
(Winter 2000)

Dr. Livingston, I Presume By T. Novan
(Winter 2001)

Daredevil Hearts By Francine Quesnel
(Winter 2001)

Prairie Fire By LJ Maas
(Winter 2001)

Hope's Path By Carrie Carr
(Winter 2001)

Storm Front By Belle Reilly
(Spring 2001)

Take Time Out By R. L. Johnson
(Spring 2001)

Meridio's Daughter By LJ Maas
(Spring 2001)

Jules Kurre, who received her Bachelor of Arts degree in English from Kent State University in 1998, enjoys writing in her spare time. She has studied creative writing for over ten years, only recently turning her ambition into reality. Some of her favorite things to do include reading, working on her web site, cooking new dishes, and traveling. She lives in central Ohio with her partner of six years, two very tolerant roommates, and her cat, Ripley.

Jules can be reached at: juleskurre@aol.com.

Printed in the United States
1730